The end is a new beginning for Prudence. After witnessing her mother's wrongful conviction as a witch in 1661 and wishing for death, she gets just what she asks for when recruited. In her new job as a reaper, Prudence must learn to navigate the delicate balance between the living and the soon-to-be-deceased. However, her duties as a harbinger of souls are only the beginning of her trials as she makes her way as an immortal through the centuries. With nothing else to care about, Prudence excels on the job, even with an ill-tempered horse demon to keep fed and jealous coworkers vying for her downfall.

Love arrives for this reaper with one of her soon-to-be-dead clients. Prudence is instantly smitten with hospital doctor Daxone, defies Death to save the woman, and pursues her desires. Unfortunately, immortals shouldn't love humans. Worse, revealing Death's secrets gets the couple banished to purgatory. Prudence settles in only to be yanked away to Salem, Massachusetts. Once there, she is forced to deal with another of Death's deadly problems. Thrust into a world of witches and dark magic, Prudence must harness her innate powers and confront a coven plotting to overthrow Death. With the world's fate and her lover's life hanging in the balance, she must find her magic and understand her past to keep the love of her life and the entire planet alive.

DEATH

AND

COFFEE

LISA ACERBO

A NineStar Press Publication
www.ninestarpress.com

Death and Coffee

First Edition, October 2025

ISBN: 978-1-64890-898-9
Also available in eBook, ISBN: 978-1-64890-897-2

CONTENT WARNING:
This book contains sexually explicit content, which may only be suitable for mature readers. Depictions of sexual assault (recounted), body horror, torture, and the death of a secondary character.

To all my mentors and friends who are part of the Western Connecticut State University MFA program in Creative and Professional Writing. There would not be a book without you all.

Because I could not stop for Death—
He kindly stopped for me—
The Carriage held but just Ourselves—
And Immortality.
~Emily Dickinson

Chapter One

Hartford, Connecticut, 1661

A frigid wind slashed the outside of the building but the chill inside the dimly lit wooden church had little to do with the temperature. In the thick press of bodies, the smell of fear and anger assaulted my nose.

"Pray, pardon me." I wormed my way deeper inside. Not a single compassionate glance or "Good morrow" came my way. The people who sat sermon with me and greeted me on the pathway a few days ago averted their gaze, tone hushed.

My father, coward, refused to attend the trial. Earlier in the morning, I'd asked him to bear witness to this day, but he claimed to be too ashamed of his family, meeting my gaze purposefully with his own.

When most attendees had seated themselves, jammed together on benches like barnacles, the minister glowered and declared, "It's time." He pointed. "Repent your wicked and reviling acts for your soul's salvation."

My mother hunched in the gloom, halfway hidden behind a burly guard. The man's hand crushed her slight shoulder before she slid to the ground like a rag doll, exhaustion and pain creeping over her face and frail body. The audience gasped but for reasons other than the jailer's brutality. They believed her collapse proved the devil.

The preacher hammered my mother with his words. "There is light in the darkness, Martha. Be repentant for the sins of your life. Ask forgiveness from God. Admit the devil afflicted you and commanded you to unleash wickedness on our community, and your soul can be free in death."

"I've done nothing." Mother's gaze found mine in the last pew. Her once beautiful auburn hair, which rarely strayed from its cap, fell lank and greasy around her face.

"You have been a practitioner of poisoning in hand and deed, but in God's house, no devil has power." The minister's voice boomed; his chin raised to the heavens. "It is the only way to possible salvation."

Blinking back the tears forming, I knotted my hands. "Please stop this. I promise my soul, my life, anything demanded of me." No one heard my whisper of pain. "If you exist, show yourself and give this horrible congregation something to fear."

Those prayers elicited no response from the heavens. The two small, low-set windows failed to remove the shadows and darkness extending beyond the rafters and into the congregation.

"God will cast the wicked into Hell. He can most easily do so, and you will be next unless you tell the truth before all your brethren in attendance."

His words were drowned in a cacophony of outrage from the spectators who packed the pews for this horrible show.

I stepped forward.

An almost imperceptible shake of my mother's head slowed my feet.

Last week, on the only occasion Father allowed me to visit Mother in jail, she'd begged me to avoid her, fearing for my life. Heart empty, I had questioned if there was life waiting for me with her gone—she, the only person who loved me in this world. Her tormented sobs made me regret those words.

Clamoring voices thickened the air as her trial dragged. Someone in town had to stand up for her. Instead, the crowd grew louder and angrier. Few still loved and wished to protect her. And, no doubt, my former friends would happily turn me over to the minister if I said or did anything here.

Rumors about my mother started in the late summer. After church one day, our neighbor Bridget complained of stomach pains. My mother had sent me to her house with tea, but the herbs meant to help had only made it worse.

In Hartford, Connecticut, when a problem occurred, everyone prayed, but prayers often didn't reach heaven, and divine intervention seldom arrived. My mother and her knowledge of natural remedies had been a quiet aid to the community for years. No one had said a word against it.

Even my father had allowed it.

However, Bridget's condition worsened, and a fever struck her the day after she drank the tea. Not a week later, she died, arms and legs flailing without consent, screams of pain echoing from her house for all to hear. My mother had been restricted to our home first, then jailed until her trial.

Bridget's death brought rumors of witchcraft to my door, and now, not even six months later, shouts of anger and fear assaulted the walls and my ears.

"You deserve to be cast into hell." The words heaved from my neighbors like boulders. "Witch. Devil's spawn."

My mother's desperate glance revealed the true horror of the ordeal; a stark contrast to the minister next to her and the pudgy magistrate who sat high on a bench, shrouded in black robes and stern expressions.

Bridget's friends and family stood and faced the crowd as they recounted her illness and the supposed potion my mother provided that led the girl first to the devil and then to death.

It had only been dandelion tea. I'd helped prepare the draught, but fear of the community and that I'd be next to my mother in jail clamped my lips shut.

The flickering candlelight turned the magistrate, perched on his bench by the altar, into a demon. This man had been a guest in our home not only to share the word of God but to ask my mother for a cure for his headaches.

"You're accused of witchcraft," he said. "How do you plead?"

"I'm innocent. I never practiced witchcraft. I swear it on my soul." My mother turned to Bridget's parents when the room had quieted. "I'm no witch. I swear by all that is Godly. I'm innocent of all you proclaim."

Charity, a friend of Bridget's, spoke. "She bewitched Bridget and made her suffer. All should have witnessed the horror of her last moments. Her lips fumbled to make a sound, teeth gnashing and mouth foaming. Her body trembled and shook before her limbs flailed, unable as she was to control them."

"Do you deny the accusations of witchcraft against you?" the magistrate asked.

"I'm a God-fearing woman, and I've harmed no one."

My push forward parted air thickened with tension and sweat.

"The evidence against you is abundant," the magistrate said. "You're wicked. A consort with the devil. All to spell innocent people. Your potions and teas are well known in town. You deserve to be cast thither. Under the law of a righteous God, your eternal soul shall be condemned to hell."

"I have done nothing wrong other than use what God has provided in nature. I'm innocent. This I swear in His name."

The crowd reared like the head of a snake, the hiss loud and damning.

I bit my thumbnail to hold back a scream, and an iron tang met my tongue.

"Do not profane his name." The magistrate called the minister over, and their conversation lasted less than a minute, but it felt like an eternity.

"You've been found guilty of witchcraft. The sentence of the court is death by hanging. Let this be a warning to all. The devil stands ready to seize our souls as his own."

"I'll die guiltless." My mother yelped when the guard squeezed her arm to silence her.

The crowd held me back. Their slurs stalled me as much as their bodies. As they herded me out of the church, I reached out to touch my mother but stumbled as those gathered pressed back to the jail. My cry filled the air, unable as I was to offer support.

The sting of my last chance at a goodbye nettled.

I hated the people who flowed around me, ignoring me as they condemned my mother. Stunned and sick to my stomach, my grief and I stood alone. When only quiet remained, a winding path walked me home.

My father met me at the door of our small wood-shingled structure. A large fireplace dominated the main room, but the house felt as cold as my father's heart.

He beckoned me into his study, a barren space with a weighty desk and two chairs. Books, the Bible, and other papers were organized into neat piles. "Sit. Tell me the decision."

The wood chair gnawed on my back. "They accused her of witchcraft and sentenced her to hang." A tear slipped along my cheek. "You need to do something."

"It's done." His large frame towered over me. "Do not question the righteousness of the church."

"It's Mother."

"I'll hear no more on this." He rounded the desk to my side.

"How can you let it happen?"

The back of his hand pounded my cheek with stunning force. "No more, child. Leave me. Get to your work."

I stood and walked out of the room with measured steps, head high. New logs sizzled in the fire by the hearth as the kettle warmed. Tears flooded, and I prayed harder than ever. Did my lack of protest make me a coward and damn my soul?

Two days of crying alone in the loft on my pallet bed and letting tears leak into every meal passed before I learned mother's fate. My father, voice distant and cold, pulled me again into his study. "She was hanged by the neck until dead and is with God now. I will pray for her soul."

Nausea built as my breath dwindled like late-night coals. My hands circled tight against my stomach, fingers digging into my flesh to staunch the tears threatening to flow. I bowed my head, at a loss for words.

"Are you listening, Prudence? You must take over your mother's responsibilities. You are no longer a child at twenty years, and I have no desire to be married again after the shame Martha put us through. You will not do the same."

My eyes had been on the floor, but now I faced my father. "Yes, sir." The words were as listless as my body. "I hear you."

"Leave me. I must retire and consider how to repair our name in the community."

How could he care more about other people's opinions than my mother? What ailed the man?

My feet padded the hard floor to my loft. Hope fled like geese in fall. I grabbed the only thing of value: a small rag doll my mother sewed for me out of scraps when I was but a child and scrambled out of the house.

I ran into the deep woods surrounding our little town. Rocks and roots clawed at the hem of my dress before I slouched against a tree trunk. My fists pounded the ground.

"I hate you, God." Tears fell and sobs covered the earth with my misery.

Hours later, numbness both from cold and my mother's death filled my body and soul. My long skirts had turned black from dirt and muddy streams I'd traversed. My scraped, bloody arms and hand marked my bodice with red. If I returned home this way, a beating awaited. If I returned home, I'd never be free.

I'd live in hell until I perished and joined my mother.

My thoughts focused on the time she'd taught me the remedy for an unwanted baby and how the same tea, if prepared differently, could cause death.

It took only a minute but, my mind calm, I hurried to find the ingredients.

Behind a large oak, the moss I needed clung to the bark. A strange silhouette appeared in my peripheral vision when I resumed my search. A bear? Something worse? Heart thrumming, mind racing, I retreated until my back rammed into the scaly bark of a tree.

"Wait, Prudence. Do not be afraid." It took me a moment to see the tall and muscular figure, cloaked in shadow, who wore a white robe and sandals. "I'm Titus. You called the heavens to help."

My mouth fell open. My mind blanked. I should have fled or defended myself, but instead said, "You're too late. My mother is dead."

He laughed, and anger bubbled in my chest.

"The gods never listen," he said. "I have another option for you. You're planning your end. Am I correct?"

The words of my demise hissed from his lips. My heart stuttered, but I did want to join my mother. This beautiful man could be an angel or a devil. His presence willed me to heaven or hell.

My mother must have been aligned with the devil for him to show up now, and I was destined for hell, thanks to her.

"I'm not from heaven," the stranger confirmed.

My knees buckled.

Titus moved close. He sat, his leg touching mine.

"Stop the crying, child." The words were gentle. "I'm here for your help. Sit and listen to what I say, and let's see if we can strike a bargain. There's a place between life and death that might please you."

I pulled my good luck poppet out of my apron pocket and held it against my breast, hoping for a last chance. No longer a child, I couldn't let go of the doll. Did it promise good luck this once?

Titus had a lot to say.

Chapter Two

New York City, 2024

My phone alarm pounds me into consciousness. Sitting up in bed, I doomscroll the internet to find a car ran into concert goers in Dallas, Texas, a plane crash killed six, a demonstration in Washington left four injured, and there's been a school shooting. Only two dead and one injured there.

Cat videos are the only cure for all the bad news. When I can take no more cuteness, I check the daily email from the boss. Damn, nineteen souls.

I work my jaw back and forth, swallow loudly in the silence, and release the tension from grinding my teeth all night. The bedsheets rustle as I shift, but otherwise the room is quiet, my only companion the hum of the air conditioner hissing cold year round.

Early gray light, already faded, seeps through frosted windows and hits ashen walls, sleet sheets, and a gunmetal coverlet. The rust brick façade in one corner and the rug under the bed are bright patches, magnified by the dance of light that peeks from between closed pearl curtains.

Scanning my smartphone, I crunch the numbers. Less than an hour per soul if eating and sleeping are still to be a part of my day.

I step into the bathroom, grab my toothbrush, squeeze a glob of toothpaste, brush, spit, and rinse. Dying is scary enough for my clients; raging halitosis is not an option.

As I move to the kitchen, a yawn escapes. The coffee maker mocks me, my need for caffeine strong, but I ignore it having lingered too long under the sheets. With so many soon-to-be-dead (SOD) to collect, my caffeine quota becomes the least of my worries. At least for now.

Heading toward my bedroom to get dressed, vowing to buy coffee en route, I wonder what today will bring and why, if there are so many other reapers roaming the city, my schedule is chock full of corpses to be.

Out of nowhere, the image of a small wood house, my mother in front of a fireplace, and a child playing with a rag doll invades. I clamp down on the recollection. Like the dying flower or the falling leaf, it's a reminder of a life long gone. No time for nonsense now, especially when the amber stone on my gold filigree amulet sparks and tickles my flesh. Its long chain dangles around my neck and burns bright red. I'm late.

My black leather jacket waits. The door handle on the way out is cold to the touch. In the elevator, the only other occupant stares at my gaping yawn.

"I need a vacation day," I say to the tall man as we ride the jerky car to the ground floor. "I haven't had one since starting this job."

"Don't we all," my elevator companion responds. We grind to a halt, the door opens, he waves goodbye, and we part company on the sidewalk.

I scroll on my phone some more. A notification about a change in the lengthy Employee Handbook I've yet to read in its entirety pings. It's all I have as my current arrangement offers no official title, job description, vacation time, or benefits program. All I know for sure is I am not alone. Many other reapers roam this town doing the same work. New York City has lots going on and needs a large clean-up crew.

Lacking an official trade union, we call ourselves reapers. We're more deathmonger or a harbinger of death than true Death. I might even go so far as to call myself a banshee, but I don't wail.

At the corner of the street, my black hybrid rests. Well, it appears to be an energy-efficient car to the humans walking by it. The reality of the situation is much different. It's an undead horse demon, a nuckelavee with fiery eyes, bad breath, and a personality to match. His name is Goose, and he's my ride.

Goose's hunger radiates the same as it did on the day of his arrival. His exposed rib cage heaves, and his eyes narrow. All he had to do was stand on the curb all night and terrorize tourists. How can he be famished?

"Let's get you a snack," I say.

A guy rushes by and pushes me into Goose. The nuckelavee snorts, and the man's pants erupt in flame. It's a small blue-orange burst, but a few bystanders stop and stare. More people wrinkle their nose at the smell of rotten eggs erupting around them. I pat the passerby's backside to put out the already dying burn and get a nasty retort for my good deed. At least only the stranger's clothes are singed; there's no burning flesh. Being that it's New York, most people have seen weirder and walk away.

"Easy, Sweet Pea."

People race to their jobs between brick buildings blackened with age and reedy bent trees. One block over, high-rise apartments grow like clusters of honey mushrooms. Racewalkers crowd the narrow pavement or stroll the already busy sidewalk. One small boy watches me, and I wonder what he sees.

"Don't obliterate anyone today," I beg. The demon's neck reminds me of a sponge. "How's my lovely Goosey?" The words pour from my mouth in a purr. He's high maintenance, and I hope the nuckelavee is in a good mood as I climb onto his back, no saddle needed. My ankles tap the demon's flanks. "Come on. Let's go."

To my extreme irritation, the nuckelavee decides he's not in the mood to move. He's lazy as shit, but this is not unexpected. Most days he's tolerable, except when he pulls this crap.

Goose snorts and chews a leftover fast-food wrapper he pulled out of the gutter.

"There's no time for this. We've got nineteen pickups, I'm coffee deprived, and not getting any younger."

He emits weird, derisive sounds that equal demon laughter.

To oblivious humans, it appears the engine starts and stalls.

My boots smack what remains of his flanks. The reins slap against Goose's exposed muscle and skeletal sides. Most days I can't smell him over the scent of New York, but he must have eaten something dead, and it is going to make for a trying few hours.

Having begun life in the sixteen hundreds, I used to ride horses and had a beautiful chestnut mare at one point. There weren't many other options until recently. While that pony could run, riding Goose is an experience like no other. He doesn't canter; he flies. Literally.

Appearance wise, he's not so hot. I mentioned the exposed muscle, right? But as far as demons go, he's okay. I've grown used to the endless darkness in his eyes and the snorting of hellfire. The sulfuric farts are something else. They turn your stomach no matter what.

Goose canters off.

"Good boy," I croon and whisper my daily prayer. "Please let the SODs go quietly and turn to RODs without any problems." It's not like this job is predictable.

A reaper can never know what will happen with individuals passing to another realm, and while it keeps the job interesting, it's also demanding work. Most SOD are compliant, but I'll wrestle the rowdy ones into the next world if it leaves me time to finagle a stop at my favorite café before noon. Other than being on a permanent caffeine drip, my main goal is to help people transition to the afterlife and move from being a SOD to a recent-obvious-dead (ROD).

SODs, RODs, whatever. Dead is dead.

Goose easily maneuvers around cars stalled in traffic or stuck at red lights. While he appears skeletal, he sure doesn't feel it. My nuckelavee rides like a Friesian, one of those expensive horses people gawk at during the Olympics when they jump over impossible hurdles. The streets overflow with racewalking business suits, stores opening their doors, yellow taxis, and bountiful life. Flying high above it all, I'm elated. Prudence on the move. Get ready, SOD, I am death.

Memories flood once again. If my mentor, Titus, had let me die when we first met, things might have been different, and I'd be another corpse decomposing in an unmarked grave, never knowing this life. Instead, he drafted me, explaining his plans to disappear. Thanks to him, bouncing souls out of bodies in New York City has become a way of life.

Another yawn escapes even though I try my best to push it away. The day-to-day grind becomes taxing without any future to look forward to. It's been hundreds of years of soul after soul after soul. Those thoughts linger as Goose gallops to my first stop—a posh residence close to Central Park. I park the demon.

"How are you?" I ask the doorman.

"Good day, Miss." He seems unconcerned by the entrance of a girl with flaming red hair dressed in a leather jacket, black jeggings, and a black T-shirt.

"Howdy." I step inside the refined entry. A tall chandelier dangles on a gold chain overhead and sends a warm glow along paneled walls.

A small man in a spiffy uniform doesn't acknowledge my entrance, which works for me. I take a moment to consider my SOD. The email from this morning gave me the basics: woman, elderly, deceased husband, and three children. While helpful, not really the most important information I need.

A bright ring lights the elevator button when I press it.

Time to meet the dead. Or at least soon to be deceased.

If someone saw me on the street and stopped to chat, they'd learn I'm a twenty-eight-year-old college graduate who works as an independent contractor for a marketing firm in New York City. My few apartment-building acquaintances have no idea sending souls to heaven, nirvana, or hell is an actual job. And while most people have heard those names for the afterlife, it could easily be moksha, purgatory, Hades, Valhalla, paradise, Summerland.

As Death tells us often, don't question them and *stay in your own lane.*

I've given up seeking answers.

The elevator rumbles on the way up.

Do souls take a similar ride? Honestly, none of my fellow reapers are sure where they go. We collect them, but what happens after the deposit is a mystery. My boss is pretty shadowy too. I've never met Death in person, but we've interacted when it comes to the job. In addition to my amulet, we communicate through email and Teams. There are regular placement changes, personnel updates, and new policies. Sometimes cell phone conversations happen to defuse those tricky situations.

With a ding, the door opens on the fifth floor. I step out into an elegant, recently painted hallway imbued with bright abstract art. Some entrances have welcome mats. A yippy dog makes its presence known. The SOD's apartment is at the far end of the hall. The doorknob turns and clicks, opening easily. It always does.

I wipe my boots at the door. Reapers don't leave tracks, but it's good to be cautious. Everything inside the condominium is bright and shiny. White walls are highlighted with some mirrors and landscape paintings. My shoes submerge into the pristine white carpets on the floor of every room.

How do dying humans see me when in work-mode? Am I a scary figure in black robes holding a scythe or an angelic form bringing peace to a person's final moments? Or do I appear human and all too average, except for long, red hair, abundant freckles, and ample rack. What can I say? The gods giveth as much as the gods taketh away.

The truth about my appearance on the job site might never be known because whenever I pass a mirror before a reaping, it's my frowning face returning the scowl. To be clear, standing and staring into mirrors is not a common occurrence. I have little time to study myself while coercing souls into another existence.

A carelessly thrown hardcover novel has me tripping across the living room. "Hells bells," I whisper and chuckle at my own lame joke.

Actually, there are no bells, whistles, or tunnels when a person dies. It's only me or one of the other reapers toiling away at the job like any other white-collar worker in New York, except our benefits package is nonexistent. It's not like we need healthcare, but there's no overtime or vacation. Benefits include eternal enslavement to Death.

I want to turn my mind off. It's stuck in a vicious loop and won't stop obsessing over the topic, but it would be great to know the age of retirement if it exists. Five hundred years? One thousand?

The kitchen is to the right, and three closed doors stand at attention like soldiers. The pull guides me to the correct one. Inside the bedroom, an elderly woman lies in bed, bedspread to her chin, daughters and son by her side. Her face is too thin, flecked with age spots and blue veins. Her eyes are half shut, and pain and fear radiate off her.

No one notices me except the dying woman.

"Is it time?" She opens one eye, and the effort drains her of life force.

Feet planted at the bottom of the bed, I say, "You betcha." The words boom from my lips. I almost jump back, concerned at the amplification. But then I clear my throat, realizing I sound callous. A lack of coffee is to blame. "Yes, it's time." After all these years, it's still hard to control the doomsday, harbinger of death vibe. "What's your name?"

"Eliza." The woman heaves her last breath, and her soul departs. Mist rises from her chest, cold as morning icicles, bright and as disorienting as evening sun setting in the front windshield of the car when driving. More than anything, impossible to describe.

It flows into a plastic soda bottle. You'd think it would be something a little prettier, maybe blown glass, but plastic is durable. Don't want to have an accident, break a bottle, and watch a soul float away.

Eliza's soul shines with iridescence and sparkles in the early morning light. There's something so beautiful about most of them. Some are murky, less than shiny, and a few fill the bottles with black goo and phlegm, making me want to get rid of them as soon as inhumanly possible. Those types of truly damaged souls give me the heebie-jeebies and, often, nightmares to follow.

This soul's good. Into my backpack it goes, and I'm out the door before the family sheds their first tears.

The rest of the day proceeds at a horse race pace. Two more collections before a stop at a local café for a triple shot large latte. Feeling better after the caffeine ricochets through me, it's time for a phone check before the next stop.

Can't keep a customer waiting too long.

Chapter Three

Aberfeldy, Scotland, 1701

"Die, damn you, die." I resisted the urge to kick the dying man lying on the ground in front of me, frustration dripping from my body. My first time was supposed to be beautiful, magical, life altering, but this experience did not come close.

Regurgitated berries soured the air, making me gag, and Scotland during a national famine did not come close to my idea of enjoyable.

For the first time since my transformation, I reaped alone and faced a soul refusing to leave its body. Titus should have been here to help, but he'd reaped for so long Death offered to give him a break.

And that quickly, Titus abandoned me for warmer, tropical places. As my mentor, he always made this part of the job appear effortless. Yet here I stood, staring at a soon-to-be corpse who'd kept me waiting for hours. The man continued to forsake death.

How dare he.

Titus made everything about soul collecting effortless: cajoling, flattering, wheedling the near dead, doing whatever it took to pull souls from skin and bone.

The emaciated SOD couldn't weigh more than ninety pounds. The best option for him would be to let go. How did he not see that? What could keep him so tethered to a hateful and cruel world that treated him without regard?

Gods mostly ignored humans. Did anyone care other than me? At least I was pretty sure I still had emotions for the souls reaped but maybe fear more than love kept me working. Or something darker.

My own near demise flooded my thoughts, and I ignored the man on the ground for a moment as I considered when passing away had become the best option, the afterlife of no concern. Shaking away the thoughts, I sealed my mother's death back into the smallest space in the corner of my mind.

What tethered this poor soul so firmly? If I'd learned anything in my short time as a reaper, it was hard for anyone, human or supernatural, to give a damn.

The man writhed in pain on the ground, balling in on himself. Now my failure at being a reaper became evident to all watching. Did Death have spies? Should I be worried? An exasperated sigh fell from my lips. "Why don't you want to come with me?" I asked. "There'll be twrkie and pease pudding there." I had no idea if this was true, but anything to convince the soul of death's benefits. "It's time to leave."

He grunted out the word, "Family."

"Family?" I turned back toward the dilapidated shack. "What if I give you my oath to take care of them, at least for a little bit?"

"Promise?" The whisper died in the wind.

"Yes."

His body sagged in relief, and his soul departed. I caught it in a plain, glass container. The milky white film, which often reminded me of a spider's web, clung to the cork top, wanting to rise.

Damn my promise. I retreated, reversed, tromped toward the shack, and glanced inside. A woman and two children rested on the floor in front of the empty hearth, all woefully skinny and keeping warm under a single, ratty blanket.

Peering into the bottle and back at the family, I knew I needed to do something, or my soul would turn into black goo. An ax leaned against a log, and I grabbed it. I hiked into the woods, not even trying to hide my presence. There were no neighbors, this family's homestead being far from Aberfeldy.

Each blow of the ax smacked deeper into the small fallen tree. Being dead gave me ample stamina and plenty of time to reflect, especially when Titus ensured I received an easy territory in Scotland to find comfort in my position.

Prior to that, I'd never known of Scotland other than by its name in my geography primer, but when I joined Titus, he appealed to Death to move us. He thought it best to get as far away as possible from the village where I'd lived and died.

The thump of the ax against wood turned rhythmic.

The man I reaped wanted so much to live for his family, not himself. I never had that. Other than my mother, the warmth and comfort of loved ones or a husband lived only in my imagination. Curiosity came with the glimpses of this precious happiness. I watched the bedside weeping of relatives and family, those distressed at the loss of loved ones on their deathbeds and wondered what they'd found in life that eluded me.

In my former life, I'd been beyond marriage age at twenty. My father had confined me to our home, his pious standing in society allowing him to get away with all his misdeeds. How my mother endured, I'll never understand. After her death, continuing to live became an impossibility. Then Titus presented eternity as an option.

I once longed for a husband and children of my own and to bear witness to romantic love. While that was no longer a choice for me, this man wanted to provide for his family. I'd help, even though my aid wouldn't benefit them for long. With winter coming, they'd not survive the lean months ahead, and I'd be back.

At the cabin, I stacked logs in a pile before carrying a few inside and arranging them in the hearth. No one woke when I searched for a fire striker. Nothing.

With a huff, I tramped out across the cold, barren heath to my cottage, the walk long and arduous, lamenting my lack of a horse.

Fire striker in my pocket, a bag of bere, greens, and eggs from my hens bundled in my small hand cart, I returned to the family. A cold pink and blue light began to bleed across the horizon.

I kindled the fire for them and left the food.

The pendant around my neck grew cold—no other souls to claim today.

The River Tay opened before me, and I pulled the glass jar from the same pocket where the fire striker had rested. It slipped from my fingers, bottled soul dropping into the churning water.

Returning to my cottage, I made some tea and wept.

The next day, the pendant still dormant, I walked back to the River Tay to ease my consciousness, reminding myself of my duty. It involved lots of soul collecting, no matter the outcome for the living. Was I capable of this task?

The narrow path turned muddy by the river. I realized Death could make it easier on me. Before his departure, Titus told of the many reapers worldwide and how some earned rewards for their service. Obviously, I had yet to please.

And then it appeared. A monster of grand proportions rose from the River Tay. Formed like a horse, its iridescent skin dripped away with the water and turned black in the sun.

Flummoxed by the creature, I forgot to scamper away.

It stared at the people walking along the embankment, saliva dribbling out of its snout.

I must have failed the reaping, and my end waited in front of me. Death wanted to claim my sorry soul and throw me into the pits of hell.

The beast continued to stalk the oblivious pedestrians with its glowing red eyes. Shaking fear and panic away, I sprinted toward it, intent on saving as many humans as possible before it had a chance to eat me.

Slowing to a walk, I held out a hand as if to tame an escaped stallion.

It spoke in a low guttural growl. "I was sent to aid you, but I'm hungry, and my meal has arrived."

"Wait. What?" I sucked in a breath and coughed out noxious sulfuric fumes. Shocked and stunned was an understatement. My mind churned. I gagged out, "Please no. Not the big ones on two legs." I pointed to the geese. "Eat as many of those as you want."

The creature tromped after the poor, unsuspecting animals.

Horrified and perplexed didn't cover my range of emotions, but I wanted to stay alive and instinctually understood the importance of both remaining strong and endearing myself to this creature. We needed to bond to work together. Time to make friends. "What's your name?"

Its hide rippled with a shrug and exposed muscle surfaced. "Your kind call me–" The monster paused to think, each syllable sounding ill-fitting when it emerged. "–a nuckelavee."

The foreign word rolled over my tongue. "How'd you feel if I called you Goose instead?"

It started to eat.

Chapter Four

New York City, 2024

The narrow Lower East Side building of brick is well kept, and the front door yields to my touch. Once inside the apartment, tasteful decorations abound. There's this crazy, yummy aura of peace and love floating around me even with death present. Intriguing.

With a toss of my curls, I hum "The Reaper" by The Chainsmokers.

The vibe in this apartment is something otherworldly. It's a love fest for death. Not me, per se, but the whole cycle from birth to death. Fear, false hope, pain, and anger fill most dying people. Peace and love have their place too, and whoever lives here appreciates what comes next on a level I've never experienced. I want to bask in it.

True believers are usually happier at their time of death, but there is insight lacking about the afterlife, and, admittedly, few of the dying welcome me. Western philosophies do little to dispel that fear. After my years at work, I'm not a huge fan of any religion, having a better knowledge of what lies behind the curtain than most.

My phone pings with the collection details, and I enter the living room to search for a body. It's an aneurysm, so it's likely the poor person's not going to be resting peacefully in bed. I hate peeping into bathrooms. Three out of ten times, the dying person is there.

Not in the living room.

For a moment, I ignore the pull. The couch looks damn comfy. I sit on it for kicks and wonder if, before I collect the soul, it would be too callous to ask what store it came from. Reluctantly, I stand and decide the question is probably in poor taste. When I meander into the kitchen, my SOD is on the floor, not quite dead.

"Who are you?" the woman asks.

"Prudence." Flustered, I realize my mistake. "Death."

The SOD is tall, even prone on the ground, and in her late thirties, with olive skin, stunning large, warm brown eyes, and long tangles of hair, so dark it's almost black. Her boxer-briefs-clad physique is impressive, but there's something more: goodness, zeal for life, and empathy. It radiates off her in waves like the bright shininess of a perfect beach day sitting near the ocean and watching the waves.

"I'm here to collect your soul."

"There's more to do." Her voice is weak. "So many people to help."

Those words are often said, but for once, I believe it. "Time to shift your soul."

Now, there's a whole chapter in the *Reaper Employee Handbook* on how to handle clients, unlike when I began. Any reaper can find Death's website with a link to the handbook, and everything is explained ad nauseum. There is even a downloadable PDF version for smartphones.

There are tips for reapers galore. Don't use the phrases "take" or "claim" when talking about souls. Be reassuring and never mention hell, Hades, eternal damnation, Gehenna, the netherworld, etc. People don't want to hear about their worst fears. Death is scary enough. There are many more rules, and they are forever updated.

The freaking handbook sucks big time.

"You'll be transitioning to a new place. Maybe people there need help. I'm sorry you're going early." It's one of the few times since starting the job I mean it.

I kneel and touch her arm, forming a connection to be able to bear witness. Curiosity drives me to relive the loves and losses of her life. What my mind's eye views is surprising. In most every other case when I've peeped, skeletons lurk in the closet. A rough childhood, a hidden fascination with the occult, or an obsession with porn, but she's as close to pure as possible. I'm stunned and a little infatuated.

I pull my gaze away, reach into my pocket, and pull out a cold metal flask. No time to think. Impulse overtakes. The bottle tilts between my fingers.

This is new territory, and I take a moment to scan the *Reaper Employee Handbook* on my phone. My other hand tingles as I shake the magic tincture. The handbook states that if there's a person who needs to remain alive and has more work to do on earth, a solution is available.

And here she is.

The woman before me is a physician. If I save her life, she'll go on to help numerous others. She's also hot, sexy, and kind. Kind should have come first along with some different adjectives, but whatever. While it's pretty obvious I'm not supposed to use this on my insta-crush SOD, I can't resist.

Now or never. I go with my gut.

"Drink this." I tip the lid. Blue liquid spills forth and gurgles down her throat. "I'm calling 9-1-1 for you." She lacks a landline. A search leads me to her phone, wallet, and keys in the bedroom. I want to take a few minutes and explore but push the three numbers on the cell phone instead.

When I return to the kitchen, I sit cross-legged next to her and take her hand in mine. I'm happy to note its warmth.

"May I kiss you?" she asks.

My mouth gapes but no words come forth.

Her other hand reaches up to touch my hair. "I want to kiss away death."

She probably thinks she's hallucinating. I'm not thrown off by her request. This isn't the first time I've heard it, but it kind of rules out the popular notion that death arrives in black robes and carrying a scythe. I sigh, roll my neck, and ready myself.

Both men and women have asked for one last kiss, and it's not always sexual. Many people lacked love in their life and want to relive desire before going to the great beyond. Up to this point, I've never acquiesced.

Today is the exception in so many ways. I lean forward and push my mouth against hers, thinking the kiss will be over quickly, but her lips are soft and inviting. I part mine, and we spend minutes exploring. The kisses swirl together like snow in the wind, soft and decadent. My hand moves to her abdomen. Part of me focuses on the job. She's warm, a good sign. The other part of me focuses on her smooth abdomen, which has nothing to do with reaping souls.

There's a tingle from my nether regions. Hey, now. That hasn't happened in a long while.

This canoodling should go on forever, but it's an impossibility. I'm death's representative after all. Still, I wouldn't say no to one more make-out session. Maybe three.

Sirens on the street blast me out of my fantasies, and I scurry from the apartment doing the walk of shame. My foot pounds the pavement outside her door at the same moment the EMTs rush in.

As I walk away, what was left behind stays with me when I try to get on with my job. It is New York City and death is always near, but throughout the day, one question reverberates: What have I done?

The nausea in the pit of my stomach won't relent. I wait for repercussions around every corner. A phone call from the underworld secretary or a nasty email from Death themselves, but none arrive. Between my fear of having messed up the balance of the universe and the fact that SOD woman will not leave my mind, my day is fucked. I return to my regularly scheduled program, drink my coffee, collect the rest of my souls, and deposit them at the end of the day into the Hudson River, AKA River Styx.

It's dark by the time I park Goose and call it a night. Loopy and discombobulated, I ask myself over and over if I collected the correct souls and if I went to the right places. My day's a blur, and I wonder if it's nerves from using the serum or something else. Maybe this is the way it ends, with my mind and body breaking down. Tomorrow I could be walking the streets, human once more, homeless and muttering gibberish.

Pins dot my skin in fear at the thought. I hope I don't turn into a raving bag lady overnight but being dragged under might be worse. I've never pulled something like this before, but I rationalize that the bottle is there for this exact reason.

I've tried to read the handbook multiple times, but it's extremely dense and certain passages are complex and hard to decipher. It's been a great remedy to sleepless nights, but a few rules stand out. Never tell anyone who I am or what I do, deposit souls daily, and respect the client, etc., etc. Other rules and bylaws exist such as when to use the tincture. Still, as the hours pass, I wait for hellfire and brimstone.

My world doesn't end, and I order a chicken salad for dinner and watch Netflix. I head to bed late. Sleep evades. Death doesn't show up, but someone else does. In my mind, Boxer-briefs Aneurysm Woman keeps me tossing and turning until dawn.

At 4:32 in the morning, I give up trying to sleep, sit up in bed, and push away the tangled sheet, chastising myself for not asking her name.

Chapter Five

Dublin, Ireland, 1728

Potatoes and pigs. I detested both after six months in Dublin. I moved through the throng near Trinity College, not hearing the desperate cries or the pitiful whimpers of hungry children but the frenzy building in the air. Beggars, some no more than wee tots, grabbed my dress, asking for coin.

Death neared. My pendant, burning into my chest, confirmed this. I crossed from Dame Street and watched a drunk man dressed in rough wool garb burst through a pub door.

"England be damned," he shouted.

"Long reign George the Second," a voice from inside screamed even when the English government ruled with a strong hand and little heart.

The small spark from the original disagreement grew into an inferno, the initial drunken cheer accented by the clang and shattering of earthenware thrown to the ground. The mob of inebriated Irish Nationalists followed in the leader's wake, deserting the pub and running into the streets. They picked up stones and debris and threw them into windows and doors.

A low growl rose from the throng and a sea of angry faces engulfed me. They stormed along the streets, hurling rocks, knocking over bins, sacks, and the occasional person, destroying anything not bolted to the ground. The air was thick with unwashed bodies; the smell of rage, bitterness, and bile assaulted my nose.

I'd been drawn here not to stem the burgeoning riot but to collect the souls of those who would die in it.

The Guards arrived. Two officers pulled away a drunken man who tried to upend a cart, and rowdy gang members brawled with police. More guards arrived, clubs in hand, and beat the drunken men into submission before pulling them toward incarceration.

Beggars, mostly women and young children, cowering in the doorway corners and on the steps, found themselves shoved into the chaos. An enraged guard swung his club ruthlessly. It slammed into a child who must have been no more than six years old with a dull thud. His mother pushed between them.

My heart ached as my pendant pulled me toward his bloody mother who had tried to protect him. She'd be my next collection. I had no fear of the crowd as I moved to its core. The screaming rebels continued to march along the street to meet the ever-expanding line of officers. These desperate men destroyed their own community and attacked one another.

I turned from the fray to drop souls into the River Liffey. Needing a break, I rounded a corner, falling behind two well-dressed men conversing in a low, serious brogue.

"I'm going to write about it," said the taller of the two.

"What about your position as dean of St. Patrick's?"

"I don't care. Look around. People are starving. They're dying in the streets, and the wealthy landlords are not doing anything to help here or in other parts of Ireland. The English government is worse than the lack of Irish leadership. Someone has to take a stand."

"Do you have thoughts on what you'll say?"

"I need to address the beggars clogging the streets, and those lacking work in the city." He fidgeted with the lapel of his jacket before speaking again. "It goes beyond that. Trade restrictions are killing those who are even trying to be self-sufficient. Profit for the landlords can't be more important than our people's welfare."

"True words. Let's discuss this project further, but I must head off now," the shorter, stern fellow said with a curt bow. "Will you join me later?"

The man nodded and continued his jaunt alone. Three quick steps brought me to his side. I'd seen too much in my time as a reaper not to say what took root in my mind, and perhaps this was my chance to help, to do good in a world filled with pain and death.

"Sorry for the intrusion, sir. My name is Prudence Barlow, and I overheard your conversation. Would you be kind enough to share your thoughts about the English landlords."

The fifty-something man turned his intelligent eyes to my face. He wore a fine suit and wig. Inclining his head, he said, "Jonathan Swift at your service. I am headed toward the college to research how best to address the unfair English trade agreements." He took a few minutes to fill me in on the unjust treatment of England's rule over the Irish, especially now the potato crops were failing.

"You do a good thing for the families here."

"I would like to think so, but I'm not sure how to best address my message."

"About the government devouring the citizens they're supposed to protect?"

He stopped, eyes wide, and stared at me. "What an interesting turn of phrase." He paused in thought. "Men eating men. It is so morbid, yet apt. You've inspired me."

"Is that so, sir?"

"It's shocking to consider the metaphor, but the English are eating away at the Irish, turning them into nothing more than a weak stew."

"Now you're the one getting creative with your words." I smiled, hoping I had, indeed, been some small source of inspiration.

We reached the gates of Trinity College, and with a quick goodbye, he departed.

I never saw Jonathan Swift again, but not many months later, I was delighted to read *A Modest Proposal*.

Chapter Six

New York City, 2024

Groggy and irritated the next morning, I check my schedule and my pendant. The stone at the bottom of the chain around my neck is a hazy sailor's moon, much better than the hot, glowing red blaze that normally tattoos my skin.

There's a staff meeting at nine in the morning followed by a full day of clients. I could gather some souls before the meetup, but I don't have it in me today, and there are no emergencies. Using my time wisely as always, I putter around my nondescript apartment. It does not represent me, but it's meant to showcase the twenty-eight-year-old consultant, not the reaper or the young woman who lived and died in the 1600s.

Only three objects in the apartment are important to me, and they're hidden away from prying eyes. Before technology, but after Lisbon, I used to carry them on my person, never sure when I'd be whisked away, but now, with the advent of the smartphone, I always have time to plan before being transferred to a new place.

I grab hold of a framed picture on the fireplace mantel. My face stares back, but it's of little value. It's pretense. A fake. A sham like much of my life. It's a younger version of me with pretend parents and sister. It thuds back in place.

My coffee waits on the counter, and I grab it, happy for something real, even if the mug proclaims "I would fight a bear for you, sister. Not a grizzly or brown bear, but a Care Bear."

Fidgeting with the warm cup in my hands, I stare at the saying, wishing a sibling existed; someone I could go to when in need of advice or comfort. While the heat, liquid, and milky sweetness are real, that's about all I can count on when it comes to my current situation.

A sip sends my thoughts spiraling. What in the world is genuinely mine? There's so little reality in my life, but centuries at this job have made it all too easy to accept. Until yesterday. A small bottle of blue liquid has me questioning everything.

I step into my living room and sit on the couch. It isn't comfortable, at least not like the one I sat on in the stranger's apartment. Through squinted eyes, the room's drab and impersonal, but I don't spend much time in this space or in any of the former apartments assigned. Dwellings have always been functional rather than personal.

New York's been my longest stay because I can move boroughs and never encounter anyone I've known prior, but before that I've traveled from small towns in Iceland to Morocco, then to California and around the world once again. I've traversed the globe so many times, I can't remember all the places I've reaped in.

I should have perspective. It's been an interesting existence, but there's no place in the world or a person to call my own, and I haven't wanted any in a long time. On a whim, I decide that a visit to Boxerbriefs Aneurysm Woman to find out her name sounds lovely. I'm claiming three souls from Columbia Presbyterian Hospital, anyway, so why not make an additional quick pit stop and get some intel.

A large swig of coffee gives me hope for a good day. I resolve to make this happen but then consider the reasons not to visit a particularly wholesome, resurrected client in the hospital. Death will not be happy. Plus, it's in poor taste to give a person another chance at life, then go back to bother them. At least, I don't think you'd want to interfere in their lives. It's not like I resurrected her for my personal pleasure, or is it?

The Employee Handbook lights up my phone but nothing helpful comes up in my thirty-second search. I throw caution to the wind and vow to visit after the staff meeting. What's the worst that could happen?

I stand and stretch, place my empty mug in the dishwasher, and head to the Neptune Diner. It's a quick walk from my apartment and even with stores and restaurants attempting to stand out, the diner cannot be ignored. Outside is framed with fishing nets, rafts, and life preservers. The door bangs open, and I peer around. The buzz of caffeinated conversations fills my ears. Inside, it's statues of Greek gods and goddesses. Clearly, the decorator couldn't decide on a theme.

The other reapers wave from their booth. Becca's tiny frame is swallowed by the overstuffed cushions. She appears larger than life with wild, sable curls forming a halo around her elfin face. Her bright, brown eyes usually take in every detail of a situation, but this morning, they are puffy and red.

"You doing okay?" I slide into the seat next to her, beyond happy we've finally been reunited after Lisbon. She's one of the deathmongers I love dearly, and we've been enjoying this gig together for a while now.

"Tough extractions. Two clients already. One didn't want to go." Her voice fills the booth, but I don't worry. Around us, the patrons cloak us in a haze of mumbled conversations.

Death moves us reapers around every ten to twenty years. Can't have the neighbors getting suspicious when we are supposedly turning forty but still appear suspiciously youthful: no wrinkles, weight gain, or even major life changes. Becca's on year eight in New York City and I'm not too far behind. The thought of the next move and a life without her stings, but I try not to dwell. Change is part of the gig and after doing the job for a few hundred years, it's something you get used to "living" with. At least Goose travels with me, but that's more of a curse than a blessing.

Paul, sitting to her right, is her opposite. He's an overstuffed teddy bear with meat hooks for hands. If you see him on the street, he'll make you want to flee the scene until he smiles. That grin melts girls' hearts faster than sun on snow.

Small talk abounds and we catch up as the group waits for two latecomers. This is our favorite meeting place, and I know the menu by heart. Still, I glance at the specials and fret over pancakes versus an egg and cheese sandwich. The waitress arrives with hot, fresh coffee, and I order the breakfast sandwich.

Paul turns to me after I order. "I heard from the boss a few days ago."

My body stiffens. "Really? Are you moving?" I bite the skin around my thumbnail.

"Believe it or not, Death wanted a chat," Paul says.

"I've heard this story already," Becca interrupts. "Death must be lonely."

"Death can't be lonely. They are dealing with souls all day, every day." My stiff neck unwinds. "Tell me every word."

"Death waxed philosophical. It unsettled me." One of Paul's large hands attacks the scruff on his chin.

"Spill the tea." I lean across the table, angling closer.

Paul shrugs. "Maybe it was the boss's way of giving a pep talk. I've been having some mixed emotions about the job lately. The Big Guy reminded me how death is uncomfortable and unsettling for humans, and I'm the intermediary, the therapist, the guru. Pretty much told me to do whatever it takes and get on with the job."

"Isn't that so unlike You Know Who?" Becca says.

I bob my head in agreement. "What else?"

"Humans need the concept of a beginning and an end to truly embrace life. It is the meaning humans create in those moments that define them and their death. They also told me there's more to come and even though we, as reapers, don't understand what happens to the souls, I need to take comfort in the fact the journey isn't over. It's just begun."

I mull over the information for a few moments and start to ask a follow-up question, but John and Randy arrive. They are twenty minutes late and bonded at the hip. Typical.

Both remind me of guys who'd roofie girls in a bar because they can't get it otherwise. John is tall, skinny, and sports slicked-back, dark hair that's as greasy as his skin. Every time I see him, I wonder what products he uses or fails to use. Randy is most definitely the sidekick. He's shorter, squatter, and dumber. He'll follow John off a bridge if asked. I have no idea how the selection process for reapers works, but someone seriously screwed up when appointing those two.

They jostle each other and slide into the booth. It's a tight squeeze. John smells of body odor and excessive Axe cologne.

"We're here. Let's get this show on the road," John announces.

Randy giggles like it's the best joke ever told.

I roll my eyes and let the hum of conversations swarming around me fill my head like the buzz of bees. I can't help but want to punch one of them; teach them respect for others. Instead, I slouch in my seat and give them my best death glare.

Before anyone can call the staff meeting to order, John clears his throat and makes a proclamation. "I want to file a formal grievance against Prudence. She's been stealing too many of my souls."

"What are you talking about?" I sit straight and push my half-eaten egg sandwich aside, appetite gone.

"These last few months, you've been storming onto my cases, causing trouble, and pilfering my souls."

The amulet around my neck is almost as red as the flush on my cheeks. We all wear similar jewelry. It can be a ring, bracelet, or necklace, but every reaper has a large stone set in gold. My stone is cherry amber. John's stone, set in a ring, is a blood-red ruby.

I take a steady breath first, and my words are calm. "I go where the amulet takes me. When it makes demands, I'm there. You know the rules."

"It calls you to assist, not steal." Randy's smile is as cruel as his eyes.

"If I collect the soul, I'm depositing it." My voice rises with each word.

"Let's keep this conversation on the down-low," Becca advises.

"You screwed my tally for the month. I'm already in deep shit with Death," John says. "You're making my situation worse. You've pocketed nine of my souls in the last six months."

"Then do your job." Anger flares, and I push back against the cushions of the booth. My breath is ragged. I count to ten and pull it together.

"Stop taking my souls." John's face turns a shade of plum.

"Do your own work then." My hand jerks and coffee sloshes onto the saucer.

"If you keep getting me in trouble with Death, I'll end you."

"I'd like to see you try."

"Okay, boys and girls, put the personal feud away. There's group stuff we need to discuss." Paul places one of his large hands over mine, and we exchange glances.

The meeting continues and I ignore John for the rest of it, hoping to never have to see him again.

If only.

Chapter Seven

Lisbon, Portugal, 1755

Some warning would have been appreciated. One moment Edinburgh Castle loomed large in my vision and the next, my gaze fell on somewhere not Scotland. In the past, Death notified me before moving day came. A simple note on my cot when I returned from reaping often sufficed. Other times, a stranger might drop in to tell me the weather turned bad in a week and a warmer climate would suit me well. They'd provide directions to a new house; the funds I needed exchanging hands surreptitiously.

This morning, I opened my eyes to a mysterious city. Buildings, pastel and tiled, glimmered in the rising sun, emerging from behind wisps of clouds, kissing the pavement with warmth. Well-dressed people headed to church. Below the array of city structures, a thriving port and a large body of water attracted more residents. Had the first of November come and gone?

Pivoting, I wondered what Death had planned.

I stepped forward. Church bells screamed in horror. The earth growled like a dog ready to bite. My foot shimmied sideways, breaking my stride. A moment later, I crashed to my knees as the walkway twisted out from under me.

A man threw his arm around a fashionable woman next to him on the street before they dropped to the ground, and she said the first words in the Lord's Prayer. I made my way over. Only her screams echoed as I stood where she'd been seconds ago.

A gaping black hole opened and consumed them. I scrambled backward, dodging a flying stone, before another tremor sent me to my knees. Every inch of my body shuddered. I feared the tremors until a realization dawned about why I'd been pulled here. A massive earthquake. Destruction one reaper alone couldn't handle. I hauled myself up, but my feet refused to steady.

The angry ground growled under me as if telling me to get to work. A few terrified residents sprinted from the church ahead. I waited for more, but no one emerged.

A piece of tile pounded my collarbone, and I cursed under my breath. Shards shook loose from the rooftops, took flight, and dove like a hawk before the kill. Around me, scared strangers stumbled into my path.

"Dear God," an old man prayed as his knees buckled. "Let me live through this."

I sidestepped the collapsed figure. Blood ran from his hands and face where they'd scraped the rough ground. I couldn't open bottles fast enough for the dying souls.

Another shock sent the cathedral steeple crumbling into the church, leaving all the parishioners who'd failed to emerge trapped, dying, or dead in the rubble. Having no time to contemplate the destruction, I pulled my wits around me like a shield and continued to gather the departed.

A moment later, I stopped, recently collected soul in hand, and sniffed the air.

I craned my neck back. Acrid plumes of smoke rose from the destroyed church. Flames sprouted like weeds in the rubble. Could fallen candles have found life in the chaos?

I couldn't be the only reaper here to deal with the situation and wondered if it could get any worse. I begged Death not to let it be so, to spare some of the dying, to spare me of this horror, but as always, no answer.

Buildings swayed on their foundations, raising clouds of dust and lime. I battled the shaking, spitting, fiery landscape, trying to stay upright. In the middle of collecting a soul, an electric change in the atmosphere halted my progress. A fleeting thought about my own possible demise made me sick to my stomach. With so much agony around, I questioned if luck led me to avoid such a fate or a curse had me relive it daily with each new fatality.

Death wasn't done, and I couldn't fathom how one location could handle any more. The city proper connected to a sailing port. The sea heaved, swelled, and spit. A huge wave plowed onto the beach. It rose over the sea wall and crested onto the avenues, saturating buildings.

Even though I was used to a daily dose of death, horror overtook me when I watched, covered in brackish spray, from my perch in the city above the harbor. Ships tumbled, tossed about on waves the size of whales. Broken cables whipped the air. Caught in a whirlpool, two small fishing boats spun like toy tops.

Whitecaps smashed into hundreds of innocent people who'd gathered on the beach to escape the collapsing buildings. Wave after wave consumed them. The shoeless woman in a ripped dress, hair wild, scream etched on her face, would haunt my nightmares from that day forward. I'd never be able to find her soul, and it left me wondering how many were lost in the dark, cold depths of the sea. The surf towered, fell, and pummeled the beach. Scrambling to higher ground, those still alive were drenched, bruised, battered, and beaten.

The bowels of the earth rumbled once more and another shock hit the city, decimating already broken buildings. Shrieks and cries rang out when a second church toppled. Small fissures rippled and opened along the ground, reeking of sulfur and hell. A fine white storm spouted like a jet stream, covering the fleeing survivors.

Smoke and sand saturated the air, turning the city into a dark and destitute hellscape. Dizziness overwhelmed me. I stopped for a moment, overcome by the smell of destruction and death. I sank to the ground as the fire blazed and started to consume what was left of the city.

"Are you okay?" A petite woman with volumes of black, curly hair and an elfin face stood before me, unperturbed by the chaos surrounding us both.

"Who are you?" I asked.

"Becca." She offered me her hand. "You must be another reaper."

"How do you know?" I grabbed her outstretched arm and pulled myself up.

"You're still alive and haven't run screaming."

"Maybe I gave up."

"Once you're older, you'll see. It's easy to spot us."

"There are more?"

"You really must be new. Come on, let's work together for a while."

*

For six days we remained in what, later, I found out to be Lisbon, Portugal, collecting souls and watching the quake work for Death. When the earth quieted, the fire burned on, claiming even more lives.

But I'll be eternally grateful Death brought me there, because I met Becca, my best friend, for the first time.

Chapter Eight

New York City, 2024

Fueled by lingering anger and diner coffee from the staff meeting, I head to New York Presbyterian Hospital. My first soul comes from the recovery room after surgery. The procedure didn't go well for the white-haired woman with wrinkles lining her face, but she's lived a good life and her soul separates from her body without a fuss.

There's no need to try to hide when I skulk down a bright fluorescent-lit hallway far from the operating suites. I'm on official business at the hospital and in death guise with two more souls to collect. I'm pretty much invisible to everyone, able to get into need-be places, and full of charged energy. It sure comes in handy.

On the job it's important to remain aware and careful, especially now that I'm unsure of what rules are in play as I search. It's not like I've ever been in a similar situation, even after all my years reaping. The woman I plan to visit has witnessed death, and there's no telling how she'll perceive me.

I could take a chance, walk into her hospital room, and attempt small talk, but what if she screams, finds me hideous, and wants me to leave? Nervous and out of sorts, odd for this reaper, I stalk the hallway.

With a few minutes before my next pickup, this is as good a time as any. Yup, creeper in the corridor here. I want to overhear a name or spot her birthday on a chart, anything to provide some intel. Sensations like this haven't come forth in a long while. Why now?

There have been some flings in the past. A girl's got to do what a girl's got to do. I'm human with needs. No, not quite true. Even though I'm no longer human, all those touchy-feely urges and desires don't go away.

As doctors and nurses pass by me, staying far away as if pulled by a magnetic force, I consider my past lovers. A steep learning curve existed for the first hundred or so years after my creation in 1661. No time for fun.

My initial foray was a brief affair with Alexandre Dumas in France. Thinking back to the year 1831, I smile. The man wrote well and had a talent for other things too. As a fledgling reaper shoving souls into bottles day after day, I'd longed for diversion.

Dumas met my needs at the time until people noticed us together. He loved attention more than anything else. Death moved me to Whitehorse, Canada in time for the gold rush to teach me a lesson. Fun times. Scandals can't happen in my line of work. Now I'm a little older and wiser, I stay away from extroverts. I pretty much stay away from all people except other reapers.

This woman and my lust for her intrigues me.

Her restful breathing is easy to see from my stalker space in the hallway. My mind tells me to fangirl for a few minutes, finish my rounds, and go home. The smart move would be to end this little crush and return to collecting souls. As soon as she heals, she'll continue saving lives as a doctor, never remembering my role in her second chance.

Another minute passes, and it takes every ounce of determination to turn away from the hospital door. My boots smite the floor as I cruise to collect a fifty-six-year-old man who dies from a blood clot after a hip fracture and an Alzheimer's patient found wandering the streets in pajamas. The soul is delighted to depart and the inside of my bottle sparkles like holiday lights.

Souls collected, I stand with the main hospital door before me, opening and closing. People enter and leave, and fear and relief from them wash over me in almost equal parts. The long rectangular lobby with its fountain, pastel walls, and soft elevator music reminds me of the fabled tunnel many New Yorkers believe they'll see upon their death. From what I can tell, the reality is quite different, but I don't have time to ponder it now. With more pickups in my near future, I should leave, but my feet don't follow my rational brain.

My loins win. What kind of word is that anyway? It doesn't matter because they prevail, and I find myself back at her hospital room. This time I venture inside and pull a chair close to the bed. One leg is wobbly. I squeak when I sit on the edge and almost fall off. Squirming, I get comfortable on a cushion so thin the cold press of metal hits my butt. "It would seem even Death and cheap furniture won't keep me away."

She doesn't respond, and I obviously don't want to wake her. Actually, I do want to rouse her but dare not. Instead, fifteen minutes sail by. No one bothers me. No one even notices my presence.

Nothing happens. She doesn't open her eyes. God doesn't send a lightning bolt from the heavens demanding I leave, and Death doesn't instantly reassign me. I drink in my fill of the still nameless woman and leave.

*

My next few days and nights take a weird turn, but in my line of work weird is relative. I gather souls and deliver them to Death as I always have done. After work, I prowl the hospital corridors, and the hallways become my second home. I already had an intimate relationship with New York Presbyterian Hospital, but now I can tell you where the dust bunnies linger.

As Death's representative, I'm on call most hours of the day and night and don't require sleep the same way humans do. Sure, I like my rest and enjoy certain sexy dreams of late, but don't need it. The same goes for food, exercise, and most other earthly necessities.

Sleep is more about trying to find balance on the job. It's imperative I retain enough humanity to not scare the living dickens out of the dying. At times, it can be hard since there's a constant pull toward the darkness and the power that comes as part of this gig.

During my hospital roaming time, I avoid speaking to the aneurysm woman or her care team, but the kiss lives hot and heavy in my memories. It haunts me more than any case of death I've had in the past hundred years.

I'm skulking outside her hospital room door when she opens her eyes. She slowly improves and I learn her name is Daxone. I'm there when she sits up for the first time, when she eats solid food, and when she walks to the bathroom. I cheer her on, but no one hears me clap.

Friends and coworkers show up. The conversations prove she's a good woman and more. I learn Daxone spends her limited free time at animal shelters walking dogs and cleaning cages. More than anything, she wants to join Doctors Without Borders and save children.

When she's released, I follow her home. I tell myself my intentions are honorable, but admit this stalking is maybe a little much. Call me crazy, but there seems to be an otherworldly connection between us, at least on my end. I continue to tell myself I am doing all of this to ensure she's everything I assumed when administering the elixir.

Damn me to hell if I'm wrong.

Chapter Nine

Nazare, Portugal, 1788

The glass bottle shattered upon the rocks. The wreckage swam at my feet. I bent and saw gossamer webs of a soul clinging to shards of glass and trying to escape to the nearby rocks. Like everything else about humans, contrasts abounded. The soul shimmered, beautiful, elegant, and delicate as the freed silken threads slowly expanded outward. The web appeared equally dangerous and detestable as it stuck to the shards of the container.

I withdrew another bottle and coaxed the traumatized soul inside. Corking it, I examined the remains. "Please, don't let it be damaged."

The rocky shore of Nazare, where I had taken the less-traveled path, greeted me with crusty boulders, slippery seaweed, vigorous waves, and deep tide pools. I'd walked away from the pristine beach area, only to almost destroy what remained of a human's life, still with little to no idea of what I'd accomplished today or on any recent day.

My arm flailed as the soul, secure in its new bottle, hit the welcoming waves. I wondered what route it took to meet Death. Lost in thought, I meandered over to a large crop of damp rocks, the briny mist filling my nose. I found a seat. The waves hypnotized my gaze. Grand, gorgeous, endless; my emptiness opposed the boundless ocean.

The updated handbook that arrived by messenger in the morning left me with more questions than answers. I'd perused a few pages, then abandoned it on the shelf for later. How Death kept track of where reapers relocated still perplexed me. My amulet was my one consistent companion. Maybe Death monitored reapers that way. Becca had similar jewelry. She was the one person I could call a friend since leaving my mentor, Titus, and Death had cast us apart twenty years after Lisbon. No warning, just a note telling me to move on and an address to go to.

Death's agenda continued to confuse me. Maybe the gods had a master plan, but they didn't explain it to any of us low-level reapers. One part of me wondered what the future would bring and if I'd ever return home to The New World, now called The United States of America, but the other part of me couldn't bring myself to care. No one I loved remained, and Lisbon secured in me the knowledge I'd never care for anyone in the future. Alas, all I could do was watch them die.

Death kept my moves local, and I puzzled if it meant anything. I'd read *The Arabian Night's Entertainments* and studied the geography of the world, but so far had stayed stationed in Europe. If a reaper's travel was significant, Death failed to reveal any answers.

Nothing fulfilled me, not that I should ask for anything. I had immortality but once searched for a little piece of happiness and contentment. Since I'd seen so much horror in Lisbon and done nothing to stop it, hopelessness and emotional destitution had crept in like the tide and never receded.

The sun sank below the horizon. The lonely, craggy strip of shore only accentuated my isolation. After living for all this time, with all this power, I'd expected some measure of pleasure. Death had given me great gifts—no pain, illness, or worry about the afterlife—but it all felt like a curse.

Deathmongering depressed me as much as dealing with the end of people's lives rather than the joy of all that came before. Without Titus, death was my only constant companion. Titus had been my sounding board and support for many years. I sorely missed him and didn't want to do this job without him at my side.

My head hit my chest. Isolation had never been so crushing.

With no choice in the matter, all this pining was for naught. Death refused to uncurse me. Could I have done something different so long ago? Memories of my mother's demise flashed, but only for a moment. I kept them locked away; no way would the lid be opened. I refused to dwell on whether there had been a better option long ago.

Mist off the ocean waves stung my nose. I inhaled deeply. If Titus stayed, he'd commiserate, and I might be able to deal with my reaper news today. He warned me to compartmentalize death and to try to understand it as a natural part of not only an individual life but the world as a whole. It was hard—no, impossible—to do. Experiencing the love and loss of others became, at times, unbearable.

Did I want to get involved in people's mess? The *Reaper Employee Handbook* didn't forbid our kind from taking lovers, and all the conditions had been fully fleshed out in *Chapter Eight: Human as Companion*, but the thought terrified me. Even after all this time, I worried I'd say something wrong or get close to the person, enjoy their company, then be forced to reap their soul. Nope, couldn't bear it.

My hand pressed into the scaly rocks until my index finger bled.

My teeth grated against my lip as I thought about being lonely for eternity and wondered if Death should pair reapers together or something. Meeting Becca and others in Lisbon helped me find a balance as I faced the void of perpetuity, but a dreadful reason existed for any of us being there and socializing hadn't been a priority.

How easy it would be to walk into the ocean, but I wondered what would happen if I did not stop. Would I drown? What would occur if a sea creature swallowed me? Would I live for eternity in its belly? I had a decision to make. Push forward or not. With no religion in my reaper life, right or good had little consequence. Hard choices I didn't want the power to make.

If I moved forward, I would need to truly shuck off my past and live this new existence as a reaper. I shook the thoughts from my head, stood, and ambled away from the rocky terrain toward the sandy shore. The next time I reaped, I would try to stay on level ground.

Chapter Ten

New York City, 2024

The caramel macchiato is hot and sweet. I sip, wait for my avocado toast, and surreptitiously check out Daxone, who is at the next table. She looks good for the ordeal. After more than a week in the hospital, she spent a quick stint at a rehab and recovery facility, then home for some rest and relaxation. She's rocking a Mets baseball cap—bold choice—and takes the time to chat with the waitress when she orders an iced tea and turkey club sandwich.

I'm brunching; she's lunching. When her food arrives, and she takes her first bites, I'm able to mark open mouth chewing off my list of potential flaws. She turns out to be a quiet chewer who uses a napkin accordingly.

My top teeth dig into my bottom lip. She must have some defect. No one is perfect. Sure, she's perfectly adorable, but there's got to be something. How could she even like me, the most flawed reaper out there, if she's close to perfect. I'm going to wait her out and find it.

There are always more souls to reap, and my conscience screams at me daily to stop this but here I am, ready to find out if she's a cheap tipper or talks insatiably. If not, she must be bad in bed. Why else would she not have a significant other?

Minutes tick by. I hate myself for acting like a creeper but can't mend my ways. The toast is tasty, my cup is empty, and my pendant is cool. I worked hard in the early morning to earn my few hours.

One crust of her former sandwich sits forlorn on the plate. She's been checking me out during her meal, and I wonder if I've been discovered. A cover story develops as I plan my escape.

Daxone turns to me and acknowledges my presence. "This is going to sound like a pickup line, but do I know you?"

I squeak in greeting. Great start. For me, it's always been hard to process the difference between my human self and death personified, and no one's ever come back from the afterlife to recognize me. I can't fathom the fractured pieces making me whole. Daxone isn't running scared so she can't remember me attempting to collect her soul. Who even knows what people envision before dying?

My insides scream *it's me, the person who gave you a second chance at life,* but when my hazel eyes meet her beautiful brown ones, I say, "I don't think so."

"You must remind me of someone." She points to the cap. "It's not working at one hundred percent."

"The Mets hat?"

Her laugh is musical. "My head."

I don't want this moment to get away from us. "I'm Prudence."

"Daxone."

"Interesting name."

"My parents were interesting people." She smiles. "Your parents were no slouches when naming you either."

"I guess that's true."

"This will sound crazy, but I'm going for it." She stares at her plate for a moment. "I have some rare time off, and I'd love to spend it with you. Are you up for a walk in Central Park?"

Time to decide. Take my crush to the next level or walk away.

My cheeks flush. "A walk in the park sounds lovely."

"Great. It's a beautiful day." Her last word falters when she winces and touches a hand to her head.

"What's wrong?"

"Headaches. The aftermath of the aneurysm. Doctor says it's normal."

My chair scrapes the floor, and I scoot closer. My eyes grow wide in pretend surprise. "Are you all right? You said aneurysm?"

Having done the research, I've learned all about the lengthy recovery. The odds aren't great. Fifty percent of people with a brain aneurysm die within three years and more than sixty percent have some brain damage. I pray to Death I haven't brought her back to face a life of intellectual challenges or to die again in a few months. I continually question if I made the right choice.

"A few weeks ago, I had a brain aneurysm. Doctors say it is a miracle I'm alive and fully functional." She shrugs. "I'm a physician myself but have a lot more sympathy for my patients after this experience. The doctors turned me into a test case. I've been a lab rat for the last few weeks, but I'm not complaining. Very thankful to be alive."

My lips part in pretend surprise. "We can do this another day if you're not up to it." *Please don't change your mind. Please.* The refrain runs through my thoughts.

"I'll take a couple of aspirin."

"You sure?"

"Seize the day and all. I appreciate the saying so much more lately."

"You're pale." I worry my tonic wasn't all it proclaimed to be. What if she relapses? Wouldn't that be worse if I only gave her a few months more? To embrace life once again only to have it ripped away.

I shake away the conjecture. There are more mysteries of life and death than any human can comprehend. Don't doubt them now.

She squints. "Why are you shaking your head?"

"Nothing," I sputter. "Thinking about how I need to do a better job at this living in the moment thing. Go on, let's hear more of your story."

"Trying to get back into normal life. Doctors said to take it slow, but that's not a speed I run on. I pushed today, but a relaxing walk in the park with a beautiful woman will help."

Usually, I'd think the words a ploy to get me into bed. As part of the death brigade, I have the best bullshit detector, which is one of the reasons dating is not my thing. Daxone means every word.

I stand. "Let's go."

We meander through the less-traveled paths of Central Park, enjoying the fall colors.

"This is lovely." Whimsical clouds cross the blue skies above the high-rise buildings.

"It's surprisingly peaceful here when you consider we're in the middle of a city."

"Why'd you decide to become a doctor?"

"I spent a couple of years in the navy. My last tour of duty occurred off the Persian Gulf. Death and destruction lived all around. There, I decided to try to make a positive change."

I move a hand over my eyes to shield them from the sun's glare. "Did it work?"

Daxone meets my gaze. "Unfortunately, there's no cure for death."

Preach. If one existed, I'd be out of a job. "How right you are."

"It's constant work to hold death at bay in my patients." Her fingers, long and graceful, run across her baseball cap in an unconscious movement. If not a doctor, she could have been a sensational pianist. "Do you worry about it?"

I want to ask her if she plays. I have so many questions. I might have forgotten how to act like a regular twenty-something living in the city, and it takes all my resolve to hold back and not blurt out everything in a stream of verbal diarrhea.

Other thoughts form in my brain and much lower too. It is equally hard to find the restraint not to push Daxone against a tree for another kiss.

She's waiting for my answer, and it takes a second to think of what she last said. Luckily, we are on a topic I have a long history with. "Death is just another facet of life."

"Not an easy one, but we can learn to appreciate what we have."

People can have a hard time addressing weighty topics like death, especially with a practical stranger. I love that Daxone takes it on with brutal honesty. "So true."

She studies me. "Sorry if I'm a little too philosophical for our first meeting. After what I went through recently, nothing seems out of bounds. I want to wrestle with all the topics I put on a shelf for when I'd have more time."

"It's good to grapple with these ideas. I'd be afraid if my doctor didn't."

Her eyes light up. "I guess we both need to question things."

I touch her hand and find it warm. "It's important to deal with these questions, even if they're hard and uncomfortable."

She takes hold of my fingers, squeezing gently. "I'm lucky to have found someone willing to listen to me chatter on about this stuff."

"I don't talk like this normally to strangers, but you make me comfortable, and that's something I haven't experienced since becoming a..." The word reaper almost escapes. "...since arriving in New York City."

"Would you like to continue the conversation tomorrow?"

I angle my chin to the sky to meet her honey-brown eyes. Staring into their warmth, I understand this is a moment. It's one of the decisions in my life that could bring significant changes and alter destinies even for someone not quite alive.

"That would be nice." Nice. What a bland, repulsive word for the moment.

We wind our way back to the café.

Considering all the souls I've collected and the passings I've witnessed, the realization of how much it's changed my perspective hits. I wonder if Daxone understands it after her near miss with death. "Do you ever feel you can't do enough even as a doctor?" How jaded had I been until Daxone came along?

"Witnessing the random nature of death can change you. You have to believe there's a plan."

"Like a greater good to all the horror and injustice."

"Something like that," she says.

"Maybe you'll be the voice of reason to make me believe in it."

She nods, and we walk in a comfortable silence to the end of a busy street. After we turn the corner, conversation ambles like we do until parting ways.

As I leave Daxone, a line from Shakespeare's *Macbeth* intrudes. "Stars, hide your fires; Let not light see my black and deep desires."

Chapter Eleven

Atlantic Ocean, 1822

A salty breeze tousled the man's hair as he stood at the ship's bow, his gaze fixed on the horizon where the ocean met the sky. I stood next to him in agony, bemoaning the fact an easier way for me to get to England didn't exist. The rolling seas were not my friend. My stomach pitched with each wave.

I groaned and leaned out over the deck rail.

"Are you okay?" asked the man.

"I will be if the seas ever calm."

"Here." He reached into his coat pocket and extracted something long and lumpy. "Take this. Chew on it."

I eyed the orange rooty substance with distaste. "What is it?"

"Ginger. It will ease the nausea."

Shrugging, I shoved it between my lips. This small act of kindness from a stranger gave me momentary hope. Often, I only saw the worst of people at near death. Here, a reminder of the goodness existing around me lived.

The stranger smiled. "You can trust me. I am a physician. Having completed my tenure as a surgeon, I'm bound for England."

"Me too. Bound for England, that is. Not a physician. My name is Prudence Barlow."

He bowed. "Edwin Linfield."

"It's a pleasure. Thank you for your aid."

"A lovely packet ship we're on, don't you think?" He surveyed the deck and the other passengers aboard.

"I wouldn't know, stuck in my cabin for most of the trip as I have been."

"That might be part of the problem. Try to come out here as often as possible. I'm sure you'll get your sea legs soon." He inclined his head. "I'll leave you now but would love to have dinner when you're up to it."

I nodded, and the man walked away. My stomach rolled, and I forgot him until a few nights later when I entered the dining room, and he beckoned me over. After I sat and exchanged polite greetings, dinner arrived. The meal consisted of roasted meat, boiled potatoes, various stewed vegetables, puddings, and cheese. The water from a pitcher smelled of tobacco as I poured it into a glass. A small bottle of brandy rested nearby, and my companion poured some into a tumbler. We ate in silence along with the rest of the table for a few minutes, but then my new friend posed the question I dreaded would come.

"What is your business in England?" Edwin asked.

My lie sat ready on my tongue. "I'm traveling to visit my ailing father."

"Sorry to hear that."

"I wish it were better news, but death is inevitable." I studied Mr. Linfield. He possessed an air of quiet strength, his eyes reflecting the depths of the sea, his ways calm.

When I inquired about his work as a physician, he regaled me with his fascinating studies. He also spoke of some patients and his time in the service. Edwin had accomplished so much in his short life. I felt like a layabout, and though normally reaping took up an inordinate amount of time, he motivated me to do more with my long existence.

Especially now that I had no work. Everyone had remained healthy thus far on the journey. The state of the passengers would change before we docked in Liverpool, but at this moment, I had plenty of time to consider a hobby. After dinner, he left me with a polite nod, and for the next few days, we shared meals and conversation during our long and now quiet time at sea.

One evening, as the sun dipped below the horizon and the ocean's expanse glowed, I found myself drawn to the ship's deck. I'd purchased a glass of wine from one of the staterooms turned public tavern and wanted to enjoy it on deck now that my sea sickness had fully resolved. I stood alone with my thoughts at the rail, the light fading as the sun withdrew from the day.

A polite cough announced Edwin's arrival. "How are you?"

"Well, thank you. And thank you again for the ginger. It helped relieve my rather indelicate symptoms." I held up the wineglass as if it proved the point.

"It is a common ailment for those not used to sea travel."

The rhythmic lull of the waves provided the backdrop to my thoughts centered on Edwin. His neatly pressed attire bagged around his trim frame. Of average height and not at all brawny, he was as delicate as his soft features. His beauty was like a piece of art, magnificent and somewhat mystical.

"Picturesque, isn't it?" Linfield asked.

The question brought me back to the sea voyage, and I turned to face him, a soft smile on my lips. "Quite, Doctor Linfield."

"The sea has a certain tranquility, a sense of endless possibility. Wouldn't you agree?"

"Indeed." I hesitated, unsure of how much to say. Most men hated women who rambled, but Edwin wanted my ideas. Still, I remained reluctant to voice them, having been muted so many times prior.

The endless possibilities, something I often ignored, were evident in this man. He'd accomplished much already in his life and still had plans to do more. Edwin pursued his passions. I, on the other hand, only lived to help the dying. It wasn't a bad calling, working hard to make sure those transitioning did so as peacefully as possible, but Edwin reminded me there could be more.

"What are you thinking about? You appear so pensive staring into the waves."

I laughed. "I don't want to bore you with my angst. Sorry. I will try to be more gay."

"Please don't, at least not on my account. Whatever you're feeling is valuable, and I'd like to hear about it."

"I thought about all you've done in your life and wondered why I haven't accomplished more. Reflecting on the endless possibilities, my lack of grabbing hold of them is rather sad."

Linfield nodded, his gaze lingering on my face. "This world makes it hard for women to achieve what's easy for men, but I agree. We often need to be reminded the world is vast and the possibilities endless."

Silence hung between us, the waves lapping against the ship's hull the only trespasser. Linfield took a step closer, and my heart leaped with excitement. I searched for words, any words to relieve this strangeness.

"Pru, I wish to confess something," he said. "Since I first saw you, I've been captivated by and drawn to you in ways I can't explain."

My cheeks flushed. "I have felt similar since your first kindness to me."

Edwin reached out and took my hand in his. "I understand if this is unwarranted. I'm not sure of your circumstances, but I couldn't let this journey pass without expressing my admiration for you."

Our fingers intertwined. "There's something about you. You're more compassionate, not like the men I usually encounter. You listen to my ideas as an equal. Most men prefer their women silent."

"I have a bold question. Do you want to come back to my cabin with me?"

"You're rather forward, Dr. Linfield."

"I would not ask if I did not think you felt the same way."

What to do? No longer a virgin or a spinster and having lived for more than a hundred years, I wanted to embrace possibilities. My time to do so lay in front of me. "I'd like to see your cabin."

The rolling waves lolled as we hastened back to Edwin's living quarters. He peered around at the door, making sure no one saw me enter. Once inside, his soft lips met mine. Soon, his tongue tempted my mouth and hands roamed my body. We undressed. The doctor shed his garb easily. He lost his jacket and pants in quick succession. When he removed his shirt and undershirt, I received my first surprise. Bandages cloaked his chest.

"Are you injured?" I asked.

"Before we go any farther, I must tell you something. Actually, show you something." He unraveled the bandages. His breasts were not at all manly. They were small and pert but womanly.

I gaped in surprise. "I don't understand."

"My birth name is Edwina." They stepped out of their undergarments, and I took in their lovely form. "I started to dress as a man because women were not allowed in medical school, and all I wanted was to be a doctor. I have never told anyone my secret until now. I hope I can trust you with it."

"You can."

"If you want to leave, I understand."

It took me a moment, but beauty and flesh remain but a construct. We'd make each other happy, even if only for a trip across the ocean, and that we did.

Chapter Twelve

New York City, 2024

It's date night. Our first. We walk along Eighth Street before Daxone pulls me into a subterranean wine bar with tables crammed into a long, thin corridor. "Let's grab a drink."

A couple sits at a high-top table, laughing. Two men dig into a small plate of bruschetta. Tomato, basil, and garlic lace the air. I make a mental note to myself not to order the dish tonight. I'll return to sample with Becca and Paul.

Scuffed wide-plan wood floorboards beckon us toward the lively bar crowd. Farther inside, log-jammed tables are wedged together to hold a larger group.

"We could go to a different place if this isn't great for you." Her brows draw together. "It's not usually so crowded or loud."

"It's perfect."

Her hand is warm on my back, and we weave deeper inside and find a seat at a small high-top table in the bar. The conversation is light as air at first. She tells me about her desire to return to work. I recite a client story from my fictional marketing company; one perfected over the years for moments like this. It's not as if my real clientele is up for debate.

"I don't have a faith," Daxone says. "I mean I have faith in a higher power but don't subscribe to a particular religion, though my parents are Muslim. It comes down to a combination of lack of time, which sounds horrible, and shifting belief systems. What about you?"

"I was raised in a community of serious Bible thumpers."

"Like a cult?" she asks.

"Similar vibe. You could almost say it was a cult, but like you, formal religion fell by the wayside. I try to be a good person every day. I'm still very spiritual." That's the understatement of the year. I don't subscribe to a formalized religion because Death hasn't revealed much. Death is real and my employer. That's all that matters.

"Spiritual is good."

With a shrug, I say, "It's the best I can do."

The conversation pauses when the waitress takes our order. Daxone's thumb plays with the charm bracelet on my wrist. "What are these?"

She touches the ship, the heart, the Claddagh, and the paintbrush. I'm mesmerized, watching her graceful fingers trace the metal. Our eyes meet, and she smiles. Exhilaration spirals as she caresses the delicate skin near my palm and the feeling lands in my loins.

Loins? Dear God, I'm regressing. Next thing you know, I'll be donning a petticoat. Putting my past aside, I focus on the present. I can't be the only one connecting. There's a lot of connection.

Heat builds under my flushed skin. "The charms represent different events in my life. I don't remember when it started. I was young and bought them to commemorate milestones." If only I could tell her how long this has been going on and how the charms are a remembrance. It's been a few hundred years, and after a while, time shifts and blurs. With the aid of the jewelry, important people and moments stay in focus.

The bracelet rarely comes off except when I shower and exercise. Well, I don't have to exercise, but I do it on some days anyway. A good run puts things in perspective. The charms make good travel companions, unlike furniture, and they don't fade like photographs.

Not that any of those still exist. Seeing myself posed in a different time might confuse people. The image could be passed off as a relative, but it takes a lot of explaining. There's only one portrait in my possession, and I'll never relinquish it.

Daxone picks out one of my oldest charms, a crown representing my time in England.

"Is this antique?" Her gaze is soft as her warm honey eyes focus on mine.

"You'd be surprised. The first charm bracelets were worn by the Persians and other groups as early as 600 years BC. Queen Victoria initiated a fashion trend with them among the European noble classes, but it's from the early 1900s. Tiffany and Co."

"Good to know." A smile touches her lips. "For the future."

With our third glass of wine, the discussion turns as weighty as the many anchors that moor souls to earth.

"Tell me about your family."

Her beautiful smile falters. "My father died of cancer four years ago, and it made me realize how important it is to live a good and meaningful life as he did. I want to share his story through my actions. Before his illness, I focused too much on my career, and I worry that I didn't value my parents or see them enough."

"I'm sorry." One thing I truly understand is loss and death.

"I miss him every day, but my mother has decided to be doubly invested in my life to make up for it. Luckily, she's not local, so she can only manage it from afar." She picks up her wineglass, then puts it on the table without taking a sip. "She would've hopped on a plane when she heard of my accident but had hip surgery, and her doctors forbade it. My sister was helping to care for her, or she would have come out as well. We talk every day."

"Would she like me?" My hand slips from hers to play with the silverware, restless.

She opens her mouth to answer but is interrupted by appetizers; a margherita flatbread and eggplant rollatini. I pull a piece of flatbread onto my plate, not at all abashed to eat my share.

Daxone barely touches the food.

I stop mid-chew and put the fork on the plate.

She says, "Who could not like you?"

Thoughts of the meal melt away. My appetite no longer revolves around food. This will be a tryst. A dalliance. I'll get my fill and move on.

Her glance from across the table leaves me breathless, and as we snack, our hands graze.

By the end of the meal, the roar of the restaurant has faded under the glow of the moment.

"Can I pay?" I ask when the bill comes.

"Next time."

The words fill me with excitement and hope.

Soon after, I'm walking by her side through the city, the sun long lost behind tall buildings. A smog dims the night stars. An unspoken question lights Daxone's eyes, and I reply by moving closer, which is all the answer she needs.

She stops in the middle of the sidewalk. Her hand on my back pulls me close. We kiss. The taste of her—red wine and spices—makes me dizzy. Her fingers tickle my cheek and heat my spirit and my skin. I drink her in, knowing it will never be enough.

The urgent and demanding kiss we share challenges me to give her more.

I pull back, faint and out of breath. "We should stop."

"We should, but I don't want to."

"Do you always get what you want?"

"Usually." Her lips hint at a grin. "For now, we can say good night here." She arches an eyebrow. "If it's what you want."

It's not. A groan escapes, and I'm not sure if it's disappointment or desire, but I muster the most rational words possible. "I have work tomorrow."

"How about I walk you back to your place then."

"Sounds good." My smile grows.

"Let's go." Daxone takes a few steps, and I hustle to keep up. We fall into a companionable silence and walk back to my apartment contemplatively.

At the entrance to my building, she kisses me again. It's soft and tempts of more. When I don't pull back, she deepens the kiss, running her hands over my arms.

I splay my fingers under her coat and trace them over her shirt. Heat beckons, but reality intrudes.

"I should go up." The building looms in front of us.

"Goodnight." The words are a whisper in my ear as Daxone departs.

Chapter Thirteen

Bedfordshire, England 1854

My Dearest Becca,

How are you? It was lovely to read that my last letter found its way and you reside at the same location. My heart is happy we can stay in contact even with the many changes to our living situations.

This current employment as a housemaid leaves me much abused even though I am one of the lucky servants, mostly out of sight of my employer. I do question why there was no place for me as a lady-in-waiting for Queen Victoria. While that was written in jest, this situation is not my favorite of circumstances.

Let me explain, as it might seem to be the opposite of reason. The manor is set far in the country, and life as a reaper is not overly taxing. For me, the worst is the travel. You must understand this, being in a similar position. Life in the country means homes are few and far between. I must travel to reap, and it's mostly the souls of the servants. When I take a horse, no one ever notices or complains, but it is often better to walk, which leaves ample time to think. I've had much to ponder of late.

My current conditions are better than most, and I often find myself fretting for the others I've befriended. With gods all around, why is the earth so mismanaged? The staff is ill-treated, and I wish there was something more to do for them. Not one of the employers heeds the servants' long hours or cares about their holidays, which are rare to say the least. Most of the household is busy from before dawn until after dark.

My only luxury is the housekeeper, most days, forgets I'm here. It makes my job easy if I can find a place to hide. Still, this situation is far from heavenly. My bedroom, if you can call it such, is in the attic. Other, higher paid staff have rooms at the back of the house; a place where visitors and owners never venture, except for the philandering second son, Charles. Some of the maids work hard to avoid him while others welcome him. I haven't figured out which is the better option.

I write this from my attic room now. Being November, the house is bleak and cold. Many of the other girls complain about their accommodations. They often fall ill without a doctor close by or a caring family member to tend them. The draught hits my bones as much as when I lived, but thanks to Death, the bite of the frost reminds me I can still feel alive even if I don't succumb to such illnesses as are common here like consumption.

On the days when no reaping takes place, my duty is

to make sure the coal fireplaces are lit and rooms are clean when the family is in residence. Luckily, since it is the high season in London, it is not too often. Alas, today is different. I'm waiting to be chastised for my idleness as the family is at the manor for Guy Fawkes Day, and the staff is in an unusual frenzy.

Allow me to go on a tangent for a moment, dear Becca. I realize anyone reading this letter other than you will think it was written by a madwoman, but I must express these thoughts I harbor to someone who understands.

While these fancy country manor homes are so different from my humble Puritan upbringing and while my memories are dull with age, there are more commonalities than I'd hope to believe. For as many steps as humans make forward, they rarely progress. People aren't faithful to God or each other, no matter what religion they follow. They aren't kind, loving, or giving. Only the seven deadly sins make a daily appearance. Should I care for these souls at all?

Let me provide you with observations from today. The master and mistress, who divide their time between London and the manor, arrived early, and I'm one of the thirty-seven indoor servants here to attend them. They have two daughters and two sons, all in residence now with their parents.

My mistress believes servants exist for her and her family, without their own rights, feelings, or opinions. Domestics are often considered little more than livestock, less than human in the minds of their employers, and must bear petty tyrannies.

Before the sun rose this morning, the dark, steep back

stairs met me. Groggy with sleep still in my eyes, I stumbled through a side entrance into the kitchen and acknowledged another maid whose name is lost to memory. I have no idea where she even sleeps and never see the woman at meals. Still, we nodded to each other in solidarity. Guilt flooded me. No one truly knows me here. Avoiding attention and connection is my aim, and as only you can understand, our job holds us aloof.

Instead, my focus is set on completing numerous daily tasks. Already this morning, I, among a brigade of others, have drawn back the curtains in the drawing room and given them a good shaking, cleaned and raked fireplaces before lighting them, washed the hearthstone, and put the coal buckets out in the hall for the footmen to collect and fill. If that weren't enough, there are small rugs and druggets to shake and furniture to rub. While the family ate breakfast, I prepared the bedchambers for the day.

Death, putting me here in the country calm, must have some reason. Does the god want to ensure I'm so busy with the minutia of life other thoughts will be avoided? They must believe the saying about idle hands.

While lesser servants, of which I am one, rarely see the masters and mistresses of the house, I'm easily forgotten and can get away with more than the others. After breakfast, I stepped into the parlor to stoke the fire and listen in to the conversation between the mistress and her two daughters.

I lingered at the fireplace, crouching to tend the orange flames. No one even considered my presence, and I listened to Mistress Hadley and her daughters, Daphne and Clara, converse. They spoke about love, something

I dare not even consider in my role. Who'd have a reaper?

Here is a retelling of the exchange in detail. I dare say I have it memorized as it kept replaying in my mind when I later emptied chamber pots.

"Now I've got some news for you," said Clara who sat at a writing table. The younger of the two sisters, she worked to contain her high spirits. She is darker in both skin tone and hair color, which is light brown and brassy. "It is excellent news, capital news, about a person we all like."

"Do tell," said Daphne, the older of the sisters by two years.

"George Shipley is in town for the celebration."

"Was he not courting Mary King?"

"There's no danger of that anymore," Clara scoffed. "She's gone to her aunt in the lakes."

"She's a fool to go if she felt something for the man."

"I dare say her family did not lean the same way."

Daphne's hand moved first to her cheek then to a delicate blonde curl as if to check its buoyancy. "But he is a fine man."

"I pray a strong attachment was lacking."

"I'm sure there was not any on his. Mary's rather plain."

It was enough. I left the room, preferring hard work to the prattle. These women spend their life in pursuit of marriage and someone dear, something I doubt I'll encounter. My heart ached a little in that moment, never having loved in the past and wondering if it was a future possibility. My jealousy, I shamefully admit, was palpable but soon relieved. I will never love.

Distracted by my thoughts, I entered one of the parlors where I ran into Charles, the cad of a son. He followed. My pace increased as I sprinted to get to the back stairwell. He had no qualms about pursuing me.

I hope what follows does not distress you, but the need to tell someone presses on me like a boulder. As soon as we were out of the public eye, he forced me against the wall. Unsure what to do or what he wanted in the moment, I struggled and soon learned. Charles made it clear enough when he hitched up my skirt. His small, pudgy hand, with long nails like animal claws, pawed my thigh. I tried to swat it away, but his bulk moored me.

My strength soon fled, and I could not fathom how as a reaper I was strong but weak against this man. There was nothing to do but bear his ugly touch and the weight of him against me. His wet kiss and his alcohol-bathed hot breath engulfed me in his rank smell. He pushed me into the wall so hard my back almost broke along with my spirit. My mind soon left my body at what I was forced to endure.

Becca, he took liberties. I realized what was happening but didn't stop it. He thought me a possession to use at will, and I let him. No more will I write about this, but all thoughts of love and a different life have fled.

Please respond with better news than what I have shared. I wait with great anticipation for your next letter.

Your friend,

Pru

Chapter Fourteen

New York City, 2024

Staff meetings and souls. The couch greets me after a tough week, but then a knock on the door makes me jump and breaks my moment of relaxation. I smooth my hair, peeking in the mirror to confirm my mascara hasn't decorated my cheeks. Daxone is on the other side. This is the moment I've been waiting for since that last kiss rocked my world.

She pecks my cheek when she enters, takes off her jacket, and spins slowly, inspecting the living room.

Heat builds under my skin. I never bring anyone here and couldn't hate this place more than I do now.

"It's nice," Daxone says as she faces me. "Very clean."

My blush spreads. "I don't spend a lot of time here."

She walks further into the room and drops her jacket on a chair. "No, it's nice, but it's not what I expected from you."

"What do you mean?"

"You're so full of life. This place seems—" She pauses, searching for the right word. "—like a hospital. Sterile."

"I guess you'd know, being a doctor and all." The words are clipped.

"I didn't mean it in a bad way."

"I'm not sure I can find another way to take it." The door bangs shut.

She plants herself on the arm of the chair where her discarded jacket slumbers. A grin creeps across her lips. "Let's begin again. I love your place."

"Thanks." I paint a smile on my face. "Want a drink?"

"Do you have a beer?"

"You betcha." My discarded leather jacket sits on my gray Bob's Discount Furniture kitchen set stool. Daxone has a valid point. The apartment doesn't represent me, but how does one explain to a new girlfriend that one never stays in one place long enough to build roots or acquire meaningful possessions?

People notice the lack of aging pretty quickly and Death has all the reapers on a regular rotation schedule. It hasn't always been that way, but technology has streamlined the process. Thank you, smartphones.

Opening the fridge door, I extract two Sam Adams. At least I'm well stocked with all my favorite foods and drinks. I liberate the bottles of their caps and bring them into the living room.

She takes a sip, and we sit for a moment in awkward silence. I mimic her, taking a sip and wondering if bringing Daxone to my place was a mistake.

"Do you want a tour?" I ask to fill the void.

"Sure." She lowers her beer onto the table but then asks, "Do you have a coaster?"

How thoughtful. Back in the kitchen, I extract two from a drawer. We leave our beers, and I start the tour.

My apartment, like many in New York City, combines the living room, dining area, and kitchen. With a twirl, it's easy to take it all in. There's the thrift store chair, a subdued brown and tan throw rug, and a television mounted on the wall. The small, utilitarian kitchen houses a narrow table with two bar stools serving as a breakfast nook and dining area.

She stares at the picture of my supposed family on the mantel but doesn't say anything. "Does the fireplace work?" she asks instead.

I shrug. "No idea. Never tried it and never want to." Those days are long gone for me. A small shudder runs through me when thinking back. What a chore it was ensuring the fireplace, my own or others, was always lit, all those endless hours sweltering, stirring the cooking pot, or hanging clothes near the flames when it was too cold to put them on the line.

Daxone moves to the bookshelf that lines the hallway to the bedroom. It's overflowing. With no time to create any type of organization, books spill from the shelves onto the floor, amassing random piles. Even so, there's never a problem finding a book I want to reread.

It's always sad when I must leave them behind, but wherever I am stationed next, there will be new authors to explore. One great thing about the modern world is that I never lack reading material.

She pulls out a romance novel and flashes the cover at me.

"A girl's got to escape reality sometimes." I point to the book next to it. "Don't judge. I read everything." There's *Kindred* by Octavia Butler. That's science fiction. There's Stephen King horror, and, of course, the classics. I whip out my copy of *Dead Souls* by Nikolai Gogol.

I take the book from her hand, drop it, and lead her forward. "This way." The bathroom has old black-and-white mosaic tiles, a white sink and tub, and a white shower curtain. Not exciting. It's a one bedroom so there isn't much else to see. I inhale and fling open the door.

The bedroom is small, and my queen-size bed takes up most of the space. The mattress is plush. I didn't skimp. A reaper needs her rest when there's time. Across from it, instead of a television, a Toulouse-Lautrec painting hangs on the wall.

Daxone draws near to it. She stares for a few seconds, turns to me, then returns her gaze to the image. "This is beautiful. The woman in the painting looks like you. Really looks like you. Don't you find it odd?"

"It's the reason I love the painting so much."

"Is it real?" Her eyes are wide.

My lips part and close. "It's a real painting."

"Beautiful." She turns toward me. "But not as radiant as you are in person."

I snort. Yup, a snort actually leaves my mouth, and it's not dainty in the least. "Now there's a line of bullshit if I've ever heard one."

She frowns. "I mean it."

Our eyes meet. "You do, don't you." I pause in thought. How can this woman be so authentic? After many years alive, I've met intellectuals and thought leaders, creatives and radicals, but people happy in their own skin are rare. "You must have a flaw, but from what I can see you're pretty close to perfect."

She laughs. "Of course I'm flawed. All humans are. No one's perfect."

"Name one of your flaws." My butt meets the bed. "I haven't seen any."

"This is pre-aneurysm. I was too career focused."

"Is that bad?"

"It is when you lose touch with everything else, and it comes at the expense of family and friends. I wish I could go back and spend some time with my dad. We used to fish together, but I blew off the last two trips he tried to plan, and now I'll never get another chance."

"I'm sorry."

"The close call has opened my eyes and changed my perspective. I plan to make the most out of my remaining days, and that doesn't mean all work. I love my job at the hospital, and there is no better high than helping people, but I need to help myself as well."

"When do you go back?

"Two weeks." Her fingers touch the long scar on her forehead. She isn't wearing a baseball cap and the hair around the incision is cropped short but almost hiding it.

"Well then, we'd better make the most of our time together."

She smiles, but her eyes shift back to the painting. "Beautiful. Can

I take a closer look?"

"Be my guest."

Daxone walks over to it. "Do you know who painted it?"

The lie stutters out. "Toulouse-Lautrec originally painted it. No idea who did my copy."

"This is an amazing reproduction."

"Thanks. Now back to us. Do you want to join me on the bed, or is the painting going to hold you captive all night?"

"It could be your twin."

"You're killing the mood here. I definitely see another flaw I'm going to add to my list."

She smiles at me but then eyes her watch. "It's late. My mom finally got clearance to fly. She's coming to visit tomorrow. I should go after I finish my beer."

A frown forms, and the perch at the end of my bed is suddenly uncomfortable. She's leaving me? There's no way I'm sending mixed signals, but now I wonder if she is. Is she not into me? That kiss the other night. Did I forget to put on deodorant or brush my teeth? I distinctly remember doing both.

Do I smell anyway? What's happening here? What's gone wrong? I'm obviously out of practice. When was the last time I had sex? The fact I fail to remember tells me something loud and clear. This supposed seduction is not happening.

"Sure." I stand and precede her out. "Come on. Let's head back into the living room."

Before I can sit on the couch, she grabs my hand and swings me to face her. "I want to stay, but I wasn't expecting my mom's visit, and there's a lot to prepare. You understand how important family is, right?"

A memory of my mom flashes, and my body relaxes. "I do."

"Thanks." She doesn't let go, and the kiss she gives me lingers long after Daxone departs.

Chapter Fifteen

Paris, France, 1882

He was a short man, and I was a whore. We sat across from each other, and he sketched me. Occasionally, his hand dipped under the table to touch my knee as we waited for the Folies Bergère to begin.

The crystal chandelier above my head emitted a dim glow, creating a beautiful illusion of grandeur in the packed theater. A high-pitched, drunken squeal from a woman dispelled that. In front of us was the stage and to the side a large bar with too many liquors to name. An ornate, gold-framed mirror extended the entire length of the bar and threw my shadow self back at me.

Glancing at the woman in the mirror, I couldn't believe I was the same person who watched her mother die, who believed in a righteous God, whose Puritan father beat her for the most minor offense. If my father saw me now, drinking and getting paid for sexual favors, he'd go to the grave, though he was already in hell if justice existed.

Waiting for the trapeze artist to begin, I caught the barmaid's gaze. Mireille and I had become friends, and she sent me a small smile before pouring a drink for a woozy, portly gentleman. The fake flowers pinned to her dress hid a small part of her ample bosom behind dark chiffon and led her customer's eyes downward to not follow the pour. Mireille handed him the glass, and he whispered in her ear. A transaction for later in the night was brokered.

Death must have an awfully warped sense of humor, turning the Puritan woman into a prostitute, but I couldn't even get mad. I had my own room and a lot of freedom in the brothel, and it allowed me to carry on my work as a reaper without suspicion. Coming and going all times of day and night was normal for my current trade and worked for being a deathmonger too.

One unexpected perk of being in Paris was I'd had the chance to spend time with some amazing people, artists, and thinkers. Most considered me an equal and listened to my thoughts and ideas, a far cry from my past.

They recognized the body is only a flesh bag that withers and dies. Well, that's true for everyone else's, but not mine. The common belief with my gentlemen friends was that they want to enjoy the time they have with drink, art, literature, philosophy, and sex.

Henri's fingers inched under my skirt. He had money and spent it lavishly on his favorites. For the past few months, it had been me. I'd be paid well for my time, much of it spent in this and other bars or his studio, with his drinking and sketching. In truth, I wasn't even sure if he'd be able to perform later.

"It's the hair," Henri de Toulouse-Lautrec said.

"Pardon?"

"Why I can't get you out of my mind and need to draw you. I can't wait to take you back to my room and have you unleash the flames."

"Will we watch the show first?"

"Of course, but I can't wait to paint you later."

"We work tonight then, rather than go back to the maisons?" I asked.

"I want to complete my series of drawings."

His hand squeezed my knee.

"Whatever you desire." I smiled.

Paris was different from my lifestyle prior; so bohemian. I embraced it, now settled as a reaper and not worried about dying or even living morally. God, I've learned, never showed face, leaving all the work to underlings like Death.

The lights dimmed, and the burlesque show amused. The trapeze artists twirled and swung. There were singers and dancers, some wearing little in the way of costumes. Henri enjoyed himself even if he drank to the point where it was hard for him to stand and walk out of the venue.

Being his preferred girl for the last few months, I'd heard his story and knew his legs, which he'd broken in adolescence, pained him. He drank to cover that pain and others, but it also led to nights that ended with Henri passed out on his bed, where the only action taking place was me tucking the sheets around him.

On the walk to his studio, I held him tight as we traversed cobblestone alleys. It took me a long time to undress in front of others without a blush in my cheeks, but now inside Henri's cramped room and with his help, I shucked off my frock, let my hair out of its coiled bun, and slid onto the bed naked. My pendant rested coldly against my breast.

He set up his colors, easel, and canvas and painted. I stifled a yawn and tried to keep myself from falling asleep as I relaxed. There were no souls to pick up for at least a few hours so I could give him time enough before he passed out next to me.

Chapter Sixteen

New York City, 2024

A big, black X on my desk calendar stares back at me. I use my phone for most things but can't give up my paper calendar or my pens and notebooks. They remind me of my history and long time on earth, of all that has changed and all that remains the same.

Three weeks of dating Daxone. A blip of time. I shouldn't be falling for the woman with such intensity, but the emotions don't hold back. The upheaval leaves my body humming and my thighs clenching. It's a relief when my pendant flares. Death's a lifesaver because a distraction is most welcome.

Goose waits for me outside my apartment. Once I've mounted him, we both follow the pull. He gallops off. The surly wind whips through the city and my hair. A trail of sparks flames the sky. To be honest, I'm unsure if they come from Goose's front or back end.

Tucked into my leather jacket, I'm toasty against the late morning chill and enjoy the ride. New York City traffic is intense at all times of day. Car horns blare, people on bicycles weave in between cars, and taxi cabs or Ubers cut through yellow lights to chase the cars in front of them. People litter the streets as well. There's a constant push forward and a jostling of those too close. Pedestrians move in endless, steady streams of life. Even patrons enjoying brunch in the surrounding restaurants eat with intensity and a longing to dredge every ounce of flavor from their food.

The thought reminds me of my desperate need for a triple latte.

"We have to stop for coffee after this pickup."

Goose shakes his mane in disapproval. He has two modes: work and rest. Everything else is an annoyance. When he stops abruptly, I pitch forward but pull back before taking flight over his head.

"Hey, there. Be nice, or I'll make you scrounge for your dinner. Do you want scraps or steak? It's up to you." He's pitched me in the past, and I'm sure he'd love to watch me pick myself off the ground bruised and battered. But not today.

We arrive in Alphabet City, an East Village neighborhood by New York University. While the university, Broadway, and the area's restaurants are some of my favorite places to hang, the apartment complexes, not so much. Like much of the city, the area has been through periods of gentrification, and bad humans cannot hurt me, but sometimes the souls from these streets have seen more pain and hurt than the average.

I park Goose by some dumpsters in case he wants a snack, then head to Avenue D and into one of the large complexes where the SOD awaits. Stale air and someone's discarded hallway garbage greet me. The pull takes me to the stairs. I'm headed to the third floor. At least I get some cardio.

The apartment door opens to my touch. The inside is small, crowded with possessions including a keyboard and guitar, but organized. A brown stain takes up a good portion of the small kitchen ceiling and floor. Someone above has a leak, and it doesn't appear anyone bothered to fix it.

Sadness invades, and the pull tells me what I am going to find. An overdose death. He's on the bed, dressed in a grubby T-shirt and jeans. Eyes closed, mouth slack, his face is peaceful, but he might not be. I'm quiet on approach, not wanting to startle him. Overdoses can leave the person and soul confused.

"I'm here to help you move on to your next journey," I say.

"Where am I?" He's pale, and his head lolls to the side as he tries to take me in and make sense of my presence.

"In your apartment. Soon, you'll no longer be among the living." It never helps to deny the truth, but word choice can make or break a SOD.

"Who are you?"

"I'm here to help you move on. Are you ready to go?"

His fingers twitch, and his hand moves, scratching the skin on the other arm, digging deep gashes. "No. I've been clean for years, but my girlfriend broke up with me, and then I got laid off my job. It was too much. I didn't mean it. Can I stay?"

I shake my head. "It'll be better now. Come with me."

He meets my eyes. "No. I want to make it right with Lucy."

"Lucy?"

"My girlfriend."

"She'll understand." I channel my inner Zen and remain calm.

"Give me one more chance to see her." His words slur together. "Ineedtoexplain."

"What's your name?"

"Thomas. Tommy." Emotions battle. Reds and yellows flare around the room, then settle back against his dying form. Light shows are rare but do happen. Most of the time it's in cases like this where there are lots of unresolved issues. Deep breath. I'm only here to transition the soul. There's nothing else to do.

"It's time to go, Tommy." The distance closes between us. "She'll get it. Lucy will understand."

"I don't know." His head falls limply against the pillow.

I need to get this show on the road. Not much time left.

"Yes, you do. Your soul understands the next step. This is a transition you must make." He's not compliant yet but soon will be if I play my cards right. SODs need someone to take control of such a huge change, and that is, after all, my job. "Here's how it's going to work. You're going to transition, and I'll find a way to let Lucy know. I'll send the message somehow if you move on now."

His eyes are filled with the pain and horrors of his past when they meet mine. He starts to say something, but life energy drains from him and "okay" is all he's able to voice.

"Okay is good." Opening the bottle, I wonder for the millionth time what it appears to be to a SOD. They can't be putting their faith in an old, empty plastic soda bottle. It must be a tunnel, channel, river, or something appealing.

The soul drifts into the container, and I pop the lid. While it doesn't resemble black goo, it's not pretty. The consistency of blood, it's tinged with brown and red. I have no idea what will happen to it, but after my cup of coffee, I'm off to find Lucy before my next pickup. A promise is a promise, and this is not the first time I've had to make a visit to a relative or loved one to leave a last message.

I do whatever it takes to get the souls to move on.

Chapter Seventeen

Chicago, Illinois, 1921

Death swooped from the heavens, a ghostly shadow, scythe glinting in the moonlight. A black cloak shrouded him from the dying man and each step echoed with the tap of the long, wooden handle against the ground.

"Your time is up," the reaper rasped. "Come with me."

Eyes wide in terror at this callous apparition, the elderly victim opened his mouth to scream, but his last gasp croaked out instead. Death's skeletal fingers captured the old man's shoulder. The brittle, dying body jerked upward before going limp. The dead man's last stare was one of bewilderment, his mouth a gaping pit to the unyielding darkness, a silent wail reaching for the heavens in protest.

The soul lifted, a transparent shimmer of spider web, and the reaper caught it with his scythe and held it aloft. Stoic, Death turned and walked away, dragging the soul with him like a prisoner on a chain. Limp on the ground, the body remained where it fell. Only the clouds in the moonlight moved, chasing the shadows along the ground.

The movie theater was thrown into light. A smatter of applause erupted and was snuffed out as quickly as a candle. I stood, stretched, and laughed as I exited the theater, a man whose name I barely remembered at my side.

"What an excellent film," my date said in his low grumble of a voice. "It's only 1921, and technology has been able to give us the pictures. Who knows what the future holds, but I bet this decade will be a turning point when industry and technology explode."

My head bobbed in assent, but I disagreed with both the movie and technological advances. The silent film was nothing like reality, and after collecting hundreds upon hundreds of souls and living through equally as many years, I considered myself an expert on the subject.

"You really liked *The Phantom Carriage?*" The producer got death so wrong. Any reaper could verify that, but I held the words back.

"The story kept my interest, to be sure, but the technology to make it was amazing. How fast the world is progressing stuns me some days."

My date, who appeared to be my same age, was a strapping lad of twenty-five with sandy, windswept hair, thin lips, and a dimple on his left cheek. He opened the theater door for me and a chill blew my long coat apart.

After a few hundred years of reaping, I learned it was best to avoid connections with the SOD, but I continued the conversation. "Are you planning on creating something that will change the world?"

"It wasn't long ago we got electricity in the city. Look at us now." He pointed at one of the streetlights illuminating our way. "I could come up with the next great invention."

Maybe I'd underestimated this man and could be reaping a soul before it had the chance to change humankind's destiny. "What about the lights have you so interested?"

"Think about all we can do. Did you know we have a turbogenerator at the Fisk Street Station."

"I did not, but I do appreciate all the modern luxuries I have. You haven't answered my question. How do you plan to leave a mark?"

He shrugged. "I'm still young, but I'm an inventor at heart. I love reading and researching about the power network they're growing. Even people outside the city can benefit from the expansion. Who knows, someday the whole world will welcome electricity in their homes."

"Think big, right?"

"Absolutely. I have been thinking about ways to improve machinery now that we have better engines. I love to tinker. Take things apart and put them back together. I'll come up with something to change the world."

"I hope you do."

Maybe all the time doing my job had left me jaded, but it was hard to connect with and have faith in humans anymore. Their petty complaints. Their big dreams never realized. Their supposed insights into the world, and of course, their take on history, philosophy, industry. The world changed slowly, and few people saw the reality. Even I, as a reaper, couldn't always glimpse the big picture.

Over the years, I'd taught myself piano and violin, read the classics and the not-so-classic literature, adventured to many countries, often on Death's command, all to try to keep my humanity intact. It was and continued to be a struggle to be sure. Hence, the young man at my side. Nothing better than a night of lust to remind me humans still had something to live for.

The beaded hem of my loose-fitting dress tickled my thighs. The change in fashion throughout the generations had been interesting to observe along with the fight for women's rights. We'd come far, but even with the relaxed mores of this generation, we still had work to do.

While sheath dresses were all the rage, they were unlike anything I'd previously adorned myself with. Made of silky, shimmering gold chiffon, with a hemline above the knee, this one highlighted my fair skin and bobbed red curls, and Don, Dan, Drake, whatever his name was, noticed.

I felt wanton, perfect for the night ahead of me. The strands of pearls layered on top of the pendant tickled the hairs rising on the back of my neck. Outside in the icy Chicago wind, the long pendant with a cherry amber stone cooled against my skin but had shone with bright heat earlier in the night.

He took my hand, and I sent him my best smile, but my thoughts were elsewhere.

The man whose name I couldn't quite recall was on my list for collection. He was the last one tonight and had a few more hours. He'd be dead by morning due to an undiagnosed heart condition. I'd claim his soul.

There was no black cloak, no scythe, but humans' fear of death was often all too real. It was a blessing this man didn't know what was coming his way. Maybe I had a little compassion left because I would attempt to give him a night to remember in the afterlife.

Chapter Eighteen

New York City, 2024

Lunches, a visit to the Museum of Modern Art, and a return to Central Park leave me scrambling to reach my quota of souls. A few weeks fly by this way, and I'm struggling to keep to my schedule after spending more time with Daxone.

This must be a relationship, at least according to the self-help articles online. But worry creeps into my head like an ant on a picnic blanket, small and unobtrusive until it either bites or carries away the food. We haven't hit the sheets, and she's ignoring my innuendos.

I'm getting a complex and vow tonight I'll make it happen. If not, maybe I've found yet another flaw, though I've not seen the first one she talked about, the inability to put work aside. She's attentive and, though she's back at the hospital as a doctor not a patient, makes time for us.

Daxone even offered to let me meet her mother when she visited, but no thank you. It was too intimate at the time, but now I wonder if I should have been braver and gone with her.

These thoughts drag me down as we sit at a two-top in the dimly lit, tiny wine bar, enjoying a good merlot and gorging ourselves on appetizers of latkes and nachos from the eclectic menu. I'm not supposed to eat this much or laugh this hard before I plan to get naked but can't help it.

"Fuck, marry, kill. Don't think about it. Let's do *Bridgerton*."

"I don't know that show." She attempts a frown but can't.

"I've lost all respect for you."

"I'm more into documentaries."

"Next time you come over, I'm giving you a romance, and you had better read it cover to cover."

Daxone salutes me. "Anything you say, my dearest."

"If only getting my way was always so easy."

"I can help with that." Her smile is sassy, and my nether region ignites.

Damn it. I have real feelings. Heart and fire emojis would be endless across my screen if I were expressing myself to her via text. Instead, leaning across the table at the end of the meal, I gather up my big girl pants and say, "Take me to your place."

I wait for the rejection.

"Are you sure? I don't want to rush you."

Is that what this gorgeous woman has been worried about? I snort. "We can't get there quick enough. You've been such a tease these last weeks."

"I didn't want you think I was here only for sex. I have real feelings for you and one-night stands aren't my thing. Nothing wrong with those if you like them, but I'm more of a serial monogamist. Since becoming a doctor, I haven't dated much. I'm a little rusty on the rules." She stands, gathers her coat, and helps me with mine. "Sorry. I'm babbling."

My thumb hits my lips, and I tease the skin, only to bring it down and put my hand in my pocket. "Babble away. I'm glad you told me. Honestly, I thought maybe you didn't find me attractive in that way."

"That's the farthest thing from the truth."

"Good to know."

A comfortable silence ensues during our walk to her place. New

York at night is special. We move from crowded streets bathed in light, clothing and luxury items on display in well-lit stores, to the more tranquil streets of brick and stone apartments. On the corner is a deli. Small trees dot the sidewalk. Our pace slows in front of her entry.

I remember her apartment well, especially the couch, but don't let on. The space is spotless. Utensils, pots, and pans are organized in the kitchen. "You must love to cook. You have all the accoutrements of someone who spends time in the kitchen."

"I'll make you breakfast if you stay the night."

"That sounds like a dare," I say.

"Take it as you will." She raises an eyebrow.

"I never pass up one of those." Unable to be put down, so to speak, I might as well embrace some challenges. These usually involve bungee jumping and sailing Goose over skyscrapers. Love, on the other hand, is a dare I'm less sure about.

She pulls out a bottle of wine from a small wine fridge, expertly uncorks it, and pours.

I pretend to inspect the place for the first time. "I love your couch."

"Thanks. Get comfortable."

Plush cushions meet my backside. "Come join me."

She hands me a glass before she sits. "What exactly do you do as a consultant?"

Not this conversation. Not now. There's only so much bullshit I can make up about my nonexistent job.

"This and that. Create campaigns for companies, edit their employee handbooks and policies, which are often a mess. Whatever is needed. Nothing so wonderful as saving people's lives. What do you enjoy most about being a doctor?" I'm proud of myself for changing the conversation with such ease.

"Helping people obviously, but there's something amazing about the human body. Take my case. Miracles exist, and being a doctor, I see them."

If only she understood the reality. "I'm sure you're brilliant at saving lives."

"Thanks for the vote of confidence. It's sad, though. Doctors can't save everyone and dealing with grief-stricken families is hard."

"Death has a place in life too."

"I'd love to see it eliminated."

"Don't think that's the way the world works."

She puts a hand on my knee. "This is not a conversation for tonight. How's the wine?"

"Wine's good and you're so right about the conversation. I have a different one. I want you and can't wait any longer for you to make the first move. You've been driving me crazy since the moment we met. Please take me to bed. Love on me."

There's a moment of staring, a long release of breath, and some shifting, but then she pulls me up from the couch, and in that instant, I remember, of all places, Iowa. She gives me the same warm feeling Aimes did. The town was a cushion, a safe place to land. This time, I pray the feeling remains for a while longer.

Chapter Nineteen

Spokane, Washington, 1933

The large, domed room hummed with nervous energy, sweat, and desperation. I lay on my cot, separated from Barry during our fifteen-minute break. Reapers don't need sleep and a few nights without shutting my eyes didn't even phase me.

Barry, the reason I entered the ridiculous dance marathon, wasn't doing nearly as well. If the Great War had confused and disheartened the United States, the downturn of 1929 left the country empty.

Death was winning this game on earth, but who else was even playing? Competition seemed scarce, and how the hell could any competitor make such awful decisions for the people? Couldn't something good happen around here for once?

A whistle screeched, and inside the marathon dance hall, contestants sat on their cots, rubbing their eyes, and preparing for the next round. We'd been at it for nearly forty-eight hours, but Barry wouldn't last another twenty-four. Yup, here to perform my job.

True, I could have shown up as he was dying and skipped the dancing, but after the Great War, I vowed to learn a little bit about each of the SODs. My schedule made this difficult and didn't allow me to do this for everyone. Barry got lucky.

My arms reached toward the ceiling in a stretch before I pulled back the curtain and found my ashen-faced partner on the dance floor in a wrinkled once-fancy suit and scuffed brown leather shoes.

Even after forty-eight hours the onlookers remained rowdy. The crowd hustled to their seats after the fifteen-minute bell rang. The first reverberations of *Crazy Feet* by Fred Astaire boomed from the Victrola.

Barry grabbed my hand, and the tremor in his flared. He pulled me close, and we shuffled along the floor, careful not to bump into other couples. His clothes were damp, and sour sweat from him and the other participants dominated the dance floor.

"Are you okay?" I asked.

"Not since I lost most of my money in the crash."

"How is any of this helping you?"

He shrugged in surrender. "It's a survival strategy until I can re-build. I do okay and take home some small cash prizes. April, my previous partner, loved the attention until a sprained ankle left her hobbled."

Unfortunately, today wasn't going to be his day to win the big money, the one-thousand-dollar cash prize.

"Now you got me as a partner." I peered into his eyes. "You sure you're okay?"

He wasn't but smiled tightly, forehead slick, eyes bloodshot, thinning brown hair matted. "Fine. We have to push through."

How much more pushing through he'd be able to do wasn't much, but he led me to the middle of the crowd. We started. No one would call what we were doing dancing. It was more of a strong shuffle. Barry got points for determination. There was no stopping him even though his lips were cinched in a tight line and his eyes were slits as he held back tears.

What I'd gathered from our conversations in the previous forty-eight hours was that he'd been single, enjoying his life maybe a little too much until the stock market crash left him near penniless.

Bankruptcy soon followed, but he considered himself a scrapper, and after small successes at the dance marathons, he planned to win big.

The floors creaked as we shuffled around, and I considered it an ominous talisman to the proceedings. And so we went, step after step, hour after hour. The crowd continued to cheer us on. They placed bets on which couples would win and roared with excitement when someone dropped to the ground. They loved the spectacle and misery as much as they enjoyed a couple's success.

With a flip of red curls behind my ears, I let a pent-up breath escape in an attempt to lessen my maudlin thoughts. There'd been many moments of kindness throughout my tenure, but the darker forces were much more powerful. Guess who was intimately connected to those. Yup, me. Death was not kind. It had been hard to turn off my emotions at first, but with every day passing and every soul I claimed, it became easier.

The shrill blast from a whistle interrupted. To wake us up, a sprint was called for. The contestants lined up on one side of the room. Another long, loud whistle shriek had everyone galloping across the dance floor. Barry was on his way back when he slowed. I turned to watch his legs buckle. His knees hit the floor. We were disqualified. There was worse to come. Life ebbed from his body.

I sprinted over, pretending to be a concerned friend, but I wanted to collect the soul and leave this place. The small glass bottle shone, and I stared, always a little astonished that something so simple could entrap a soul's ethereal elements.

The light in Barry's eyes faded as I held his hand. He was ready to move on. The desperation of the dance marathon mirrored the fear surmounting his life after the Wall Street crash. Without a word, his soul rose from the body and sank inside the bottle. I capped it and stood as the nurses ran out to check on him.

They ignored me and I disappeared from perception. Walking out the door, I was happy to leave the humans to their ways, yet the questions of how much good existed in the world still haunted me. Dance marathons had not revealed what I searched for.

Chapter Twenty

New York City, 2024

It's hard to trust anyone, to make friends, to be lovers, but my faith rests in Daxone.

I repeat my words. "What are you waiting for? Please take me to bed. Love on me."

Her eyes grow large, but then she grins, grabs my hand, and leads me into the small bedroom with a large bed covered in a dark-blue duvet and a wide, antique walnut chest of drawers.

Her hands roam my sides. "I didn't want to come off as aggressive, but all I thought about tonight was ripping your little black dress off."

"How about you unzip it instead."

She eases the gold zipper along my back and the sheath dress slips off. I pirouette, giving her a view of my red bra and matching thong.

"You're amazing. Beautiful."

"And you'd look better naked. Let me help." I want to explore every part of Daxone's body and splay my fingers against her neck, running them down her retro graphic movie T-shirt sporting an image from *The Breakfast Club*. Heat beckons and I reach under, enjoying her searing skin.

She pulls back. "Are you sure you want this?"

"I've never been more sure." I kiss her, pulling at her T-shirt. It's hard to angle it over her taller frame, but I manage with a little help and throw it to the ground. Melding us together, I reach for her jeans, which I liberate easily.

Clothes forgotten, Daxone draws me close again and brushes her fingers against mine.

More please. Much more. My reserves shatter, our bodies come together, and my hands caress her arms. Daxone is everything I need. Is that even possible? Because no one can be everything.

When she pulls my mouth back to hers, tugging on my lower lip before deepening the kiss, my thoughts flee. She's glorious in only black panties and bra.

We kiss, our lips exploring. She tastes like wine and wilderness, and smells of strawberries. A pleasurable vibration passes through me, and I clench my thighs together. Cool air caresses my shoulders, but I need her heat. Desperately.

And heat I get. She nuzzles my neck and presses her palm against my breast. Daxone pushes away my bra and pulls me close. Her lips tug at my nipple. My stomach and a wee bit lower knot in anticipation, and I gasp at the sharp, overwhelming need that invades.

Her lips cascade along my stomach, but I pull her upright and take her mouth against mine. The kiss is sincere and full of wanting. This moment should last forever. I'm at home and in heaven all at once.

The amazing woman continues to kiss me, tempting me with a flick of her tongue against my lips. I part them, inviting her closer. She wraps her fingers through my curls, and we linger in the moment.

When I can take no more, I guide her to the bed and we crash, a storm in the making. We rid ourselves of what remains of our clothing. Naked upon the small bed, I gaze at every inch of her, but my eyes linger on the triangle of curls between her legs. It beckons my touch.

She places a finger under my chin, and our eyes meet. "Let me love on you."

How dare this woman turn my words on me when I want to kiss every inch of her body, every smooth curve and cleft. Still, I can't refuse. She could ask me anything right now and I'd acquiesce.

She presses me against the mattress, and we kiss for an eternity before her mouth roams over my body. One finger slides between my thighs, finds my heat, and nurtures flames. When her kiss returns to my lips, my groan escapes against her mouth. Unabashed, I buck when her fingers stroke my core, wanting her more. Wanting her closer. Much closer.

One palm cups my breast again. Her lips leave a delicious breeze along my neck, and her skilled fingers work my heat. I let go and my body is racked with pleasure undulating through me.

It takes a few minutes, but when I finally recover, I twist to my side. "My turn."

I straddle her and pull her hands over her head, intertwining mine with hers. She could easily free herself, but why would she want to? With the other hand, I trace patterns along her arm and over her stomach. Finally, I caress her thigh.

"Don't torture me," Daxone grunts.

"I won't. At least not too, too much."

She breaks free and reaches behind my head to pull my mouth toward her. My hair falls like mist around us, and I return her kiss. Pulling away, I slink backward. I trail a hand across her ribs before my finger finds and threads along her inner thigh. My eyes memorize each detail of the moment. "Is this okay?"

"More than okay. You are a witch and have me enchanted." The words, barely audible, are ragged and halting.

Witch, no, but that might be somewhat of an apt portrayal. I do have supernatural powers but don't so much deal with earth elements. It's life and death, baby. Close enough. To prove I'm okay with her description, I kiss the top of her curls before nestling between them. It's only a few minutes before she groans; soon after, releasing a rough and wild energy.

It's not long before Daxone returns the favor, and I go over the edge with a shudder and a sigh. Spent, we settle, her final kiss soft and teasing with the promise of more blissful nights to come.

Chapter Twenty-One

Ames, Iowa, 1956

The view from behind the wheel of the car was idyllic. I gazed out, my gloved hand poised for a final wave. While a smile sat on my lips, my heart drummed irregularly, pain attempting to break through. The soft hum of the engine filled the air.

Ames, Iowa, had been my home for the past ten years, but it was time to move. When you don't age, people notice. This time it stung. Life here had been different, somehow simpler.

After the horrors of World War II when reapers galore had been pulled into Europe, my return to the United States and settling in as a secretary at Iowa State University seemed a blessing. I'd never forget the war, and I wanted little to do with humanity in its aftermath.

I hated calling myself a reaper as well. Thoughts of corpses strewn on bloody battlefields still littered my nightmares. My daytime reminiscence wasn't much better. So many reapers, drawn together by such excessive death, drank and danced, celebrated and copulated, consuming dying as if it were the drug of choice.

Ames had become a sanctuary, with my books and my music and

a few acquaintances from the college. I could live in the campus library for days, snuggled in my favorite corner with a huge history tome as I tried to figure out why humankind acted as it did.

Here, I'd withdrawn into myself, focusing on my job, my routine, and the passing of the endless eras. Even so, after ten years, I couldn't help but connect with a few reapers in the same state who felt like me. Now, it was time to leave it all.

The sun rose from behind the buildings lining the street. It cast a bright, golden-red glow in the early morning. A cold breeze rustled the remaining leaves of one of the only trees that flailed in front of the apartments and store fronts. Bacon- and lard-scented air escaped from The Griddle Diner a few doors away when people entered and exited.

"Ready to go, darling?" Becca asked as she made her way to the car. She'd been my lifeline. If not for her, I doubt I would have been able to continue, but Death threw us together when I needed someone. How Death knew this was beyond me, but now I had to leave her.

I pushed a strand of my short, red hair behind my ear and adjusted my hat. As I nodded, my smile slipped a little. "I'll miss you. You've been a wonderful friend." The lump in my throat threatened to choke me and I had to turn my attention to an imaginary spot of dirt on the steering wheel.

My knuckles ached as I gripped the wheel with all my might, blinked, and put my smile back in place to mask the sadness swelling like whitecaps inside me. I couldn't let Becca know how much I'd miss her. How much I needed her as a friend. After living many lifetimes, she was one of only a few reapers I trusted.

When I turned the key in the ignition, the car rumbled to life. With a final brief wave, I pulled from the curb. The tires crunched through the frost. In the rearview mirror, I watched the place I had called home for a short time in my long history fade from existence much like I would be doing in the minds of everyone there.

As I drove through the town, I wondered what life would be like in the next place. The weight of the thought pressed against my heart, and tears fell in ugly streams. *Pennsylvania, here I come.*

Chapter Twenty-Two

New York City, 2024

My amulet grows hot against my throat, waking me. These days, it's usually an official email and backup text in the morning with the names and addresses of my clients, but the amulet is the way it began, old school.

It's also a failsafe for times like this when a middle-of-the-night emergency happens. I haven't worked the night shift in decades, but someone must have a problem. I don't even have to fathom a guess who that someone is.

Daxone's cheek is warm when my lips touch it. "Got to go," I whisper.

She pulls me close. "No."

"Sad but true." I push away. "Call me in the morning."

She mumbles a response, but the cold floor meets my feet. The discarded panties and black dress heap the floor.

My fingers find the amulet as I exit Daxone's place. I'm not all too sure how it works. It just does. You follow it, and it leads to death. I ride the subway toward the problem since Goose isn't close. I don't worry about being attacked or robbed. When on the job, people tend to ignore and avoid me. It's as if there's a warning signal: "Death on the warpath."

Go figure.

I arrive at the nondescript apartment complex. The elevator chugs to the ninth floor, and the door opens upon my command, but once inside, I almost back out as quickly. The air is stale and hot as hell, making it easy to tell a battle rages between soul and reaper.

John scowls at the bedroom door. I'm right once again. If an emergency call comes in from my district, it's probably him.

Whoever chose him to work for Death has some serious issues, but I was there in World War II when reapers danced in blood and made love as humanity sank into madness. Maybe *I* shouldn't be here. Still, he's as incompetent as they come.

John's angular jaw twitches when he sees me, but his slicked-back hair doesn't move an inch. He stands no taller than my five feet five in his black leather trench coat. There's a cruel twist to his lips, and his hands curl into fists. His eyes, quick and nervous, narrow in his sun-baked, fake-tan face.

"What's the problem?" I ask.

"You again? Same old, same old," He barks the words. "He doesn't want to go."

"The clients don't get a say in this."

"No shit. You think you're so amazing because souls jump into the bottle for you. It's not like that for everyone."

"Don't blow a fuse," I say. The image of him going ballistic at some innocent SOD, sparks flying from his overly greased hair, setting fire to the scene, leaves me wanting to giggle and heave in equal measure.

"Stop saying things like that. If you'd ever let me fuck you, you'd know better."

"Ease up there. Do you want my help or not?" I'm used to his attitude. He's a misogynistic pig, and none of that changes on the job. I've rebuffed his hookup offers often enough that our relationship is anything but friendly, but I can't refuse a call or let a soul suffer in limbo.

"Fine," he grumbles.

In the bedroom, an old man is shriveled between the sheets. A wheezing last gasp emerges from blue lips. "Time to go." My voice is firm.

"My family didn't come." He doesn't need to say the words. I still hear them. "No one made it."

The cases when family and friends live far away or don't care enough to return is one of the worst parts of my job. "They'll mourn you. It'll be okay."

"No one is going to mourn this grumpy, old bastard." John's hot, sour breath fills my ear.

Yuck. I shoo him away.

"They never cared enough." The old man's words fade into a ragged gasp.

I move close. "Sometimes family can't show their feelings. That doesn't mean they don't have them. Remember, this isn't one person's fault or sole responsibility. Life's an entanglement. But with death, all is forgotten. It's your time. Everything is about to change."

"I can't," he says, but the words are weak.

I cover his withered, veiny, paper-thin hands with my own. "Time to go on to the next adventure."

"I like you better than the other one."

I laugh and extract the soul catcher. "They all do." With that, it's done. I stand, turn, and find John glaring. He's heard it all.

"They all do." He mimics. "You really are a bitch sent from hell. A soul-stealing succubus. You have them fooled, don't you, but not me. I know the truth, you sneaky little slut."

"I helped you out. Do you think I want to be here in the middle of the night doing your work? Why don't you try and show a little compassion? That might get you a lot further with the dying."

"Compassion is for the weak. Death is a god, and gods do what they want when they want."

I roll my eyes and head toward the door. "That explains a lot of your problem. You're not a god."

"Not yet. Give me my soul."

"I collected it. I'm keeping it."

"I'm on duty. It's mine."

The bottled soul rests in my open palm. "Then take it from me." I've trained in all martial arts and can make this idiot beg for his mama.

He pulls out a knife. "I will."

"John, what the fuck? You can't be serious. We're on the same team and work for Death. Souls all go to the same place."

"Then hand it over."

"Not at knifepoint. I'm going to report you."

"Not if you're dead." He moves close.

I'm trained in self-defense, but he's got some pounds on me. He slashes out in the air, and I pocket the soul and step back, avoiding the blade. The soul is in my hand, and I could give it to him, but there's a bigger issue here. You don't attack your coworkers. It's a pride and principle thing. Even if I report John, I want him to understand what a dufus he's being. Unfortunately, I don't carry a weapon. Working for Death usually protects us from unexpected human violence.

A large book with a glossy picture of a classic car shields me from the blade. He jabs through the cover with the knife and pulls it from my hand. I run into the living room and dodge behind the coffee table. John pushes it aside and lunges. Loud steps echo on the old tile floor as I sidestep and flee into the kitchen. A mealy apple leaves my hand. I aim for John's stupid scowl, but he ducks. There's a coffee maker, a couple of dirty dishes in the sink, and some utensils in a large pottery holder. I aim them all at his head, but only the spatula hits true. He curses, and I throw a whisk, but it's hard to have accurate aim when dodging the end of a knife.

The cabinet doors flail open as I pull out a cast iron frying pan. I wield it as a shield and make my way to the front door. It's time to exit this madhouse. I'm close, fumbling with the doorknob, when the knife rips into my jacket. I drop the bottle at his feet and flee out the front door.

John sinks the knife into my side. Pain explodes. I stagger down the long hall. The freaking coward knifed me in the back. But I'm death. Can I die? He slices with the blade a third time, and my knees buckle in the hallway. I gather the strength to rise and stumble down the stairs.

My hand reaches around to my back, and my fingers return warm and sticky. At the building entrance, I open the door, leaving behind a trail of red, and launch myself onto the street before I twist and stagger.

John follows me out and rams the knife into my stomach. Pain overwhelms me and I fall to my knees once again. Vision blurring, I intuit more than see him standing above me. He shakes the soul in the air, bends, grabs my phone and wallet, lets out a long, slow whistle, and strolls away.

My sight tunnels. Daxone's image appears, and I relive our last moments together. Her face turns fuzzy. A pinprick of light shines brightly in her place, a star that slowly fades to soft gray. Before drowning in darkness, I wonder who will collect my soul.

Chapter Twenty-Three

Mapleton, Canada, 1975

The Ford F-100 sputtered to a stop in Mapleton, Canada at the same time as my pendent flared blood red and hot. Having collected souls for three hundred-plus years, I intuited I had twenty minutes to spare, perhaps thirty.

The truck door squeaked open, but I didn't move, allowing the fall chill to enter the heated interior. Canada was as cold and barren as my love life, exactly how I liked it of late. My most recent loss, more than ten years ago during the early years of the Rhodesian Bush War, still stung.

Three-inch platform heels crunched dead leaves and polyester bell bottoms swept them into the air as I exited the truck. My blue, yellow, and red mountain puffer jacket held the wind at bay. The Mapleton Taxidermy and Cheese store loomed large before me.

The ramshackle wood structure's door creaked open, and I stepped inside. Half the building was an homage to death. Deer heads, raccoon, possum, fish, fowl, and hides covered every inch. Animals, bones, and skins crammed the walls, shelves, and floor, a disorganized cacophony of life and death. A refrigerated glass case full of long rows of cheese hummed electrically on the other side, immaculate and neatly organized. Crackers, jams, and spreads stocked the nearby shelves.

My stomach growled. Once I retrieved my SOD, I planned to take a break and snack. For ten generations I'd gathered the departing and no longer had strong emotions about ripping a human from their life. Eyeing the remains of the many creatures on display, however, gave me pause.

I touched a gray, slightly tattered squirrel pelt. *Is this how everyone ends up? A petrified remnant of a life once lived, slowly fading into decay despite being carefully preserved.* I shook away the questions. I had a job to do, goddammit. Thoughts like these, after so many years on the job, were as worthless as the dying trying to cling to life.

In the corner of the shop, a man had been arranging a bear hide. Noticing my entrance, he stopped, slid his hands against stained, faded jeans, and walked over.

"Chuck Peel, owner," he said proudly, extending his hand for me to shake. His palm was cold to the touch.

"Saw the road sign and I had to see the shop." It was a lie. I stopped because someone was dying and it was time to collect a hide of my own, so to speak.

"The sign draws a lot of customers," he said. "It's good marketing. We've become a roadside curiosity."

"That's an understatement. Cheese and taxidermy." I pivoted around the room to take in the ambiance. "How'd the shop come to be?"

"Started out doing taxidermy, then several years ago, the cheese factory in Mapleton closed. My wife, love of my life, married forty years now, used to work there. She saw a need and so we expanded. Closest supermarket is miles away and they can't do it as well as we can. The cheese that is. No need for taxidermy with your groceries."

I nodded in full agreement. I wasn't convinced there was any need for what I saw around me.

He went on, not noticing my distaste for his craft. "We decided to sell cheese from the same shop where I did my taxidermy. Wife's home next door with the sniffles today, poor thing, or she'd be behind the counter. Can I help get you anything?"

"Maybe in a few minutes. I'd like to take it all in." I had to stall for time, waiting for my soul pickup.

"I have some hides to work on out back. You're welcome to come with me and see how it's done. Sorry if that's weird. I'm all for explaining taxidermy to people, but most don't get it and don't want to."

"I'd love that." I couldn't believe those words came out of my mouth, but he was right. I didn't get it. I followed Chuck out and watched as he cleaned a deer hide. "Nowadays, folks bring me everything they can find. This one was shot." He worked the deer carcass, skinning it, cutting away the meat.

"The meat goes to the owners and then the hide goes through the tanning process. I save the jaws. There's a market for those too. Sorry if this is too much information, but I love to share. Wife calls me a chatty Chuck."

I watched, hating to admit I was fascinated. After a few minutes, my attention turned to the owner. He was an older man, tall and reedy, with muscled arms from all the physical work he did. He appeared in good shape, with only a small gut over his belted jeans. I wondered if that came from enjoying too much of the cheese in the cabinet and the fresh venison he sliced away in front of me. Maybe that drove his cholesterol high.

"How'd you get into this line of work?" I asked.

Chuck shrugged, admiring the brown deer hide under him. "I've always found it fascinating. It's a way to preserve the beauty of the natural world."

"Isn't the natural world all around us to see?"

His eyes met mine for a moment. "Most people don't notice until it's staring them in the face."

I thought about his words. "It's a way to see something new in what's common?"

"That and to appreciate what God has put on the earth for us lowly humans."

"Like a memorial. Similar to a shrine for the dead or a tombstone."

He shot me a glance. It was a weird conversation, but he was the one who admitted he loved to chat. Plus, when you've been around for centuries, you lose many of your inhibitions, especially when collecting souls. People tend to tell you fuck all before they die. As someone who has to move often and has trouble making lasting friendships or holding on to relationships, I might as well have interesting conversations whenever possible.

He pointed his blade at me before returning it to the carcass. "It's an art too. I like to think people appreciate the fact that I can take something ugly, like roadkill, and turn it into something beautiful. When you go back into the shop, look at the animals I preserved. Notice the details."

"I'll do that."

He warmed to the subject. "Taxidermy is all about skill and precision. The animal's skin and fur have to be carefully preserved but then it takes a knowing eye to create the natural pose and a thing of beauty. There's a lot of art and science that goes into it."

"I bet you need a good understanding of anatomy and biology."

"I've never had a lot of formal schooling, but I've studied it on my own."

I liked this man, his viewpoint on life, and his passion for his craft. Chuck had obviously been doing it for years and still enjoyed it. I, on the other hand, never found something or someone I enjoyed nearly as much. It would be a loss when it was his time to go.

He continued to work the hide. "It's all part of the cycle of life. I mean humans need to survive, and the animals provide food and clothing." I could rationalize my part as a cog in the world's endless wheel just as good as any other reaper.

A glance at my Omega watch made me aware time had gone quicker than imagined. "I have an appointment and need to get going. I'd love to get some cheese curds for lunch."

I almost added "after the reaping" but caught myself.

We headed inside and I peered around at all the mounted heads. "You don't find this unsettling. I mean you're surrounded by death all day, every day."

"It doesn't suit everyone. Some people find it macabre, but I celebrate life more than death."

Red Swiss Army knives, the kind with all sorts of gadgets attached, perched in a basket by the checkout waiting to be sold.

The owner picked one up and started clicking open the different elements: a corkscrew, a wood saw, scissors. "Do you have one?"

"Me? No."

"Everyone should."

"Really?"

"You never know when it will come in handy. It could even save a life."

"Save a life, you say." I pondered his words for a moment. Could this knife one day change the course of history? Save a life that might otherwise be slated for reaping? "I'll take one. Add it to my tab."

I paid for the cheese and the Swiss Army knife and stuck out my hand again. He responded in kind and we shook, the tremor in his hand palpable. "It was nice meeting you, Chuck."

"You too," he replied.

I was no mind reader, but he seemed like he had a few more good years before a reaper, possibly me, showed up to claim him.

I walked out the door and across the street. Not bothering to knock, I turned the handle and slid inside to meet the soul patiently waiting for death. Waiting for me. Poor Chuck. I wondered how he'd go on without her, his beloved wife.

Chapter Twenty-Four

New York City, 2024

I wake in the hospital. Daxone is standing over me wearing official doctor garb. She's adorable, but a groan of pain greets her.

"You had me so worried." She frowns and sits in a chair next to the bed. Her fingers stroke my arm where the IV is not attached. "But you're not out of the woods yet. Is there anyone you want me to call? I don't know your family and friends."

My mouth burns like brittle briars. "Water." She puts a straw in the cup and brings it to my lips, and I drag a long sip. "What happened?"

"You were stabbed."

It replays in my mind with a wave of pain. "Right."

"Do you need more morphine?"

"No." I scan the room, the bedside table, and the open closet door. All empty. "Where's my phone?"

"You didn't have anything on you when the ambulance brought you to the hospital. No purse, no phone."

"That's not good." Fear invades me.

"Do you remember anything you could tell the authorities?"

A hysterical laugh bubbles up, but I choke it back. That's a great question. Can't tell everyone my evil coworker stabbed me because he's jealous I deliver too many souls to Death. Now is not the time for the truth with Daxone. "I was jumped."

"The police will be back when you're ready. They interviewed the couple that found you on the street and called the ambulance. What's weird is you weren't even close to your apartment or mine." She pauses, considering the next question, then asks. "Why'd you leave me in the middle of the night in the first place? Do you even remember how you got to where they found you?"

"Tired." No more lying right now. I'm in too much pain, on too many drugs, and would probably say something stupid or incomprehensible.

"Rest now. I'll check on you later. We need to talk about your condition and what happened last night."

My eyes close. Daxone rises from the chair, her sweet lips touch my cheek, and she's gone. Once I'm alone, the struggle to sit up is as real as the bandages curling around my stomach. Something's wrong. As Death's employee and someone not quite mortal anymore, I have the power to heal, but I'm not improving. If anything, each minute makes the hot pokers in my body multiply. The morphine does little to ease the throbbing fire.

I rip back the bandage.

My mouth drops. The wound is raw, oozing pus, and turning black. John must have somehow found and used an enchanted knife. Yes, magic exists. I mean, the pendant guides me to do what I do. That's only one of the many spirited items out in the world.

If it's the blade recently gone missing that Death highlighted in the monthly employee newsletter, my demise is hours away without intervention from the boss. A dude like Death, with all their connections and colleagues in high places, must be able to find out what made these wounds and procure a cure. My other option is to stay here and pray, but no way will these human doctors find the right treatment in the short time left.

I'm not even sure how to reach Death in my current pain-ridden, cell phone-deprived state. Fellow deathmonger Becca would come to my aid even if it meant pissing off John and putting her life in jeopardy. Or I could put my trust in Daxone.

I push off the bed and wobble like a broken toy car with three wheels. Dragging my IV along, I attempt to channel invisibility in the hallway. The nurses don't stop me; they don't even peer up from their computer screens. It could be me in death mode as I am literally dying, but they're likely too busy and overworked to care.

I scuttle, hunched over, every movement causing a hiss of pain, into the next room. An old man sleeps through a conservative news broadcast on the television. The three anchors debate the death and destruction to come. For once, I'm in complete agreement. I search the man's belongings but find nothing. No cell phone, and the other bed is empty.

I hobble around, glancing into different rooms, until I find a sleeper. I stumble through the door, antiseptic in my nose and a sheen of perspiration lining my forehead. There's a young woman in the bed, and her cell phone sits on a tray next to her uneaten meal. I walk in, grab the phone, head back to my bed, and dial one of two numbers committed to heart.

"Hello. Who's this?" She sounds hesitant.

"Becca, it's me."

"What's wrong?" There's fear in her voice. "Are you okay?"

"No. I've been stabbed."

"That's a relief. Take some Tylenol. It'll heal by tomorrow."

"This is different." Pain eats at my stomach. Bile rises. I swallow it down. "It was John. He stabbed me with some hoodoo voodoo blade. I'm not going to make it out of here unless you come."

"I will put that bastard in the ground. Prick. Scum."

"Thank you, but let's deal with the scum later. I'm at Columbia Presbyterian. You have to contact Death and get me out of here. These doctors can't help. I want to leave, but don't have the strength to walk. Down the hall to find a phone was hard enough. No way I'm making it to an exit without collapsing or spewing whatever is left of my last meal."

"Let me see what I can do. Why don't you call Death's admin now? That'll get you fixed up right away."

"Barely hanging on as is. I can't take the lecture I'm sure I'll get from them. Worse, they might put Death on the phone." A shudder passes through me. It could be the wounds, but I'm doubtful.

"Got it. I'll tell them what happened. I have three emergency pick-ups. Probably because you're incapacitated, but I'll get to the hospital as soon as I can."

*

Three hours later, covers pushed back, IV ripped out, I decide not to wait any longer. Becca promised to come to my rescue, but where is she?

I need to exit before I'm forced to tell Daxone the truth.

Chapter Twenty-Five

New York City, 1988

"Rex," the woman shrieked. "Look at that building."

"That's the Chrysler building, honey." The man patted the woman's arm.

The two gawking tourists dressed in I Love New York T-shirts blocked the sidewalk. People from their group exited the bus that held up traffic on Forty-second Street and formed a wall.

I threw up my hands in exasperation, plotting a path around the sightseers or through them. Rex was tall and had once been athletic, judging from his jackhammer arms. He'd probably played college football but now preferred to watch games with a few beers, as the paunch under his too-tight T-shirt indicated. White knee-high socks and black sneakers made him appear older than his years. His wife, petite and curvy, sported chunky, zebra-striped, blonde highlights under a visor. She wore Bermuda shorts, and her matching T-shirt was cinched tight with the aid of a fanny pack.

Going around the zebra-striped blonde appeared easiest, but the wall of I Love New York T-shirts grew as more tourists pushed out of the bus. I'd have to go in between. My arms circled my waist, ready to elbow through the couple. I race-walked forward, my lips forming a determined line. I drew so close I could smell Rex's Old Spice. My pendant flared. Not the usual hot red, but fire brick orange, the normally bright flame of death muted like embers in the fireplace at the end of a long evening.

With no idea if my pendant was malfunctioning or trying to tell me something, I pushed through them and turned back. The ruby pendant wasn't calling me to Rex's death, but it sure the hell wasn't silent either. This had happened a few times in the past, and I'd ignored it. This time, schedule light and my curiosity piqued, I followed the couple to seek the answer.

The tour guide, a stringy, hyper man, stood on the bottom step of the bus, shouting, "You have time to explore. Our hotel is only five blocks away. Very walkable. Be back there and ready for dinner at six. We have a reservation. Don't be late."

The group parted, and the couple ambled off gawking at the buildings. At the same time, real New Yorkers took a moment to return the favor, ogling the out-of-towners, smirking at their otherness.

I trailed them, trying to embody a private investigator. A few minutes later, the couple entered the lobby door of a hotel and checked in at the front desk. Could the bus ride and all New York had to offer have worn them out that quickly? The little miss, whose name I learned was Janet, headed upstairs while Rex sauntered into the red-and-chrome-toned bar, mirrored walls highlighting his bulk. He nursed a beer. Then another.

This was a waste of time. Three beers and twenty minutes of nothing. A yawn escaped, but I stayed and was soon rewarded when a woman entered, peered through the scant crowd, and joined Rex. Her hair, glossy, black and wavy, reached her midback. A nearly backless gold dress glittered under the disco ball lighting.

She flashed a smile. "Rex?"

"Yes. Want a drink?"

"No thanks. I'm ready to go upstairs if you are."

He stood and paid his tab. "Let's go."

This was getting weird fast, but I followed them, nonetheless. Could Janet be asleep? Maybe Rex drugged her to get her out of the way or maybe she was going to join the festivities. That still didn't explain my pendant, warm and waiting, but for what, I had no idea.

They rode the elevator back to the hotel room in silence and went inside.

Doubt took over. Who was I to judge what married couples did on their vacation? I hung outside their door for a few seconds, but my curiosity overrode my moral concerns. I let myself inside. No one noticed.

The woman sat on the bed, hands over her head as she slipped out of her dress. Rex watched but only for a moment. His eyes met Janet's when she emerged from the bathroom, her I Love New York T-shirt worn as a nightgown, a grandiose oversized knife in hand, and I asked myself what souvenir shop sold the weapon to her.

If she hadn't procured it in New York City, had it been hiding in her luggage this whole time? Did the rest of the group know about it? Was this some new kink going around the Midwest that I was unaware of? My love life was nonexistent at this point, but I had no desire to live vicariously through these two.

"Whore! Blasphemer," Janet screamed, brandishing the weapon overhead.

Rex grabbed another serrated knife from the nightstand drawer at the side of the bed. Premeditated murder much?

My mind exploded with questions, but mostly I wondered who these people thought they were, and what the heck was going on. I had no clue, and I thought I'd seen it all over the years.

Their guest didn't move from her spot on the bed, but her mouth dropped into a black oval. A gurgle escaped its depths.

"Don't talk," Rex said.

With a flurry of rabid animal movement, the weapon and Janet were at the woman's throat.

"Your kind goes against all the heavenly laws," Janet wailed. "We can't rid the world of every evil doer, but one less sure can't hurt. It's our mission. On every trip we take at least one sinner out and return them to hell where they belong." The knife twisted closer.

This speech sounded familiar, and my mother's face surfaced. I pushed the memory back into the dark corner where it belonged. That was the past. This was the present.

Rex grabbed the woman's arms and secured them behind her back with zip ties that had been in his pockets. If I had to give them any props, they did have the whole murder thing well planned.

From the moment these two stepped off the bus and blocked pedestrian traffic, I guessed they were evil. Peering into the souls of the three people in the room, something I normally loathed, I saw Janet and Rex's were black and twisty. The woman on the bed, while not incandescent and pure, was in a heck of a lot better shape than the other two.

The knife at the woman's neck drew blood. She whimpered as it leaked a red line in between her breasts. "I have a son." The words barely escaped her lips.

"Better for him to grow up without a whore for a mother." The blade pressed deeper.

I pirouetted away and drank in ten calming breaths. This had nothing to do with me. I wasn't scheduled to pick up the woman's body and the murder was so not my problem. Calling the police struck me as an option, but, no, not part of the job description either. My hand reached for the doorknob. Despite the city heat, it was icy, frozen like my heart had been for the past hundred years.

I turned back and pulled out my blade, the Swiss Army Knife from the taxidermy and cheese shop. Not that I needed a weapon.

"Stop," I roared.

"What?" Rex stuttered. "Where'd you come from?"

"Let her go." With each step, my determination increased.

"Grab her." Janet aimed the knife at me. "She must be another one of them ungodly whores."

"Wait a minute now." My off-the-shoulder neon T-shirt flared in the mirror across from the bed. It was 1988, and I was fashion forward, dressed appropriately with low-rise, ripped jeans and a tangle of curls held high with abundant hair spray and captured in a banana clip.

After reassuring myself my clothing choices were perfectly acceptable, I pushed Rex aside. He fell to the floor with a loud groan of pain. Rushing Janet, I liberated the blade from her grasp, grabbed the dazed prostitute, severed the zip ties with my Swiss Army knife, and hustled her out of the room. "Go home to your son," I ordered.

I closed the door, and my focus turned to the crazed killers. Rex, face mottled and sweaty, eyes like black caverns, drew himself off the floor and faced me. My tiny knife slipped in my sweaty palm. I had no experience using the gadget as a weapon. The corkscrew, screwdriver, and scissor accessories were the only ones regularly opened. I should have taken my taxidermy lesson from years ago more seriously. Brandishing the tiny blade like actors do in the movies, I put a psychotic sneer on my lips. Anything to scare the insane couple away or at least give me time to think of a plan.

Then everything got weird.

The hum of a vacuum filled my ears, and the air whirled and twisted, as if it were all to be sucked from the room. Maybe I'd go with it? Nothing like this had ever happened before in my time reaping. Rex leaped at me, but like some cheap science fiction film, his approach slackened, and his run turned into a slow-motion slog. He halted mid-stride, and the two killers were stuck in time like grotesque statues.

The phone screeched, causing me to jump. I scampered to the side of the bed and picked it up with trepidation. "Hello?"

"You're not supposed to interfere with the humans," a cheery female voice intoned.

"They were planning to kill her."

"Doesn't matter. No interference. It's on page two thousand seven hundred and sixty-four of the manual. Haven't you read it?"

"It's rather dense. And long. It must cost Death a shitload of money to print for all the reapers. To be truthful, it's a little confusing and complicated. Maybe some revisions?"

A sigh from the other end. "You'll have plenty of time to study it now. You've been demoted."

"What?"

"Pack your bags. We're sending you to Cape York, Australia for ten years. It's remote and filled with crocodiles. Have fun."

"Fun?"

"Have a lovely day. Ciao, bella." The voice disconnected.

Chapter Twenty-Six

New York City, 2024

Pain clouds my mind when I stand and shimmy to the other side of the room. I still can't believe John tried this and I promise to take him out of the game for good. What an idiot.

Clothes sit on a shelf in the open closet. They aren't from my apartment but appear as if they will fit. I pull off the flimsy paper gown, wondering what happened to the shirt I arrived in. Burned, I hope. My leather coat has been spared, even with the slash marks. It's on a hanger. An oversized long-sleeve shirt and sweatpants are waiting.

Now all I have to do is make it out of the hospital without getting caught, Uber to my apartment, find my backup phone, and explain to Death what happened. While I was able to call Becca from the hospital, when I finally roused the courage to call Death, no answer. The phones that come with my job as reaper must be different. There's a backup cell phone at my apartment, and that's where I'm headed since my bestie is delayed.

Clothed and ready to be sprung, I dial Becca's number. It rings once before the call goes to voice mail. Where is that woman? Probably dealing with the mess of souls I left behind. Signing myself out is an option, but I want to avoid the hassle. Escape it is. I inch to the door, biting my lip to avoid crying out with each step. It's midday, but in the hall, everything is quiet. I hug the wall, taking one gut-wrenching step at a time, and make it to the elevator before her voice reaches my ears.

"What are you doing?"

The shock on Daxone's face almost makes me smile. "I'm leaving." My voice is calm, even as my heart accelerates.

"That's crazy. You're not well. Your wounds are fresh."

"They're turning septic. I know someone who can keep me from dying."

"You're delirious. Come back to bed." Her hand covers my arm when she catches up to me, and she steers me back to the room.

I stand firm, even though it hurts like hell. "Do you want me dead?"

"This is a hospital. We're going to help you heal."

"You can't. I'll be in a body bag by morning."

"Don't say that. You can't leave. They have you on high doses of antibiotics and painkillers. You're not thinking straight. Everyone here is trying to help, and the medicine will cure you."

"The drugs won't do anything. I'm fucking knocking on death's door."

She steps back, not used to my language. "Of course they'll help." She moves close once again, forgiving my outburst, blaming it on the pain or my delirium.

Our eyes meet, and even with everything going on, all I want is to be lost in her gaze and stand here until the last of my life drains away. I can't live without Daxone and can only hope she agrees. I'll have to survive to find out. It's only taken stab wounds to foster some clarity, but it's time. I love this woman even though it's been a short relationship; a fleeting moment in my long life.

I have to tell her who I am. Damn the consequences. Daxone has to understand human drugs cannot cure me. I'll be a ROD without contacting Death. But the real reason I want to show her is more obscure, rooted in the fact that I need her to love all that I am. "Come with me."

"I'm working, and you should be in bed."

"Get on the elevator. I need to show you something. After you see it, if you want me back in bed, I'll go, but you'll change your mind." The elevator arrives, and I pull her inside with me. Luckily, we're alone when the door closes. My index finger hits the key for the bottom floor.

Her lips are soft and supple when I pull her close. They taste of mint tea and honey. I drink her in. Damn, there will never be enough kisses. I stop the elevator mid-floor, wanting a few extra minutes. This make-out session might be our last.

A buzz as loud as locusts fills my brain when I pull away. A few deep exhales banish it. After collecting souls for so long, my human form and the deathmonger are closely intertwined. But I need to conjure the reaper. Every ounce of dwindling strength focuses on death, my true form.

The reflective elevator walls scream back at me. While not skull and crossbones terrifying, my image is something to behold. My hair becomes a halo of flames framing my face, and my hazel eyes turn into endless pools of inky darkness, a reflection of the eternal struggle. While I don't feel taller, my image fills the small space, yet I'm not all hellfire and damnation. The smell of honeysuckle and cut grass fills the elevator. Death is equal parts love and hate, redemption and damnation.

Daxone turns white and sags against the elevator wall, which proves I'm a scary bitch when I want to be.

"I'm death." My reaper retreats, and my human form stammers in awkward explanation. "I mean, not really. I don't want to take credit away from my boss, but I am a soul collector, a reaper."

She stares.

"Are you okay?" I ask.

"No," she mumbles, wide-eyed.

"I'm the reason you lived when you had the aneurysm."

"I'm having another one." Her body slumps against the wall. "This is all a hallucination."

"It's not."

"What are you? An angel? A demon?" She rubs her temple. "No, this is all in my mind. I need help. Am I dying?" She begins to pray.

I recognize the words from so many souls collected.

"I'm not sure what I am, but to answer your first question. I collect souls."

"You're Death?" Her hand touches mine and jumps back as if exposed to flames.

"Not really." I throw my hands up and spread my fingers like angel wings. "There are those above or below me. I don't know what to call them or how to describe them." I shrug. "Their names all depend on your religion."

"This can't be real."

Nerves tingle under my skin. I ramble. "There are many characters in folklore associated with death. Various death-announcers and death-dealers, but they aren't actually Death. I'm a death-dealer. A reaper."

"We're both sick." Her face is ghostly.

"You're not sick. Only me. I need to find the cure, but it's not here. I have to get my cell phone. Do you believe me?"

"No."

"Do you want me to show you again?"

Daxone takes a step away from me. "That's okay. I prefer this version of you."

I shrug. "I'm not too scary for you, am I?"

It's her turn to shrug. "I don't know. I might be hallucinating all this." Her shoulders slump. "I prefer that it's all in my mind." She shakes her head. "I'm not sure what the other options are."

There's nothing more I can do to convince her now, and I have to find a cure before my reaper days are over. "I have to get my cell phone and call my boss."

"Cell phone?" She shakes her head again to clear it. "I can loan you mine." She looks at me. Her eyes are glassy. "Are you here? Really?"

Signs of shock are easy to see, but I can't deal with two crises at once. This was the worst idea ever. "It'll be okay. Really. I need my cell. It has a direct line to Death."

"Then you better go get it. I'll even play along, hallucination or not. Let me come with you."

"Finish your shift. I'll meet you at your apartment later today." The elevator dings, and I step out.

I Uber back to my place, step inside, and tumble on my couch. My body aches, the wounds throb, and chills cause me to tremble. For a moment, I'm stuck, having no idea how to proceed. Then I search my closet, find my backup phone, and scroll through my contacts.

Death is going to be pissed. Is there anyone else to call in a case like this? I'm staring at the screen when the phone rings. "Hello?"

"There are consequences for telling Daxone your secret. You have two days to be together. That's a gift for years of faithful service, but then you both die."

"Who is this?" I ask.

"You know who this is." The voice on the other end booms.

"Let her live," I plead. "It's John who is at fault. If he hadn't knifed me, life would be good."

"Both of your fates are determined. John is no longer employed, but that does not excuse your actions."

"Is there anything I can do?" My body slumps to the ground.

"You've done more than enough."

"Please. I'll make it up to you."

There's no response. The line clicks off. Stunned, it takes a minute to realize I'm no longer in pain. I hitch my shirt up, and my wounds are healed, not even a scar. Unfortunately, bigger problems lurk around the corner.

I retreat into the bathroom. The spray from the shower scalds. I want it to wash everything away, but it can't. I imagine what Daxone is thinking. Scenarios churn like the water running down the drain. Does she really think it's another aneurysm and she's going to die? Does she believe my story? Most of all, I wonder if she'll be there after her hospital shift. Is there a way to stop our fate? I, better than anyone, understand there's no way to halt the arrival of death.

Finally, the question everyone asks themselves at some point surfaces. If you had forty-eight hours to live, what would you do?

Chapter Twenty-Seven

New York City, 2009

The door swished open, and Poster House's light-filled lobby greeted me. I paid admission and took a sticker for my black leather jacket. It had been a while since I'd last visited any museum, but this was a retrospective of Toulouse-Lautrec's work. I'd been friends with Henri, more than friends, and I owed him at least this much.

Espresso and pastries from the small café on the lower level and the scent of old paper swirled around me. I walked into the open galleries. Posters of all sizes and colors decorated the walls. Linen-backed, professionally framed, they barely resembled the mess of sketches that had littered Henri's small studio floor.

Faces of the people I once knew mocked me. So much time had passed, yet here I was. The same. No better or worse, a cog in Death's endless wheel. I created no art, even though I'd learned to paint and sculpt, studied the masters in books, and later my computer, yet never become proficient at anything. For all my long years on this earth, I was forgotten.

This attempt to revisit the past might be a fool's errand, but I needed to try.

The winter wind whistled an ominous tune against the large entry windows in the other room. The ghostly serenade had me retreating farther into the galleries. I meandered around the first corner and found Henri's biography. Most elements of his life were accurate, but the stories I could tell about him... A smile touched my lips as I regarded his famous posters hung on gallery walls for review.

In the corner, on loan, were some paintings. I drew ragged breaths and sat on the bench before *Woman in the Window*. I'd sat for Henri as he sketched at my back. He'd been drunk on cheap bourbon some sittings, kind and funny others, but I'd never seen the final version. The painting loomed in front of me. When had that been—1892? 1893? A tortured breath escaped. It didn't matter. I was no more enlightened than long ago when I stared out the window and contemplated my life while Henri painted.

Times had changed; some might say extensively. My biggest transformation: joy and sorrow escaped me. I existed in an emotional chasm that I wanted desperately to understand.

A visitor crossed the gallery to view the poster *Moulin Rouge*. My eyes followed him momentarily before settling on the painting once more, and I whispered to Henri's ghost. "You were a man of emotion. Does my lack of emotion have something to do with all the time I've spent on this earth?"

Did I even bear to contemplate this fate as a reaper? I had chosen it but now detested the constant taking of souls.

"My life is death. Why?" I asked the spirit of Henri, or maybe I hoped my painted self would turn and respond. Nothing from either the ghost or the woman on the wall.

If the other visitor saw me, he'd think I'd lost my mind, and maybe that was true, but he stood in the far corner contemplating a poster of a woman kicking up her heels. My quiet rant continued. "If I was less thoughtful about the whole shit show maybe I'd be able to go about life without considering my actions, but everything is in question now. It must be true, what my dear artist friend said long ago. Contemplation destroys the harmony of the mind. I must live on, not think on."

I hadn't expected my painted self to turn around and answer, but stranger things had happened, and, like always, I watched for a sign from Death. A clue to everything or anything. As usual, nothing out of the ordinary occurred. I, the woman who talked to the painting, was the biggest curiosity. My fate was sealed for eternity unless, like Titus, there was a loophole I could find; a way out to exploit.

The figure was so close, the paint tempted me to touch. "Henri, you lovely drunk, remember when you told me the aim of any life should be self-development. I've tried and failed miserably. Look at you, your passion on full display. People normally cover their sins, but you painted your wicked ways for all to see. Your truth is on display forever. But here I am, now a supposed business executive living large in New York City, and everything about me is a lie." My eye twitched.

Again, no response. "How does that Dunbar poem go? Oh, yes. 'We wear the mask that grins and lies...'" A strangled laugh caught in my throat. "My mask never fades. My true nature, reaper, will always be hidden. Here's the big question: Am I evil, doing what I do?"

Words fled for a moment, running like a startled rabbit. Minutes passed as I sat and stared until I calmed and returned to my diatribe. "What does anything in this life mean after emotions have disappeared? So many encounters throughout the years, but none that I can truly call my own." A gruff, near hysterical laugh escaped. "You can't ever truly experience all the world offers you if you feel nothing, have nothing, are nothing."

An errant thought bulldozed. Crazy, irrational, wonderful, and daring. I rose from the bench, color draining from my cheeks, heart galloping. Did I have the courage to steal the painting?

The artwork glittered in its golden frame. "I cannot change so why not do something for myself and take what I want." Would there be any repercussions? The *Reaper Employee Handbook* didn't say anything about art theft. It mostly focused on SODs, RODs, and soul collections. Did it have a conduct clause? I couldn't remember.

How hard could it be, but why did I want to do something illegal and wrong? Why couldn't I try to be good and live a life loving another person more than myself, or any of that bullshit. The answer was simple. My job as a reaper didn't allow it. This was my lot in life.

The gallery lights were as somber as my thoughts. Gaze intent, I took in the locations of the emergency exits and back door. I could slip out and blend into the crowd, which I did well as a reaper. No one would be able to track me and since I didn't exist, no one could find me.

Security was lax in the gallery, the posters too large and unwieldy for anyone to steal. The paintings were the exception rather than the rule.

The only way to eliminate this temptation was to yield to it. The words come right out of *The Picture of Dorian Gray*, one book I've read and reread. His philosophical ramblings are pertinent to my current situation. My life had been, up to this point, a constant fight against temptation, and it was time to embrace the dark side.

I circled the near-empty gallery again, then headed back to the painting, questioning how to extract *Woman in the Window* from the frame. As luck would have it, I carried my Swiss Army pocketknife, which I considered one of humankind's greatest inventions. I grabbed the knife, clicked it open in my pocket, surveyed the near-empty gallery, and moved close to the picture.

There was no hesitation. My knife cutting through the canvas reminded me of the earlier wind against the windows. Slicing the sides of the fabric was easier than expected, and I pulled the painting out of the frame. Seconds later, my boots slapped the floor as I hightailed it to the back entrance.

"Wait," the other patron who'd been in the gallery called out. "Stop." His steps gained momentum as he sprinted after me.

My pace quickened. The back door appeared much farther away than it had a minute ago.

"Stop," the man yelled again. "Museum security."

Bam. The door crashed against the building. I threw myself onto the sidewalk, ran two blocks, slowed, and merged with the other nondescript New Yorkers.

Only the fading voice of the disgruntled security guard alerted the world to what I'd done. Hopefully, Death wasn't listening.

Chapter Twenty-Eight

New York City, 2024

I pace the sidewalk in front of Daxone's apartment, unsure if she'll show up. It's her building, but she might take an extra shift to avoid me. With each minute, the hum of desperation buzzes louder in my ears. Finally, I catch a glimpse of her walking up the avenue.

What if she rejects me? Worse, what if she thinks I'm insane? Maybe I am for having told her the truth in the first place. I shake, unable to take my eyes from her, fearful this might be our last encounter. She could tell me to go to hell in a minute, and she'll be gone from my life forever.

She's mute when she arrives at my side.

"Is this going to be a good or bad conversation?" I ask.

Her forehead furrows. "Not sure yet."

"Do you believe me?"

"What to believe isn't easy to figure out right now. I'm late because my coworkers ran all the medical tests on me again and rushed the results. Everything came back normal. That means there has to be another explanation. I trusted you. This isn't some weird game, is it?"

"A game? What would be my end goal?"

"Maybe I misjudged the situation. You could have escaped from an institution, and this is what you like to do: drive lovers slowly insane."

My mouth pops open. I don't have an instant comeback for that, but I don't need one because Daxone is on a roll.

"Is this a prank? Some weird shit you're posting on YouTube or Instagram?" she asks. "Though I couldn't find you anywhere on social media."

"Not a trick. It's real. Do you want a repeat performance for proof?"

She takes two steps back. "No, thank you."

"I don't know what else to say."

She stares. "If you're messing with me…"

"Of course not."

A grunt escapes her lips. "I'm not sure the supernatural even exists. I want to trust you, but now what?"

"Not sure." I hitch my shoulders. "Go back to girlfriend status?"

Her laugh is hard. "I have doubts about everything after what happened in that elevator."

"If you don't want to see my transformation again, I'm not sure what other kind of proof to provide. Death isn't going to speak to you, and the knife I'd been stabbed with is long gone. That would have been interesting for you to inspect." The pendant on my chest looks like normal jewelry. Nothing otherworldly going on there. Where's a reaping when you need one?

"I guess I believe you, Pru." She scratches the incision on her skull. "But it makes no sense. Whatever the truth, I assume you'll tell me all about it as soon as possible. I can't believe I'm saying this because what I saw in the elevator isn't possible, but my tests came back normal." She frowns. "If this is an epic episode of psychosis, I'm glad you are in it with me."

"It's real, but there's another little problem."

She frowns harder.

"Death's given us forty-eight hours together." The part about eternal oblivion remains unsaid. "We should part ways now. It might spare you what's to come."

"Do you want to do that?"

"It's the smart thing."

She scoffs. "I didn't ask what the smart thing to do was. What do you want to do?"

Time to admit my true emotions? After showing her all of me, I might as well disclose the rest. My next words have been picked with care. "I have feelings for you. Deep feelings, and I want to spend all my last moments with you if you want the same."

"Are you trying to tell me you love me?"

"Yes." A smile overtakes my lips.

"I have more questions, but I'm giving you the benefit of the doubt because I've never felt this way with anyone else. Come up, and let's continue the conversation."

"I'll counter your visit upstairs. Do you want to get food? I have a plan but work better when fed and caffeinated."

Daxone pauses. Her expression sours with distrust, but she acquiesces, and we head out for food and a daring escape plan. It's a long night.

*

The next morning, I check my bank account. Thanks to Death, I have funds but not a lot of time. The first few hours after my phone call with my boss had been wasted peering over my shoulder, waiting for another deathmonger to show. When no one arrives to claim my soul, I relax and decide to believe we can outrun fate.

Daxone decides to come along for the ride. It's a miracle she accepts my job as a reaper or wants to continue with what she thinks is a shared delusion thanks to her aneurysm. Either way, the fact that she's willing to leave with me blows my mind. I'm still not sure which of the two is more improbable. Yet today begins a daring escape plan to avoid Death with the woman I love.

Becca and I text. Me with updates, her with the gossip surrounding John. It does not sound good for him. Au revoir, sucker. She's busier than ever while my pendant is cold as the Arctic, but my bestie makes the time to see me off and commandeer Goose.

"I promise to take the best care of the smelly, attitudinal nuckelavee."

"He's a handful but no match for you." A tear slips from the corner of my eye. I change the subject to something happy. "John's gone?"

"I'll kill that asshat with my bare hands if he ever surfaces, but I don't think that's a possibility."

"I hope there are serious repercussions for what he did. You can't go around stabbing people."

"The official memo from Death's people says he's no longer employed, but according to the gossip, the severance package was pretty harsh. If it hadn't been, he'd have to face me, and it wouldn't have gone well for him." Becca straightens her back. While barely five feet tall, she appears to be a giant before me. "If Death didn't end him, I would have, and there would be blood. His blood and lots of it."

"This is why you're my bestie."

When Becca breaks into tears, I join her, and we have a long hug and an ugly cry.

Finally, she pulls away. "Got to go. My list of souls is growing by the second. Without you or John and no backup, Death is piling on the work. I'll be back for Goose when my shift ends."

We hug again, and she's out the door. Restless, I grab the vacuum but realize there's no need since I'm leaving. What will the cover story be? Another girl who disappears on the New York streets, or will Death somehow fabricate a company transfer?

Overwhelmed, I tumble onto the couch to wait. If nothing else, my goal over the next two days is to show Daxone how much I love her. It's another twenty minutes before she arrives at my apartment wearing a long-sleeve flannel, faded jeans, and hiking boots, and carrying a duffel with her stuff for the trip. She kisses my cheek and steps back. "I put in vacation time, packed my bags, and here I am ready for adventure." Her brow furrows. "There's been so much on my mind, I forgot to ask you how you're doing. Are you even up for travel?"

My black shirt slides up, and my cargo pants sit low on my hips. There's nothing but smooth skin where the injury should have been. Her mouth falls open. I flummox Daxone again after the big reveal in the elevator and take a little too much pleasure in her perplexed gaze. This kind of showing off is what landed us in problem city to begin with.

"You're healed." Her hands roam over my stomach and back, and I can't help but enjoy their warmth.

"All better," I purr.

"How is this possible?"

"Perks of working for Death."

She runs a hand across her face. "I'm a doctor. For you to heal this quickly is an impossibility."

"After everything that happened in the last day, why even question?"

"Because it makes no sense."

"Call it magic."

"You're the miracle." She leans in to kiss me, and I return the favor, moving close so that our bodies connect and the heat sparks between us. I wonder if the flames are in my mind or real, the experience is so hot. I don't want to stop, but after many minutes, I pull away.

I groan, grabbing my black leather jacket and small suitcase off the couch. I packed light. Enough clothes for two days, toiletries, and the only other items that matter: my Swiss Army knife, the *Woman in the Window* painting, and the doll my mother made for me. "We have to go."

Chapter Twenty-Nine

New York City, 2014

I patrolled the hospital lounge. Strangers' hearts pounded loudly as they waited for news of loved ones. We were all anxious, and I grew tenser by the moment. Four hours had passed, and the elderly grandmother car accident victim now surrounded by family in intensive care failed to give herself to death. The woman was nothing if not stubborn, clinging to every last minuscule ounce of life.

Huffing an inelegant breath, I paced, irritated that the dying woman was throwing off my schedule big time, but no one even batted an eye at my dramatics.

The bang of a door to the right of the waiting room caught my attention. A tall physician with warm, russet skin walked through. Her black, cropped hair stood in short spikes, a dramatic contrast against the white of her lab coat. She fumbled with the files in her hands.

"Are you Jill?" Her honey-brown eyes met mine.

I'm usually ignored in death mode, but her intense scrutiny found me. This was new. My heart skipped a beat when she faced me. "You're talking to me?" Normally more composed, being caught off guard had me reaching for words and the pocketknife in my black leather jacket.

No weapon needed, I quickly realized. I calmed a decibel but couldn't fathom how this woman saw me clearly when I was a shadow to most others in the room.

"Are you okay?" Her lips narrowed into a thin, confused line. "Should I have a nurse come check you out? Maybe shock?"

"Yes. I mean no." Something in her concerned gaze made me jump to clarify. "I'm fine. Not in shock is what I meant to say."

She cleared her throat, a surprisingly musical sound.

The desire to extend the conversation even if under false pretenses had me ask, "How's the patient?"

"He had a TIA. It's similar to a stroke."

"I'm Prudence."

"Daxone. Sorry, Dr. Saber. I'm a little scattered. This is my first day of residency."

"Congratulations."

Her lips twitched, and I watched her mouth work; it was soft and full when not concerned. "Thanks."

"Will he be okay?"

She straightened her spine and turned all business. "Your father's stable. He's going to be okay today, but you need a plan from now on."

A pretend sigh of relief escaped. "Thank God."

"I'll take you to see him now." She turned away. "From what I can tell, he works too much and exercises too little. The smoking doesn't help him either."

I stalled, desperate for a rational excuse not to go into the room of a man I didn't know and a soul I couldn't claim, at least not yet. As death's minion, I'd scare the bejesus out of him. "I'm waiting for more family. I'll be there in a minute."

Daxone's eyes narrowed. "I can send someone out for them. Don't you want to see him?"

"They'll be here any second." I stepped back, shifting my gaze to the lobby entrance.

She acquiesced and stood at my side, a glacier among rocks.

"What are you doing?" My heartbeat picked up its tempo.

"Staying with you."

"You don't have to do that. I'll ask the nurse to page you."

"Would you like some more information about your father's condition while we wait?"

"Um, of course." What I'd like was for her to leave now. The old lady was slipping away, and I had to move. It did not matter that she was damn cute, or that she was tall, sexy as sin, and soulful. Hell's bells, what does soulful even mean in my business? But she had it, whatever it was. And young, new to the business of doctoring. Normally, I could enjoy it. She was, after all, the one who decided to stay, but I had a soul to collect.

"It's going to be important he makes some life changes to move forward in a healthy manner," Doctor Daxone said.

A nervous wisp of a woman walked into the waiting room, and I intuited the real Jill had arrived.

"Here she is." I pointed. "Glad you made it so quick."

Wringing her hands, the new arrival peered between us, confused. Daxone shared the same information, and I moved away, and in a few seconds, it was like I never existed. Following the pull, I hustled farther along the corridor, the grandmother finally ready to let go of life and embrace death.

I slid into the room, opened my backpack, and pulled out a plastic bottle. The transfer was simple. People at the old woman's bedside didn't notice me, the redheaded girl dressed in black jeans, black boots, and a long-sleeve T-shirt. I collected soul filaments and departed before the first tear was shed.

Bottle top tight, I darted through the hall. The thump of my body against what felt like a hundred-year-old tree trunk had my gaze going up.

"Sorry," I said. "I wasn't paying attention."

Doctor Daxone stood there. Her hand touched my shoulder, steadying us both. "My fault." Her head tilted to the side. "What are you doing here? Weren't you going to see your father on the fifth floor?"

"I got turned around,"

"Are you doing okay?"

"You asked that already." A smile hinted on my lips. "Dad brought this on himself." The reaper in me knew death and how people often helped it along. After all these years, I'd given up trying to understand why and accepted that there was nothing I could do to stop the universe's endless cycle. Some late-night moments had me wondering what made individuals hasten the end. Then, I only had to think about my story before realizing I should not question others too deeply.

She eyed her watch. "I have a fifteen-minute break coming soon. We could go get some coffee, and I can tell you more about your dad's condition. Or is that too forward? I'm sorry. Never mind." She backpedaled.

Impersonating a sick man's family member to have coffee with a hottie doctor was wrong, very wrong, but I relented. I was, after all, Death incarnate. Why shouldn't I indulge my wants and foibles? "I'd love it."

The café was only a few doors away, and we sat in a comfortable booth. Fifteen minutes turned into thirty as Daxone shared her life, dreams, and hopes for the future. I, for a few minutes, felt human. I'd almost forgotten its warmth. For the first time in decades, maybe longer, I enjoyed the emotion.

When Daxone glanced at her watch and stood in panic, I resigned myself to letting her and my emotions dissipate. While there was something special about the woman, nothing in my world could hold on to the moment.

She walked out the door and out of my life, and it was craptastic. As I sat and finished my latte, my pendant flared a new color, one I'd never seen, fire orange, then black before its return to amber. Having no idea what that signaled, I vowed to ask the crew at the next staff meeting for a little clarity.

Chapter Thirty

Hardwick, Massachusetts, 2024

The lovely, nondescript four-door sedan I rented for our trip waits. The road out of New York City is forever busy, and we inch along the highway into Connecticut. Daxone power naps, which is good because there's lots of plotting to do and driving allows me time to outline ways to save her. I don't care about myself, but her continued existence is a priority.

Maybe we can flee, leave all this behind, and not get caught. Perhaps Death's radius is limited to New York City. I call bullshit but don't have a better plan. We'll run. Seriously, I've been moving around for centuries and can outlast and outplay others of my kind. But for how long?

I'm slightly bummed I'll have to devote my last two days with Daxone on the road but refuse to tell her what our soon-to-be future holds, only that we need to be somewhere else. Death will not be claiming her soul.

Massachusetts is the stop for the first day, and that evening we visit a local winery near our hotel. I'm trying to find some enjoyment while watching the seconds tick away.

We spend an hour walking through the vineyard, sipping a red blend, sitting on a blanket, and talking. I twirl a leaf between my fingers and think about what our future might be like if I can find a way to get us out of this situation. So far, Daxone has avoided further discussion about my alternate elevator self. She's still processing, but I want to learn everything I can about her in case these are our last moments together.

Normally, thinking about kids makes me sad. As a reaper, I'm not even sure if it's an option, but rug rats with Daxone might have been enjoyable.

The light fades around us, and she scoots closer. "The winery is going to close soon."

I shrug. That's the least of my worries. "Did you ever want children?"

Her eyes widen for a moment. "There are so many things to think about with them." She runs a hand through her hair, causing the pieces near her scar to stand on end. "I can't imagine not having a family at some point, especially after falling ill. I value the time I have left so much more than I used to." Her smile falters. "It would be great to share it with others."

I've taken that from her. How do you tell someone their life might be over in a few hours?

"I'm not sure I want them, but I had a cat growing up, and she wasn't too hard to take care of."

She lets out a hearty chuckle. "How much harder do you think it is to have kids than pets?"

"Owned a horse once, sort of. Goose was ornery. Kids can't be that much more complicated, right?"

She pats my hand. "Children aren't like pets. Maybe like a dog in some ways, but not like a horse unless talking costs. They're both expensive, but children take constant supervision."

"Maybe I need to consider my options and start with a puppy." *Don't make plans,* my mind screams. *Dumbass.*

"If you had a crystal ball and could learn the truth about your future kid, what would you want to know?" she asked.

I gape, close my mouth, and blood drains from my face. "I wouldn't want to know anything. Seeing the future sucks."

"Sorry. I guess I didn't consider your job. Still getting used to that. You're pale. Are you okay?"

"Fine." Her happiness is my priority, and I plan to make our time together special and oh so memorable. With a little death magic, I shield us from prying eyes. No one will notice the blanket or people on it before they close the vineyard.

The sun recedes, falling into the horizon with an epic display of reds, yellows, and orange, and we're finally alone in the field. Two moths flicker in the fading light.

I draw her close. We kiss, but my mind remains stormy. Sitting back, I attempt selflessness. "You should get away from me. Take the car tonight after you drop me off at the hotel and head back to the city."

"I will not risk losing you again." Daxone crushes me against her.

With my body pressing on hers, the little resolve to let her go disintegrates. "Show me how much you mean that." My response is muffled; cheek pressed into her jacket. She releases me. The sky shoots from dark orange to navy blue to black in moments.

Daxone's lips are back on mine, and even though it's cool, the air heats.

"Is something wrong?" she asks when I pull away.

I can't tell her I'm afraid of what tomorrow will bring, so instead, I plan to enjoy each moment. Straddling her lap, I tuck my long legs around her and lean back. "Admiring the view." My lips dance over hers. She slides off my jacket, and her body meets mine. Her hands trace my arms, tickling my exposed flesh.

My fingers work along the edge of her jeans as I consider the best way to liberate what I want from its confinement. The button pops. The zipper skids down, and I release her from those tight thigh-huggers. My gaze now focuses on her shirt.

"Wait." She grabs my palm.

"No waiting." A pent-up breath escapes.

"Here?" She laughs the word.

"Why not?"

"Let's wait until the hotel."

"Thank you, but no. No one will notice. Trust me." I tackle the buttons on her shirt, and my nails leave a path along her shoulder.

"You have my full attention at this moment." She offers no resistance, reclines on the blanket, and lets me have my way with her. Her hands ravage my hair.

I lean in. "Let me show you what you do to me."

We kiss, and hers is no longer tender. My hands slip to my sides, and we both fall back on the blanket. Her hands move over me. Her smile is mischievous as her fingers find the edge of my cargo pants. Rational thoughts flee. My thighs clench. I'm hot, wet, and ready.

"I'm healed. One hundred percent," I say. "Don't be too nice." Our eyes meet. There is nothing more to say. Only action will do—no more waiting. I seal our lips in a kiss and take advantage of her nakedness.

Her hands work my curves, taunting me, and one drops low and massages the inside of my thigh. Whispered words tickle my ear before her lips leave a trail of butterfly kisses along my neck. I'm lost in sensation; her fingers are magical on my heat. I wrestle for control but, unable to hold back, I go over the edge.

Daxone cocoons against me on the blanket, and I'm reluctant to move. The idea of getting dressed holds no appeal. I want to stay in this perfect fantasy for a moment longer, but we have much to prepare if we are going to leave for Maine in the morning, then Canada.

I move from her protective embrace.

She groans. "Do we have to go?"

"Let's head to the hotel."

The drive is quick and quiet. Upon arrival, we check in and drop our bags in the room. I don't unpack, not knowing how much longer we have or what tomorrow will bring.

I pace. "I'm not tired."

She's sitting on the bed, eyes pensive. "Me, either."

I need to get out of this room and out of my head. Focus on the physical. "Do you want to hit the hot tub?" I ask.

"That sounds relaxing."

"I had something else in mind."

"I can do that too." Her smile is wicked.

It's the middle of the night, so there's not much activity in the hot tub. We undress, neither having brought a bathing suit, and slide in. I should shield us with a little death magic but don't. Part of me wants to get caught. The thought alone arouses me, and I put my legs over her in the steamy, bubbling waters.

For a moment, we both stare out the large glass windows and listen to the silence only interrupted by the motors jetting water against my thighs. That's not the only throbbing going on when Daxone's hand runs up my leg. It takes mere moments for me to dissolve like liquid and float in heaven for a few minutes before returning to Daxone on earth.

My turn now. I crush my mouth to hers. My kiss is urgent. I nibble and suck on her lips and hope my desire and delight reveal my deep love. She is my eternity, and my body burns with a need only she can satisfy.

Chapter Thirty-One

The Netherworld

I sit and drink hot, sweet lobby coffee on my hotel balcony. Daxone sleeps inside and I'm in no rush to get ready for the day. After mind-blowing hot tub sex, we decided not to run but to spend our time here with each other, the present being most significant.

The tap on my shoulder causes me to hitch in fear and nearly spill my drink. My gaze travels up. Death stands behind me.

"Follow me. The hour of your departure from this world has come."

"No introductions needed." I stare at my boss. My blood runs cold. "Already? It's too soon."

"It's time." An imposing figure in black robes; something much darker hides behind them. Skeletal features frame the mask of paper-thin, gray skin. "The moment you told Daxone about us, your time on earth was limited." Death's voice booms inside my head.

I can't fathom a response or witty retort. I should be more scared for myself, but my worry is directed at Daxone. I've lived a long life. Death might be welcomed, but my love has so much more to give.

I surrender to my fate and follow Death. "Make Daxone a reaper. She deserves time."

"No."

"Why not?" Am I actually going to pester Death now?

"It is not her calling."

"It wasn't mine either."

"Not true."

Death grabs my hand, and the next thing I know, I'm part of a long queue in a mammoth cavern. It's dark, except for the flickering candle flames that sit aloft on ledges and craggy shelves. Small groups of souls huddle in inky blackness. Tunnels narrow, then open into small rooms. You'd think Death would have upgraded to electricity by now. They must be old school all the way. The crunch of receding footsteps is louder than the soft whispers. The only good thing is Daxone is not with me.

The chamber's ceiling is massive. There's a soft rumble, and bats explode from above, announcing Death's arrival. Some of the other people duck their heads or huddle together, but I watch the display of flight. In their own way, the bats are beautiful and powerful. The draft of bats lifts after a minute, and they spiral high until they are finally consumed by the black chasm. As the processional moves forward, it's cool and damp with millions of candles lighting the route: some leaping and dancing, some slowly burning, others extinguished.

Death sits on a throne made of bones, human, animal, and other, some grotesque. The monsters they conjure are the stuff of children's nightmares. Death's minions, ordinary people dressed in business casual, sit at cheap metal desks below or hustle the deceased through different tunnels. It's a surreal contrast, and I blink twice to make sure I'm not hallucinating. The skin around my thumbnail turns rust color; the tang of blood on my tongue. Is this where I'll spend eternity? My heartbeat thuds loudly in my ears at the possibility.

Men and women in front of me chatter and protest, offering reasons why they should be spared. I stay quiet and watch, noting they are sent through different dark corridors. The line staggers forward. My eyes meet Death's, my mouth dry and my heart beat loud and erratic. Everyone in the cave must hear it echoing off the walls, though I am probably the least scared person here, having worked for so many years under this god's tutelage.

Death ignores most of the other arrivals but speaks directly to me. "With each birth, a candle is lit, and each time a candle grows low and is snuffed out, a life is ended. This one is yours." They point to a candle that has burned to a pool of wax.

"There's an apt metaphor. Here's one in return." I should shut up. This is not the time for snark, but I can't help it. I'm sure I'll be doomed to Hell for speaking, yet I do. "For many years, I served you. Light a new candle for me so I can stay with Daxone."

Death gazes at me. He's not amused. I pale. A sheen of sweat breaks out on my forehead.

"I cannot change what you did," Death intones. "Daxone can no longer be of earth knowing the truth."

Daxone appears by my side, and in front of us, the gaping mouth of a cave reveals impenetrable darkness. Finally, tears flow. This is her end, and Daxone doesn't deserve this fate.

"Each of these candles is a human life, at any moment ready to be extinguished." Death pulls one from the many and holds it in front of me. It is no longer lit, but the last of an orange glow on the wick remains. "This is Daxone. You cannot save her again."

"We didn't have enough time."

Daxone peers around, speechless.

"You should not have fallen in love with her in the first place."

"But I did. Take my life for hers."

"I cannot, but I can make an exception for your years of service." Death stares at the woman by my side. "What is it that you want? She has served me well. I can return you to your life with no memory of Prudence."

Her hand finds mine. "I want to be together in death," she says. "Life without her in it is not worth living."

"Don't say that. You have to return. Don't follow me."

"No, Pru. You can't make this choice for me."

"I don't want you to die."

"I can't live without you."

"Stop." Death says. "No more. Her decision is made. You do not know what lies beyond this chamber. There may be nothing for you both. Even I cannot predict everything that will happen after this moment."

"There must be more." I stare into the endless nothing. "You're proof of that. My work on earth speaks to that." I have to hope. This can't be our end.

"You have served me faithfully, and I will repay that with consideration." Death ushers us toward the inky blackness.

The shadows call, ready to cloak me in eternal forgetfulness. I face Daxone and make one last attempt to get her to reconsider this fate. "You don't have to do this. You can go back. Do you want to spend eternity here? There's no guarantee of anything."

"There's nowhere else I want to be."

"It is done." Death snuffs out both candles from the stack in a single movement. "You cannot cheat death, even for love." They send us away with a flick of the wrist. "Go, my unwise apprentice."

With those words, pain courses through me where my wounds had once been, and I crumble. When I open my eyes, Daxone stands before me, more beautiful in death than in life. We are at the mouth of a distant tunnel. Turning, I see the chamber, the candles, and Death hard at work.

"Ready?" Daxone asks.

"Whatever comes next, we'll be together from now on."

Joining our hands, I take a last moment to admire the billions of glowing candles lighting the faraway chambers. The dark mouth of the cave calls me to explore death with the one I love. I'm ready to be with Daxone in heaven or hell.

"Don't get too comfortable," Death's voice is in my head. "I might need you one day soon."

Chapter Thirty-Two

Salem, Massachusetts, 2025

I wake in a comfortable bed, the mattress firm under me and the cotton sheets soft. I sit up ramrod straight, and my glance darts around the small room. Where am I, and why am I naked?

Standing, I sluff off the cover and survey the surroundings. The bed where I currently reside is sandwiched between two light-brown nightstands. The dresser holds a flat-screen television, and there's a brown chair, a small table, and a bland dark wood desk. Tasteful pastel landscapes decorate the walls.

I shake off sleep, stand, and head to the closet to see if I have clothing. When I push back the sliding door, a hanging white robe beckons, and I slip it over my shoulders and knot the sash. On the desk, a notepad welcomes me to Hotel Salem.

Salem. The word brings a rush of memories. This is Death's fault. Every bad thing in my life—and some of the best things—are Death's fault. I'm not sure which direction this little adventure is heading, but the memories of my arrival flood back to me.

Daxone and I have acclimated to our new life in purgatory (the netherworld, shades, Tartarus, whatever it is named), finding it manageable if not as pleasant as being part of the world above. The positives of my situation down under—we have eternity to bond, but the lack of stellar coffee here—a definite negative. Purgatory brew can't compare to a cup of New York City grinds. Not that I even need to eat or drink, but some habits are hard to dispense with. Sustenance makes me feel human. I don't want to lose that.

Purgatory lacks amenities for sure, but Daxone and I haven't given up. Back in my reaper days, I hit the gym, enjoying my treadmill and elliptical time. No gyms, running clubs, or online forums for Peloton and iFit enthusiasts. Personally, I find it important to stay in shape anyway. Down under, I improvise workouts. My last run became the catalyst for ending up here, wherever that is.

With all the time in the world, my runs have become pretty extensive. Today, along the way, the only "life" I've encountered is the baying of the hellhounds. After two hours, I stroll through the graves in the underworld, cooling down from the twelve-plus-miler. I'd waved at our one neighbor, an older man who resembles Einstein and lives in a dilapidated shack a few miles south of our homestead, and reminded myself that Daxone and I meant to have him over for tea. Neighbors are few and far between, and it would be nice to be social. My guess is whoever runs this place prefers to keep all the residents secluded. That said, plenty of mountainous outcrops, dead trees, and dried, brown grass are available for our viewing pleasure. Also, rampant weird critters, but they are as scared of me as I of them. If I pretend not to see their squishy gray shells or black, mold-spotted fur, they leave me alone. I doubt they'd make good pets, so I ignore them as well. They make me miss Goose.

I watch my feet, careful not to trip over the buckling concrete path. Gnarled, leafless trees guard the exit to the cemetery. Silence rules, the only noise my angry breath. Each exhale sends a frosty mist into the gloom. Purgatory lacks restaurants, galleries, and television, to name a few of the creature comforts people above take for granted. There are no wild parties, not even a dance hall. It's an extremely boring place under all circumstances.

I pause to wipe the sweat from my brow with my gray T-shirt, my clothes all being the same color in purgatory. I hustle a few steps in reverse when Death, in black robes and wearing a skeletal smile, appears.

"Well, hello there." My body shakes, and I'm hoping exercise exhaustion is the reason. I put on a brave face and smile. Death has left us alone since the banishment, and I haven't missed that cheery presence one bit.

"I have a mission for you." Bone-thin lips stay fixed in a haunting scowl, but the words scream in my head. "Three witches want to disturb the balance of the universe by taking souls, my souls, to raise an immortal. You must stop them."

I blink. "Not into pleasant greetings or small talk? Did it ever occur to you to start a conversation with, 'You appear well, Prudence. Glad to see you adjusting to the underworld after your banishment. Anything you need?'"

Death's immortal, hellfire eyes are hidden under the hood, not that I want another view. One glimpse was enough for a lifetime, but I imagine them narrowing at my impertinence. The brittle, dead grass under my shoes suddenly appears interesting. "Why me?"

Death remains mute. Have I pushed my luck too far this time? More silence. My sneakered foot crushes the dead grass, and it sounds like broken glass under my heel. I need to learn to respect my elders. Maybe tomorrow. "Do I have a choice?"

"No."

"Alrighty then. Fill me in, oh benevolent one."

Death's voice invades my head, and I'm sure to end the day with an awful headache. "Three witches are attempting to sway the powers of the universe against the balance. They cannot complete their task. It's your job to stop them. You need to defeat the coven."

"What fun." I'm less than enthusiastic about this little side project. "How?"

"You'll be able to figure that out when you reach Salem. You have time to tell Daxone you're leaving, and then I'll be along to fetch you."

"What? Daxone's not coming with?" I pout. "I'm coming back here after, right?"

More silence.

"What are you not telling me? Don't hold back. Inquiring minds want to know." Nerves have me spewing verbal diarrhea. "She's staying here because it's safer, but she'll be fine. This is a short-term gig, and I'll return soon?" My words trail off when I realize I'm not going to get answers. Never had in the past. Why would anything change?

"All will be revealed. Go now, or we leave for the surface."

I sprint, even though I've completed a multitude of miles, and my muscles ache. What to say; not a lot to do here other than self-improvement. Isn't that the point?

I stand for a moment outside the dwelling I now consider home. Shocker, it's carved out of gray rock. A faint glimmer of light flickers behind the drawn curtains, not that there is anyone around to peep. The inside is plain, furnished with the basics, a kitchen that opens into a living room. Two additional doors hide a bathroom and a bedroom.

Food appears in the fridge, and gray clothes are in the bureau, which is fine. There are no seasons or any change to the damp, overcast coolness. The endless sea of gray T-shirts, shorts, and joggers matches the slate skies and dreary drizzle. In some ways, life is easy, with no utility bills or rent, and once in a while, if you wish hard enough, a book or game magically appears on the shelves to ease the tedium. Daxone and I jumped for joy and played The Game of Life for nearly a month when it showed up.

I approach Daxone.

"I'm leaving." I crouch to catch my breath. My hands drop to my knees.

"What?" Her gorgeous brown eyes meet mine.

"Death is making me fight evil above." I bite the skin around my thumb so hard it bleeds. My nails are a disaster for so many reasons. "You're staying underground."

"I can help." She stands and puts Dante's *Divine Comedy* on the stone table next to the gray chair.

"Death didn't offer that option."

"How long will you be gone?" The frown on Daxone's lips causes worry lines to form on her brow and at the corner of her eyes.

I hate to see that, but there are no answers. I shrug away the guilt to survive the moment. "I'm not sure. Death didn't supply a lot of information. Three witches. World domination. The balance of nature at stake."

"That doesn't sound like an easy assignment."

"Based on the job description, there's a chance I might never return."

"Don't say that. Not even as a joke."

"I'm sure Death has an aftercare plan for you."

"You're not funny."

"I'm a little funny."

"This is not the news I've been hoping for. Why couldn't you have run in here to tell me we were taking a vacation on the surface?"

"We don't always get what we want."

"There's a Rolling Stones joke in there somewhere."

"You have no sympathy for the devil at this moment?"

"That's an understatement if I ever heard one."

Daxone grimaces. I understand her concerns. The only thing we both want is for Death to reconsider our eternal stay in purgatory and return us to New York. Unfortunately, Death runs the show, and there's not a damn thing I can do about our current predicament. The Evil Under-Lord has given me no other choice.

In the middle of our kiss goodbye, Death whisks me away. When I wake, I am naked in Salem, Massachusetts. My mother's rag doll is nestled beside me.

Chapter Thirty-Three

Hartford, Connecticut, 1648

The floor in the house's main room was cold even with the bear-hide blanket under me. My father still enjoyed retelling the story of how he bargained the trader down to almost nothing for it. Outside, a blustery wind whipped our wood-framed home. Despite the insulation of wattle and daub, the cold embraced me and kept hold.

Yarrow and dried herbs hung from the rafters. The furnishings were fine but sparse. Years later, I learned that my father, the youngest son of a wealthy landowner, had come over from England to make his fortune. While prosperous and respected, he had found his new life in the colonies challenging, especially after his young wife, whom he'd hastily married before the trip, failed to produce anything but a single daughter.

I inched closer to my mother and pushed up on tiptoes to see what she was doing.

She was a tiny, bird-like woman, but her nature was the opposite: strong willed and easy to laugh. She understood the woods around us better than anyone else in the village but only shared her knowledge with me.

I rarely saw her hair loose, but when she brushed it, it didn't match mine, which grew redder each day to the displeasure of my father. Her hair was the color of the sandy shoreline by the river. It appeared brown but contained strands of gold when the sunlight hit upon it. She smiled in her close-mouthed way, self-conscious of a crooked front tooth. To me, she was the most beautiful woman ever, and she banished the chill that tried to crowd around me.

"Prithee, my love." She patted my head. "What are you up to?"

I shrugged. We'd finished gathering firewood and bundling it by the hearth. I'd played with some small sticks, throwing them into the flames when my mother had settled in a rocking chair by the fire to do some mending.

"Can I help?"

"'Tis good you want to learn, little one." She threaded a needle for me and handed me a scrap of cloth to practice on. "But you should play too. Life will be difficult for you soon enough."

The tiny needle kept slipping from my fingers, but I tried my hardest to make a line of straight stitches and almost succeeded. Time slipped by that way, and I didn't even notice when my mother put aside her mending to start a new project.

"Pray, little one. I made you a poppet." She handed me a rag doll.

"Gramercy." A smile broke out on my lips. "She's beautiful." My mother had somehow pieced together scraps of material to make a doll like her with a cap, apron, and a warm smile.

"Take good care of her. You will need her in the future more than you know."

I bit my thumbnail, not sure what she meant by that. She gently removed my finger from my mouth.

"You're too young to understand now," my mother said, "but I have sewn your heritage into the doll."

"I'm seven," I said proudly.

She took my free hand and guided me to her and my father's bed. My pallet was across the room and closer to the warmth of the fire. It was not until I was much older that I moved to the loft, happy to give up the warmth for a modicum of privacy. "You are a big girl. You need to listen and remember my words. They're important. Can you do that, prithee?"

The red curls that escaped from my braid bobbed under my cap. "Yes, Mama."

She pulled up the doll's apron to expose writing in her neat, tiny stitches along the hem of the skirt. I stared but couldn't decipher what had been sewn even though I'd mastered the alphabet and numbers up to ten. Not only were these words long and complicated, but they didn't make sense.

"It's Latin," she said.

"What's that?"

"I'll teach you someday soon."

Before my eyes, the words faded.

"They're gone?" My finger touched the fabric where the words had been.

"They'll be there when you need them."

The door banged open, and my father, Caleb Barlow, entered, bringing a draft with him. He was tall and rangy, and his once hand-some face held lines of disappointment and cruelty. A frown hid behind a thick beard. "What are you doing? Idle hands find time for the devil." He eyed us skeptically.

"I was mending your woolen coat, the one that got caught on the fence post last week. I only stopped for a moment. Prudence is practicing her stitches."

"The farm work never ends on these hundred acres." He took off his hat, shaking his head in distress. "These indentured servants do what you ask, but they aren't family. This place is supposed to be my inheritance to a long line of Barlow men, but there are none. It doesn't look good to the community."

He dropped his hat on the large, ornate table that filled most of the room. Made of carved wood, it seated eight people. We cooked meals, prepared my mother's poultices and teas, and supped at the table, as common a meeting place for my mother to host friends from the community as for my father's political conversations.

"Your daughter will grow up to be an educated and pious young lady. She will also be an advantage to you."

He nodded, moving closer. "'Tis all fine and good. We can solidify our connections to the Connecticut Colony when she is older with a good marriage, but sons would have been more helpful. I should hope to be governor one day and having sons shows I am strong and worthy."

"This is not the time for a conversation of that nature." My mother went back to her mending by the fire.

"Maybe not, but we will have it tonight."

"Did the supplies come today?" Mother asked.

My father shook his head. "They were delayed. I was expecting correspondence from my family, but word from them will have to wait." He eyed the meager living space. "Sometimes I wonder if I made the right choice coming here." He kicked the pile of wood by the fire. "It's cold. Can't you even keep the fire going?"

My mother jumped to her feet and added a few more logs to the already blazing hearth. "Pray pardon. Why don't you go into your study, and I'll bring you a hot cup of tea. I made cornbread earlier. Would you like some?"

He nodded and left.

I hadn't realized I'd returned my thumb to my mouth and ripped the nail with my teeth. In my other hand, I clenched my new poppet tightly, afraid my father might take it away.

Chapter Thirty-Four

Salem, Massachusetts, 2025

I return to bed, stare at the ceiling, and list everything I remember. My name is Prudence Barlow. My mother and I died the same year in 1661. My father was an asshole. Death recruited me to reap, getting me out of that hellish situation. I did well at my job of claiming souls until I met Daxone. Who could have fathomed falling in love meant certain death? It wasn't all bad. Daxone and I were able to strike a bargain and hang out in the down under, and I don't mean Australia. If you like gray and damp, Purgatory is the place to be.

Sitting up, I face the mirror hanging over the bureau and sneak a peek, wondering if limbo has aged me. Nope, my cover still stands. Still me. I'm average in so many ways: height, weight, breast cup size. My hair, on the other hand, has grown even longer and redder, if that were possible. It's the color of hellfire if the biblical perceptions are true. Being stuck in limbo, I still don't know for sure if other realms exist or what they entail. They could be full of puppies and rainbows or pay homage to Dante's *Inferno*. Both options are equal possibilities.

Will I even need my cover story? I'm pretty positive I won't be meeting any friends or associates in Salem. I don't know anyone, and it's not like I have coworkers I need to meet with. It's kind of liberating to no longer pretend to be something I'm not. I can be a lone wolf.

That's not true anymore. Daxone. God, I miss her already. The tears that didn't come with thoughts of my mother's death surface now. She was happy with me—the entire package: good and bad, reaper and human—and that's what matters. That's why I'm here and will fight for my return to her.

My pendant hangs low around my neck, and I'm overjoyed to have it back. An amber stone is encased in gold filigree and shaped almost like a heart, but the top is smooth. The necklace hangs on a long, lacy gold chain. The stone glows red when a soul is ready to depart to the underworld, and the necklace is a large part of my identity. I missed not having it in the afterlife, but I'm confused about why I'd need it now if I'm not here collecting souls.

An alarm buzzes, and I spot a shiny new phone on the nightstand. Death can be cruel, but he can also be kind. It's the latest iPhone. There's a reminder set, and it shouts, "Time to find the three witches."

How the hell am I going to find and track three broom riders in a town where being one is more normal than not?

My new phone informs me it's a Monday morning, and the July sun leaves a hot streak on the floor of my hotel room. I have no idea how to find the witches or what to do when I encounter them. I've never been to Salem and don't even have a map. Worse, I didn't see any other clothes hanging in the closet but didn't investigate thoroughly. I'm not stepping foot out of this room in the robe, soft and cuddly as it is.

I'm overwhelmed, but Death could be watching. I attempt productivity or at least pretend to fake it until I make it. I emit a sigh of relief when a suitcase appears in the corner of the closet on a low rack with camo shorts and a black tank top inside. Bras, undies, and other essentials are mixed up in the clothing. Someone needs to learn how to pack. Did Death pick out the thongs, or did he have an assistant do it? Under the suitcase on the floor, combat boots and sneakers reside.

The phone rings. Death's voice booms. It always does, and I have yet to get used to the reverberation. "Get ready to start the job. It's imperative you find a way to stop the three witches. They are stealing my souls, and that's inexcusable. I'm sending help. This isn't a one-person job."

"Don't need an assistant. I work best alone." I drop the clothes on the bed.

Death disconnects, and there's a knock on the hotel door. Random thoughts bombard me. How long is the room paid for? I hope she's competent, this assistant of mine. Does the hotel have a spa?

Hand on the doorknob, I hesitate. Death better not have sent a John wannabe. One guy stabbing me in the back was enough. Whatever happened to that bastard coward anyway? I hope Death fried him in the pits of hell if they exist.

All this before the door opens.

My hopes for room service are instantly dashed when I peer at the largest chest on this side of the afterworld. My eyes travel up and meet hazel ones filled with snark. He's a giant with tan skin, a shaved head, and the most extreme neck muscles known to humankind.

"I'm the help." His smile is full of attitude.

Oh my God. "I don't need help. But I'll always take it from you."

"I missed you, *parva soror*."

"You promised never to call me that."

He shrugs those massive shoulders and steps into the room unbidden. He moves in for a hug but then realizes I'm still in a robe. "Get dressed."

Blushing, I hug him anyway. "Titus, I am so happy to see you. I missed you so much and can't believe you're here. Didn't you retire?" I pirouette away. The clothes on the bed call me to dress. "What have you been doing, and why are you here?"

"That's a lot of questions all at once. Death called me out of retirement, and you know I'd only come for you. There's no time for chitchat right now. I'll fill you in later. Did you hear me say get dressed? We've got a lot to do."

"A little less attitude, please." I suck in some air. "You have your own hotel room, right? You're not staying here. I gave up everything for Daxone. It's true love and nothing's spoiling that."

"Death filled me in. Sounds like a Disney classic." Titus draws his dark eyebrows together. "I've got my own room, and at the rate you're going, I'll be living in it for a very long time."

I humph and grab the black T-shirt and army print cargo shorts. At least Death or an assistant understood my style preferences. I decide to ask Death how they knew during our next conversation. "What's going on in the world since my departure?" I head to the bathroom. "What's the year?"

"Twenty-twenty-five."

I turn and stare.

"Yup. That's the year." Titus appears bored.

"I've only been in purgatory for six months? That's not possible. We've been living there for what feels like forever."

"Time works different in the afterlife."

I squint. "How would you know that?"

He shrugs his massive shoulders. "Are you getting dressed soon?"

My toothbrush and other necessities are in the bathroom. I make short work of it, throw my hair into a messy top knot, head back into the room for the black combat boots to complete the ensemble, and I'm set. "Let's go. I'll do the talking, and you can be the muscle."

"I don't think so."

Before leaving the room, I snag the poppet and put it in my pocket.

Chapter Thirty-Five

Hartford, Connecticut, 1652

Honeysuckle reminded me of my mother. I plucked off the end of a fragrant flower, pulled the sepals, and touched my tongue to the sweet drop of nectar. Out in the fields and forest, I'd begun to help her collect plants at an early age. She used them for her remedies and our meals.

The hot sun directly overhead hit my neck. I let my cap fall back. The strings under my chin held it there. My poppet was in my pocket. I was too old for dolls, but this one was a comfort, and I still carried it, hidden though it might be. The field we combed through edged the forest on part of Father's land. My mother collected jewel weed for our neighbor who had a rash. Also in her basket were wild blackberries.

My basket held dandelions, from flower to root. The flowers for tea, the greens for cooking or salad, and the roots for something else. Still learning each plant's use, I wasn't sure what she did with them, but my mother instructed me to dig them up along with burdock in its entirety. Burdock she applied to those with stomach ailments. At least my dirty nails would keep me away from biting them, a habit both

Mother and Father tried hard to break.

"Prithee, come here." She beckoned me close. "Nature's beauty abounds. See how the cycle works?"

I moved close, my light bodice and skirt sashaying as I walked. A caterpillar climbed the prickly ash. "I don't understand." It was an ugly worm. There were some things about my mother and her love for nature that didn't make sense.

"It's the pattern of life. This caterpillar eats the leaves of the prickly ash, which helps it turn into a beautiful butterfly. Nature provides for it and us." She picked the prickly ash branches, making sure not to disturb the caterpillar or the nearby cocoons. "This will be good for Mr. Johnson's toothache."

At that moment, a swallowtail butterfly landed on my arm, and I wondered if my mother was right but then dismissed the idea. The butterfly took off in search of a softer place.

She wasn't done with the lesson. "The butterfly is trying to tell you something. Listen to the world around you."

I loved Mama, the person who understood me best, and respected her more than anyone else, but she was different in the wild. At home, she read the Bible, attended church religiously, and obeyed my father. Out here, she seemed free and unorthodox. It made my eleven-year-old mind uneasy, and this she could tell, but we explored often, and these adventures never went without a lesson.

People trusted her knowledge of plants and came to her for all kinds of concerns. Therefore, I vowed to have confidence in her too, and put my doubts aside. There were no doctors in the village, and my mother was the most skilled of healers, but it also set her apart. Still, I fretted and almost put a nail in my mouth until I saw the black dirt that clung to it. My father was extreme in his demands, and I constantly tried to meet his expectations. It put this part of my life at odds with others.

"What did you learn from the butterfly?" she asked.

I rolled my eyes.

"Don't be cross." She smiled mischievously, her crooked tooth peeking out from the gap between her lips. "You're old enough that I can show you a secret."

Unable to resist, I moved close. "What?"

She put a finger in the air and drew. With each movement, a golden light trailed behind.

My eyes grew wide, and I stepped back in fright. No words escaped.

"Don't be scared, little one," she said.

"What was that?"

"That's our secret. It's a spell."

"As in magic?"

"You might call it that. My family liked to say we harnessed the power of nature."

"I don't understand."

She tilted her head. "The best way to describe it to you would be to call it witchcraft, but we aren't evil or of the devil. We're of nature."

"We?"

"My family has a long history of relying on what is of the earth. We see the world in a way that is different from other people. Mother Nature shares her power with us. Now you are old enough to understand the gift as well."

"It must be of the devil if it is not of God." I stepped back from my mother, suddenly frightened.

"No, child. There is more to the world than a god and a devil. There is Mother Nature to be sure, and other wonderful things we cannot even fathom. Come here. Trust me. Have I ever shown you evil?"

I thought about her words. My father had been the only one in life to show me malice, whether it was his harsh words or the branches that he made me gather for my whippings when I displeased him. Mother had always been kind. There couldn't be evil in her, or if there was, I'd rather follow her than my father's notion of what was good. "Show me."

I moved close again and waited expectantly.

She drew a golden line in the air, then her finger crossed back through it, creating a complex pattern I could not track. At the same time, she said a prayer, but the words were nothing like I had heard during our long services.

"What was that?" I asked.

"That was a protection spell. I asked the earth to keep you safe."

"Me?" I squeaked. She had put a spell on me? My heart thudded with worry.

"I have done so since you were little. This is a harsh world and much goes wrong. I wanted to ensure you had the best chance to live long and prosper in it."

When my heartbeat faded from my ears, I asked, "Will you show me?"

"Come close, child." She held my hand in hers and extended my pointer finger. "The first thing you must learn are the ancient runes. While my family now lives in England, our ancestors came from Ireland. These runes were our original language. I will teach them to you." My finger flared along with hers as we wrote in the air.

Exhilaration, joy, and delight swirled through me as the bright light found its place within my soul.

We spent the next hour in the dirt. My mother would write out a rune, explain the meaning, and I would practice it.

She made me promise never to show anyone or inscribe any of the runes.

"Why?" I asked.

"Our neighbors would not understand. This language and practice are ancient. People here would think them primitive and dangerous. It is best to keep them to ourselves. Prithee, promise me that."

"I will." I did not know at the time, but it was a promise I would not keep.

Chapter Thirty-Six

Salem, Massachusetts, 2025

We exit the hotel and weave our way through waves of tourists. The humid summer heat is already driving the temperature into the eighties, and I'm not loving it after my stay in the constant gray and cold of the underworld. Bad hair day or not, I'm on a mission with the giant, and I want it done quickly so I can be reunited with Daxone. Even better, maybe I can convince Death to reunite us here.

Titus and I stroll the streets. A police car, adorned with a witch logo, passes. A couple of teens jostle as they meander along the sidewalk, fast food bags in hand. One of the boys wears a band T-shirt advertising The Witches. The whole theme is out of control in this city.

I stop to read a placard about Gallows Hill, once believed to have been the site of many public hangings, including those convicted as witches. It is now a park and used as a playing field for various sports. Titus strides ahead and I jog to catch up. The only noise is my huff of indignation. We march, and the prolonged silence between us begins to make me uncomfortable.

"So do you like returning to work for Death?"

He grunts in response.

"You don't have more vacations, do you? I want a vacation from down under. Don't let anyone fool you into thinking it's a nice relaxing getaway because it is not. Daxone and I talk about visiting Hawaii someday."

"If you're stuck in purgatory, I doubt you're going to make it there."

"Don't be a glass half empty kind of person."

"I'm sure Death is planning your vacation right now."

I change the subject before I haul one off and punch this beloved partner of mine. "What's the plan?"

"End the three witches. How hard can it be unless you get in the way. Do you remember the time you almost lost that soul when you were apprenticing?"

"Can we not go there, please." I jog to keep up with his long strides. "Why do you think I'm going to be the problem? I have no idea of your witch hunting qualifications. I, at least, was born in that era. You could be a dud. Thanks for nothing, Death."

"Let's find the witches and see what we're up against," Titus says. "Then we can decide who's the dud."

Sweat drips under my bra. "Where do we start?" Skipping a couple steps helps me keep his pace.

He pulls out a similar phone to mine. "If you read the memo, you'd know that we have an address."

"I woke up in a strange hotel room after a long hiatus. It takes a few minutes to get back into the swing of things. These lovely witches, do they work together, live together, eat, sleep, and spell together? I mean what does a coven do?"

"A coven doesn't mean the witches live together. That would be like me moving into your hotel room." A wicked smile graces his lips. "But according to the memo, they're the exception and are cohabitating."

"Great. Let's go. Where to?"

"What exactly do you think is great? The possibility of sharing a room?"

"Yuck. No. That would be like living with a smelly older brother. The ability to find these witches and stop them so I can return to my life with Daxone. Not perfect is better than not at all."

"We're going to 33 Forest Street." He grabs my wrist and yanks me around a corner. "You're heading the wrong way."

The streets are typical New England: quaint and touristy with stores stacked side by side in low single- or two-story buildings. Unlike New York City, there are no skyscrapers. Some fronts have small wooden placards announcing their wares. There's a bookstore, over-priced clothing boutiques, a candy shop, and a tarot card reader in a neat line.

People stroll along the narrow sidewalks, and it leaves me longing for the rush of the vibrant New York City streets. The people here are nice and relaxed, enjoying their vacation. Smiles abound and some tourists hold hands as they amble.

No one bangs into me or pushes me aside with a rushed apology or grunt. These tourists lack intensity, and the New York City part of me doesn't quite understand it. Even in purgatory, I rarely relaxed. There was always some new territory to explore, a new run to complete, and of course, sexy time with Daxone.

I stumble after the hulk, narrowly avoiding a collision with an elderly couple when I catch up, and he hip-bumps me. "I'm calling Death if the abuse continues." Titus is going to be a pain in my ass.

"Like that would make a difference. Get your act together, and we'll be fine. Incompetence doesn't do it for me."

Something unintelligible sputters out of my lips before I shake my anger away. "Not incompetent. You're looking at a model employee with one of the best rates for reaping souls in my unit, at least before meeting Daxone and banishment."

"No doubt you were good at your job. Remember, I trained you. Death wouldn't be ill tempered enough to make this job harder by sending me, what did you call it, 'a dud.' There's a reason he needed you, but I didn't get the intel why." He wipes away a drop of sweat from his cheek with the back of his palm. "Try to remember we're dealing with witches now not dying, angsty humans."

Holding back further comments, I toy with the pendant around my neck.

Titus notices me fiddling with it. "It's still tuned to the souls of the dying. It'll glow when we get close to some. If the witches are stealing them, they'll be nearby the souls."

"That makes sense. I wondered why I got it back, not that I'm complaining."

"Don't you read any of your memos from Death?"

"I've been busy. Can you fill me in with the details I've missed?"

He whisks me around another corner. "Sure. Anything to help you, my favorite apprentice." Perfect white teeth shine like the blinding tunnel light to the other side. Someone has good hygiene. The attitude, on the other hand, I can do without.

My step halts midstride on the sidewalk, and I take in the aroma I've missed more than life itself. The door is open to Brew and Bakers. The theme, no surprise, is witchcraft, but my nose fills with the most tantalizing smell and my stomach growls on cue. "We are so going inside." I pull on the sleeve of his pressed, immaculate pink shirt that does not cloud his masculinity one bit. "I haven't had good coffee since being you know where. Must have java."

He doesn't even try to stop me. I order an extra-large mocha latte and two chocolate croissants. He orders an espresso shot and oatmeal. Once the order arrives, we sit, and I savor everything with New York intensity.

Titus stares. He's not sure what to do with me after so many years apart. I admit I've changed a big bit but don't care. Coffee consumes one hundred percent of my attention at the moment.

"Amazing." I take the last sip. "You cannot, I repeat, cannot get food like this in the place that shall not be named in public."

"Is that what people are calling purgatory nowadays?"

"Do you want me talking about purgatory with so many innocent people around?"

He tilts his head. "Good point, but they'd think you were crazy, and you might be. It's been a while. Ready to go?"

My gaze turns toward the bakery display case. "I could take something with us. Another latte?"

Titus opens his mouth but doesn't have a chance to say anything. My pendant glows at the same time as the jewel on his ring lights up.

"Showtime." He stands.

He guides me to his Porsche. "Here it is," he says and opens the door. "After you."

"Seriously? I'm stuck down under and you're driving around in a Porsche?"

"We all make our own choices and live with the consequences."

"Truth." I cannot argue and wouldn't trade my love for Daxone for any number of cars. Still, sinking into the seat and resting my head against the leather, I wonder how I was lassoed with a flaming-eyed, metallic breath, bad personality nuckelavee demon while Titus got a Porsche. My thoughts begin to unravel. Where is my beloved horse demon these days anyway? I need to find that out soon and wonder if Becca has the same phone number still.

We travel thirty minutes outside of Salem into the middle of nowhere. The few houses soon spread farther and farther apart. Otherwise, the landscape is full of trees and grass and nature. It's rural and empty and perfect for the witches' evil doings. "Where are we?"

"The sign said Middleton, Massachusetts. I follow the pull."

Titus finds a spot on the side of the road where the vehicle can hide behind trees and parks the car. Once outside, I follow him across a narrow, overgrown path.

"This is nature-y." Trees, rocks, and rotting logs dominate the landscape. I scramble over them, listen to an occasional bird call, and wait for the dense foliage to diminish and let the sunlight in. "Do you know where you're going?"

"Nope. Following the pull."

I sense it too. Memories of my past invade my thoughts, and I stumble.

Titus treks along the rocky single track without issue.

"How long have you been back?" I ask.

"Not the time for questions." He comes to a sudden stop and surveys the scene.

We arrive at a dank and dreadful bog at the edge of a larger lake. He waves me forward. Nerves ignite when I traipse deeper into the void. What if this is a trap? Here I come weaponless and without a plan.

The path slides away into mud, and I miss the stepping-stone. My boot sinks into the muck, and I glare. "Nature's the worst. This isn't what I expected from Death at all. I hail from New York City, and this is too much country for me. Why couldn't witches hang out in Boston. Is that too much to ask?"

"Yes."

"Why is it so important witches perform their craft in the middle of the forest. Is it the whole 'connecting to Mother Earth' thing?"

"They don't practice in the woods all the time. Witches live everywhere. These three happen to reside in a farmhouse near a lake. With what they're planning, they need more privacy than the average crone."

"Great, but we don't even know if this is the witches' doing or if it's a soul ready to depart."

"Let's find out."

I'm wondering what I got myself into, and it's making me a little concerned. Purgatory is sounding better and better. "You first."

"We're close." His back is to me, and the wind muffles his words.

When I hear rustling by my side, I stop. Growling rumbles behind me and fangs glisten in my periphery. "What the—" The rest of my sentence falls away when two huge, dark beasts emerge from behind a craggy rock outcrop. These aren't your ordinary pups. "Dogs," I croak. My skin prickles and goose bumps pimple my arms. "Scary dogs, not like cute puppies at the pet store."

Chapter Thirty-Seven

Hartford, Connecticut, 1657

He smiled as he came closer, and I was lost in it. We'd been liberated from the morning church service, which had lasted more than two hours, and my parents were socializing. Strategizing might be a better name for what my father did; always attempting to improve his standing amongst his peers to further his political aims.

"Trusting in God you are in good health," Thaddeus Walker said. He was tall and thin, and his hair and eyes were a similar shade of brown, but much was covered under his cap. His crooked smile held an abundance of cheer, something woefully lacking in my father's house. I had had a crush on the lovely and charming Thaddeus Walker for the past two years.

"Good morrow." I dipped my chin. My wool bodice and ankle-length skirt were brown, the sleeves white. My father always preferred my mother's and my dress plain and modest. A long-sleeve fitted waistcoat had been secured over my clothes for warmth, but the bodies in the church had made the room steamy, and I regretted my decision to add it this morning. My hair, as always, was pulled tightly back, and gathered under a hat.

"Pray, remember me to your parents."

"Of course." I smiled tentatively. "Prithee, how is your mother?"

"Good. It takes a lot of her time to make enough food to feed her sons." Dressed in his Sunday best, he stood out in the crowd in a long-sleeve, off-white linen shirt with a collar that buttoned in the front but was much covered by a doublet. Close-fitting, it highlighted his lithe, strong figure and broad frame. A cloak was draped over his shoulders. His breeches extended to knee level while the rest of his legs were covered by wool stockings and high-cut leather boots that accentuated his strong calves.

"Your poor sister. It must be lonely being the only girl with five brothers." Even though I said it, I wished for siblings. As an only child, there were so many expectations. And so many disappointments.

"We make sure Nellie Helen is always occupied."

My eyebrow rose. I had heard of the mischief the boys in his family attempted. "I'm sure you do."

"How's your father's farm? Ours was most rocky at the time of planting, but the soil is fruitful, and it appears our harvest will be fine this year. My brother and I have been working the fields daily."

"My father's harvest looks fruitful too." I dragged my eyes away from him, which was harder than expected. Shameful as it was, I did not want to lower my gaze. I promised myself I'd say extra prayers tonight, asking God to forgive my wanton abandon. But this man, if he could be called that at seventeen, was beautiful in appearance and kind at heart. He'd be the first to help a small child crying when they lost their toy or go far out of his way to walk an injured neighbor home if the ground was icy.

"That is good to hear."

"Aye." Not sure of what to say, I watched his small movements, a private grin forming inside my head that I was unable to share.

"The cattle thrive well here." His eyes grew playful.

My chest thundered with my loud heartbeat. *Is he teasing me? Is this what it is like to love a man?* I was so new to this, so uneasy, I did not know how to engage. At sixteen, I was plenty old enough to marry. Would Thaddeus be a good enough match that my father would approve? I was hopeful that this might be the start of something.

"Yes, they do." I held his gaze, bold and reckless.

"Have you been to the river to fish?" His boot scratched the rocky pathway.

"Father would not think that appropriate for me to try."

Another grin. "True, you are a well-schooled young lady."

"I heard there should be a new ship arriving with over twenty-five passengers and supplies. That will be a most enjoyable encounter. It will be nice to receive word from family in England."

"Yes, it will. We all appreciate the supplies and updates."

"Prudence, come here. We're leaving for home." My father called me to his side.

"Good morrow, Thaddeus." A blush rose in my cheeks as I said his name and left.

"Good morrow." He returned it with a dip of his head.

I failed to hear any of the conversation between my parents on the way home. My thoughts were lost in replaying every word Thaddeus said to me.

My reverie continued into the night, and I decided to do something. For him. One of the first spells my mother had ever shown me was a protection spell. I would cast it on Thaddeus to make sure he remained safe, make sure that there was a chance for us in the future.

The moon was high and half full when I slipped from the loft steps and headed outside into the chilly autumn darkness. My mother had told me it was the best time to cast fertility spells, but I hoped the same went for protection. Skulking away from the house, I bundled the blanket around me. I had not bothered to dress; my stay outside would only be a few minutes.

Under my favorite oak tree, I recited the words my mother taught me. A tingling traveled up my fingers and through my body. As I continued the spell, my hand danced through the night and left a trail of golden sparks in the air. Goosebumps brandished my skin, whether from the chill or the spell I was not sure.

> *Mother Nature, I say a prayer for Thaddeus.*
> *Preserve his soul thou created.*
> *His sense of joy and delight*
> *His strength and vigor in times of plight*
> *Bring ease and freedom to him*

(and here I paused, all at once remembering our conversation and how he appeared so rugged and handsome as we spoke.)

> *Hand, eye, ear, and limb*
> *From thy bounty provide support so he may sup*
> *From your full table and overflowing cup*
> *His heart holds no sorrows, his body no pain*
> *Only the joy of gain*

The sensations dissipated as quickly as the last word left my lips. The world around me shifted and I communed with nature. Words cannot do justice to the feeling of the wind and the land becoming intrinsic to my soul, comforting and kind. But most of all, powerful. My mother had warned me many times over that the gift must only be used for good and to gently tug at the power of nature, not pull too hard. Unpleasant consequences waited for the people who tried to do evil or use too much of nature's power without offering to replenish it.

I lingered in the night and never saw my father slither from the shadows and return to the house. When I went inside all was still: the fire low in the hearth; the sound of my parents' breathing calm and steady.

Chapter Thirty-Eight

Salem, Massachusetts, 2025

Behind the drooling dogs, a shadowy form solidifies, faces us, and bows her head in acknowledgement. She seems civil enough. Relief floods through me. My pulse drops a notch, and I hope there will be little to worry about here. I'm sure we'll come to a reasonable solution. The matter, solved quickly, will please Death, and back to my love I'll go. Maybe, Death, so grateful, will return Daxone and me to the topsoil.

The woman in front of me bucks all the conventional wisdom about witches. She's no hag, lacks warts and a tall black hat, and doesn't hold a broom. Young and attractive, with long, wavy brown hair, supple curves, and ample breasts.

"Let me introduce myself." Her mesmerizing big, brown doe eyes are framed by long lashes. "I'm Lulu, one of the three sisters. These are my trusted watchdogs, Alder and Ash. They're Rottweilers, if you couldn't tell, and will be your companions on our little excursion."

"Alder and Ash like trees? Gentle, green, blowing in the breeze trees? Aren't there more appropriate names like Hulk and Hellion?

Death and Blight? Fang and Fangier?" I ask, not appreciating the way the dogs' small black eyes focus on me like I'm a chunk of meat. While my pulse has quieted, it's not returning to normal thanks to them. I shift from leg to leg, and the damn beasts track the motion.

"Like the trees, my two friends here are constant companions, a most important part of the circle of life." She beckons to us. "They're also trained to eat your innards on command. Follow me. We've been expecting you."

"We?" I mouth at Titus.

He shrugs and we're ushered forward. The dogs flank us. My heart pounds again and there's a lump in my throat. Scary Ash, as big as a bear, trails behind, sniffing shrubs. In front of me, Titus is engrossed in conversation with Lulu, making it impossible for me to send him a pointed look of distress. A chuckle escapes his lips, which unnerves me even more.

Did she spell him? Is he enthralled and only thinking about Lulu's amazing eyes or other body parts? Does he remember the reason we came? Or is enthralling someone a vampire thing? Maybe witches can't even do that. Does that mean Titus is a double agent? Did he lure me here only to sacrifice me on an altar in some ritual? Death would be so mad.

The urge to yell something overwhelms me, but I don't know all his methods yet. He might have changed since we worked together long ago and take my shrieking the wrong way.

Titus might be working on a well-thought-out plan. Only God knows.

I refuse to be the dud on this mission. It's high time I developed my strategy to end this craziness. And soon. I want nothing more than to see Daxone's face again, but my coffee and pastry this morning were kind of over the top yummy. Could we at least get food trucks in purgatory?

Focus is clearly needed. I peer up at the dense canopy of treetops that shade us. "Where are we?" I don't expect Lulu to answer, and I'm a little shocked when she pulls her eyes away from Titus to meet my gaze.

"My grandmama's farm. It's been in the family for many generations, back to when women were making potions to help others through childbirth and a whole host of other ailments. Our ancestors came here after the events in Salem in 1692 to escape the madness."

I trip over my feet. Our histories sound too familiar for coincidence. Is that why Death dragged me here? To commiserate? "I'm a little rusty on what went on in Salem that far back, but I sure know some other towns from that time period."

"I'm sure you do." Her smile is seductive.

It makes me nervous, and I word vomit, "I should have found out more about what happened, but I was pretty busy at the time."

"Were you now? How interesting."

Titus gives me a withering glare. Did I reveal something I should not? Maybe I'm the dud. I twist back to check on the hounds and see they're still at my heels.

"Fill me in," I say. "What happened to your ancestors?"

"It was a tragic time for female empowerment. No one should ever forget." Lulu turns away from me to Titus. "A local physician, a man of course, diagnosed several teenage girls as bewitched, which resulted in twenty deaths, mostly by hanging and mostly women. My grandmother was charged but, lucky for me, not convicted. She got the hell out of there, once released from prison." Her gaze returns to me and reaches into my soul, creeping me out. "I like you, and you hold a lot of power. More than you can dream. Join the coven."

"Thanks, but no." I swat at the swarming gnats in my ear. "I'm here to stop you from whatever evil misdeed you're planning."

"I already know." Her laugh is a church hymn. "Follow me."

Trees dissipate around us as the tall grass and wildflowers tickle my legs. There are fields, stone fences, an apple orchard, and a large white house perched high on the hill. It's a ramshackle collection of architectural designs with black shutters and moss on the roof.

"Let's take a quick tour of the grounds before we decide your fate." Lulu motions us forward.

The dogs release a menacing growl. A few rapid steps put space between me and them.

Lulu leads us to a barn. It's hard to decipher the paint color. The wood is worn, bleached by the sun, and in need of refurbishment. She pulls the doors back and candles blaze in the interior. Cobwebs highlight the corners, old hay bales fill the empty stalls that line each side, and a huge table sits in the middle. From the smell of molding hay and earth, I doubt livestock inhabited this place of late.

"All those candles must be a safety hazard. Is this the best place to light them?" I ask.

No one responds. Two other women standing near the table aglow in the candlelight stare. They're also attractive. One is older, in her forties, and could have been a daytime television star. She's taller than I am, and her black braids are shot full of gray, which only makes her more exotic and attractive. The other woman is mid-thirties and dressed as if she never left the 1970s. I give a wistful sigh, remembering some of the fun times I had so long ago. Extensive blonde ringlets fall to her buttocks and are crowned in daisies. She has blue eyes and a peaceful smile.

"This is them?" Hippie Woman asks.

"Present and accounted for." Lulu strides to the table.

Titus and I pose awkwardly inside the barn. The dogs sit in front of the door, guarding against any attempt to flee.

"We have a problem." I focus on Flower Power. "Let's come to a solution and go our separate ways in love and peace."

"I'm all ears," Blondie drawls. She fidgets with her white dress, fluffing out the full skirt. There are spots of red splatter. "These stains will never come out. Any suggestions to remove blood?"

"Sorry, no," I stutter. The creep factor is high here and a chill runs down my back. "Not a domestic goddess."

"Me either." Hippie Woman's smile is nearly as enticing as Lulu's, all bright-white teeth and cherry-red lips. "We have so many other important things to accomplish. Who has time to do laundry?"

I don't return the smile. Her comment reminds me how

uncomfortable I am in addition to everything else I'm feeling. Mud has encased my ankles, my socks are damp, my boots heavy. I casually stamp my foot, hoping to evict the mud off the boots, and think about my argument. A few seconds later, I push my shoulders back and get to the point. "You're pilfering souls from Death, and they don't like it. That's an understatement. They are pissed off. The soul stealing needs to stop." I pause, then add, "Please."

"We've been sent to make sure that happens." Titus puffs out his chest and stands tall.

I glare. Being all masculine isn't going to work here unless he wants a date. How can he not tell that?

"What can we do to make that happen?" I ask in my most appeasing tone, happy I don't trip over the words.

The three women put their heads together and confer. Their voices blend into a sing-song melody.

"This is promising." I elbow Titus as the minutes tick by and no one dies. "I'm going to earn brownie points with Death and be home with Daxone quicker than I thought. I'm bringing her coffee and croissants." Actually, I plan to stock up on a year's worth before going back.

"We've discussed it." Lulu closes the distance between us. "While my sisters and I understand Death's concern, we have a valid mission. The only way to complete it is with the souls of five men." She ignores Titus and reaches out her hand to grasp my arm. "We could use your help."

Every pore in my body tingles. I shiver but can't believe I have power. Unsure if it's me she wants to join the coven, I turn to see if some other woman is standing around who I failed to notice. Nope. I'm alone with Titus. "Me?" I ask when I turn back.

"The three of us can all sense your power," Lulu says. "You might not understand it yet, but you could be a valuable asset, and a part of liberating women from the unfair and degrading patriarchy they've endured."

"I'm all for feminism, but I don't think that requires human sacrifice."

"We're freeing all women," the older witch with braids continues. "Many don't even understand or accept how bad their existence is because of a lack of empathy by the opposite sex. Feminism is a fine movement, but we're talking about something much bigger. We're talking about women taking all the power from men and designing a new world where they rule. It'll be so much better."

"Join us or die," the blonde witch says, moving close. Her gaze makes me the most important person in her world. "Here's the thing. We need souls to power our spells. We're working on some important magic to change the world. Death will have to do without a few. I'm sure he won't even notice them missing, but I'll tell you all about the plan when you join us."

I'm momentarily entranced but then step out of her reach. When I can think clearly, my ears ring. Irritation fights with fear. "I'd love to help and all, but Death's been my boss for a mighty long time, and I don't want to piss them off. Plus, Death's got my girlfriend locked up in purgatory. Can't leave her there to suffer alone."

Chapter Thirty-Nine

Hartford, Connecticut, 1658

Thaddeus and I stood before my father, Caleb. My heart pounded. With others, this might have been a joyous moment, but I only knew fear. The evening sun cast long shadows across the wooden floor of the homestead, and I wondered if it was an omen of ill. I raised my hand to my mouth, wanting so badly to tear at my fingernail, but then shoved it to my side, telling myself not to fidget.

The heat from the hearth radiated off my mother, who couldn't contain a grin. She almost bounced each step when she joined my father at the table. While not the decision maker, I was happy she was present; a positive influence against my father's frown.

"Mr. Barlow." Thaddeus raised a hand in greeting, trying to banish my father's stern countenance. "I come to you with the sincerest of intentions and seek your blessing. I hope you will consent to Prudence becoming my wife."

My father leveled a withering gaze on the younger man, skepticism and disbelief evident. He adjusted his hat, his farm-sore hands on the brim.

"You want to marry my daughter, Prudence?" he asked, voice low. "You're a decent lad with a proper family. I have observed your conduct with my daughter but thought it barely a friendship. I would have stepped in sooner, had I discovered something else was happening."

"I love your daughter, sir. I'll work to make her happy."

"I'm sure you would, but marriage is a solemn covenant, not to be entered into lightly. Have you considered what it entails?"

Standing in silence, I could only watch the exchange.

Thaddeus nodded. "I have, sir. I understand the responsibilities that come with marriage, and I am prepared to shoulder them. My father said he'd provide me with some acreage to begin my own homestead, and I'm sure the community would help in the building of the house like they do for all the newly married."

Caleb arched an eyebrow. "I'm sure they would. Members of the community in the right standing deserve a prosperous start."

Thaddeus hesitated a moment, unsure of what to say next. "Mr. Barlow, pray pardon, but I am diligent and hardworking. With time, I will establish myself in the community and provide for Prudence and the children we may have."

My father's gaze turned to my mother. He squinted, as if trying to see under her skin. "That is the question, isn't it. Children are a blessing, but they are also a legacy. It's important to consider that."

"Yes, sir. Your family is held in high regard. I'm sure any children we have would be the same."

My father regarded him for a long moment. "Your words are earnest, but I cannot say yes to this union."

I gasped. What reason would my father have to disparage the union? Thaddeus and I loved one another. With marriage, I could leave my father's home and find happiness. I might even be able to appease him with male grandchildren. I didn't understand. Disappointment gnawed at me, but I refused to yield to despair too quickly. Could this be a test? Was he pushing Thaddeus to see if his intentions were true? I was sure my love would fight for me.

Thaddeus tried once more. "I understand your concerns, sir, but

I'm willing to work tirelessly to prove myself worthy of Prudence's hand. With your blessing, I'm confident that we can build a wholesome and blessed life together."

My father sighed, and I thought his resolve faltered.

"You are a good lad, and I harbor no ill will toward you. But my duty as a father is to safeguard my legacy, and I cannot in good conscience sanction this union. You may not understand why, and I cannot explain it to you. I'm sorry, but Prudence will not marry."

My mother gasped. "Why do you say such things?"

"Martha, do not contradict me. My word is law in these matters. You and I both understand well what the problem is."

My mother took a step back when I had expected her to champion me. I swallowed the lump that had formed in my throat. My hopes could not be so easily discharged. Emotions raged and crashed like a wave against the rocky shore.

"I don't understand, sir," Thaddeus said with resignation. "But I shall respect your decision, though it pains me greatly. Would you reconsider if I return? Maybe after considering the matter, you will change your mind."

My father placed a hand on Thaddeus's shoulder, showing him more empathy than he'd ever shown me. "Don't lose heart. There are many pious young women in the town and many paths in life. I will not change my thoughts on this matter but keep faith, and all shall be well in the end."

My father guided Thaddeus to the door, bid him farewell, and I watched through the crack as the first man I ever loved trudged away from the homestead, his footsteps heavy on the ground.

The weight of unspoken sorrow bore me to the floor; my chance at happiness carelessly discharged.

"Why?" I asked when my father turned to face me.

"Your mother has corrupted you," he replied. "I let her have her herbs, teas, and potions. I thought it was harmless and that she was helping others and never realized she'd teach you the art. I see now she plans to take you down the path of evil with her."

"Father, I'm not evil."

"Nor am I." My mother, tiny and thin, had never appeared fiercer. Her hands were clenched into talons.

"I will make sure that you both do not engage in the work of the devil."

My mother stood tall. "We would never."

He stalked toward my mother and raised a hand to strike her. "You say that, but I saw Prudence out in the middle of the night, casting a spell. Her fingers glowed. My eyes did not deceive me. It had to be your influence."

"I would never hurt anyone," I said.

My mother sent me a careful glance, and I stood silent.

"You must have been mistaken." Mother drew near Father, hoping to take his hand, but he stepped away.

"I was not mistaken." He paced the floor around where I had dropped to my knees. "I will not let Prudence marry, nor let whatever evil you have unleashed continue under my name."

"This is unfair to her," my mother said.

"You are the cause of this." He aimed his finger at my mother." If anyone is to blame, it's you. I thought you used the bounty of nature, what God had put on the earth for man, but I see I was wrong. You delve into unnatural things, and it will occur no longer. Prudence will not marry. I forbid it."

My heart rebelled against the notion of surrendering my happiness. My mother had hushed me, but I couldn't remain quiet and give up my only chance to leave the confines of this harsh, stifling existence. Thaddeus offered me a chance at happiness and love.

"Father." I took a deep breath, steeling myself against his anger. "I love Thaddeus, and I cannot bear the thought of a future without him. He is a man of integrity and kindness, and I would always do the right thing for his family and ours."

"Prudence." Anger radiated off his skin in a slick sweat. "You and Martha are the cause of your fate. You'll never marry. There'll never be a Barlow legacy in America as much as I want it to be. I'll not unleash more of your mother's evil onto the community."

Father stalked outside. Unable to stand, I stared at the crackling embers of the hearth. My fate was sealed. I'd be alone forever, trapped in this small house, this isolated existence. My ears rang, a sob built in my throat, and dizziness threatened. One part of me wanted the darkness. I smashed my knuckles into the floor to stop it.

"Forget, dearest Prudence," my mother whispered, coming to my side. "Abandon this encounter and your abilities until they are needed."

The spell was the last thing I heard. When I woke, I'd forgotten Thaddeus proposed and couldn't remember any of the spells my mother had once taught.

Chapter Forty

Salem, Massachusetts, 2025

Lulu runs a finger through my red curls. "Such a shame." She shrugs and walks back to the other witches. "Guess you both die then. Sisters, let's go and leave these two to their fate."

Three witches and two dogs walk out the door. Titus and I are left standing, very much alive, in the middle of the barn. It's quite atmospheric with all the candles.

"This isn't as bad as I expected," I say. "I get they're witches and all, but they're pleasant."

"It's not over. You heard them say we're going to die." Titus turns to the door. "They're up to something."

He twists back when a deep guttural moan emanates out of one of the stalls. A once beefy man with a mullet leaves a trail of pus and guts along the floor as he limps closer. The odor of three-month-old cauliflower and dog poop brings my hand to my nose. I take a few steps back. "What the F is that?" The living dead staggers my way.

"Walking corpse," Titus answers.

"They don't exist." The shock of seeing a dead man walking causes bile to rise in my throat. Dread floods the pit of my stomach like runoff and oil form in a puddle after a sudden storm. I want to hide, bend over, and heave, but can't take my eyes off the advancing monstrosity.

Titus sends me a "you're not the brightest bulb" look. "You've seen crazier things, I'm sure."

"Since you're the expert, what do we do?" I manage to put one foot behind the other and an idea pops into my head. I'm suddenly thankful for the candles. "We could burn it."

"We'd go up in flames. There's hay and dried wood everywhere. I suspect the door's locked too."

"Other options?" I'm stepping backward, heading for the exit. The zombie lumbers, in no hurry to eat my brains. Either it knows we are trapped, or my innards aren't prime pickings. That doesn't stop my pulse from pounding.

"It's not like I fight zombies every day. My guess would be the witches take the soul and then reanimate the body. Bad, bad magic."

I squat and pick up an old shovel. "Let's talk about that later. We need to behead it or de-brain it or something."

Titus surveys the zombie, then the barn. He grabs a pitchfork leaning against the wall.

I hold my shovel like a bat. "You first."

"Ladies first. I insist."

"I'm an equal-opportunity feminist. Go for it. Don't get bit or scratched or whatever."

Titus steps into the path of the undead. "I don't think these are the infected kind. Reanimation is different."

I shrug. "You're the expert."

Its face is full of yellow pustules, some popped and leaking. I try not to study the extent of the decay, wanting to keep those croissants in my stomach where they belong. The zombie ambles like it has no worries other than tearing us apart, and well, I guess that's true. It's dead and sans a soul and ripping us limb from limb is its main agenda item of the day.

Titus spears the undead redneck with leaking boils and purple mottled skin in the belly. A pitchfork to the stomach makes sense in theory but what leaks out has my breakfast in my throat. I turn away for a moment only to hear the squelch of pitchfork retracting.

"You should try the shovel," Titus says. "This is a no go."

Metallic, acid taste still dancing on my tongue, I go to bat. I swing at the zombie's head. The crunch surprises me. I'm stronger than I appear, but the mess is way worse too. The shovel slices right through the matted mullet, skin, and muscle to meet bone. It doesn't carve all the way through but makes a damn good dent.

Unfortunately, the undead is angered by almost losing its head. Go figure. "We need to work together and fast." I jog a few steps back, holding onto the shovel for dear life as the redneck limps closer one icky step at a time. I don't even want to fathom what makes each footfall squelch. "Use the pitchfork and then I'll bash away."

"Teamwork. That's the spirit." With a nod, Titus hoists the pitchfork and lets out a war cry. He runs at the creature, plows it over, and impales the pitchfork in its meaty beer gut.

Trying my best to ignore the wafting aroma of bowels, I smash the shovel into the zombie. It screams out in an inhuman voice and attempts to commandeer my boot. I kick out and slam the tip of the shovel into his neck. The zombie's head lolls to the side, but its teeth continue to chomp. I repeat the motion. After five times, it stops squirming. I continue to bash at the thing to be sure.

"It's dead now," Titus says. "Only pulp and liquid remain."

I squat and huff in breath. "This is a lovely welcome to Salem."

We relinquish the farm tools and head to the barn doors. My mouth drops when they open into glorious, non-zombie sunshine. I peer through squinted eyes, body braced, waiting for more of the horde or a secondary attack. Maybe some familiars or fairies. Not sure what to expect, I'm slightly disappointed when I get nothing.

"The witches must have had a lot of faith in their zombie," I say. Lulu and companions are nowhere to be seen. "I'm sad they thought so little of me as an opponent."

"You'll get over it. Come on."

I put the thought out of my mind, and we sprint back through the bog and the trees, happy to leave nature far behind.

The car ride is silent, both of us lost in our thoughts and trying not to inhale. I can't help but wonder if Titus is worried about the interior of the Porsche but I'm not opening my mouth to ask.

Thank goodness the hotel lobby is empty. If anyone sees us, they'd be likely to call the police. It appears we either tried to commit murder, or someone attempted to kill us, the latter being the truth.

"Do you want to get a drink?" Titus points to the bar.

I pull at my grimy shirt covered in zombie bits. "Nah. Too tired. I'm going up to my room to crash." I wave goodbye and head up in the elevator. I lean against the interior wall. I'm bone-weary, nauseous, and disgusted with myself that I lost a soul to Lulu and couldn't save the zombie man's life.

Back in my hotel, I shower off zombie guts, my body succumbing to the aftermath of the fear and adrenaline rush. I have little left in the reserve tank and can barely hoist the pajamas that have magically appeared over my head. I manage to dress and call room service. Not long after, a hamburger, fries, and more fries arrive, along with an entire bottle of wine for me. It's a wine night most definitely. If anything can revive me, it will be a quality glass of merlot.

I'm sitting on the bed, shoving my face full of French fry goodness and attempting to dry off my hair all at the same time when my new smartphone rings. It's an unknown number. "Hello?"

"It's me, Dax."

"Oh my God, how'd you call me?"

"Death's assistant came by and dropped off a cell phone. He said I could phone you to keep you motivated. How's it going?"

"There's a bakery with amazing coffee and pastries."

"That's good, but the witches?"

"A little setback today, but don't worry. We're on it. The witches are wilier than I imagined, but we'll get them tomorrow."

"That's not the news I was hoping for. Wait, you said 'we.'"

"Daxone, I miss you so much. It's unfair you have to stay there while I'm here. Titus agrees Death should have sent you with us."

"Titus? Who's that?"

I shrug, then realize Dax can't see the movement. "Death sent me some help. He used to be my mentor. Titus, you remember. I'm sure I told you about him."

"I don't think you did. Please tell me he's five foot two and has a handlebar moustache."

"Five foot three, but yes to the moustache."

"Tell me he isn't at all attractive."

I consider Titus's six-pack abs, dark hair, and tall frame and lie, hoping my chances of exiting purgatory aren't diminishing with each word. "Really heinous. You're not the jealous type, are you? We didn't discuss those little details on our whirlwind romance." My voice softens. "You're my one and only love."

"Keep telling me that."

"The witches are misguided." I change the subject. "I can reason with them and adjust their perspective on resurrecting a god. We'll find some middle ground and then I'll be home."

We chat for a long time, until I yawn into the phone. "I have to go and make plans to destroy these witches. I want to be home with you more than anything. Call often. Every day. Twice a day. Okay?"

"I will. Love you."

"Love you." I hang up and fall onto the pillows, damp hair spilling around me. I'm so over the witches and this assignment and fall asleep wondering what I'm going to have to do tomorrow to get the broom riders out of my life.

Chapter Forty-One

Hartford, Connecticut, 1660

"What are you doing?" I asked my mother, Martha. She'd sent me off to find some willow bark by the stream. I'd scoured the trees but had been unable to locate a willow. Both my mother and I knew about a copse of them not far away, so I wondered why she'd dispatched me on a fool's errand. On my return, I found her by our favorite tree; an ancient oak that provided ample shade and whispered wisdom when the wind exhaled. There was a hollow at the bottom, and she'd been pushing something into it.

"It's nothing."

"I saw you put something in there."

"The sun must have been in your eyes."

My mother and I had always been close, more like sisters. We shared everything, or at least I thought we did. Concern didn't drive my questions, only curiosity. "Pray, do not lie to me, Mother." I flopped in the grass next to her crouched form.

"Fine." She pulled a book from the hollow of the tree, dusted it off, lovingly stroked the front as if petting her favorite mouser, and handed it to me.

"What is this?" My eyebrows furrowed as I squinted at the weighty, ancient tome.

"You wanted to see. Now you can decide."

As I studied the rich, dark leather cover with small ripples and eddies, an embedded amber jewel caught my attention. I ran my fingers over the stone and gasped when they tingled. I opened the book and stared at the page, flipped to another, then through the rest. "It's blank."

"It was meant to hold things special to me."

"A journal?"

"Aye, something like that."

"Why's it empty?" The page rippled in front of me, and words formed, soft and blurry like a faraway shape. I touched my fingers to the soft parchment and warmth, like a summer breeze, spread through them. "There's something here."

My mother ripped the tome from my hand. "Now is not the right time. I'm saving this for you, but for later."

"I wasn't done," I grumbled.

My mother was rarely rash and never reckless, and I didn't understand her rush to take this treasure from me. I'd never seen anything like it. The paper we used for letters and correspondence seemed ordinary when compared to this.

"Another time."

"Why not keep it in the house? Then, you could show me it again." I couldn't explain it to my mother, but the book called to me. It wanted me to study it. That sounded absurd, and I'd never tell Mother these thoughts, but still wanted it close.

"Your father would not approve."

"Even he could have no concerns with a journal. If you let me write in it, I'd muse on the long Sunday sermons and the crops. There'd be nothing to offend him."

She stashed the book back in the tree trunk, stood, and pulled me up next to her. "I say we don't chance it and not tell him. Our secret, yes?"

I shrugged. "That's fine, but I don't think he'd mind."

"You never know what he ends up fretting about. This is the easier way."

We walked back home in the cool autumn after collecting the willow bark. Once there, I stoked the fire in the hearth. It crackled to life. The small windows let in the last of the afternoon light and turned the interior warm and smoky. While the harvest had been completed, my father was out with the livestock and wouldn't return for a few hours.

I sat at the wooden table while my mother brewed us tea.

"How did the Walker birth go?" I asked.

My mother's gaze softened. Thaddeus had married a lovely girl named Rebecah and she'd had a baby. Usually, I'd go along to help my mother with the birth, but she'd asked me to stay behind.

"All went well. The baby boy and mother are fine. The father most proud."

A moment of sadness hit me, as if that should have been my life, but I forced it away. I had my mother and was learning her craft. I was healthy and content and had plenty to be thankful for. I'd pray tonight to ask God to forgive me for wanting more than my lot. "That's wonderful news. I hope I can be as skilled as you one day when it comes to birthing and all your healing ways."

"You are already so much more, my dear. You have a kindness and bravery that surpasses any skill." She set tea on the table and sat across from me.

I tilted my head, sensing melancholy in her. "Is something wrong? You seem sad."

"It's nothing. An old memory."

I reached out and held my mother's hand, the weight of unspoken truths and secrets lingering. "I love you, Mama." I hadn't used that term since I was a child and watched her face light with a myriad of emotions, eyes swelling with tears.

"I love you too, Prudence," Martha said, her voice choked.

"I didn't mean to upset you."

"The opposite, dear child. You're the most precious thing to me. I take joy in you every day."

Changing the subject, I hoped to lighten the mood. "Then tell me what's going on. I can't get the book out of my thoughts. Even now, it lingers. I must sound hysterical to you."

"No, but I must ask you not to speak of this to your father. There's been talk in the village of late and we need to be careful." Having finished her tea, she stood and emptied the basket of herbs, flowers, and willow bark.

"What talk?" I asked.

She ignored my question. "Prithee, do you remember what to do with the willow bark?"

I smiled at her test. "Of course. You must first strip the bark and use the innards. Boil it in water for at least ten minutes and let it stand for thirty more. Then strain the mixture and add cinnamon and honey for flavor."

"What does it help with?"

"It's helpful with aches and pains and to reduce inflammation. Don't try to change the subject. What have you heard in town that you're not sharing?"

"The town is beetle headed. There's silly talk of witchcraft. The bad harvest has left everyone rattled and concerned. It is nothing."

"Witchcraft? What does that have to do with us?"

"Nothing." Her words were forceful. "But your father is concerned that my applications and healing teas might be viewed as not from God."

She passed me some of the willow bark and we stripped the rough wood into fine lengths. "You've only ever used your knowledge to help people," I said. "The town would never turn against you. They're all our friends."

Her fingers worked swift and sure. "Let us hope."

Chapter Forty-Two

Salem, Massachusetts, 2025

An obnoxious beeping from my phone wakes me. I'm confused until the barn, the zombie, and my conversation from the prior night replay in my mind. I sit and swipe the hair out of my eyes and the drool from the corner of my mouth. I text Daxone some morning tenderness, stretch, stumble out of bed, and vow to reset the alarm to more dulcet tones.

The shower is lukewarm and reminds me of my stay in purgatory where everything was tepid, except for the love of my life. I comb the tangles out of my hair, but after using the hotel's tiny bottle of shampoo and conditioner, my locks imitate Merida's from the Disney movie *Brave*. I head to the closet. It's another day in uniform: army cargo shorts, tank top, and black boots. A Devils' baseball cap sits crushed at the bottom of the suitcase. I wedge it on.

Titus and I plan to meet at the bakery at 8:00 a.m., grab a latte, and strategize some more. I hustle downstairs to make it there early, wanting to beat him at something. The hotel mimics a grand, modern colonial house. The lobby's décor includes overstuffed couches, dark wood tables, chrome, and mirrors. When the glass front doors slide open, humid air greets me.

After getting lost, I spot Brew and Bakers on the far side of the street, duck into the café, order an extra-large latte, and stare into the pastry cabinet filled with croissants, bear claws, apple fritters, and donuts. I almost go for a green tea donut but a cinnamon bagel with cream cheese calls to my empty stomach.

The little café is bustling, and I people-watch as I eat. A couple sits under a pair of crisscrossed broomsticks. They share three donuts. One takes a bite, then offers the treat to the other. Both perch on stools at a small high-top table. Their love is disgustingly cute but likely to lead to diabetes. An older woman appears to be a repeat customer. The man behind the counter waves and greets her by name when he calls her order. She reads the newspaper on her iPad. A family of five with a little girl dressed as Elsa from *Frozen* devours pancakes shaped like witches' hats.

The cute family breeds thoughts of my previous conversation with Daxone and images of the deeds we did after the talk flood my less than pristine mind. I'm enjoying my daydreams, food, and drink so much I don't even care that Titus is late. It's all so normal and lovely after dank, dark purgatory.

Breakfast accomplished, I reconsider my time with the zombie and realize it was as horrible as I initially thought. I'm glad I stayed up late talking to Daxone. Otherwise, that lesion-covered, dead-eyed zombie would have kept me twisting and turning most of the night on my more-comfortable-than-in-purgatory bed.

I order a second latte to combat my lack of sleep and stare out the window of my new favorite bakery, really the only bakery I've tried in Salem. As I slurp the caffeine infused drink, Titus continues to be a no-show and my concern heightens.

Did the witches conduct a sneak attack at the hotel last night and take him out? It's a possibility and one that leaves me alone to fight and without my beloved mentor. Shaking my head, I'm ninety-nine percent sure that Titus is indestructible, but three witches against one reaper aren't fair odds. I pray Death didn't put him on another job and hope he shows soon. They would have notified me, right?

To ease my anxiety, I text Daxone another cheery morning hello with coffee and food emojis. She responds right back, and my day is instantly shinier.

How's life going on the flipside? Daxone asks.

Great coffee and bagels, less than perfect no show sidekick. Wish you were here. I add lots of heart emojis.

I'm running extra miles to be buff on your return and planning a couple surprises to show you how much I miss you. She adds a few heart emojis of her own.

You're so sweet. That's why I love you.

There's not a lot else to do here except pine away.

Don't pine. We're having a wonderful little romantic moment right now. I'll be back with you soon. I promise. I'm not sure what emoji to send next. *I hope we can finish this disaster of an assignment today, and I'll be back in your arms tomorrow.*

Can't wait. Love you. She sends a face blowing kisses and then a devil and flames.

I spend a few minutes pondering what excitement might be waiting for me back in purgatory, but thoughts of Titus invade. The man is tightly wound and checks his watch every five minutes to ensure we remain on schedule. He's not the "dude" type who would casually stroll into the bakery still slightly intoxicated after a rough night of drunken debauchery. He's imperative for this assignment and cannot be witchnapped or dead. As much as I'm a lone wolf kind of gal, three witches might prove a little too powerful for me.

I'll give Titus five more minutes before I emergency dial Death.

Since I'm no longer a reaper of souls, I consider a title change as I wait. Death's personal assistant is already taken. Brainstorming on a napkin, I end up with Death's All-Important Aficionado. It sounds significant but is vague enough to encompass whatever we need to do today. I cannot wait to explain my reasoning to Titus, and I hope he'll take the title on too. We might even want to petition Death to legitimize it.

At 8:30 a.m., Titus saunters in, bedroom eyes still drowsy with sleep.

"Did you just wake up?"

"Yes." His words sound gruff. "Some of us had work to do after our meeting with the witches. I've slept an hour at most." His lips prune. "What happened to your hair? It's bigger than normal."

Ringlets of red frame my face. "New shampoo. Want a latte? My treat. Actually, Death pays the bills, but I'll order it for you."

He grunts. That means "yes" in the land of Titus and so I head to the counter. It's so unfair that he wakes up and hauls ass out of bed appearing attractive and manly. My look takes time. Not too much time as of late since Death didn't supply makeup and the few changes of clothes are close to identical sets of black jeans, T-shirts, army fatigue shorts, and sweatshirts. Death splurged for the Devils' cap, one leather jacket, and a pair of boots. Waiting for Titus's food and drink, I consider a shopping trip might be in order, desperately needing some hair products to tame the frizz. Hello. We're talking July in New England.

"I assume you haven't gone gluten free." I drop the coffee and bagel in front of Titus and watch him inhale it all. "You want to go back to the farm today after we stock up on supplies?" I fidget in my seat, lattes working their magic. "You think we can surprise them? We might be going back too soon?"

"It's as good a plan as any. We have one stop to make first. Death emailed this morning. I'm assuming you didn't read it."

"I forgot to check my emails." My cheeks burn. "There hasn't been a need to do so down under. What do we have to get?"

"I'll know it when I see it."

"That inspires confidence. As if our ingenious plan wasn't going to stump the witches, this surely sounds like a showstopper."

He pushes the empty plate away and stands. "Ready?"

Chapter Forty-Three

We head out the door and into Salem proper. Derby Street is busy with tourists, making us skirt around them. I hoof it to keep up with Titus's long strides and scroll through my phone as we walk. "There's a witch museum and a satanic temple. Do we have time to stop?"

Titus drags me away from the crowds beginning to flock and into a side street. He's obviously searching for something. We enter another bustling neighborhood.

"This is Witch City." He pulls me through the doors of a shop called Wonderful Witchers. Inside there is everything metaphysical and wiccan related.

"What do we need here?"

"Advice."

Titus says hello to the goth woman working the cash register. They chat before he leads me to a room at the back of the store. His knock is loud on the closed door.

"Fortune teller" is etched onto a faded wooden sign hanging crookedly.

"Enter," says a voice behind the barrier.

I've dealt with many strange things in my lifetime, but goose-bumps hit my arms hard without good reason. Burying the unease, I follow Titus.

Inside, it's muted with flowing wall coverings. The fabric sways from a light breeze coming through an open window. I could get lost in the ripples of reds, oranges, and yellows. Festive. We tunnel through the veils to the end of a long and narrow room, and I suppress the urge to grab Titus's hand.

Behind a broad, scratched table, a large man stands, head bowed in prayer, eyes closed. He sports long brown hair tied in a man bun and a shaggy beard. He looks like a gym rat Jesus. Tarot cards, bones, runes, skulls, and a crystal ball clutter the space alongside other relics.

My words to Titus are hushed. "Isn't this clairvoyant stuff all parlor tricks?"

"Like Death coming to claim souls or witches raising corpses?"

"Next you're going to tell me there are vampires and Franken-steins still running around Antarctica."

"You never know. By the way, Frankenstein was the doctor, not the monster."

"Whatever." I sit, refusing to acknowledge him or my hurt pride, while Titus stands next to me at the table.

The man shakes Titus's hand. They chitchat, and after a few seconds, it's clear to me they've done this before and have a working relationship. The fortune teller ignores me, but I'm overwhelmed once again by the abundance in the room. His flowing golden robes shimmy and blend into the gently swaying rainbow scarves and wall-hangings. Elements of the occult are stacked chaotically on shelves and appear as if they'll topple with the next strong gust of wind. He collects incense from a large glass container and matches from a drawer before setting the aromatic sticks in a holder and lighting them. The smell of lavender and sage are soothing. In the background, faint carnival music plays.

With nothing else to do, I question my sanity and then Titus's and wonder why Death paired us together once more. Must be the need for Titus's mastery of networking. I mean, he found this guy. As if reading my thoughts, Mystery Mystic Man clears his throat. His eyes are closed, but his gaze focuses on me. "Wanting something more than intended is the key to ruin." He finally sits at the table and Titus perches next to me on a too-small stool.

When he opens his eyes again, they're pure white. My mouth drops. His hand snakes out to grab mine before I can pull away. Leathery fingers travel over every inch as if there's an important message on my palm, knuckles, and nails. "No one wants to be happy with what the great beyond has bequeathed them."

"How do you know what's inside the crystal ball if you can't see it during a reading?" The question slips out of my mouth.

Titus's fingers squeeze my thigh. "Rude much."

"Sorry."

"No apology needed." He shakes his head. "I am able to see in my mind's eye. There is no need for physical sight."

"That makes sense." I scrunch my nose at Titus.

He gives me a not-so-subtle kick under the table at the same time the fortune teller releases my hand.

"What is this world coming to?" The mystic adjusts his man bun, and the reading begins. I wonder if that helps focus his inner sight when he says, "These witches should realize there are no shortcuts in life."

"I guess Titus has filled you in."

"Yes. A dangerous situation for both of you." The supernaturally sensitive fortune teller grabs the crystal ball in both hands. "I can see why Death chose you to battle them. It will be hard, but you can do it. You must stop the evil from rising. They want the power of the souls without returning anything to the universe. Nature is a balance that goes both ways. If they succeed, the balance will be lost forever." He sits the crystal ball back on the table and has no problem finding my face with his hand. He takes my chin between his warm fingers. "You need to be a quick study and learn."

"What do you mean?" It's hard to speak with his hand squishing my cheeks.

"Remember your mother's lessons. At the same time, it's imperative you grasp the witches' practices in the now to save the future. Find out what they want and how they plan to get it. Then, it will be up to you to stop the three of them. You're connected to the witches in ways you will soon come to understand. Use your gift. That's why Death chose you."

"What about Titus here? He must have a role in all this."

"He does." Soothsayer says no more.

I huff. "Why me?"

"There's always a reason."

I pull my chin from his grasp and push my chair back. "What reason? I'm one of many people Death could have called upon. I'm not that special."

"You are." He leans over the table, closing the distance between us. "Throughout history, many struggled to attain the same power the three vie for now. If they get all the souls, the witches' power will be unimaginable and terrible. If humans could see into my crystal ball, they'd do anything to stop them. You can, being one of the few special souls with a great inherited gift."

"Okey-dokey." I study the figure seated across from me. He's dressed in a traditional fortune teller costume with a glitzy gold robe and crystal ball that was clearly purchased on Amazon. The room screams tourist trap. How can he know all this information?

"I offer help to anyone who wants a glimpse of the bigger universe." He answers the question I didn't ask. "Is this your first time?"

"Yes. Shouldn't you know that?"

He's quiet and I study him, trying to learn anything that might help me make sense of what is happening because Titus, for once, is silent. I'm not sure if that or the mystic scares me more. The reading must not be finished because the freakish fortune teller presses his fingers into my arm and moves it until he reaches my hand again.

Chills hike up my spine. "How long have you been doing this?" The question distracts me from his touch along my palm.

He grabs my wrist, his iron grip burning my skin. "I've been at this location for many years. Time has little meaning anymore since my mind can travel beyond this plane of reality. I have been shown the deeper levels of existence, and they are not bound by the hours."

"Right." I pull away. "What did my palm tell you?"

"Death is near, but you are stubborn. A natural survivor and a witch." His yellow fingernails slide across the table. "Pray for eternal peace if you fail to find and destroy the witches' spell. Hopefully, Death will not let you suffer. I can guarantee it will not be painless if the three have their way with you."

"I'm not a witch." The edge in my voice highlights my discomfort. "You haven't told us anything that will help us stop them."

"You'll never leave the farm alive"—Mystic Man stands, turning his back on us—"unless you pick the right book and remember your mother's words. Your poppet will help."

"What? The doll my mother made for me?"

He nods.

"What book?" I ask.

He shrugs. "We're done now. It was a pleasure to meet you. I truly hope you survive."

Chapter Forty-Four

We walk back into the store, and I browse the strangeness. I mean, I've seen bizarre when I go into people's houses and worlds prior to their death, but I've never been in a wiccan shop. There's a vast array of daggers and knives alongside jars of herbs, weeds, bugs, concoctions, and other strange stuff. I cannot pronounce the names of at least half the items stocked around the store. Amulets line shelves that lead into more ledges stacked with candles and crystals. A dark crevice along the back wall is covered with animal fur, bones, and skulls.

I breathe deep to hold it together. "What did the mystic man mean when he said pick the right book? Is that anything like *Let the Right One In*?"

"Good movie." Titus nods in approval.

"Get serious. If I pick the wrong one, am I doomed to an eternity of misery or something worse?" I point to shelves full of scrolls and books. "Here they are."

"He said you need to pick the right book. I don't have any additional information. You were sitting next to me."

"You two had a brotherly bond going strong. Did your bromance bud tell you anything extra in your conversation prior to the reading?

Color, size, shape, or title of said book?"

"Sorry. The fate of the world is resting on your choice of reading material."

"I'm beginning not to like the supernatural speaker of beyond space and time."

"That's a little derogatory, don't you think?"

"He didn't tell me his name. What do you want me to call him?"

"Psychic, medium, or clairvoyant would work, but his name is Sam."

"I'll remember for next time, which I hope will never happen." I pull a book from the shelf, flip through the pages, and put it back. I do the same to a few more. "I'm not feeling anything. They're books. This is an impossible task."

"Give it time. The book might not even be here. There are plenty of other stores in Salem."

I groan. "One store is more than enough unless it's for a new wardrobe or food. We can always shop for food, but no more scary stores. It's got to be here." I peel one book off the shelf after another, but I get nothing. The worn leather covers range from stiff and cracked to soft and broken. Pages smell of musty paper. Some have writing, others are blank. Old time journals sit alongside almanacs and children's stories from the 1800s.

I grab a heavy, clunky book and my fingers tingle. It's got a slick, dark-brown leather cover with a burnt-orange amber stone in the center. Moons and stars decorate each corner. There's writing, but it shifts in front of my eyes so I'm not able to read the title.

"What is this?"

Titus appraises the cover. "It's a journal. Most witches would use it as a grimoire, a place to collect and write spells."

A kaleidoscope of strange letters and symbols weave and shift in front of my eyes. I reach to touch one of the symbols, but it darts away, appearing to hide behind the amber stone wedged into the smooth leather. "What does the cover say? I can't read it. The letters keep moving. Crazy, right? I wonder how the printer did that?"

"What are you talking about?" Titus reaches to take the book from me. His hand touches the stone on the cover and traces one of the illustrations of a moon etched into the corner. "There aren't any words on the cover."

"Right there." My finger touches the spot under the flaming orange stone. Heat radiates from it. "Ouch. That burns. Why is the universe out to get me today?"

Titus touches the amber and runs his fingers all over the cover. "Nothing. This must be the right one. It's calling you."

"It burned me. That doesn't sound like it wants to make friends."

"Didn't you notice that the gem matches the one in your amulet? They must be linked somehow."

I pull out my amulet and study the two stones. The colors are surprisingly similar. "My amulet isn't evil, but the book is. It has a bad temper to be sure. Maybe the book and Goose, my horse demon, are distant cousins? I wonder if I should introduce them. They've probably already met somehow in the great beyond."

"Are you talking about the book as if it were a person?"

"No," I hedge. "But it could house a demonic relative of my nuckelavee. I did say it was bad tempered."

"This is it." His expression is unreadable. "I'm sure about it."

Titus walks the book to the checkout and hands it to the woman behind the counter. Her hair is dyed black, her eyes cloaked in black eyeshadow and liner, and her costume (I mean clothing) consists of a black, long-sleeve shirt, leggings, and matching tutu.

"We'll take it." Titus smiles at the woman and her cheeks turn pink, a nice contrast to her somber outfit.

"You understand I have no idea how to use it." I lean against the counter and fiddle with the Harry Potter wands.

"You'll figure it out."

"That's asking a lot from me. We've only been working together for two days now. You don't know what I am capable or not capable of accomplishing."

"I remember well." Titus grimaces.

"Stop that. I was the bestest mentee ever."

The girl at the counter studies the book, opens the cover, and flips through the pages.

"These make great journals. I'm using mine to write my romance novel. It's almost done. Enemies to lovers."

"Where do you write stuff?" I ask.

She squints. "On the pages."

"But they're already full of writing."

The saleswoman narrows her eyes at me, takes the credit card from Titus, processes the sale, and hands me the grimoire. "Enjoy."

On the way out, he whispers, "She can't see the spells and probably thinks you're nuts."

"Someone has it out for me today. Do you think the witches put a curse on me?"

"Never say never."

We hoof back to the hotel but when I try to enter, Titus stops me. "Where do you think you're going?"

"Inside. I have to pee after the two lattes, and then a nap."

"A nap?" The worry lines on his brow deepen. "We found the book for a reason, and that purpose is to use it against the witches."

I shuffle from one foot to the other. "Can I at least use the bathroom before we decide the fate of the world?"

He nods and I see disappointment written in his eyes, but my bladder does not care. I hand him the grimoire before hightailing it to my room. On the way out, I notice the rag doll on the bed and put it in my pocket.

Back in Titus's Porsche, I settle in with the book as he drives to the witch farm. Studying the spells, I dare not read them aloud, scared to say any of the words, especially those not in English. I have no idea what will happen. What if I blow us both up?

Titus glances away from the road. "What'd you find?"

"Spells." Now that the book isn't trying to take me out, I've come across flying, cleansing, childbirth pain reduction, and rain spells on my first flip through, but none of those seem likely to help us in our current predicament. Personally, flying sounds awesome, but falling out of the sky, not so much. I'll tackle that one once I get my witchcraft wings. I cannot help but wonder how the doll my mother gave me so many years ago connects to all of this.

"Keep reading and take these." He hands me zip ties.

The way my day is going, I don't even question his gift when I stuff them in the pockets of my cargo shorts. "Even if I find the perfect spell, it's not like I know how to cast it. What if we need ingredients or something? What if I say it wrong and turn myself into a toad? This is dangerous."

"We're on the way back to the farm. Figure it out."

I stare out the window and watch Salem fade away in the rearview mirror. A police car with a witch emblem whizzes by a double decker bus proclaiming ghost tours. The busy streets full of people, cars, and buses slowly morph into the suburbs, then nature takes over.

I'm ecstatic for the air conditioning as the temperature gauge in Titus's car reads ninety-eight degrees. Even the leaves on the trees we fly by are heat oppressed and saggy. As we head along the road cruising at speeds well above the limit, the greens and browns blur into waves.

I return my gaze to the book, and the spells mimic the outside, all waves and ripples. It's hard to make out individual words, let alone full incantations.

"Maybe I'm getting car sick, but the book's not playing nice. Couldn't we get guns or machetes or some other type of lethal weapon instead of relying on my spell skills? A flame thrower might be nice. Isn't that how they kill zombies on all the shows?"

"The zombies aren't the problem. The witches and their plan to rule the world have become the problem."

"I don't know. The walking corpse was pretty scary. Plus, my necklace hasn't lit up since then. I can't help but notice your ring is quiet too."

"Death has them set only for souls that the witches target. I don't know how he did it so don't ask, but he's Death."

"Better not to question." I take in this new piece of information and vow to read my emails. "Why are we going back exactly?"

"Surprise attack. Catch them unaware. We're being stealthy. They'll never expect us so soon after yesterday."

I roll my eyes. "I can't believe I trusted your judgement for so many years when you were my mentor. We're being stupid. What about appealing to their kindness and reason?"

His silence is loud.

Chapter Forty-Five

The overripe, humid air is tempered by the slight breeze and the tall foliage. Old stone walls crisscross some of the deer paths we use as guides to return to the farm. Unfortunately, mud and slime creeps through my only pair of recently cleaned boots and gnats sing a discordant song in my ears. I'm beginning to dislike these witches and silently plot even more dark and dirty revenge if our present plan fails.

There's a problem with our current strategy, and that's that we don't have one. I've got a spell book and Titus has muscle, but everything else reeks of spur of the moment decision making. I've always wanted to be a spontaneous person, but admittedly, I'm seeing the downside.

We head in the opposite direction from where we met Lulu yesterday, which I take as a good sign. I follow Titus, who appears knowledgeable about the landscape. That, on the flip side, is a little concerning. Has he been here before? Is he in league with the witches rather than Death, but has me fooled? Did I even get a memo about working with Titus? Damn emails.

Reaching for my phone, I have a moment of self-doubt but then remember my initial call with Death. Titus must be legit, but so much has happened in the last forty-eight hours, I'm beginning to forget the details. Maybe I'm suffering from early-onset Alzheimer's. I mean who knows what living in purgatory does to a person?

I revisit the discussion. Actually, Death said they were sending assistance but never supplied a name. Titus showed up at the door, but he could be a ninja assassin who took out the real help that Death sent.

Alder and Ash bark in the distance, and I shake my distrust away. "Can they smell us all the way out here?" I'm concerned for my appendages. Overthinking my situation is hard work, but I put it aside for later, promising to tackle this quandary if I survive the dogs and whatever else awaits. If Titus helps me do that, I'll assume he's on my side. If he turns me over to the witches, spell book and all, I'll learn an important lesson about trust.

"I've scouted the area," Titus says. "They're doing their dog thing."

The stream we follow empties into a lake. There's a small rowboat at the end of a rickety wooden dock, and I wonder if it could take me back to Daxone. Facing death by witches has me missing her even more than normal.

"Get in. I'll row." Titus throws his backpack into the bottom of the boat.

"How do I even know where we're going?"

"This is the Ipswich River. Remember, we're trying for a surprise attack. They won't expect us from the rear of the house, and, hopefully, the dogs won't sense us until it's too late."

"Are you sure this boat is seaworthy?"

"We're on a lake, not the ocean. You'll be fine."

"What if I can't swim? Did you even ask? What if there's a monster in the water that upends us, or a magic storm rises, and we're pelted by wind and rain?"

"It's not like the tunnel scene in *Willy Wonka*."

"That's a doozy." I jump in the boat. "The entire movie terrified me, but my dearest reaper friend, Becca, thought it hilarious."

"Thanks for sharing." Titus unties the skiff and off we go.

"How come we never watched movies together?"

Titus eyeballs me. "We met before the television was invented."

"Right." The ride's not so bad. Woods line both sides but nothing is out of the ordinary. The dog howls remain distant, but birds trill from the foliage. In another life, this would be scenic and rather pleasant. I consider grabbing an oar and helping, but no thank you. On the other hand, the paddle could become a makeshift weapon. Other than the grimoire, I've got nothing. Though the tome is weighty, it seems like a stupid decision to face three evil witches empty handed. Maybe Titus is hiding a weapon in those tight jeans he's wearing, but I don't see any of the pockets bulging. Must be in the backpack then.

Once more, I second-guess Titus's allegiance and his intelligence level if he's failed to bring a weapon. Unfortunately, that reflects on me too. I did follow him into the situation without question. If I make it out of here, I vow to curb my trusting nature, and I also need to be able to defend myself. I want something big that everyone will see when I'm coming. I can't imitate Death with his scythe and a flamethrower seems a little messy, but maybe one of those big guns from *Die Hard*, the best Christmas movie ever.

"Do we have anything for protection?" I ask.

He glances at the backpack. "Don't worry, I have us covered in that department."

My thoughts continue to career like the boat as we travel for another fifteen minutes listening to howls that send chills along my spine. If I survive this little field trip, I plan to send the dogs back to hell where they must have come from, or at least, find them a decent trainer. We come to a bridge and Titus pushes the boat up on the bank, grabs the pack, and slings it over one shoulder. I follow him out and onto semi-dry land.

The white, rambling, all-too-normal colonial house perches on top of the hill. I peer around, but we're alone, surrounded by nature and numerous old stone walls. The small mountain we need to trudge up looms, and the woods fall away to gardens. The witches grow their own herbs and some other crops too. By no means an expert, I recognize the large, swaying corn stalks. Closer to the ground, I can make out a few blueberry bushes. The rest of the plants remain unrecognizable. There's one with dark-red flowers and thick thorns that I avoid like the plague, or like any other zombies that might be rambling the property.

In the back yard, a wraparound porch sweeps across the foundation of the house. Numerous windchimes fill the air and the pillow-covered Adirondack chairs appear comfortable.

I imagine myself with a cup of tea on one of the small side tables, sitting in the chair with a book, and almost wish it was my life with Daxone. Then I remember that the witches plan to end everything in this world and I'm back on task.

"Where are we going?" I ask.

"I want to check out the house and see if the witches have any weaknesses we can use against them. Let's pray we can get in around back without anyone noticing. I heard from a store manager they usually come to town for supplies today."

"You really did have a plan. I'm impressed. Sorry, I might have underestimated you a little on the boat ride and silently cursed you for dragging me along."

"Totally understandable. I should have explained earlier."

"But dogs, remember?"

"I got something for them." He pulls dog treats out of the backpack.

"You think those are going to tame Alder and Ash?"

"They're gourmet. Cost me as much as a filet mignon."

I shrug. No better options present themselves.

We skirt through the hilly woods, attempting to find the best vantage point and the least conspicuous way up the hill to the house. The scent of pine from the forest and mulch from the gardens cleave to my senses, but as we near the back door, something rotten permeates.

Titus takes shallow breaths, and I can tell he got a whiff.

Chapter Forty-Six

A corpse greets me. The dead man is propped against a rock, face tattooed with unrecognizable symbols, body broken, bent at odd angles. One part of me doesn't want the full story but I ask anyway. "What's going on? My pendant never lit." My tone is measured, but I hold back a shudder. "If he's recently dead, we should have been called here."

Titus's face is grim. "If I was a betting man, I'd say they're at least two souls into their plan. First a reanimated corpse and now this. The soul's no longer here."

"Remind me, how many souls do they need?"

He sighs. "It was in the memo from Death. Why don't you read them?"

"That's what I have you for. Fill me in, Big Man."

He's silent.

"Please, this one last time. If we live to see tomorrow, I'll do better. It's been a little harder than expected to get back into work mode after living in purgatory. I forgot how vivid and wonderful things can be. I'm missing Daxone and dealing with all the horror of death and destruction once again. Purgatory is bland and boring, but it's also calm and peaceful in its own way." I point to the man's body. "This is not peaceful. I'm readjusting, I promise."

"To get you to stop talking, I'll tell you. Five souls."

I nod. "At least, we still have some time if these are the first two souls the witches got their hands on." The unnaturally broken corpse creeps me out even though I've seen many before. The way the body's been defiled makes me sad. It weighs heavily on my thoughts. I rescue souls all the time, but something tells me that while this poor man's body is broken beyond repair, his soul is still being tortured.

A fantasy fills my head, cutting out Titus's voice. He's laying a plan, but I'm thinking about running away. Once I'm back in the Porsche, we'll drive off and head back to Salem. I'll tell Death this is over my paygrade, and he'll find a new recruit. Down under appears better and better, and I'm ready to go back. Plus, I'm missing Daxone huge. It's only been two days but could have been a lifetime.

Lost in my daydream, I don't even realize I'm climbing the hill to the back of the house until I huff for breath. Pulling my thoughts together, I turn and glance at the corpse we left behind to ensure it hasn't decided to reanimate. I'd hate to find it stumbling toward us. That would feature in my nightmares for weeks. To be honest, this entire trip might replay there for a while. All I want to do is end this little charade and get back to Titus's car alive.

A moss-covered stone wall and sprawling lawn lead to a ramshackle white colonial house, which appears to date back to the Salem Witch Trials. Somewhere in the late 1700s the family started renovations and restorations that didn't seem to end. It truly is a hodgepodge of styles and aesthetics. There are numerous windows, some stained glass, few of standard size, staring at us. I pray no one watches from them or that the cantankerous canines don't sense us behind this wall and beg to be put out to play.

My amulet glows, the stone turning from golden amber to ruby red. Titus's ring shines too, alerting us to the dire situation. I study his ring for the first time in centuries. It's gold, the band around his finger simple, but the stone is large and dark. There are symbols on the cage that binds the stone. It could almost pass for a college ring for those who aren't in this line of work; the symbols could represent a fraternity. Something nags me, and I want to ask more about it, but now is not the time.

"A soul is waiting for us. We have to save it from whatever the witches have planned." My nail hits my teeth, and I tug at the skin until pain sprouts. When I realize what I'm doing, I cradle my pendant instead. "Let's make sure this one is ours, not theirs."

"Watch yourself." He leads me over the crumbling stone wall.

"Duh." I expect the stones to be smooth, but they slice into my palm when my hand lands on one for balance. Climbing the last bit of hill to the house, I crouch. It's not that the witches would do anything as mundane as shoot me through one of the windows, but it's better to be safe than sorry.

The steps to the back porch appear squishy, with worn wood dangerous to stand on. "Some of these are rotted. If I fall, can I sue the witches? If I take everything they have, that'll put a dent in their plans."

He shakes his head. "Be careful when you climb."

I precede Titus up the steps, placing my hands against the wooden rail. The wraparound porch has a pair of rocking Adirondack chairs and empty mugs adorn the tables, but there's no sign of witches or dogs. The wind chimes are louder here, and the tinkling bells drown out the bird songs.

A black door marks the entrance to the house. I point toward it and Titus nods. It creaks open at my touch, and I pass through the mud room into the kitchen.

What the hell?

It's that smell again, reeking of dead flesh and decay. My eyes scan the room, searching for another corpse, but there's nothing in sight. I turn to Titus. He's got one hand over his nose and mouth and pushes me forward with the other one.

That's when I see something squirm. It's a man, bound in ropes. He's on the floor, propped against the corner of the wall. His face is covered with bruises and sores. When he opens his lips to beg for help, I see only a few remaining teeth. I'm flummoxed. The book of spells slips in my suddenly sweaty hands, but I hold tight. I run over and try to untie the ropes that bind him, but the knots are complex and every time one loosens even an iota, it stiffens back up as if they're enchanted.

A dark shape fills the doorway, then the person belonging to it moves into the light. It's not Lulu, but it's clearly one of her sisters. She's equally as impressive with dark-brown skin and braids that reach below her shoulders. Warm honey-brown eyes dominate her thin face. I'm downright frumpy compared to her toned body in skintight leggings and burgundy tank top.

She directs her words at me. "I remember you. We were never formally introduced. I'm Bebe and his name was—" She pauses and shrugs. "—doesn't matter. We needed him. His soul is ours tomorrow during the summer solstice." Her voice is a lullaby in my ears. "You met our first victim. I assume you passed the second on the way in." She points to two jars on the mantel. "I will say I'm impressed you managed to escape the undead."

"Thanks so much for setting him on us." I stand, grimoire in hand, and step back toward Titus, the door, and my possible escape.

"We had the important thing, his soul. My sisters and I figured you could deal with his body. It was a new experience for you, was it not?"

"Not one I appreciate so I won't say thanks."

She follows my steps. "Tomorrow night we'll have another and soon after we'll complete our collection." She peers at the desperate man slumped on the scratched hardwood floor. "Sorry, but I can't let you have him."

Bile rises in my throat, but before I step back again, Bebe grabs my hand.

I have no idea how she reached me so quickly. Flinching, I pull back as if shocked by an electrical outlet, but she's strong with a vice-like grip. "Lulu told me you were interesting, and she was right. Oh, the power inside you. We could use you on our side."

She lets go. The prisoner wails mournfully. My head pounds and my vision blurs into a cascade of spots. Panic overcomes me and it takes all my will to keep standing.

"What did you do?"

"Read you. Be calm. Here, sit." She leads me to the table, and I take a seat. Bebe does a good job ignoring Titus, and I wonder why he's not doing something. He's the muscle after all. Where's the testosterone when you need it? I'm waiting to see sword brandishing and hear the hail of bullets ripping through the room's furnishing and slugs embedding themselves in the walls. Instead, it's Bebe's musical voice in my ear.

"Let me explain what we're attempting to do. Once you hear about it, you'll appreciate our plan and maybe even want to join us. Tea?"

I shake my head.

"Lulu, Hen, and I are a lot older than we appear. We've seen the struggles of women from before the times of the Salem witch trials. While the trials were a tragedy, they weren't even the worst of times for women. We want to make a change, a lasting one. It took a long time for us to figure out how to do so, but we finally did. My sisters and I plan to raise Lilith. It's possible once we get five human souls. Men's souls."

"Her name is Hen? Like in chicken?"

Her eyes glint and narrow. "That's what you took away from this chat?"

"Lilith? Isn't she in the Bible?"

"Some people think Lilith's a demon, but we understand she's going to be a savior to women everywhere. Men have ruled too long and done so much wrong. It's time for change. Are you following? You're a little glazed."

"You need men's souls to raise a demon."

"She's not a demon to women. She will be the beginning of a new era, one in which women rule. My sisters and I will be Lilith's immortal emissaries, keeping men in check. If men don't obey, they'll die. Isn't that often how history treats women?"

"Let me summarize: You plan to raise a demon, enslave all men, and recreate the world?"

Chapter Forty-Seven

Purgatory appears better and better, but I worry for Titus. He wouldn't do well under the Lilith regime.

"Doesn't that make you as bad as the men who subjugated women?" I ask Bebe.

"Lilith will rule wisely and compassionately," she says.

"Did you have a bad breakup recently? Boy problems?" I scratch my head. "I went a long time without a significant other. Took me hundreds of years to find a good one. Got to say, you sound a little bitter."

"Ready for a change. Men have ruled the world and worked hard to destroy it. Now it's time for women to improve it."

"If you say so." I glance at the bound man. "And to make this happen you must sacrifice five men?"

"I'd sacrifice hundreds to raise Lilith."

"Women power is great, but I'd like to go home now and think this over."

"Where exactly is home, dear?"

No answer leaves my mouth, but what would I say? Hartford, New York, purgatory? Did I ever have a place to call mine? Daxone is more my home than a physical location, and boy, is she calling me back. I have a sinking suspicion the witches already know that and have more information on me than my name. "We should be leaving," I say, hoping beyond hope there is a chance she'll let me go.

"We're taking this guy with us," Titus says.

For a moment, I forgot he was there.

"The fun's begun." Bebe's smile is blinding.

Her perfect white teeth grow large in front of my eyes and suddenly I'm spellbound, unable to pull myself out of the trance. I have no idea what she's done to me, but I'm happy to let her guide me by an elbow.

Her eyes graze over me from head to toe. "Surprisingly strong. When you come into your power, you'll be glorious. If you survive that long."

Titus steps between Bebe, me and the door. "Prudence isn't going anywhere with you. Neither is this guy."

The man's bound wrists are bloody, and I realize he's been a prisoner for a while. His horrid condition and worse fate clear my head. Bebe must have put a spell on me because, for a moment, all her talk about Lilith almost made sense. Finding a way to free the poor prisoner is the priority. It's more than my job. I wholeheartedly disagree with Bebe and the rubbish she's spouting. Paul and Titus are two examples of all that's right with the world. The man on the floor is another good soul, and I have to find a way to save him.

Titus bends and tries to unbind the tangle of knots that ensnare Bebe's next sacrifice.

"The rope's enchanted. There's no way to loosen it," she says. "Since you still hesitate to join us, I must be going. There is so much to accomplish before the solstice. Sorry, I can't let you have him." She pulls the man up like he's the weight of a feather. "I hope you like the little surprise I've left for you here since you wouldn't be gracious enough to follow, and I don't have time for your shenanigans right now." Her gaze meets mine. "Such a shame."

In a classic puff of smoke, she and the man disappear in front of us.

"Where'd they go?" I ask.

Titus stands from his crouch, ready to sprint after the witch. "We need to follow and rescue him." He takes a step but then stops. The pantry door creaks open.

"Hello?" Inky blackness spills from the closet. A spindly leg slinks out of the door. Then another. And another.

I gasp and brace myself for whatever exits.

Long, segmented appendages emerge.

Air refuses to leave my lungs. I don't know which way to step, how to escape, or if fighting this monstrosity is even possible.

Titus doesn't seem to feel the same. He pulls the backpack's zipper apart and grabs a knife. "We have a problem. Can you tell what that is?"

"Duh, and no. Never seen anything like that before."

A black bloated cephalothorax emerges, and finally a head, with multiple beady black eyes that focus on me.

I squint. Its stare appears almost human, but the fangs dripping venom are most definitely not of this earth.

My pulse flutters, then races.

The spider creature skitters the rest of the way into the kitchen on eight spindly legs. Ridges along its spine make it appear to have slumped shoulders and a hunched back.

It crouches for a moment, makes a clicking noise with its fangs, and jumps on top of the table I'd been standing near moments ago.

My ears burn as taps, snaps, and metallic clicks create a cacophony of sound.

It's my turn to scurry away. I bump into Titus when putting distance between us and the spider creature. "Where's my knife?"

"Use the book."

"What book?"

"The spell book you're carrying."

The book of spells is heavy in my shaking hands. I'd forgotten the tome even though I clutch the leather as if it were a life preserver on a plane crashing into the ocean. "What do I do?"

"How do I know?" My mentor brandishes his knife. "It's your grimoire."

"It's not my book." I open it and a few pages flutter by. "Don't do me dirty. Help me find the right spell."

While I'm distracted by the myriad possibilities, the spider jumps and bowls us both over. I'm flat on my back staring into the dagger-filled mouth of the creature. I'm gasping, choking, trying to draw in air, and throw my arm in front of my face for protection. A drop of venom hits my shirt, scorches it, and a cry of pain explodes when the bubbly acid eats the flesh away.

Titus kicks out and the creature wobbles. He repeats the motion, foot thwacking against the spider's hard outer shell, irritating the gorilla-sized arachnoid. It turns, fangs chattering, and spits at him. His shirt starts to dissolve before the demon reaches out with two spindly legs to impale him.

Titus slashes with the long, serrated blade and the end of one leg falls to the ground. He swings again and another clatters when it hits the tiled floor.

One of the creature's remaining legs careens through the air and a red streak appears on Titus's chest. He jumps back to avoid being impaled as another leg shoots out.

The larger-than-life spider turns to me, chittering in anger. It scurries close, eyes mocking. I'm weaponless, and because I'm panicking, I do the most stupid thing I can think of. I scream and thrust the damn grimoire into its mouth with both hands to avoid being eaten. Fangs clamp around the leather cover. Green goo as thick as oil pours out of its mouth and it screams and drops the grimoire before skittering back toward the closet.

It takes a moment before I realize the book burned it. I love my grimoire.

Titus throws his knife at the spider, and it impales the creature in the back, but the arachnoid doesn't care and continues to scamper across the floor, a little slower with the loss of two legs. I watch as the knife dissolves into quicksilver.

"Read a spell. Any damn spell." Titus huffs. A quick glance reveals venom holes stinging his shirt. That must hurt.

I pull open the cover, and pages flip themselves to a spell called repulsionem. I read words without understanding what is coming out of my mouth.

The skittering spider takes a step back, then another. Its abdomen shrinks and expands, pulsing in the afternoon. There's a sudden blinding light and the demon detonates. Spider pieces explode across the room, drenching Titus and me with molten-colored slime, skeleton, and guts.

"This is disgusting and smells rancid." I peer at my unsalvageable outfit. I hate the fact that my body will not stop trembling.

"At least you're alive."

"What about the hostage?"

"We need to figure out where they took him and the ceremony's location."

"Ceremony?"

"To raise Lilith. Haven't you been listening? I have no idea where Bebe went in a puff of smoke, but I might have a way to find out. Then we can rescue him. Let's go back to the hotel, shower and change, and then I'll go talk to my contact."

"You have a contact?"

"I have many contacts."

"Can I come?"

"No."

"Will you at least pick up pizza?"

"Sure."

"I want pineapple."

"That's sacrilegious."

"Try it. It tastes amazing. By the way, I like the grimoire." The inane conversation has calmed my shakes but I'm still amped on adrenaline as I walk out the kitchen door. "It's a keeper."

"We'll need it again soon, but please learn how to use it. At least a little bit."

"I've got nothing better to do than stay up and study it tonight. After I call Daxone to tell her I survived the day."

Titus leads me across the yard and back toward the boat. "You do that. Don't tell her tomorrow might be worse. I don't want her coming after me for putting you in danger."

"No promises there."

Chapter Forty-Eight

Heaven is the word for the smell of garlic, tomato sauce, and yes, pineapple wafting through my hotel room. Pushing the poppet off the pillow, I slide into bed with my leftover pizza feast. I've cleaned up, called Daxone, and now it's time to open the grimoire. I expect to put in a few minutes of study while I eat, then vegetate in front of the television before falling asleep and forgetting my awful day.

The poppet is sitting next to me. Creepy. I pushed it to the end of the bed and now wonder how it found its way back. Enchanted doll? At this point in my life, nothing would surprise me. When I pick it up, the small figure stares back at me. Its clothes are tattered and dirty, the stitches that make the face are threadbare, but the memories it carries of my former life are deep and precious.

My hand tingles, and I almost drop it. I grab the cloth arms, one in each hand, and scrutinize the toy. Maybe I'm suffering a head injury after the spider incident because the figure begins to glow, a halo forming around it. Golden words form, a drastic contrast to the ratty dress.

They aren't in English, but I have no problem reading them. Memories flood back so hard I fall onto the pillow. My mother was a witch. She taught me about herbs and spells. Growing older, I learned to use my powers, found her grimoire, this book, in the tree, and there was a boy, Thaddeus, who I loved so innocently and long ago.

Knowledge of my past and emotions for the people I cherished and left behind overwhelm me. I tremble, head against the pillow, tears in my eyes. A missing part of me has been revealed and confusion sets in. I'm in pieces and at a loss. How could I have lived so long without this understanding?

The grimoire calls me. Sitting, fingers scrolling the pages on instinct, calm fills me. Here is my history. I'm not anywhere near all right, but the threads of past and present don't seem as discordant when my hands are on a remnant from my heritage. I read a few spells and my mind circles back to the past until the book takes over.

My body hums with a new power. I'm hooked on learning the incantations, the grimoire demanding more from me with each passing minute. There are pages of history and recollection. Charms, remedies, curses, and elixirs for everything from menstrual cramps to love potions to improving crop production crowd my noggin as pages turn.

Skipping crop production, I locate the juicy stuff. Every sheet holds multiple entries dating back to fourteenth century Europe. Gently turning through yellowing parchment decorated with the loveliest illustrations of flora and fauna, I land on entries from the time of my life in Hartford and wonder what happened to the book after my mother's death? How did it find me? The grimoire doesn't want to divulge that secret yet.

There is a spell to put your enemies to sleep.

> *Find the edge of the dark*
> *where dreams begin*
> *Look and step there*
> *Enter in unaware*
> *Take down your guarded wall*
> *Be wakeful no more*
> *Enter the gate of death's pall*
> *Somnus*

And another about bringing death. This is one spell I hope to never use.

> *Some die by disease or disaster*
> *Some die silently in bed alone*
> *Some die desperately wanting to forget*
> *Some die suddenly unable to postpone*
> *No matter how, no matter why, no matter what*
> *Death is final*
> *animam agere*

A spell to see beyond the veil catches my attention. I'm not sure what exactly that means or when I might need it, but the spell calls me.

> *Most see the beauty of the world but lack clarity*
> *A tree is a tree*
> *But today, for this hour*
> *I demand the sky for mine*
> *The stream for mine*
> *The stars for mine*
> *And for a moment, your eyes for mine*
> *And for a moment, the bird's eyes for mine*
> *Along with the wolves*
> *For a moment, I demand the sun's view of the earth*
> *Sapere Aude*

And finally, a spell to break something down.

> *Crumble, crush, grind, pound*
> *A fundamental process*
> *Organized decay*
> *From form to dust*
> *Turn to elemental rust*
> *Collapse*

Speed the way
To decay
Swiftly fall
From solid to ash
This I ask
Disrumpo

It's well after the witching hour when I push the book aside and fall into a dark and dreamless sleep.

A raucous banging and morning sun hitting the table through the large windows wakes me. I'm not surprised when the pounding is Titus.

"What?" I quickly dress, open the door to my hotel room, and yawn in his face.

"We have a fighting chance to take out some baddies today."

Stepping back, I let him enter. "I've been hard at work studying the grimoire and catching up on emails." Another yawn escapes. "See, my tired state proves I spent a late night learning me some new tricks."

"Your boundless knowledge is only going to get us so far."

"Coffee will do the rest."

He hands me a cup, appraising my sleep-deprived countenance, and frowning. "I hope so. You might need these too." He produces more zip ties.

"If only Daxone were here."

"You'd be too tired to do anything with her."

"Don't mock. I pulled an almost all-nighter," I say.

We settle in at the small table and debate our next move over bagels. I practically hum in delight as I lick cream cheese off the edge of the toasted goodness before biting into everything bagel decadence.

In the middle of swallowing too large of a bite, my amulet flares. At the same time, Titus's ring lights up like a firework. The heat and light rising from my necklace are unexpected. It's been unnaturally quiet since I got to Salem except with witchy interference. I'm used to the hustle of New York where people are dying constantly. Salem's been more of a slow burn.

"Time for work." My hip slams into the wood table as I stand. I dart to the bed, grab the grimoire and the poppet, and shove them into a backpack Titus gifted me. Coffee comes with me too. Prepped and ready, we head downstairs, Titus's weapons peek out of the duffel he'd lugged to my room.

We're in the lobby when I notice the three witches outside the large window. When they see us, they scatter. This puts a kink into the plans we came up with.

"They must have a soul with them for my amulet to light," I tell Titus.

"Let's go." We head outside. "You take the blonde one. I'll nab the other two."

"Why do you get two?"

"You want them?" He shrugs his massive shoulder.

I don't think the answer over too much. "Nope. Sorry I questioned your judgement."

We sprint in opposite directions.

Chapter Forty-Nine

Hen's a willowy and wily one.

The excitement of my amulet working drips away along with hopes of rescuing that close-to-dead guy from the farmhouse kitchen. Instead, it's a game of chase that leaves me in a bad mood. Witch hunting is not my jam.

Hen flies through the narrow streets doing an amazing job of avoiding the tourists, and I cannot help but wonder if she has an athletic trainer. Damn, the girl is fast. Death didn't provide any extra prowess to deal with witches, but I kept up with my fitness goals down under and upped my running time during purgatory. Fitness and loving on Daxone took center stage since there's not a lot else to do without Netflix and good coffee.

Air exits my mouth in a ragged stream that sounds more like a train horn with every passing second. How can Hen be in such good shape? What potions are part of her daily routine, and where are they sold or brewed?

Asphalt turns to cobblestone sidewalks. Bustling crowds of tourists create walls. "Out of the way." I push them none-too-gently and get an earful of less-than-kind words in return.

"Sorry." My boots maim the grass lawn of the First Baptist Church of Salem. Sheltering trees and a blue door beckon me inside, but my mission calls. Most definitely in need of spiritual guidance, I promise to return. I pick up speed. There's no stopping now.

Hen beelines to the wharf. I can't catch her even though I run like demons are on my heels. Thoughts of the witches' innocent victims who didn't deserve their unfortunate fates keep me motivated.

She jumps a wall without even a smudge on her daffodil-patterned skirt or an ounce of sweat seeping through her blouse. As I plod over the same wall, sweat trickles across my cheek. I take a leap of faith, speed up, and close in behind. Hen snags a flowing shirt sleeve on the end of a gate and momentarily slows. Victory is mine when I snare the back end of her luminous skirt and pull. She stumbles, and we both end up in a heap of limbs on the ground.

Calling what happens next a girl-fight would not be in any way disparaging or understatement. I slap and poke, and when that doesn't work, pull hair and pinch.

Hen takes fighting seriously. Her fingernails turn into insta-claws that rake my arm.

"Get a manicure." The softness of her skin surprises me after such sharp nails, but I shove away before she can scratch my eyes out. Pulling herself up, she tries to rise and run, but I grab onto the voluminous skirt again and yank it to her ankles. She trips over the excessive material and ends up on her knees, granny panties exposed. I jump on her like a little kid who wants a piggyback ride.

I'm not heavy but she's waif-like. For someone so slight, Hen's resilient, almost throwing me off with all the kicking and flailing. Somehow, she ends up on her back and I'm sitting on her stomach. Her elbow finds my boob.

"Enough," I grunt in pain.

Fingers curling, I send a right hook into her cheek. It stuns her for a moment so that I'm able to flip her on her stomach, wrangle her arms behind her back, and push her head against the ground. I hope without free hands or spell book close by, there is little additional damage she can do.

Whispers wash over me, and I see bodies in my peripheral vision. So used to being alone in purgatory, I hadn't expected a crowd. With my bleeding arm, her bruises, and our grass-stained clothes, our shenanigans demand attention and receive it.

"Nothing to see here," I say. "She's the other woman, and I'm letting her know he's married." How many more lies will I need to tell to make this stop?

Tourists snap pictures, and making the tabloids becomes an actual concern. I'm not sure how Death feels about publicity. Others exchange whispered words about my methods (they're rooting for me, but not my tactics). One man offers to help, but I shoo him away with a gruff, "No thank you. Not today."

"Prudence?"

The bright sun blinds me, and I'm unable to see or fathom how someone knows my name. Hen squirms under me, but I rock my knees on her back a few times and she settles.

When my eyes adjust to the glare, I see a halo of dark curls.

"Becca?"

"What are you doing here? You disappeared off the face of the earth. No one could contact you. I was so worried." Her petite frame appears tall from the ground, but her narrow eyes are sharp and angry.

Truer words have never been said. "It's a long story. Can I call you later?"

Her mouth is a straight line. For a moment, I think she plans to tell me to F-off and she has the right. I did abandon her, but Death didn't give me time to say goodbye or offer cell service in the down under.

"Fine." She wags a finger at me. "You better call and explain everything."

"Promise. What are you doing here in Salem?"

"Another long story."

"Same phone number?"

"Yes." She points the same finger at my nose. "You'd better call me today."

"Absolutely."

Finally, people turn away. We wait. I get Hen to sit up but keep a hand over her mouth until every last curious lurker leaves. I pull the zip ties out of my pocket and bind her wrists behind her. That's when the wail of sirens reaches my ears. Someone dialed 9-1-1.

We stand and I drag her to the side of a building under renovation where there are no prying eyes. Scrunched under the scaffolding, I catch my breath, my plans to interrogate Hen ruined with the cops' arrival. They wouldn't appreciate my methods, and I want to avoid the inside of a jail cell.

The door to the building opens to my touch. A small part of me recognizes that I should be cautious, but I want to avoid open spaces right now. I shove Hen into the cool gloom.

"You're causing me a lot of problems," I say. "Can't we all just get along? By that I mean can you not end the world?"

She mutters something unintelligible, smiles, and turns her head. Bebe and Lulu enter the room from the depths of the murk. Titus walks docilely behind like a well-trained dog. My eyes trail him for a moment. Watching makes my stomach clench and my jaw drop. My spit dries up and my throat tightens. Not that it matters; words elude me.

Chapter Fifty

Suddenly, I'm unable to move my body parts, any at all and not an inch. A snap of my fingers or blink of my eyes is impossible. Frustration builds as my body resists even the easiest command. Titus must be experiencing the same thing because he halts in his tracks when Lulu raises a hand.

Bebe meets my eyes, and her licorice breath envelops me. "Don't make me kill you because I don't want to. You can still have a seat next to us on the throne. But I will destroy you if you push me too far."

I try to speak but can't.

"Oh, right." Bebe snaps her finger. "Go ahead and say what you must."

"No, thank you." I'm rather polite after beating up Hen. The witches most definitely incite mixed emotions.

"Well, then. I guess that's all for now. Maybe you'll change your mind if you manage to survive our little surprise."

Lulu frees Hen of the zip ties, and the three disappear, blending into the shadows of the building in front of me like Macbeth's witches into the ground. Silence greets my ears, and it's as if the entire world has been forced into stillness. For a beat, nothing moves. Another beat and I hear a bird, then grunting.

My fingers twitch and my ears register the clang of falling metal like someone pulled a shelf full of pipes onto the floor. After a little more crashing around from whatever is in the next room, I can move my entire arm. By the time my legs twitch, the echo of feet shuffling and stomping along is loud in the gloom.

Turns out it's not a stray cat. Hell's bells, I'd take a rabid racoon. There's a slow moving, hulking figure coming our way. The smell of week-old garbage hits first. It's hard to see clearly in the old building; the only light comes from a small line of dingy windows, the glow of my pendant as dead as the zombie.

Horror holds me rigid this time.

The creature shambles close, and the face of the sad man in the kitchen comes into clarity. He smacks sore-ridden lips together, revealing his remaining teeth. The witches have turned him into another undead, and he's here to chomp some brains. Mine are the first in line with Titus as dessert.

"We can't let it get into the crowds." Titus's muffled voice rises from a few feet away.

I break out of my fear. My limbs work now for the most part, and I peer around for a weapon.

What had once been the tall man in a button-down blue shirt and jeans is now a hulky piece of rotting meat. Ripped fabric and popped shirt buttons reveal a bloated, distended stomach. The corpse's face shrinks in on itself, like a molded peach; a mottled mask adhering to the bones underneath.

"Anything in the book?" Titus yells in my direction.

The undead sways and shifts, staggering toward Titus's voice. It trips over the shelving it demolished on its entrance and falls to the floor. Splayed out like a child throwing a tantrum, a mewling whine escapes it, and the remnant of a nose puckers, sniffing the air, savoring its next meal: me and my sidekick.

It heaves itself into a crouch and crawls closer, one limb moving at a time.

"I didn't have time to find zombie-be-gone spells before our lovely meet-up with the witches. Sorry." I'm thankful the creature is the slow-moving shambling kind and not the quick running kind or my noggin would already be nothing.

"Now would be a good time to try, don't you think? Do what you did last time and let the book pick a spell for you. I'll be the distraction." Titus searches the debris in a can of garbage and jerks a discarded piece of pipe into a batting pose.

My backpack has stayed attached through the entire run and girl-fight. In all honesty, I had forgotten the book. I'm not used to being a reaper witch or witch reaper; not even sure of the correct order. Thanking God and Death that my limbs now function, I grab a strap but curse when my fingers slip off the nylon, twitching in dissent. I choke out a grunt, utter some rather rude language, try again, and the pack slips from my back. I unclasp the hooks and release the grimoire.

The corpse points its chin to the sky and takes in a long, raspy breath through decaying, black lips. Unblinking eyes stare. The undead stands and closes in. With a growl, it launches at Titus. "Hurry," he shouts.

"Help me oh wise book." The cover opens on command to my unsteady grasp. My knees feel ready to buckle. I want to slump to the concrete but will myself to stay standing.

The monster pushes aside a pail in its path and reaches out with a fist.

"Those witches did him wrong." He swings low and hard but misses. "Wow, he reeks. Anything?" Titus swats at the corpse. A squelch of decomposing bowel lets me know contact's been made.

"Pages aren't turning." The book remains still and heavy in my hands. "Want some help bashing it?"

The zombie growls as if in answer and stretches a mottled, sore-ridden arm to grab Titus.

"I'm a fine distraction. Keep looking." Titus kicks out and connects with the creature's stomach. There's a soft pop, then green and yellow goo as thick as honey leaks from its belly button. "This is disgusting. Hurry up, please."

"The smell is strong over here." Stepping back doesn't alleviate the odor, and I fan my hand in front of my nose. "Levitation, guiding, light show. None of these are helpful."

The corpse staggers back but then surges forward.

My heart stutters along with it and lurches into my throat.

"Come here, big boy." Titus steps away from me toward a pile of rubble in the middle of the room. The risen dead trails him, its once tight jeans sagging to reveal a whole lot of ass crack.

"That's something no girl ever wants to see." I return my gaze to the unhelpful grimoire. "Come on, almighty book. Do your stuff. Rescue us."

"Focus on finding a spell, please." Titus swings out. The pipe connects with the zombie's head. The loud crack bounces off the empty walls. The creature's entire body twitches, head lobbing to the left. After a second, it shrugs off the blow, mewls, and takes two steps closer to its prey.

Dead fingers grab Titus's shirt, pulling it from his chiseled stomach and tearing it away.

"That's all you got for me?" Titus steps forward, hoists the pipe, and whips it at the undead. This time the pipe slams into the side of the zombie's face, taking out an eye. Titus steps back but the corpse, unconcerned with the lack of vision, closes in for the kill.

"Did I mention you should try to speed things up?" Titus dodges the lumbering monster. "This thing doesn't want to die."

"Help me out here. Please," I beg the book. The pages flutter, turn, and still on a spell called liquesco.

Titus skids to me, slashing the pipe like a sword side to side, holding the creature at bay. "Why won't you die?"

"Maybe you have bad aim." The words wheeze out of me. "Or it could be that the corpse is already dead. I found a spell. The book wanted me to be polite and say 'please.'"

Titus frowns. "I have great aim, and not only when fighting zombies."

"Rude."

"I'm rude? The book demanded you be nice when the creature is trying to eat us alive. Do you want to discuss who is being rude?"

I wave him away. "Take care of the zombie. Let me concentrate. I have to read the spell from the beginning and get every word right."

Titus moves behind the writhing creature and the monster spins to face him with one soulless, staring eye. Huffing out a breath, my mentor jumps back. "It seems to like me but I'm not in a good place to date or die at the moment."

"Solid no more. No wood, rock, a barrier be. Liquid it should free." The last lines are in another language. I pray my pronunciation is correct with each haltingly pronounced word. "Spell read." My voice is barely audible above the corpse's whining. "Now what?"

"Haven't a clue." Titus continues to brandish the pipe. "Are you sure it worked?"

My shoulders chug up and down.

Muscles bulging under his shirt, lips set in a firm line, and a determined gleam brightening my once mentor's brown eyes, he continues to hold the creature at bay. The zombie swivels to me, probably deciding I'm the weak link if it can think at all. Or maybe I smell better than Titus. Who knows.

The grimoire becomes my weapon. "Stay back or I'll use this book. I mean I have used the book, but it's heavy and will hurt if I swing it. Why is the spell taking so long?"

"Are you sure you said it correctly?" His words make the undead pivot back around. "Time to put you out of your misery." Titus takes a step closer, pipe at the ready, and bashes its skull. The force of the pipe swing tips the living corpse's head to the side and its cheek lodges against its shoulder.

Using the pipe as a baton, Titus pounds into the monster's skull. This time, his hand sinks into the soft remains of brain matter. Suddenly, skin, bone, and brain start to liquefy. Like melting candle wax, the zombie's head decomposes in front of my eyes and slides down its torso and to its feet. The rest of the body follows. Seconds later, all that is left on the ground is a puddle, albeit a putrid one, but a puddle, none-theless.

"That was a fun morning." I step back from the pool of remains, sink to my knees, bone weary, and upchuck all that remains in my stomach.

"Thank God for that grimoire." Titus drops the pipe.

The loud clang reminds me of church bells and the fact that we're squatting in an abandoned building. "You were doing fine."

He reaches out a hand and pulls me into a standing position. I wobble and lean against the wall, still holding the grimoire close. "I was concerned for you, not for myself."

"Sure, you were." My body won't stop spasming.

"We better get moving. I'm surprised no one's here doing work on the building. No doubt the witches spelled the place."

"I need a shower." My grass and other stained self is less than fresh. "Let's go back to the hotel for now and regroup there." I put my thumbnail to my mouth but quickly pull it away. *Nope, not sure what's on it.*

Titus puts a hand in front of his nose only to withdraw it quickly. "Normally, that shower comment might tempt me to make a less than appropriate quip, but after what we witnessed, a naked human body might not be appealing for some time." Closing his eyes, he shudders and shakes his head. "I have some errands to run after I clean up. We can meet for dinner."

"Fine by me. Let's take the side streets and try and avoid the crowds."

Chapter Fifty-One

The hotel mimics a grand, modern colonial house. In the circular driveway sits Goose, my nuckelavee. He's seventeen hands and sleek, with a glossy mane. Sure, the exposed muscle brings back some recent distressing zombie memories, but I push them aside. Happy to see him, I move in for a hug, but it's hard to ignore the flaming red eyes and metallic breath.

To all the curious onlookers, a disheveled, smelly, dirty woman hugs a shiny black, energy-efficient hybrid car. They can't tell it is a disguised undead horse demon, and I must appear crazier than a vampire in the sunlight. I hope they let me back into the hotel.

"Did Becca bring you? Are you as happy to see me as I am to see you?"

Goose narrows his eyes before releasing hellfire, charring my hair. His snout is warm to the touch. He snorts, and I pull my fingers away. I suck my burnt thumb to relieve the pain.

"Where'd you come from? Becca with you?" No answer. "Fine. Be that way. I'll be back. Need some sustenance to deal with you. Don't cause any trouble and move yourself to the garage, please." I almost lean in for another hug, but my hair smells like burnt toast and my fingers throb. The smell of damnation must be my new normal because it's not so bad.

I proudly show Titus my ride. "Goose, my nuckelavee, is back."

"Nice." Titus squints.

"I'd offer him as an alternative to the Porsche, but he's kind of a one-woman demon."

"You don't say."

"He doesn't like me much, but we tolerate each other's eccentricities."

"Just like us?" The smile doesn't reach his eyes.

My grin falls a little short too. It's been a hectic, dismal day for the good guys. At least Titus is trying to see the humor in all this. I let out a dramatic sigh, turn, and walk into the hotel, shoulders slumped.

A few minutes later, zombie guts run into the drain. The smell of my singed hair is replaced by lavender conditioner. This shower is the best I've ever had, and it takes a full twenty-plus minutes for me to exit into the steamy bathroom. After cleanliness, Daxone is my priority. My fingers dance on the phone keys. She picks up on the first ring.

"Hello, my love. It's been a day," I say.

"Fill me in because one day here is like every other."

"Goose came back. It was nice to see my horse demon again."

"That's good someone gets to visit. I'm slowly dying without you."

"Don't say that. Think about what our future might be."

"All the time. Lazy Sundays together and traveling to new places full of color and light. We are never, ever painting anything in our house gray."

"Promise. Soon we'll be exploring the world. Or, at least when I get back, it'll be just us, enjoying the quiet moments and the baying of the hellhounds."

Daxone chuckles. "I'll take what I can. Down under is dreadful without you. These phone calls are my lifeline."

"Stop." I press my thumb against my lips. "You're strong and it's only been a few days."

"Time moves different here. It feels like forever since you've been with me. This being alone thing sucks."

This is my fault, and my heart aches. What can be done for the person I love? I dragged Daxone into this situation and there's no way out for her. Tomorrow, the witches are goners, so I can go home, which is anywhere my love is. "I'll be back soon. You're my missing piece and being away makes me miserable. I can't wait to return and fuck you senseless."

Daxone snorts. "Such a romantic. But seriously, I miss you. Love you more than words can say, Pru. You're my everything."

"Put it all out there." Guilt expands in my chest. "Ditto. And you're mine, Daxone. Forever and always. I'm all in, Dax. For eternity and beyond."

"Is that from a Disney movie?"

I ponder it for a minute. "The phrase is 'to infinity and beyond.'"

"Right, Buzz Lightyear." She laughs. "Thanks for not forgetting me."

I fill her in on my day and we finally hang up, with a promise to talk more later. I dial Becca next. I explain the whole crazy situation and invite her to dinner so she can clarify why Death moved her from New York City to Salem.

It's still light outside when Titus arrives a little before seven in the evening. He's clean and handsome in his tight white T-shirt and jeans. A gold chain circles his neck, highlighting his tan. He holds a pizza box and two swords.

"What's with the swords?"

"One's yours. It's for protection. We don't seem to be doing too well in that area without a weapon."

The sword is heavy in my hand. "Good idea but we need a real plan."

"That's what the pizza is for."

"Pizza and a planning session. Sounds like a fun night, but I've also been catching up on my missed TV shows. The hotel has great cable channels, and my favorites are streaming. Can we play something in the background?"

"You were deprived down under." He smirks. "Poor baby, but no. I need your full attention."

"Now I remember why I don't like you."

The knock on the door is loud. Titus frowns, but when I let Becca in his eyes light. Her masses of dark curls fall from a high ponytail. For someone chasing souls all day, she is surprisingly comfortable walking around in three-inch heels.

"Surprise." I wave her inside. "This is Becca. I worked with her in New York. I'd love to tell you more, but I have no idea why she's in Salem."

Becca smiles at Titus and turns away, flushed. "Death called me up one day and said that the Salem reapers were disappearing, and he needed help in the area. He thought because of my years of service and my stellar track record, I might be able to help them figure out what was going on."

"Reapers disappearing?" My mouth drops open. "I've never heard of that happening."

"Scary, right? I couldn't refuse the transfer to Salem. No one refuses Death."

"Have you found anything?" Titus asks.

"My pendant has lit up a couple times and then petered out. It's like souls disappear before I could even get on the road to collect them. Other than that, nothing too strange."

"We have." Cheese falls from my piece of pizza as I transfer it from box to paper plate. "I'll tell you more, but not before I get the New York gossip. How's Paul? Do you keep in touch?"

Becca plays with a long curl that escaped her ponytail. "He's good. We talk on the phone every so often, but you know the job. It keeps you busy."

My lips firm into a tight line at the thought of the next names that come to mind. "What about John and Randy? You know, the guy who stabbed me and his dumbass sidekick."

"That was a bad situation. I'm not sure what happened to them. You disappeared and a woman from Florida was moved up to New

York. Her name's Ann. She's older, loud as heck, but nice overall. John and Randy disappeared. They could have been relocated or something worse. Death doesn't keep us in the loop. Their replacements were fine, but I didn't have time to get to know them because I ended up here."

"As much as your reunion is sugar on sweets, we need to focus on the present." Titus grabs another slice before he sits. "The witches are more powerful than we thought and already have three souls. We can't let them get more."

The small table in my hotel room becomes our battle station and feeding ground as we chomp through some excellent cheese pizza. It might not be New York's finest but after living on purgatory food for a while anything tastes like heaven. I vow to bring some back for Daxone.

It's as if she knows I was thinking of her because my phone rings. I answer.

"Missed you. Had to call again. This place is hell without you around."

"It's less than an hour since our last call."

"Can't help myself. Again, time's different here. Feels like it's been days."

A few steps is all the distance I can put between me and the others. "It's not much better up here without you."

"Hey!" Becca says through a mouth full of cheese, sauce, and crust.

"Present company excluded." My gaze shifts to Titus. "Sometimes."

He smiles and takes a bite of pizza.

"That guy is there again?" Daxone asks.

"Yes, and surprise, Becca is here too. She's another reaper from my former life. We're going to stop the witches tomorrow now that reinforcements have arrived. The sooner we do that, the sooner I get back to you."

"I don't like this entire situation."

The room is small and it's hard to put space between Titus, Becca, and me. "You know what I like. I like when you do that thing in the morning."

Her voice turns sexy. "What thing?"

"You know when you wake me up by putting your lips—"

"Other people in the room." Titus's voice is loud. "Please spare us the details."

I sigh. "Got to go. Miss you so much and love you more. Be back soon."

"Miss you and love you too." Daxone hangs up.

"You two are disgusting in love." Becca bites into her slice. "Almost ruined my appetite."

"We're an adorable couple, aren't we?"

"Let's get back to the plan," Titus grumps.

Chapter Fifty-Two

The last slice of pizza is no longer warm. For a few seconds, the only sound in the room is chewing. I open the grimoire, doing my best not to get greasy prints on it. Easier said than done. This time, I carefully peruse the spells. Some of them shift under my gaze and I realize they're layered. When I focus on my needs, the spells in the book reflect that. There must be hundreds of spells per page.

"Do you want to hear my ideas on the grimoire?" The crust from a slice sits on my discarded plate, and I don't wait for an answer. "People used the grimoire as a journal over the years instead of a spell book if it fell into non-magical hands. Those wants, needs, and desires are somehow translated into spells. Each page holds numerous layers. It's pretty cool. Not everyone can read them or use the book, but everyone who owns it, adds to it."

"How can we use it to our advantage against the witches?" Titus asks.

"I'm not that skilled yet." Fidgeting under his scrutiny, I face Becca. "I've been a newbie witch for like forty-eight hours."

Conversation lulls and we don't really have a concrete plan. The day has left me distraught but afraid to sleep. I'm guaranteed a visit from the undead in my nightmares. "Want to get a drink at the bar?" I ask. "I'll be awake all night after that zombie this afternoon and that stupid alien spider. Alcohol will help dull the memories."

"Alien spider?" Becca asks. "Aren't you dealing with witches and stolen souls?"

"Did you not tell her about the kitchen incident?" Titus asks.

"Didn't want to scare her too much. It's a good story for after a few drinks." I point my finger at Titus. "Coming?"

"Why not? We still haven't created a plan and need to sooner rather than later." He stands and stretches, stomach muscles tightening.

Becca stares.

I'm more interested in the remnants of cheese and grease on my paper plate. "Maybe you two should get to know each other better."

Becca shushes me.

The deserted long hallway greets us with quiet and reminds me of *The Shining*. Thank the gods for company tonight. Elevator music hums on our ride to the lobby. The grimoire is nestled in my hands. I'll study it while playing matchmaker. Overstuffed red chairs nestle around small tables and contrast the exposed piping in the plush hotel bar. A quiet corner waits for us, and I study the crowd once settled.

An attractive woman nurses a fruity drink; hair falling glossy brown and wavy. She wears a silver dress that glitters seductively. Pale, unblemished skin peeks out from under her hair. The glistening bar, decked out in silver and gold, with mirrors lining the walls, lights her up from all angles. She's radiant, near perfect, and hard to ignore.

A dufus in an ugly, ill-cut two-hundred-dollar suit approaches, but she waves him away. The other men in the bar, including Titus, watch her like she's ready for the picking.

"Can I have your attention here." The grimoire thumps against the tabletop.

Titus pulls his eyes back.

The waiter arrives. "What can I get everyone?"

"What do you have on tap?" Titus asks.

After hearing the list, he picks Harpoon Summer Style.

"Good choice." The waiter faces me.

The wine list is extensive, but a light zinfandel calls my name.

"Piña colada, please," Becca adds.

Once the drinks arrive, we banter ideas around like a tennis ball in a game.

"Trying to rescue people isn't working for us." I take a sip and sigh with contentment.

"We're always one step behind." Titus swirls his beer in the glass.

"What if we focused on the souls they already have?" The wine tastes too good and a pleasant warmth fills me. I'll need another soon.

"That could delay them," Titus says. "They wouldn't be able to release Lilith."

"Can't they get more?" Becca asks.

"I don't think it's easy for them to collect souls. That poor man we found in the woods was covered with symbols. They must have to do rituals to pull the soul from a body. It's got to be a lot of work."

"It would buy us some time so you can get more proficient with the grimoire," Titus says.

"Tomorrow, we try to find the three souls they have and send them Death's way. Done and done." My chair swivels to Titus. "We have a plan even if it is a rather sketchy one. That's a relief. Now you two can get to know each other better. You should tell Becca your story."

He shrugs his massive shoulders. "Not much to tell."

"Liar, liar, pants on fire. Come on. She deserves to know and would love some intel into her partner in crime or partner in crime-undoing."

He peers at me through hooded lids and lets out a grunt before facing Becca. "I was a gladiator for a while."

"Like in the Roman Colosseum?" Becca asks.

"Exactly. I was a warrior, a prisoner of war, and trained in the way of the gladiators. It was brutal, but not every battle ended in death. We wounded rather than killed more often than not, but my win streak was long. At first this made me immensely popular, but then the crowds became bored."

Becca leans in. "How could anyone get bored of watching you?"

"Let him finish the story." I nudge her back.

"They set me up in an unfair fight. It was three against one. I held my own until a spear lanced my sword arm. I was down and one of the other warriors was basking in the audience's appreciation before delivering the final blow. Death picked that moment to show up."

"That must have startled the crowd." I said, thinking about my interactions with the black robed, skeletal figure.

Titus's massive shoulders shrug. "No one else saw Death, and it's unclear what happened after that. My body died on earth. Death took me on as a foot soldier. There's been plenty of evil before the witches and I'm sure more will come after. Death's only one of many entities, and they're pretty petty. Along with outside evils, there are many internal problems needing to be fixed."

"Like what?" It's my turn to lean in. This is all new information to me.

"Territory rights, ownership rights of trinkets and artifacts, and of course, the occasional play for world dominance. Listen, while this has been fun, my story isn't that interesting or that important."

"But we want to hear more," I whine.

"Let's focus on the problem at hand," he says, "and get back to taking out the three witches and recovering the souls."

We order a second round and finalize our plan. After a few minutes, Becca and Titus discover they share a lot of common interests. With gazes focused on each other, they begin to discuss their love of The Beatles.

My drink keeps me company until only a single sip remains. The mesmerizing woman at the bar locks eyes with me. Those eyes appear familiar. She smiles. Titus's gaze diverts from Becca. He's staring at her too.

A seductive finger calls him over. Becca frowns. My hand reaches for his arm to hold him back, but Titus is out of his chair faster than a shark on attack. The waiter returns and I'm left paying for the drinks.

The bar isn't too far away from our table, which lets us overhear the conversation.

"What a lovely night, isn't it?" Her voice is silk.

Titus flashes his pearly whites. "It's much better now."

My spidey sense is tingling. I stand, walk over, and put myself in between Titus and this woman. "I'm Prudence."

"Men like you have a lot of needs." She ignores me, focusing on Titus. "I can fulfill them tonight."

He raises an eyebrow. "And I'll give a woman like you what you deserve."

"Gross." I white knuckle the spell book so hard permanent fingerprint marks are a possibility. "Who are you? We were in the middle of an important discussion." I push my body between them. "You interrupted us." Hand on Titus's arm, I try to force him toward the exit, but he doesn't budge. "Time for bed, big boy."

He ignores me.

The woman locks eyes with mine. "I get what I want and tonight, it's your friend."

Chapter Fifty-Three

Something isn't right in Oz. Maybe it's the spell book clutched in my hands like a lifeline or my new witchy powers, but a veil lifts. The supposed stranger is all a glamour. Her face keeps popping in and out of focus but sitting before me is one of the sisters. Stranger danger. I'm sure of it.

"You're not taking him out of the bar," I say.

"Try and stop me." She turns to Titus. "You want to party? I'm ready." Her red nails trace a line up his leg.

He pants like a dog.

Pushing her hand away, I chide, "Stop that."

"A woman who knows how to get to the point is so sexy." Titus is infatuated. "I have a room upstairs."

I want to slap him.

"Something better is right around the corner." Musky perfume flowers the room. She leans in and whispers in Titus's ear. "My place is close and there's a surprise for you there." She giggles like a school-child. "I'll share my special secret, but only with a man like you. It'll make the rest of the night so much more, shall we say, stimulating. Up for a little enjoyment?" Her gaze falls below his belt.

"Becca, a little help here," I beg.

My reaper friend stands and we both stare at the glamoured witch. How powerful is she that she possessed Titus while he sat at our table? It's totally unfair. Frustration builds. I dig my fingers into his shoulder.

He comes out of his stupor for a second to peer at me. "What's up, little one?"

"Little one?" I'm insulted he used my nickname from when we first met but give him a pass because he's spelled. "Let's go upstairs now. It's time to call it a night." My best stink eye lands on the witch and I'm wishing for that sword Titus brought me, but it's in my room. Plus, bloodshed in a crowded bar might make the evening news. "We have a lot of work to do and you're wasting time." I tug on his T-shirt but he's a boulder and refuses to move.

Titus stares blankly. "Here's good."

"Nope, you're coming upstairs."

"I can make up my own mind, thank you very much." Titus turns toward the woman.

"Can you?" I clench my jaw. I'm not sure what to do next. It's not like he's easy to move.

He ignores my question. "Always up for a good party and fun times."

"That's not what we're here for or what she has planned for you. Trust me on this one." Another tug on his shirt, but he's an unmovable tree rooted to the floor with those size twelve feet.

"I thought you'd say yes." She makes it sound like he won the lottery. "You stand out in the crowd. A real man in a sea of guppies." The stranger swallows the last of her fruity drink, licks her lips, stands, and sets her glass on our table. Her eyes roam the length of Titus. "Yummy. We should go."

"Lead the way." He looks like a puppy waiting to go on a walk.

This entire conversation is so not like the Titus I know and care about that I shake my head, wondering what she's done to him and hoping Becca understands he's under some kind of enchantment. "He's not like this normally." This is too much, even for me. Titus's arm convulses when I squeeze it and plead, "You don't want to end up the next soul in a bottle, do you?"

He pushes me. I stumble. Becca gasps. The witch takes Titus's hand, and they walk toward the exit sign.

"I'm so happy I don't have to go home alone," the witch says. "Until you walked in the bar, my night was unfulfilling. You changed it all."

"Can't have you unfulfilled. I'm here to please," Titus says.

"This will be fun." Her smile twinkles under the dim lights of the bar.

I slam the grimoire on the table and flip through the pages. "Don't fail me now."

They move to the exit. My fingers slide along the parchment and grow hot at a spell named subsisto. The words flow from my lips, and the book's power courses through my body, warmer than the two glasses of wine in my stomach.

Titus stops at the bar exit, peers around, stares at his hand clasped in the stranger's, and his lips draw down into a frown.

"Ready?" she asks.

"I can't go." He turns back.

"Why?" Her fingers trace a line up his arm.

"Not sure, but I need to stay here."

I grab the book and Becca and walk to him. "Come on, big boy, time for bed."

The three of us head toward the hotel lobby, my arms linked with my mentor's.

The witch huffs but does no more. She probably doesn't want to draw attention in the crowded bar.

With some distance between us, I backpedal and face the witch and mouth, "How'd you know we'd be here?"

She shrugs and stage-whispers back, "I was sent to do recon in your hotel. I didn't even expect to see you both in the bar, but it was a little extra fun to play with that man. I'll show you the spell if you join us."

"Which one are you? Lulu?"

"How'd you guess?"

"The eyes. You're beautiful in real life but you're beyond stunning now. Your eyes didn't change though."

"Thank you, sweetie. That's so kind."

"If only you weren't evil and sent zombies and alien spiders to kill me."

"All that will stop when you come to the coven."

"If that's anything like come to Jesus, I'm good." I wave my hand with false bravado. "Shoo, now. Got to go and put this hunk of man to bed."

"He doesn't know what he's missing."

"I'm sure he'll be glad to be alive tomorrow."

"He'd have no regrets and would have died happy."

"Gross." It's the first I've heard from Becca.

"A little late to chime in now." My words trail out of the exit with us.

Back inside the hotel room, Titus sits docile on the bed, and I order a bottle of wine from room service with two sides of French fries. I'm sure Titus is hungry after his near-fatal run in, and my adrenaline from the encounter crashes.

"Seriously, recon? What is that?" I ask.

Titus splays a hand through his hair. "No idea. I couldn't stop myself from going with her."

We toss around theories about what spells Lulu could have been using until the food and drink come, then we settle in to enjoy the late-night fare.

"We need a better tomorrow plan." I wag a French fry in front of his face. "This is getting serious. They're on our home turf."

He grabs the fry and shoves it in his mouth. "It's beyond humiliating not being able to control yourself. That was twice today. Can you imagine what would have happened if she got me back to the farm?"

"Don't even want to envision it." Becca is perched on the end of a chair, sipping a glass of wine, but leaving the fries to us.

Images rush through my mind of Titus dead, soul taken, but I banish them all. "How do we find the stolen souls and get them to Death?"

"I was supposed to be their fourth victim," Titus says. "Let's hope Lulu doesn't have enough time to find a replacement. They have three, and our priority is reclaiming those and stopping them from getting the rest. Nothing in the book?"

"I'm still not sure how to use it properly. It only works when I'm in desperate need of something, but it came through tonight." The adrenaline has slowly faded, and drowsiness is overtaking. Still, I'm impressed with myself for saving Titus and that's keeping me awake.

He runs his fingers across his chin. "You're one of the lucky ones who can read it. It's all gobbledygook to me. Why don't you peruse it now?"

"The more I focus on what we need, the more the spells reflect that. I have no idea what I need right now. Maybe sleep." A yawn escapes me.

He ignores me, gaze focused on Becca, smiles, and asks, "What do people need late at night?"

"Yuck. Is this you flirting?" I say. "After everything that happened?"

Becca, on the other hand, smiles back.

"You guys get a room. I'm sleeping with the sword in my bed."

"After you find a spell to help us." Titus is at the door with Becca trailing after him.

"I'm on it. Now get out."

Chapter Fifty-Four

The clock radio blares. The lack of light from behind the curtains has me putting a pillow over my head to drown out reality. When Daxone's face comes to mind, I call her. After we chat, I drag myself out of bed, take a shower, and get dressed. Comfortable underwear is today's priority. These thongs are not appropriate attire for witch takedowns.

My outfit choice is the same as yesterday. I wonder how a clean set of clothes magically appears but then again, I've faced a lot of weirdness lately and can't extend too much energy on the problem, especially before coffee.

I'm out the door, on the sidewalk, and thinking about all the breakfast caffeine and deliciousness when I sense a presence next to me. And there Titus is.

"Creepy," I say.

"What?"

"You sneaking up on me like that. Weren't we supposed to meet at seven?"

"Thought you might want some breakfast company."

At the Artisan Bake Shop, apple fritters and an extra-large latte are my jam. Titus gets coffee and oatmeal.

"I need advice," he says.

"On what? You're the expert."

"Becca."

My eyebrows rise. This I can handle. Maybe. "What kind of guidance, oh skilled one?"

"Want to ask her out," he mutters. "Not sure if she'd say yes. Do you know if she's seeing anyone else?"

"Speak up. Morning ears. They aren't working yet and can't hear what you're mumbling about." It's so odd seeing Titus all insecure about anything. He's usually the in-charge, confident leader. This is a side of him he refused to reveal when I apprenticed with him and I'm digging the vibe as he repeats his query. "Becca hasn't said anything about a man, and she wasn't seeing anyone special when we were in New York. You, of all people, must understand how hard it is to have a normal life and work for Death."

Titus nods. "I have a good feeling about this."

"Go for it."

"I will."

It's as if the gods were peering at us because Becca makes a dramatic entrance at that exact moment. I nudge Titus with my knee under the table and flash a Cheshire Cat grin. Surprise replaces the smile when he flushes. He's doomed. Becca's charms have ensnared him.

After another latte, plans for rescuing souls, and some titillating personal conversation, a first step for Titus to be sure, Becca and I leave the bakery. We're on a mission to find some much-needed personal items and the ingredients for a potion, one found last night in the grimoire, that's supposed to help. The enchantment should enhance my natural abilities or at least amplify the cherry amber stone hanging around my neck.

Like a medium gets messages from the dead, and they are sometimes clearer than others, this potion is going to lead us straight to the souls. We all know who they'd be with and now we can hopefully locate where the evil trio stashed them on the farm.

Not long after, I'm perusing cute pajamas sets in Target at Hawthorne Square while Becca has moved a few rows away to ogle sports bras. Shopping is serious business, but a sudden coldness has the hair on my neck standing at attention. The sleepwear goes back on the rack. I turn and find myself staring at Bebe.

"Hello, my lovely," she croons like Elvis. "Follow me."

Without hesitation, I do exactly what she asks, and a few minutes later find myself sitting in a restaurant next to Bebe drinking another coffee concoction. The sugar and caffeine rush amazes for sure, but I'm confused about my arrival. One moment snuggly night-time wear is of utmost importance and the next moment it's time to dine with the devil.

Don't get me wrong, caffeination is always a high priority, but I never made it to the apothecary to find spell ingredients. Shopping distracted me with makeup aisles and sales racks. There are no department stores in purgatory and Target is kind of like putting a sugar addict in front of a plate of donuts.

"Let's be reasonable." Bebe places a hand over mine, and there is an instant tingle throughout my body. Good tingle or not is still undecided.

My hand itches when I pull away and gulp my drink. "Reasonable would be not killing innocent people."

"Believe me, they aren't innocent, but that's beside the point. You need to see the bigger picture. We're restoring the rightful balance to women as the protector of the earth. When Lilith rises, she'll make sure men know their place."

"Through death and destruction."

"If that's what it takes." She purses her red-painted lips. "Don't give me that judgmental look."

"You could pass for a teen when you pout like that." I tilt my head to the side. "Actually, how old are you?"

She waves her manicured hand in front of my face. "Two hundred and something."

"Did you say thirty something?" I shift in my seat.

"No, two hundred plus."

"How is that possible?"

"Let me explain, dearling. Maybe that will help. To understand my life as it is now, it's important to appreciate what happened at the Salem Witch Trials."

"You can't be that old."

"Of course not." She rolls her eyes. "They occurred in 1692, but I'm the descendent of one of the first accused."

I sip before speaking. "No shitting me. We have that in common, but I'm from Hartford."

She nods her head, affirming what she already knows. "After I explain what happened, you'll change your mind and want to join us. You're so formidable but can't even comprehend the extent of the power. I'll help you channel and use your innate abilities."

"Tempting. Fill me in on the history first." It must be the great coffee, more likely a spell, or possibly the combination of both, but nothing could get me out of the chair. Her story is as enthralling as she is. And even though Bebe's a killer who has attempted to end me and my buddy Titus a few times, I order another drink like nothing is amiss in my world.

"Let me share a little context about the witch trials first," Bebe says. "At the time of the accusations, there were already ample stresses of seventeenth-century life in the Massachusetts Bay Colony. There existed a strong belief in the devil and the supernatural."

"Please, no history lessons. I was never a good student."

"I'll be succinct. What few people know is that trouble existed between families in the town and rivalries between Salem proper and nearby areas. At the time, tensions were running high and then a smallpox outbreak happened, making everything grimmer. I'd be remiss if I didn't mention the Native American tribes weren't too happy with the settlers either."

"Got it. Big bad going on."

"I am a direct descendant of Tituba. She survived the Salem Witch

Trials after admitting to preparing a witch cake."

"A what?"

"A witch cake. Her charge, Betty, had been in pain for weeks and no one could figure out why. Tituba was from Barbados and was well versed in good magic. A witch cake took the urine from the girl—"

"Wait. Pee? She took the girl's pee."

"If you stop interrupting, I'll explain. Rye meal was mixed with the girl's urine, baked in ashes, and then fed to a dog."

"That's disgusting."

Bebe sighed. "The dog, bewitched by the cake, would reveal the name of the witch who spelled poor Betty."

"Did it work?"

The witch's shoulders slouched. "I don't know, but it set off a chain of events that ended up with the death and incarceration of more than one hundred and fifty men and women from towns in and around Salem. Tituba was lucky to survive after admitting to the practice of witchcraft. She also made sure her ancestors would be strong enough to seek revenge. That's what I'm doing now."

"Why'd they let her live? I mean didn't she pretty much get the ball rolling for the witch trials?"

"She denied using any witchcraft prior to making the witch cake." Bebe drummed her fingers for a moment on the table. "No one had evidence she'd performed other rituals or rites before the fateful incident that set the witch trials into motion."

"What does this have to do with me?"

"Can't you see how many women were mistreated, accused of the devil's work, and put to death because they were women and men didn't want them to have any power, not even the ability to help others of the same sex."

I wag a finger at her. "It's more complex than that. You said so yourself."

"It comes down to men and their refusal to see us as powerful. There continues to be a total, undeniable, overwhelming lack of respect for that female power. In June of 1692, a court in Salem heard the cases of witchcraft. Bridget Bishop was the first to be tried, found guilty, and hanged. Thirteen additional women quickly followed her to their death, many of them convicted based on spectral evidence."

"What was that?" Dregs of coffee remain in my cup.

"Evidence the girls dreamed or claimed to see in visions. At the time, there was also a belief in the power of the accused to use spirits to torture their victims."

"All of this happened in the past. Times have changed. Why are you trying to raise Lilith?"

"She'll ensure men never take advantage of us the way they did during the Salem Witch Trials. We'll be powerful warriors, ready to take our rightful place in history as queens."

"Aren't women doing this on their own?"

"Not enough." Her lips are a flat line. "In too many places, women lack control of their own destiny. Lilith will change that."

Chapter Fifty-Five

It's my turn to wave my hands in front of her face. "You do know you and your vision are a little scary."

She smiles, flashing perfect teeth. "That's a good thing."

"Is it? You might want to consider rebranding. Maybe it would improve your following."

"Right now, you're the only person I am worried about following me."

"What happens to Titus and Daxone?"

"It doesn't matter." She shrugs. "Some people will die, women will rule under Lilith, others survive to be servants and slaves, but I could put in a good word for them, and you could keep them as pets."

"They're not livestock. If we do this, we'll be as bad as men who see women as less."

"Women are meant to rule. We're kind and good and magnanimous."

"Right, you're so sweet already, and power never goes to the person in charge's head."

Bebe meets my eyes. "Are you in?"

"As much as I admire your bold plan"—sarcasm hisses out of me—

"I can't be part of it."

"Then you will join the men in their fate."

Released from her spell, I push away from the table and stand. Bebe does the same. One moment the slip of paper with our food bill rests on the table, the next moment it disappears under a pile of cash that materializes from nowhere.

Afraid her plans include smiting me down, I stride to the exit.

There is no smiting.

"So be it," Bebe says.

The door bangs shut behind us and Bebe is lost in the crowd. Our meeting annihilates any hope of putting this issue to rest without more death and destruction, possibly my own.

Even though Bebe's ancestors suffered in the Salem Witch Trials, in no way is her killing five men okay. Sure, she says they're not innocent, but they aren't axe murderers either. The coven tried to take Titus, and he's one of the good guys. He's my mentor, for Death's sake, and Lilith's ruling style doesn't sit well with me. Titus and I have always had our differences, but he's an upright guy. Not to mention what might happen to Daxone. She could be safe in purgatory, but maybe not. I saved her soul once, but I doubt Lilith does second chances.

Texting Becca, I explain what happened. To clear my head, it's back to shopping, needing time away from everyone to further consider my conversation with Bebe. I pick out a polka dot five-pack of hipster underwear, jeans, T-shirts, a cute pajama set, shampoo, conditioner, toiletries, and other staples.

All the while, my thoughts return to Lilith's resurrection. Women ruling the world. Would that be so bad? Um, yes, if Lillith is in charge. I'm all for woman power, but she sounds like a bitch. Socks are so perusable, but the impending end of the world refuses to leave my thoughts.

Personal shopping complete, Herbal Heaven Apothecary comes next. Bebe has me all mixed up, and my cranium hurts from too much thinking, but the search for the needed ingredients must go on. Deep breaths. My basket fills with packets of dandelion leaf, nettle, black sand, candles, and coffin nails. A small part of me understands why the witches want to shake things up but good and honorable men such as Titus exist. If they were strangers and my father was a role model, I'd be tempted to join the witches, but no thank you.

A little later, the numerous shopping bags thump and spill onto my hotel bed. My companions are not in their rooms but canoodling by the pool. I explain my disappearance thanks to Bebe and decide to grimoire the heck out of the ingredients from the apothecary before we head back to the farm on our search to find souls and send them to peace.

The new jeans and a V-neck retro T-shirt that proclaims love in rainbow colors are much comfier than the camo shorts and G-string. Candles lit, dandelion leaf, nettle, and black sand sorted, the potion making begins, but creating a potion in a hotel room is hard work.

There must be a difference between a potion and a spell, but as a newbie witch I have no clue. The grimoire is curiously silent on the distinction. When I become a master witch, all of this will make sense, but for now, I'm flying by the seat of my pants without a broomstick.

Dandelion leaf combines with nettle. It takes two attempts to get the Bunsen burning to heat things. I open the grimoire and chant:

> *By ancient right and earthly grace,*
> *I seek a power to embrace.*
> *Realms of old and mysteries deep,*
> *Grant me strength, my spirit replete.*
>
> *Embolden me with celestial fire,*
> *Supply me with all that is required.*
> *Mixing elements of death and life,*
> *Awaken a power deadly as a knife.*
>
> *Let heaven and hell blend,*
> *Make it be, from end to end.*

My beaker smokes and shakes, and I can barely hold on to the tongs that spare my fingers from the Bunsen burner flame. Snap, crackle, pop. The slate smoke recedes and a darker gray liquid drips from the beaker onto the floor. It's done, or at least I think it is. A headache settles in the front of my noggin, and I remember my mother's words about balance. No more potions today.

As I stare into the beaker, a smile flits across my lips. I did it. My first potion. They really did sell everything a person needs to create a decent enchantment at Herbal Heaven Apothecary. I'll leave an excellent Google review and a large tip for whoever cleans the room because there's a stain in the carpet that will never come out.

*

Twenty minutes later, the Porsche engine roars when Titus shifts gears entering the highway. My backpack holds all that's important to me: pocketknife, poppet, and grimoire. Not only are they keepsakes like my charm bracelet that clanks on my wrist, but they've come in handy; some could say my salvation throughout the ages. If only Daxone and Henri's canvas painting of me had been transported to my side, life would be complete.

The late afternoon sun obscures my vision of Becca in the back seat. She's sharing the space with the backpack that holds my spell concoction and grimoire. Titus wouldn't let us leave the swords behind and they're balanced beside her too. He better not get in an accident because those things are sharp and could cause some damage. And there is a good chance this might happen. His driving makes all the coffee consumed feel like barracudas trying to chew their way free of my stomach.

"They have three souls and need two more," I say.

Titus floors the gas. "That's why we're heading back there." There's not a lot of rush hour traffic, and he speeds away from anyone doing less than eighty miles an hour.

"Hate that place." My stomach aches, whether it's from the memory or the excessive acid isn't clear. "We need to find those last two men, before their execution, and I'd like to avoid another zombie encounter."

"Maybe they didn't have time to round up more specimens." Titus speeds up.

"Let's make sure, and if they have, we'll stop them." It's the first I've heard from Becca.

"Here's to hoping." Relief floods as we exit the highway, and Titus stays within the speed limit to avoid undue attention. We pass the driveway. The farmhouse sits pretty; charming exterior hiding the horrors within. A copse of maples shades the barn as the sun falls lower on the horizon. Titus parks far enough away to still see the house, but out of anyone's direct view.

Before heading inside, Titus sheaths his sword on his belt. Who knew they still made sword sheaths. I wonder if it is original or if he bought it on Amazon. I search for the bottle of newly concocted augmentation potion and extract it from the backpack.

Staring into the gray liquid swirling at the bottom of the bottle, I ask, "What else do you think this could enhance?"

Becca raises a single eyebrow. Titus remains mute.

I pull off my pendant and pour a few drops onto it. It steams, shimmers, then the liquid vanishes. We repeat the experiment on Titus's ring, and I offer the potion to Becca. She declines, having been drafted as lookout. If anyone arrives at the house after us, she'll call my cell phone.

"Let's hope your spell works." Titus walks toward the trees on the side of the house, attempting stealth.

Silence greets me, the hounds of hell quiet. "No dogs?"

"Maybe it's nap time."

"They could be on a walk."

"They're quiet. You should be too."

Chapter Fifty-Six

The kitchen is spotless, all signs of the alien spider scrubbed away. The grimoire is in my backpack along with the last dregs of the enchantment, a bottle of water, and a candy bar from the hotel mini fridge. You never know when the need for refreshments will strike.

Nothing jumps out as we tread deeper inside but my amulet and Titus's ring glow. I'm carrying a sword but it's two-hands-worth of weight, and I have no idea how to brandish it. From the way Titus holds his it's easy to see he has a lot of experience with the weapon.

"Are the swords magical?" I worry my bottom lip. My thoughts return to our recent monster interactions.

"Nope."

"Do you know how to wield it?"

"I wield all my weapons well."

"Are you flirting with me at a time like this?"

"Do you want me to? I'll do what it takes to get your mind off the possibility of our death."

"Keep at it then, but maybe you should focus your attempts to be charming on Becca."

He surveys the living room from the doorway before we step

inside. "Does my sword wielding tempt you a little bit?"

"I've known you too long as my mentor to be interested. Plus, there's Daxone. Let's have a conversation about you taking advantage of the power dynamic if we survive this."

"I was a Roman gladiator," he huffs. "Different norms and expectations."

"Get with the times. That's what the *Employee Handbook* is for."

"Have you actually read that thing?"

"I've tried."

The ground floor reveals nothing. My glowing pendant guides us up, and we climb the stairs. It's light, airy, and modern, but this could be a glamour spell. Three bedrooms highlight each of the witches' distinct personalities. Lulu's is sleek and modern. Hen's room basks in sun, airy and full of fresh-cut flowers, and Bebe's is decorated in hues of royal purple, sumptuous and lush.

"Let's go back to the barn." Titus exits the bathroom. "There's nothing here."

"Please, no." I twirl my sword. "There are zombies in there."

"Not anymore. We killed it."

"What if they made more?"

"I have a weapon now. I'll protect you."

"So, you admit I've been the one doing that up until now."

"You coming or do you want to stay here alone?"

Down the steps we go. I'm not letting Titus out of my sight.

I think we've been stealthy, but my stomach curdles when Bebe greets us at the barn. An overweight man stands behind her. He's wearing a ragged, stained suit that hangs off flabby, sagging skin.

"This is not good." My whispered words travel in the wind.

His nose is red, eyes bloodshot and swollen, his lips chapped and frowning.

"Come, come." Bebe waves us into the barn. "You know this place well."

The man steps aside as if under a spell. We enter. A chain clinks. An iron cuff anchors the captive's ankle.

"Can you believe he weighed nearly three hundred pounds when he got here? We fed him to see how much he'd consume, and thought he'd eat us out of house and home. People need to have control over things like that. If not, maybe they'll serve another purpose. Do you wonder what color his soul will be?"

"You'll never know," Titus growls.

She purrs back. "You obviously don't have the same problem with food. What are your vices?" She licks her lips. "I'd love to find out. Your soul would have been the prize in our collection. It's sad you resisted temptation when Lulu came for you."

"I prefer to keep both life and soul," Titus says.

"No fun, are we?" She points to the shackled prisoner. "He was our first collection, and we kept him as a pet for a while. Now it's his time to help us achieve greatness. He didn't originally appreciate his role in raising Lilith, but he's coming around after begging to be freed for the longest time. We keep explaining his name will be remembered in the new era, and it might have gotten through all that excessive flesh finally."

My heart bleeds for the prisoner. "You can't do this. To anyone. It's inhumane. Insane."

The man turns to me but doesn't say anything. He's more a bleached crustacean shell long left in the hot sun on the beach than a functioning person.

"It's time. Join me."

Without any other immediate options, we enter and scan the barn for the other two witches. It appears empty, but appearances can be deceptive.

"We can't let you do this." Titus raises his sword.

"Sure, you can," the witch answers.

"Let us take the man and go." Titus's sword slices through the humid air. "I don't want to have to kill you."

She laughs. "We have others. Remember we need five, and men are so easy to come by. Even if you take him, there'll be more. But no. You cannot have him, and I dare you to try and kill me with your little weapon. I hope it's not a reflection of other things."

"Why is everyone picking on me today?" Titus asks and rushes at Bebe.

She holds out her hand and whispers something I can't hear.

Chapter Fifty-Seven

Titus stops in his tracks.

"What did you do?" I'm too shocked to be scared, but that only lasts a moment.

"He's fine. I immobilized him. We need him alive if he's going to be a sacrifice." Bebe studies me. "I'm not usually so magnanimous, but I'll ask again. Join us? You might not know the extent of your power but it's impressive. Supernatural energy is rolling off you in waves right now."

"Death's my boss." A whine fills my ears, and I start to shake. It's anger. I'm done with all this bullshit.

"What have they done for you? Banished you to Hades and given you a life of servitude. With us, you'll be free, formidable, and understand all the gods' powers."

"Tempting, but if it involves killing innocent people, no thanks."

"He's not innocent. Believe me." She pushes the man deeper into the barn.

As I follow her, strategies for possible success run amok through my thoughts. Attacking her with the sword didn't work too well for Titus, and I'm not nearly as skilled. She might notice the grimoire if I reach for it in my backpack. Playing along a little longer and hoping for brilliant inspiration sounds like the best plan.

"I need to go check on some preparations," she says.

"I'll come with." Staying close to Bebe is my only option now.

"Stay with your friend and ponder your fate, which is join us or die. We can't take his soul until midnight. It's not even dark. You have some time." She moves close. Her rich perfume reminds me of emeralds and palaces. Caught up in identifying the fragrance, I don't notice her hand in my pocket or the fact that she's stolen my cell phone until it's too late.

Titus doesn't even raise a finger when she grabs his phone and heads outside. The barn door slams. Murky light seeps in through the stall windows. One step toward the door and my canine buddies, Ash and Alder, saunter in from where they have been napping in the hay. The two dogs sit at my side, issuing low growls as if to remind me of their presence.

Sending them my best stink eye, I hunker down on a bale of hay, not wanting to vex the duo of demons. All the recent life changes are flabbergasting. From collecting souls, to finding true love, to residing in purgatory. Now it appears I'm slated for true death. How to defeat the witches remains a mystery, which reminds me that Titus is still immobile.

I stand. Moving slowly, creeping close to my mentor, I try not to evoke the ire of the puppies.

"Titus." I shake him. "Can you move?"

A head bob.

"Try again." Minutes tick away. My patience crumbles with each new growl from behind me.

I refuse to engage with the demon dogs.

His fingers twitch. A few seconds later, he opens his mouth and hums a catchy toon. "Duhm duhm duhm da da."

"What is that song?"

"Duhm duhm duhm."

I sing along. "Downtown by myself, duhm, duhm, da da, sit and think about myself. And there Death was, like evil incarnate, yeah there death was, like totally irate." Pause. "I smell death and coffee, here, mmm." Drum roll.

Titus groans loudly.

"That's good. The spell must be wearing off. Keep going."

It takes about thirty minutes, but he's finally mobile. "Crazy, right?" Titus leans against the barn wall.

"Agreed," I say. "Catchy tune. Haven't thought of the song in ages."

"You got the lyrics all wrong."

"Nope. I got them right."

The dogs watch intently as if they understand the conversation.

"I have no idea what's going on." Titus runs a hand through his hair. "I've always been able to defeat the baddies and never had to struggle this much for the win. That's why Death sends me."

"Maybe that's why we were teamed up. It can't be normal to pull someone from purgatory after being banished."

Titus shrugs. "There's no way to explain what's going on with Death, but I'm glad you're here."

"Speaking of that, how do we escape with him?" My head tilts toward the prisoner who sits placidly against the wall, eyes glazed, drool leaking from the corner of his mouth. "Why couldn't she leave us our phones? We could've played Wordle or Candy Crush to pass the time."

"We would've called for backup, that's why. There's got to be another way. You'd think I'd have a solution considering I've been Death's foot soldier for a long time. Usually, it's just hack up a demon or three and get out. After doing this for more lifetimes than I can remember, the witches have me stumped."

"Right there with you, but you were great with the alien spider."

"Killing things was kind of my specialty before I shifted to soul collector. Did you know my nickname from my war days was 'The Impaler'?"

"Not sure that's a compliment."

"Of course it is."

"Let's debate it later," I say. "Got all your strength back?"

He flexes. "Think so. Have to ask if we're being played right now. The witches have been one step ahead of us this entire time."

"You think we're pawns in their game?"

"Wouldn't put it past them. We didn't surprise them today."

I slouch to the ground. "If that's true, it doesn't bode well for us. Maybe I should consider joining them."

Titus glares.

"Kidding."

"You're as dead as I am." The imprisoned man's slurred words have me jumping off the ground. "I was optimistic about escaping, at least for a little while. We're all going to die. Hope it's quick and painless."

Titus faces the bound man. "There's no way this is my end."

The dogs growl.

The Impaler growls back at them, and they stop, confused. He meets the prisoner's gaze. "What's your name?"

"Bob."

"It's time to go." Titus swings in a circle, surveying our situation. "An entire life spent fighting Death's wars. I'm not letting three witches and two dogs stop me. It's almost as bad as that three-headed troll in Norway."

"Three-headed troll?" I tilt my head to the side, trying to conjure an image. "Should I ask?"

"A story for later."

"We have time. They said they're leaving us here until dark."

Titus sighs and spills. "Long story short, I was in Norway and ran into a mountain troll, you know the kind depicted in *Lord of the Rings*. They're large, dumb, and brutish, and this one had three heads. I wasn't even there for the troll, I needed to pass through their territory. Anyway, I impaled it on my sword. Story done. Can we get out of here now?"

"Who knew that trolls existed, but the retelling needs some work. Draw out the action and add a little romance."

"Focus on our escape, please." Titus turns away.

"Talking helps me think," I babble and open my backpack, which, surprisingly, the witches left along with Titus's sword. They must think so little of us. Perusing the grimoire, I search for a spell to call Becca and have her come to our rescue. When that doesn't materialize, I keep looking.

In the background, Titus paces as he recounts a battle with a demigod who wanted control of Hades. Once you get him going, he doesn't stop tallying those long-ago victories.

My mentor moves close and peers over my shoulder. "Was that retelling better?"

"Sure."

"This is unbelievable." He resumes pacing, each of his footfalls heavier than the last. "I killed demi-gods only to end my time stuck in a barn with two mutts and an incompetent witch. What's my life come to?"

"Hey, new witch here, not an incompetent one." Page after page flips by.

The soon-to-be sacrifice in the corner finds his voice again. "Don't you see? You're what the witches detest. Forced into servitude for someone else, doing their dirty work. You're complicit, following some greedy, heartless super entity. Death doesn't care about those he employs, the souls collected, or even the state of the human world. It's time to consider how Death's actions impact others. You're brainwashed, empty shells, and the witches see right through you. They'll bring about needed change."

"How do you know any of this?" I ask.

"The witches want me to know how important and vital my sacrifice is to the world. They filled me in about everything, even that you'd try to rescue me. I resisted them for a long time but see the truth now. That's why I'm a willing sacrifice tonight."

"You don't want to be rescued?" I squint, trying to see inside this man's head. "Then why are you chained up?"

"To prevent you from interfering with the witches' plans."

"Bullshit." Titus coughs.

"Excuse you," I reply.

"We're the ones fighting the war for the good and righteous." Titus retrieves his blade. "It's the witches who have twisted the truth. Lilith is a demon, not a savior. She'll destroy the world. You're coming with us." He slams the blade into the chains. It takes a few swings but one of the links comes loose.

"Nifty trick," I say.

"Special sword."

"Is mine special?"

"Not like this." He grabs the man's elbow. "We're out of here."

The dogs growl at us.

"Maybe we should stay." Alder and Ash nip at my ankles. "Bad dog," I say to Ash. "Sit."

Ash lunges at me and sinks its teeth into the leg of my jeans.

A squeak leaves my mouth, and I wait for the pain, but nothing. The animal shakes its head dramatically.

"Hey. These are new." I smash the dog on the top of the head with the grimoire. It growls, thrashes its massive jaw, and yanks at the bottom of my pant leg, pulling me off balance.

I stagger but manage to stay upright.

Making a stabbing motion, Titus says, "I can kill them."

My gaze shifts to the dogs. "It's not their fault they were trained to follow the witches' commands."

"We can't stand around here all day. I'm stopping this and getting out of here. Too long, I've played nice. The Impaler's back and ready for action."

"Hold on there, Big Man. Maybe I can spell the dogs. I've been practicing."

"Try it. The other option is to kill them."

"That's not an option." I make sure the sword Titus gave me is still at my side and he's not brandishing his. Nope. Both accounted for and not thrust into any living creatures.

"It is. You have one spell. One chance and that's it."

Chapter Fifty-Eight

The spellbook falls open and the poppet rests like a bookmark on top. Power morphs under my fingertips, surging and retreating. "That's new."

"What?" Titus's confusion etches lines across his brow.

"Fill you in later." The next words come out in a whisper. "Sit and stay spell, please." Pages turn. Unexpected to say the least. Maybe there must have been a dog-trainer who journaled in the book at one time because there is said spell. It's a crazy coincidence to be sure, but I recite the words.

The dogs sit, and this seems way too easy. Their smooth fur bunches at the hackles making them both appear as if they have spiked armor rising from their backs. They growl, glued to their respective spots, white fangs dripping saliva. We back out of the barn.

Titus sheaths his sword, picks up the soon-to-be sacrifice, and carries the brainwashed man. The former prisoner pounds on his back. Angry howls follow the beat of my footsteps toward the driveway.

"Woods," Titus yells.

We sprint in the direction of the river.

"Why?" The word is a puff of air.

"Don't know if Becca's still around with the car since we couldn't call her. Safer in the trees under cover." Titus's voice is strained. The prisoner does a slow slide down his back. I forage through the undergrowth, staying on deer paths leading me away from the house, refusing to stop. My sense of direction is less than stellar, but I attempt to lead us back to Titus's car. He follows on my heels.

Evening cloud cover has set in, distorting the moon, and I can't believe we languished in the barn for so many hours. Darkness might shield me from the three bad witches, but it sure won't help my trek. It must have been another spell of some kind.

Logs and rocks jump out of the gloom. The dense tree canopy throws creepy shadows to every side, bears down on us, and whips me with branches, tearing into my hands and face. My knees buckle, but thoughts of being caught spur me forward. Short, sharp bursts of air contort my cheeks as I dodge obstacles.

The path turns rocky and steep, and that's when I hear the howl. It's close. Ash and Alder sat and stayed, but obviously not for long enough. Spells need to come with specific durations.

I pick up the pace, my heart thudding as another loud whine from the canines brings the reality of the situation home. Lost in the wood, our situation is bleaker than the sky. This isn't a pleasant diversion from the underworld, not at all.

A jagged rock appears in front of me. I step back, bump Titus, and he pushes me forward. "Fuck me. Fuck the witches." Pebbles dig into my palms and knees.

Titus grabs my elbow and pulls me from the dirt. "Language, young lady." He clucks his tongue.

The whine of the beasts keeps me silent and trotting through the undergrowth, away from wild and rabid dogs.

"They're coming." Those are the first words I've heard from the man slung over Titus's shoulder since we left the barn. At least the escape hasn't killed him. My breath heaves and I pause to consider my surroundings. We've been running blindly, and I'm confused, second guessing if I'm heading in the right direction. It's hard to see anything now that night has fallen.

I puff out a pent-up breath. The farmhouse lights are a distant memory. "We've got to be close to freedom."

"Once we cross water those hellhounds shouldn't be able to track us anymore."

Deep growls close in from behind.

I falter, catch myself, and feel the heat crawl up my neck, not sure if it's caused by embarrassment or fear.

Marathon training in purgatory pays off. My sprint is strong and I'm able to sing a spell between ragged breaths, having no idea where it came from. The grimoire is safe in my backpack, but words pour forth. Nothing happens after I scramble over a log and race forward. Well, that was a dud.

"Keep going," Titus huffs.

Panic sets in but then my senses expand. The snap of the wind against my cheek lessens the howls of the dogs closing in. My heart explodes in my chest with each loud beat that echoes my footfalls. A flashlight sweeps to the left. The witches are after us and they're close. Too close. I promise myself we'll reach the water and run on, limbs aching, teeth gritted. The rush of the river grows loud. The spell gives me the extra strength to drag the damn heavy sword along with me.

Not even thinking about it, I splash into the murky wetness when it rushes to greet me. It's colder and deeper than expected. Shivers rise from my toes all the way up my back. Snarling dogs crowd in on my side. I hear a scream, turn, and see Ash bite deeper into the prisoner's elbow and drag him to the ground. Alder leaps at Titus, teeth centimeters from his throat, powerful jaws dripping saliva on his face. The guttural growl is low but loud in the night. The iron tang of blood and the smell of sweat rush at me when the wind shifts.

A whistle explodes in the darkness, and the dogs sit, one on top of Titus and the other on the prisoner. Titus tries to wrestle the dog away and Alder sinks his fangs into his hand. Blood spurts from the wound.

Another step into the river has Ash growling and crouching, ready to take me out. I hold up my shaking hands in defeat. Panting dogs, my ragged breath, and the captive's whisper swirl in the darkness.

"Don't move." Lulu's voice is silk as she stands over Titus. "The precious puppies are trained to remove any part of your body I want them to. They can bite through a hand, a foot, or your manhood. You lost a small chunk of your palm. It could get a whole lot worse. You don't want that, do you?"

Titus shakes his head.

She turns her flashlight beam to me. "We need to talk. This has gone too far and the both of you are causing too many problems. To-morrow, meet me at the pastry shop you so like."

"How'd you know my favorite place?"

"I know a lot more than you think. Tomorrow. Nine in the morn-ing and don't be late."

She heads over to the man on the ground, ignoring Titus. "That's a good boy. Get up and let's get you back to the barn."

"You're letting us go?" Titus asks.

Lulu laughs and prods the captive up with her walking stick. "Come, come," she says. "The night is still young, and we have lots to do." She addresses me. "Right now, you're like a fly in my ear. The buzz is annoying, but you can't do any real harm. Go back to the hotel, stay out of our business tonight, and I'll let you live to see tomorrow. He's a different story."

The dog steps away, and Titus sits up.

Lulu is unconcerned and points to her prisoner who has wobbled a few steps in the direction of the house. "Tonight is this man's special time. He'll be part of the resurrection, and his soul and the souls of the other men will usher in a new era." She scratches the dogs behind the ears, letting them know they've done well.

I can't help but ask. "You have all five souls already?"

"We will tomorrow, and the last one has to be of a very high cali-ber. Perhaps your friend here, but my sisters and I have some other thoughts."

"I'm bleeding real bad," the man says to Hen who pushes him along the path.

"You made the choice to run." She shrugs off the captive's dog bite as if it is no more than a kid's scraped knee. "You're going to die tonight anyway."

Lulu ushers the prisoner back toward the barn and there is nothing for us to do. I want to save him, but the dogs crouch and growl, low to the ground and ready to strike. Their eyes are trained on Titus, ready to take out a large chunk of his leg. My best bet for survival is to call it a night, find Becca and safety, and regroup.

Hen and Lulu wander off with their prisoner as if on a moonlit stroll. Before they are out of reach, Lulu turns back to me. "I'd run now. A special surprise waits for Titus, and I'd like to see you alive in the morning. If you stay close, plan to die alongside your friend."

The dogs don't follow the witches. Ash stares me down. After a moment they both back up but don't leave.

That's when the change begins.

Chapter Fifty-Nine

"Can I kill them now?" Titus stands.

Black eyes blink and glow red. Alder and Ash's bodies twist and torque. Their ears elongate along with their teeth and claws, more akin to dragons than dogs. Black fur stands on end, forming spikes.

"Hellhounds! Really? Wherever they show their fangs, fear and death follow," I say.

"Guessed that already." Titus brandishes his sword.

Their bodies are the size of bears. Alder huffs out a growl, scorching the ground. Fur blends into the darkness. Fire leaches from their lips and lights the air. The dogs snort a sulfurous odor that reminds me of Goose, which makes sense since they are from the same place.

"This is not going to be fun," I say.

"You should run."

"Leave you here? Never." I shake my head. "But how'd the witches do this? Only Death has the power to control the creatures of the underworld. He'd never loan out his hellhounds to the witches the way he's loaned me Goose."

The monsters rage.

I flail about.

"Now is not the time to wonder. You're going to need your sword for this," Titus says.

The blade in my hand swings from side to side, and I pretend to know what to do with it, but my heart jumps higher than I can lift the sword. Ash jerks its head in my direction, and a sharp hellhound howl roots me to the ground.

Red eyes glint. Ash arches its back and tenses to jump. There's a beat of time and then the hellhound flies. It lands at my side. Its huge paw glances off my arm, sending me sprawling. I crab-walk farther away, grunting, panting, fear pounding in my head.

The sword shakes in my trembling fingers as I grab it off the ground. My arm should be in ribbons but it's not, probably so the witches can have their way with me later. Titus, on the other hand, isn't faring as well. The other hellhound rears on its hind legs, spreading its paws like a bear grasping at a hornet's nest. Titus is entrapped in Alder's deadly grasp.

I'm too preoccupied swinging my sword and evading Ash to see how Titus escapes but he ducks, rolls, and is up again. He's fast, but the hellhound is faster. A flick of a paw and bloody gashes appear on his arm. I'm too far away to prevent the hound going for the side of his jugular, but his sword is up in an instant, separating teeth from skin.

Refusing to cooperate and submit, Ash launches at me. I keep my sword in front of me. The beast deviates midflight and lands on my other side. Angry teeth snap, narrowly missing my cheek. I put my hand up and the hellhound tears into it, creating deep punctures in my palm. Pain rips through me. A scream erupts from my throat as the monster drags me away from Titus. Blood drips down my arm as flesh rips away. I pull back. White-hot needles of agony erupt from my hand. A horrible snarling erupts from the hellhound's mouth when the monster releases me.

Alder bleeds on the ground.

Ash abandons me and launches at Titus. The hellhound swipes at his sword, which is held high and aimed for a killing blow. With the flick of a paw, Ash sends the weapon flying and into the dense undergrowth. With another swipe of the same paw, Titus falls under its weight, knocked to his back.

Running to help, I brandish my weapon. "Sit, stay, down."

"Cast a spell." Titus's hands are deep into the hellhound's fur, holding back sharp teeth from tearing out his eyes.

"They're not dogs anymore." I poke it in the ribs, but the sword doesn't penetrate its armored hide.

The beast turns and sprays me with fire. I jump back, clothes and skin singed and smoking.

Titus pushes the hound off and rolls away. "Sword. Throw me your sword." The beast's teeth draw close to his nose. Alder wobbles and rises from the ground.

The sword sails through the air to Titus, and I sing-song the sit and stay spell but the hellhounds don't obey.

"The book. Find something in the book." His words sound far away over the snapping jaws and deep growls.

I'm on the ground pawing through the pages while Titus is back on his feet and using the sword to keep the two hellhounds at bay.

"Hellhounds, hellhound," I yell. The pages refuse to move. Titus stumbles back and nearly trips over me.

"Do something."

"Weakness. What are their weaknesses?"

The pages shuffle and turn. I don't even look at the spell but read the words that flash before me. Something drops on my shoulder. It's white as snow. "What?"

"It's salt." A smile crosses Titus's lips. "They hate salt."

It must be true because the hellhounds retreat a few steps. Every grain of salt that touches their skin sizzles as it embeds itself in their fur. The line of salt begins to extend across the ground as far as the eye can see and beyond.

"They won't cross it," Titus says.

"We should run." I set off, racing across the stream and along the path on instinct, and we reach the Porsche when the first howls hit the air.

Becca stirs in the back seat. "You guys were gone so long." She yawns. "I took a nice, relaxing nap. All good?"

"Drive." I thump the console.

Titus floors it. Darkness surrounds us. There's nothing but a moon-soaked sky above and a dark forest surrounding both sides of the road. I cannot see one house for the life of me. The Porsche hits 80 MPH as we cruise back to Salem.

Becca sniffs. "It smells like you were in a fire. What happened?"

Our three phones ping at the same time.

"New update to the employee handbook," I read. "Do not kill magical creatures unless absolutely necessary. Demons can be disposed of on a case-by-case basis. Contact your manager for additional information."

Titus moans.

"Alrighty then." I slump in the car seat.

Chapter Sixty

Titus drives at super speed so I assume he sees the urgency in taking down the enemy before the witches let Lilith's freak flag fly.

"There's no way I want to fight more zombies and hellhounds. I've had my fill of decaying skin, erupting bowels, and flaming death dogs." I shake off my fear and loathing. It almost works.

"They have four souls," Titus reminds me.

"And we have zero rescues."

"We can't give up. Let's plan."

"I can't. I just can't at the moment." My mind is overloaded and in extreme chaos. I need a reset and subject change. "Do you think Goose could go this fast?" I yawn, letting out all the tension, only covering my mouth in an afterthought. "Maybe we should bring him along next time. A demon horse could be helpful and he's just rotting away in the garage."

"What?" Titus glances away from the road, obviously preoccupied by more important things.

"Goose. How fast can a demon go?"

"Should I know that piece of trivia?"

"Don't get cranky. I'm making conversation and you know all sorts of things, but you seem a little tense. Your shoulders are hunched and bunchy." I put a hand up to massage one, but he shrugs me off.

"Saving the world puts me on edge, thank you very much." Titus's brow matches his shoulders. "You should feel the same. Do you know what happens if we don't come through? Lilith rises. Great for the witches who'll be rewarded and sit at the side of her throne, but for all the other poor shleps like me it's not going to be nearly as pleasant."

"You don't need to mansplain to me." I pause in thought. "Maybe the mansplaining is one reason the witches are doing this."

"That's not their main motivation."

"How about after we're done with saving the world, we race Goose against your Porsche and see who's faster. I'm curious." I turn in my seat and face the back. "Becca, you're awfully quiet on the matter. Goose or the Porsche? Who'd you bet on?"

Becca mulls it over for a moment. "Goose is high spirited, and he doesn't like to lose. I'll put my money on him."

"Good choice."

We return to the hotel to strategize, change clothes, and fuel up on pizza. I call Daxone, catch her up, and grab an early morning catnap while waiting to leave. All too soon, it's time to meet the others and head back to the farm for what I hope is the final showdown. These trips are wearing me out.

I organize the backpack and place the poppet and pocketknife on top of the grimoire. The weight of all my favorite things feels comforting against my shoulders. Once we're on the move again, there are at least twenty moments where I think my life will end during another thrill ride in the Porsche. I'm almost happy when Titus pulls to the side of the road two blocks from the farmhouse. But then I remember the three witches.

"We're going to hike from here like we planned," Titus says.

I'm fueled on coffee and pizza, and the door rebounds a little too hard as I force it open and exit the car. Armed with the grimoire, I'm ready. The others are too. Titus has his sword and Becca her spunk, and my former sword. I was useless with it.

Minutes later, on the trail, my boots are once again covered in slime as I slog through the mud. I stumble, recover, huff a ragged breath, and peer around into the emerging light for Ash and Alder. I don't let it out until I'm sure they're not close.

We hike and hike some more until, across a narrow, rocky lane, a dilapidated shack comes into view.

"This must be the outskirts of their property," I say. "I don't think we've been here before. Go ahead, try it." I motion to Titus.

With a dramatic sigh, he pushes ahead of me and fumbles with the doorknob.

I'm slightly shocked but not disappointed when there's no jump scare. The door squeaks open, releasing the moist darkness. Other than that, it remains quiet. The inside appears to be a large potting shed the size of a two-car garage. As we head into the gloom, the interior is lit up by my amulet. I peer around. Becca's necklace and Titus's ring burn bright as well. On a small windowsill sit four clear glass bottles. Souls ranging from clear to murky gray are trapped inside.

"We found them. Who would have thunk it." I move toward the window and grab a bottle.

"The bottles are glass," Titus warns. "Be careful."

Becca and Titus pull down the others.

"What do we do with them?" Becca asks.

"We'll deal with the souls later. For now, keep the bottles close. It'll be best to put them in different places." I shove one bottle in my backpack and the other in a pocket. "That way the witches can't get them all."

Once the souls are safely stored away on different people, we trek back to the barn. We aren't disappointed. Hen's inside and Lulu strolls in soon after we arrive. A man sits in the center of the building on a dried-out bale of hay. Someone sits next to him. I step back involuntarily when I see who it is. Daxone is shackled to the spot.

She smiles at me. I run to her, but about one hundred paces away, my feet stop and I'm unable to take another step. How is this possible? She was underground. We'd searched for an exit the entire time we were there. The witches have found what we'd been unable to do. I can't process it. She's here. Daxone, my love, is so close yet I can't touch her, which is all I want to do.

"What the fuck?" I say instead. The upper half of my body wobbles, but I still can't get any closer to Daxone.

Bebe steps into the barn with Alder and Ash and locks the doors. "We thought you needed some additional incentive." She smiles at me before shifting her gaze. "I see the rest of you are here for some fun." She contemplates Becca. "It's been a bountiful week." The witch claps like a little girl waiting for birthday cake. "You're another interesting specimen. Not as powerful as Prudence but most definitely worth keeping. I can offer you the same deal. Join us and sit at Lilith's throne or die."

Becca's mouth drops open, but words fail her.

"Tick tock. Time's a-wasting," Hen says.

"Here's how this is going to work." Lulu moves center stage or in this case, center barn. "Hand over the souls you've taken." She whistles and Alder and Ash crowd Becca and Titus. Alder bites into Becca's calf.

Becca screams in pain before trying to push the dog off her leg. When that doesn't work, her cry descends into a whimper.

"Was that necessary?" My gaze shifts between Becca and the dog that still has her leg in its jaw.

"Like I said, it's incentive." Bebe looks away from me and finds Titus. "We don't care who ends up being soul number five." Her gaze roams between Titus and the other man. "They're both excellent specimens."

I should be horrified at what she uttered, but seeing Daxone tied up has the rage inside me working overtime.

Hen whistles and Alder and Ash join her.

Becca sinks to the ground and wraps her hand around her bleeding leg. She won't be running anywhere fast.

Her pain makes my stomach hurt. There's so much blood.

"Why don't you and I take a walk?" Bebe snaps her fingers.

I can move again and oblige her. Anything to stall because I have no idea what to do next.

We head out to the other end of the barn. "We're so close to starting a new world. It puts me in such a good mood. Hen and Lulu can watch the rest of them and make sure they behave."

I bob my head, afraid of what might exit my mouth. We walk in silence for a few minutes until we come to a large pond. "Take a look at Lilith's version of the world. Sit and peer into the water."

Shadow and light rise from the depths. The water swirls and begins to paint a beautiful picture. It's indeed a paradise with Lilith high on the throne, and I'm enraptured and enthralled by the scene. Little girls play in open fields, running and laughing. Their joy surges through me. Older women work in harmony and happiness, picking fruit from apple and pear trees, kissing in the shade of the pine groves. While men are lacking in the vision, no one in this utopia seems the least bit bothered. I wonder, why should I care then?

A small nagging sensation that something is not quite right reminds me of the spell I'd studied one night at the hotel room. It feels like a lightning strike when the words hit my brain.

> *We see the beauty of the world but lack clarity*
> *A tree is a tree*
> *But today, for this hour*
> *I take the sky for mine*
> *The stream for mine*
> *The stars for mine*
> *And for a moment, your eyes for mine*
> *And for a moment, the bird's eyes for mine*
> *Along with the wolves*
> *For a moment, I demand the sun's view of the earth*
> *Sapere Aude*

The water twists and bends and a new vision comes to light. Lilith remains on the throne, but the rest of the scene has changed into something out of Hieronymus Bosch's *The Garden of Earthly Delights*.

A chosen few naked women frolic in a pond, playing with one another's hair, braiding strands into unending coils while on land men in chains groan in pain, shackled together. Other women repose on the ground, men fanning them. Further on the landscape, monsters roam, taking down anyone who dares to rebel. There's no sound but my body fills with the anguish and pain of the universe. It hurts so much, I jump back from the vision, closing my eyes against it.

"Once again you're full of surprises," Bebe sighs. "We should get back to the others. You're obviously not going to be persuaded this way."

I follow her back to the barn, shaking off the anguish and focusing on the current dilemma. I try to come up with a miracle or at least a strategy. Inside, it's as if time stood still. Daxone is shackled, sitting on the bale of hay, and Titus and Becca are being guarded by the hellhounds.

"Time to get this show on the road," Hen frowns and points at me. "Your persuasion spell obviously didn't work on that one."

"You pick." Lulu's gaze is on me. "Who do you want to die to complete the spell and raise Lilith? Will it be your faithful mentor who has saved you on numerous occasions and earned your admiration or the stranger? Tough choice, isn't it, but life is full of tough choices."

My lips pucker but words fail me.

"We don't have all day," Hen adds. "Pick now or we'll pick for you."

That's when my night with the spell book comes back. This is war and I'm starting with the hellhounds. I don't want to kill them and would love to return them to Death unscathed, but they must go down so Titus can be of some use to me. Gaze focused on the angry, drooling beasts, a sleep spell flares behind my eyes. I pray it works on humans and non-human entities alike, unlike the other spell I previously attempted.

> *Find the edge of the dark*
> *where dreams begin*
> *Look and step there*

Enter in unaware
Take down your guarded wall
Be wakeful no more
Enter the gate of death's pall
Somnus

The air changes and light flashes in the corner of my eye before a headache takes over. Maybe I'm using too much magic, or maybe I'm not good at it. Bile builds in my throat, red stars rake my eye, and my temple throbs.

A cool fog rises and shrouds the mutts. The creatures wobble and crash. The witches are momentarily flummoxed but then jump into action. They grab Daxone and the strange man, both of whom are barely functional. What have they done to them? The thoughts make a red haze of anger flood my vision.

Freed from the guard dogs, Titus grabs his sword off the ground and runs after the witches. Becca joins in the chase, but before they make it to the door, the wood slams in their faces and the three of us and two sleeping dogs are trapped inside the barn.

Slumping to the ground, I try to control the nausea since there's nothing to do about the pounding in my head. I didn't pack any Advil. Silly me.

Titus hacks away at the wood, leaving barely noticeable scratches.

"Let's hope the spell keeps the dogs down for a long while," I say.

Chapter Sixty-One

Gulping back bile, I rise to my feet on wobbly legs. Daxone is out there alone with the witches. A spell twists and turns in my brain until the words appear in my head. "Let me try something."

I aim my hands at the doors.

Crumble
A fundamental process
Organized decay
From form to dust
Turn to elemental rust

Collapse
Speed the way
Decompose today
Swiftly fall
From solid to black ash
This I ask
Disrumpo

Wood cracks and splinters, decomposing before our eyes. Outside, fresh air hits us before the last board litters the ground. Rain and hail pelt my throbbing head. A tree trunk shelters me as I heave up my last two lattes.

My head and stomach shriek, demanding an end to this. The skies growl louder than the dogs ever could, but nothing will keep me from Daxone.

Titus growls something unintelligible, grabs my arm, and we run toward the river. He's fast and it takes a lot to keep up with him. Becca arrives at the water's edge a minute later. We're out of breath, gasping for air. We wait as Titus pushes the same small boat we spied earlier into the churning waves.

"They're headed for that island," Becca wheezes and points to an immense crop of rocks with a bulbous dead tree in the middle.

"In." Titus directs.

Fear floods, but I obey. My hands are a death grip on the edge.

This is in no way going to help settle my stomach. "Is this the same body of water we were on before?" No one bothers to answer, too busy with other tasks like rowing and not capsizing.

Choppy waves and murky depths remind me of a stormy sea, not a New England lake. Spelled by the three hags that way? I'm sure of it.

Hand shielding my eyes from hail bullets, I search out the witches in their much more durable motorboat. Lulu's gesturing with her hands and the water under us turns even more murky as silt and sand funnel up from the depths.

"What now?" I ask.

Titus focuses on paddling and keeping the small canoe heading for the island. We tilt and swirl like we're on a carnival ride. I white knuckle the sides. Something glances my wrist and slithers around it. There's a tug. Another powerful yank heaves me over the canoe's edge and into the water.

A scream erupts but water pulls it back. Waterlogged, clothes heavy, dense black water surrounds me. I drown in panic until I see a glimmer of light.

I kick, swim to the surface, and sputter. I turn in place to try to get my bearings. Cold seeps into me. The weight of the water drags me down. Titus has stopped the canoe, but he's pointing and yelling rather than paddling back to get me. Twisting, I tread water. Waves frost over me as I try to find air before sinking beneath them. I cough, inhaling more water into my screaming lungs even as I try to keep my lips clamped.

A fin surfaces first. There's a single moment before the creature rises above the waves. The front half is shark, and the back half is squid.

Sharknado, Jaws, and *The Meg* pale in comparison. This thing is worse. Much worse.

A scream sticks in my brain.

It hunches its back like a dog, annoyed and ready to attack.

"Here," Titus yells before he throws a knife. I stretch out my hand but the weapon lands in the water. Luckily, I grab it before it sinks and thrust it into my pocket. I need both hands to stay afloat. The monster spins. I'm afraid to turn my back on it and swim, so I tread water and listen for Titus's paddle strokes, but he's battling a supernatural current that's sprung up.

I'm gasping, choking, trying not to inhale more water.

"I can't get near you. The canoe's stuck," he yells.

Becca's inventive swear words ring loud and clear through the chaos. I applaud her gusto.

Pulled straight from the murky depths of deep-water hell, this is a damn big shark squid monster—somewhere around fifteen feet. I watch its head rise out of the water; its jaws are wide open, white teeth bigger than my fist littered with bits of its previous meals.

There's a splash in front of me. Becca has thrown an old cooler from the canoe, trying to hit the monster on its deformed, razor-toothed snout. I appreciate the attempt, but her aim is awful, and it misses. Without stopping, the shark-squid grabs and lifts the container out of the water. It shakes it like a dog would worry a bone before flinging it away.

The hum in my ears intensifies even as the air around me goes silent. Waves churn as the creature submerges. I want to cry, scream, and rail against my fate. I cannot die this way. I wonder if Death will greet me when I die by this horrendous tentacle. An immense force strikes my back. The monster turns and sinks sharp teeth into my leg. I'm pulled under.

My scream leads to a mouthful of muddy water. I gag under the waves, only making myself choke and panic at the lack of air. The shark-squid releases me then grabs me once again with its tentacles and drags me through the water so quickly it hits like a car crash. Whiplash is most definite with all the thrashing back and forth.

The monster releases me for a moment. It throws me from the depths. I belly flop back into the waves, the pain barely registering against the others. I flip and float on my back, drag in long breaths of air, catch a glimpse of the now close island, turn, and swim toward land. For a moment the water is calm, and I thrash forward, stroke after stroke, with strength I didn't realize I had. A trail of blood from my wounded leg follows in my wake.

My bloody and beaten self manages to climb onto a rocky ledge. I ignore the pain in my scraped hands as I desperately pull myself higher. The shark-squid rises from the water and opens its impressive snout. Between mega teeth, a tongue covered with smaller razor-edged canines emerges, ready to slice and dice me into a meal. It moves closer.

The boat floats far in the distance as Titus paddles tirelessly to get to me. Even out of the water, it's not safe. The shark-squid chomps its teeth, and I reconsider a mad sprint toward the canoe. Nowhere is safe and I'm not putting their lives in danger.

I'm puffing hard, breathing like a steam train, beginning to hyperventilate, heart banging in my chest, blood running down my leg. The shark-squid launches out of the water. It flies at me and lands on a rock to my right. I pull the serrated bowie knife that Titus threw me out of my pocket and attempt to protect myself with it. It's laughable but it's all I have other than my backpack, and I'm not stopping to open and inspect that now.

The monster rages. It lurches forward, propelled by squid tentacles on land. I lift the knife high and slash at the demon to fend it off. The weapon makes a shallow cut on one of its puckered sucker legs, a tiny slice of red on the massive beast, so insignificant I doubt it registered. No way the weapon is going to save me, but I have no alternative.

The shark-squid rears up again on its tentacles and lashes out with a long limb. It sends me flying onto the rocky island shore. Pain rolls through me as my back hits the jagged stones. Stars float in my vision and a groan gurgles out of me. The knife clatters in between the rocks, lost.

Witch magic burns in my soul, releases my pain, and tells me this is not my time to die. The poppet and grimoire burn bright in my backpack even if I can't see them. My mother and her family are somehow here, protecting me, guiding me.

The spell comes out of my mouth without hesitation, muscle memory from the generations of witches before me.

> *Death comes by blade or blood*
> *Or silently at night alone*
> *Death ends the desperation of wanting to forget*
> *It's stealth something unable to postpone*
> *No matter how, no matter why, no matter what*
> *Death is final*
> *animam agere.*

An unholy scream issues from the monster's mouth. Its skin begins to peel back on itself, and it slowly sinks into the water that now churns red with its blood. When the creature rises to the surface one last time, its head lolls to the side.

I sink to the ground. My first thought is that I need to get up and save Daxone. My second thought is that I hope I'm not in trouble with Death because I didn't contact my supervisor before killing the demon. The overwhelming pain comes in third. Everything hurts, making me afraid to move, but I shake that away and focus on standing and saving the love of my life.

Less than a minute later, Titus pulls the boat to shore and Becca rushes to me. I'm battered and bruised but able to stand. My wobbly leg is a tattered and bloody mess in need of stitches.

Titus takes off his shirt, rips it into strips, and binds it around the wound. I lean heavily on him. The gesture is much appreciated but I'm not sure it's going to help much.

The island is little more than rocks and hilly patches of sand and soot. The ridge is steep, my legs are weary, but I hobble along with help from my companions. At the top of the hill, we step into a small grove of grass. Daxone and the stranger are tied to the dead tree.

"You do make this a challenge," Lulu says. "The three of you won't die, will you? Death does know how to pick them, I'll give them that, but I'm getting bored of this game. We must get our last soul before night falls, and you have become an annoying distraction. Sisters, let's end this."

I clench my shoulders. First, they try to kill me, and now they want to execute my one true love. I've had enough. I can't take any more of this shit. The magic roars to life inside me and this time I don't try to taper it or stop it. Its full power flows through me and consumes me. My pulse stutters. It's almost like death, or what I assume is death. The ringing in my ears, pins and needles in my arms and legs, a shock wave that rocks my body, and a heat that consumes my soul before it spreads outward.

"You're glowing!" Becca's voice is so far away it sounds like she's in another world.

Chapter Sixty-Two

I near the tree, the love of my life, and my possible death. Titus keeps me from stumbling and crashing to the ground. Anger and power radiating from the grimoire and poppet in the backpack focus me. These witches have cost me too much already.

Ahead of us, the coven members skip through the gloom like elves, out of reach but enjoying the show as we climb closer. Only at the top does sharp, spear-like brown grass wave in the onslaught of the wind. Straggling shrubs have taken hold and try to grow but with little success. In the center of the island is a mammoth tree with black bark and twisted vines for branches. Daxone waits at the base.

I stare into my worst nightmare and can't believe I once mistook the witches as misguided, beautiful, and determined. The truth is they are evil, bloodsucking, world-ending devil spawn.

"This is it for your one true love," Hen calls to me in her musical flutter. "I offered, but she didn't want to bed me. No getting her jollies off one last time. She loves you. Like your boss, you do know how to pick the good ones. Too bad she has to die to get you to understand. She'd make a pretty toy."

"Save yourself. Run." Daxone's words are weak. There's a long gash on the side of her head that continues to drip red.

Electric spots fill my vision. "No way I'm leaving this little shindig until it's over once and for all. There's no more soul stealing happening, no more murders, no more raising Lilith. We're done with all this today." I sway on my feet. Blood from my wound has caked Titus's shirt strapped around my leg. It hurts like demon spawn and spurts with every step.

A streak of lightning flashes across the horizon, allowing me to clearly see the horror movie I'm living in. The island is larger than it appeared from the canoe. A smooth white path reaches to the middle where the dead tree looms. Another flash illuminates the haunted conifer, branches erratic and broken like skeletal hands reaching into eternity. The trunk is stained red and black. I don't want to think about what caused it.

Daxone is slumped, chained to the prickly bark, wedged against the aged wood that arcs like a scorpion's tail.

I move closer, my mind swirling like the clouds above me and the magic in the air surrounding me.

A knife flashes into view. "Not another step," Lulu says. She holds the blade to the love of my life's neck, and I watch a new gash bleed red.

"Stop," I scream and my steps halt.

"Shouldn't you be thanking us?" asked Hen. "We rescued your lover from purgatory. Yes, we plan to kill her, but we brought her back to you first."

Her question seeps through the pain and anger. I must admit I'm curious. The three witches managed to do something I was unable to. "How?"

"It wasn't easy," Bebe said. "Death runs a tight ship, but when the three of us work together there is little we can't do. That is why you should join us."

"Will it save Daxone's life?"

"After Lilith rises you won't need her for anything."

"That doesn't answer the question."

"She's a sacrifice you need to make to prove your loyalty to Lilith."

"Pass. I don't know why we continue to circle back to this useless conversation."

"Don't say we didn't ask."

"More than once."

Bebe steps forward, disrupting my view of Daxone. "Have you ever wondered what it was like to be pressed to death? Most of the witches were hanged during the witch trials but some, like Giles Corey, were pressed to death. It seems fitting since we need to build a shrine to Lilith at this tree, your love's body and soul will be the base of it." With a flick of her wrist, a stone the size of a honeydew melon lands in Daxone's lap.

"While we don't have two slabs like the used in the trials, we'll make do. In the past, the person they wanted to press became a human sandwich, squashed between two large flat stones. A bunch of smaller ones will do for us." Another stone rises into the air and thuds against Daxone's chest. She huffs out a breath.

"It's reported that it took days for Giles Corey to pass away even at the ripe old age of eighty-one. We don't have a lot of extra time, so we'll speed the process along." Another small boulder lifts in the air. The stone falls and clinks against the others.

Daxone huffs, cheeks red. "Save yourself, Prudence," she wheezes. "I love you forever."

"You will not die on me, Daxone. I saved you once. I'll do it again. I'm not spending time in purgatory without you. Titus, help me out here."

Titus's upper body lurches forward but his feet refuse to move. "I'm stuck in my spot. Let me know when you got a plan."

"This is your last chance. Join us and we'll kill your lover quickly. Defy us and she dies, well, like this." There's a *plunk* of stone as another hits the growing pile.

"No matter how many times you ask, my answer will not change. No." The words are soft but purposeful. I'll happily sacrifice my life for Daxone and derail Lilith's rising no matter what it takes.

Another stone hits Daxone's lap and she groans. The tree buds. Small black flowers shine as the drops of rain hit them, illuminated as if by magic.

When another rock lands on Daxone's ankle, she screams.

Bile fills my mouth and fear fills my soul.

"You've been buzzing around us like a fly for too long and you've become much too annoying," Lulu says. "This is over now."

"I agree. Let's do this." I raise my foot to run to Daxone, but my legs will not move. I'm immobile, stuck like Titus and Becca. I howl, my rage swirling the wind into a magical storm. Leaves and twigs dance around my head. The rain lashes at me in sideways splinters.

I try to pull my foot off the ground but cannot. A leaf hits my cheek, and I bat it away.

"I hate to see such power go to waste." Lulu raises her hands to cast a spell. "If only you understood your magical history. You could be the most powerful witch in existence, even more powerful than the three of us."

She stares at Titus, then Daxone, before her gaze returns to me. "Her first." She points at Daxone.

"No," I scream.

"You had your chance to join the winning team."

A stone the size of a grapefruit rises from the ground and drops with a *thud* on Daxone's chest.

"Enough." The ground rumbles around me. My foot lifts into the air. I don't know how it's possible and don't care. I'm able to shift the other foot as well and take one wobbly step after another closer to the tree and my true love.

Lulu hisses out a spell and another stone drifts into the air.

Fear gives me strength, and I launch myself at the tree, a spell flooding my mind. Water rises from where it meets the land, spirals up, and drenches us.

When it quiets, I wipe my eyes and spit grit and sand from my lips. I created little more than an unexpected rain shower. Surprising, but in no way deadly.

"I didn't realize you were already so strong." Hen is drenched but unhurt. She runs her hand through her soaking hair before walking to Daxone. "Be careful what you try next, or I might have to retaliate on your girlfriend."

"Stop wasting time. Tie them all up or kill them. I don't care, just do it." Lulu's white teeth and malice stain the night.

Bebe's feminine giggle swims through the darkness. "I'm on it."

I step toward Daxone and Hen, but my mind is blank. No spell fills it, and I've no idea what to do. And worse, the three witches treat me like I'm not worth their contemplation. First, I'm powerful but now I'm like the trash, useless and discarded. I don't know how to take the insult, but don't have time or energy to dwell on it. It will be a good starting place if I end up in therapy after this. A big if, contingent on survival.

"Sisters," Bebe says, stretching her arms into the air. "Are we ready?"

There is a pause, then they join hands. "It's time." Lulu's voice hushes the rest of the group.

"No!" Instead of moving closer to Daxone and the evil threesome, I race-walk backward and grab Titus and Becca's hands. A simple spell enters my mind, and I pray it works. Words that expel my anguish, fear, and pain issue forth in a primordial scream. With Titus and Becca's natural talents enhancing my own ability, the binding spell flies forth.

> *With helping hands, I command*
> *In this tree, Bebe,*
> *I will enslave your power*
> *Forever bound*
> *From now until time's end, Hen*
> *Grow as one*
> *Three sisters forever twined*
> *Never shall you leave*
> *But forever be blue, Lulu*

> *Captured in the roots and trunk*
> *Souls trapped as permanent as the trees*
> *Buffered only by the breeze*

"Say it with me," I yell over howling winds and storming rains. The three of us chant it together. Too late the witches realize it's a spell with their names attached to it.

My wrist burns. A quick downward glance reveals my charm bracelet lit up like fireworks. Sparks fly and fall. Heat radiates from each life event I've encapsulated in a metal symbol. My Claddagh charm from time spent in Ireland melts first, then my paintbrush, a small sailing ship, and a sneaker, followed by the key, the leaf, the tree, and the horse. They all flame and spark, searing my wrist and the air, but the pain doesn't reach me. Finally, the last charm erupts. It is a small gold heart to remind me of my mother.

Slow at first. Too slow, but as our voices reach beyond the wind and the rain, so does the spell. It grows, blossoms, and shoots forth. Spidery branches reach out to ensnare the three witches. They're unprepared. Their weak attempts at individual magic aren't strong enough to stop my linked spell.

Hen goes first, body pulled into the trunk of the tree, her scream forever imprinted in the bark. Bebe is next, body coiled in branches, spun like a ball of yarn until there's nothing human left to see. Lulu fights the hardest, slashing away at the branches that reach out, shooting spell after spell at the endless twigs that grasp like tentacles, but she tires. A branch snags her foot, and she stumbles and falls. Roots erupt from the ground and drag Lulu under the mud.

We keep chanting the words until there is nothing left to see.

Finally, my body, mind, and soul spent, the void greets me.

Chapter Sixty-Three

Cancún, Mexico, 2025

I wake up in a hotel room but realize it is not the one I've come to know and love so much in Salem.

Did I get transferred again?

The walls are painted bright yellow, and the light spread on the bed is covered with bold flowers. The window is open, gauzy white curtains swaying, allowing a tropical breeze to flutter inside on butterfly wings.

Much stranger, there's a warm body in my bed. My heart pounds against my rib cage as I strain to hear any sounds around me other than the gentle snores from the sheet-clad figure. Memories flood.

Where is everyone? What happened to Becca, Titus, and Daxone?

I'm afraid to pull the fabric back, but there's no other way to calm my racing heart. I lift the sheet and peek under the covers. A huge sigh of relief escapes. It's Daxone, and she's breathing steadily. Her ankle is bandaged and there are bumps and bruises on her torso and face, but otherwise she's healthy and alive. I stare for a moment. For a person who was almost crushed to death, she looks good, better than good.

She's so damn hot and attractive. There's no way this moment is passing me by.

I bend over and plant a gentle kiss on her cheek to wake her. She continues to snore. I try her neck, shoulder, and finally her ear. That does it. The bed is cushiony; the soft morning light rides the breeze, outlining her curvy figure. She's slept in the nude, and I enjoy the view.

"Hey." Her eyes are hooded, and a soft, sexy smile greets me.

"Are you okay?" I ask.

"Better now. I don't know how you did it or what magic you have inside, but it must be very powerful."

"I'm wondering what else my magic might be good for." I stretch none too casually and watch her eyes widen as she follows my movements.

She sits, releasing a small grunt of pain.

I hesitate, but only for a moment before throwing back the covers further and carefully dragging myself onto her lap. She's pale from time down under, which makes the purple and black bruises more glaring. I want to kill the witches again but suck back the anger and focus on my love in front of me.

She clears her throat. "Where are we? This is not down under."

I shrug, considering what I want to feast on.

Her hands roam over my arms and legs, fingers tickling with each movement.

"What's this?" Her fingers trace my wrist.

"I don't know." My eyes scrunch as I stare at the black burns that lace my wrist.

"Where's your charm bracelet?" She pulls my wrist to her. "Wait, it can't be. Your charms are tattoos. When did you do this?"

"I didn't."

"How'd they get there?"

I pull back my arm and stare at the permanent black band that circles my wrist. Each charm is delicate, as if inked with the finest of paintbrushes on my skin. I count them. They're all there.

"It can't be. The magic did it." The charms move under my gaze, alive and restless.

Daxone calls my name. "Are we back on the upside for good?"

"I don't know. No idea how any of this happened." Spreading my hands, I embrace the room, wanting to enjoy every minute. "We're here and safe. I don't care about the location and I'm not checking my phone. Let's hope Death doesn't make contact about our future, at least for a little while. We're together and the bed's super comfy."

"Free of purgatory and here with you." She kisses me. "I hope to God it's permanent."

I shrug. "I have yet to figure Death or his stupid employee handbook out. I'm happy we're here now. We should take advantage of the time."

"Absolutely. Fill me in on everything that happened, including your new friends."

"That wasn't what I was thinking."

Her expression is blank for a second, then a wicked smile reaches her lips. "Oh."

We kiss, our lips exploring, and she tastes like wilderness. A pleasurable vibration passes through me as her tongue explores mine. Cool air caresses my shoulders, but I want her heat. She traces my nipples with exploring fingers, then cups my breasts in her hands before her lips take over from where her fingers have been.

She pulls me off her so that we are side by side in the bed. I tremble when her fingers find my core. Her touch makes me want more, forever more.

I need her. The thought scares and thrills, and when her fingers push inside me, pleasure pulses. A moan escapes, and I try to slip away, but she won't let me, one hand against my lower back, anchoring me against her.

I thread my fingers through her hair. She shifts her weight again and her lips caress my belly, tickling my skin. She licks the inside of my thigh before she kisses the same spot. Her mouth moves higher as her kisses become an exploration. She finds my heat with her tongue, and her hands caress my buttocks. She holds me captive in ecstasy. She licks and sucks. Tremors course through me.

"Stop. Torturing. Me." I gasp the words.

"You mean like this." A finger replaces where her tongue has been. Wet, white heat erupts, and I moan. "Or this." She adds another finger.

I command life and death. Control is my thing and it's hard to let someone else lead the way, but it feels so damn good that I don't resist. In my line of work, I take and take. For once, I want someone to take me, at least for a few long, luxurious minutes of selfish, mind-altering pleasure. Finally, and it takes a lot of effort, I push my desire aside to think about her needs. I anchor my hands on her arms. "Let me reciprocate."

"Not right now—I am worshipping you, and there is nothing you can do about it."

I open my lips to protest, but she crushes her mouth to mine. This kiss, raw and real, ignites my body and soul, both already aflame. My heartbeat skitters when she cups my breast in her hand. Her tongue is between my lips, exploring my mouth. I lean into her, nipples hard, and moan. Her lips demand more.

Her hand tangles in my hair. She tugs. Waves of pleasure shoot through me. My fingers explore her shoulders, kneading them. She rips her mouth from mine and paints my neck with a trail of kisses.

I run my nails up her arms and grip her shoulders, clawing to close the distance between us. When her mouth meets mine again, the kiss pushes my head onto the pillow. I drink her in, fulfilling a need I didn't know existed. Or one I'd long buried since taking on my role as death.

"You're the most amazing person I ever met," she pants. "I've loved you since the first time our eyes met in that restaurant." Her fingers inside me take away sensible thoughts. An earthquake builds within me and waves of pleasure cascade until I melt away.

It takes us a long time to leave the hotel room. There's a lengthy hot shower and a quicky on the desk chair, not to mention that it seems we arrived at our new hotel room without clothes, and Death is not providing anything this time. I almost miss those damn camo shorts.

We hang around in the hotel robes until an employee delivers some gift store basics.

Finally, dressed in colorful T-shirts saying "Cancún, Mexico" and bright jogging shorts, we exit the hotel into the early afternoon. It's glorious. A crisp ocean breeze whisks away any thoughts of witches. Birds chirp symphonies from nearby trees. The perfect day. I let the sun warm my face for a few seconds before I surrender to my fate, whatever that might be.

In front of me the white sand beach is dotted with umbrellas and lounge chairs. They look like an artist's rendering as they spread to the turquoise-blue ocean. The smell of brine and suntan lotion infuses the air. People bob in the waves; some relax at the high tide line, letting the salty water soak their feet. There's laughter from the tourists at the bar and splashes as children cannonball into the deep end of the pool. Employees in bright-pink shirts walk along the shore offering cold, watered-down drinks, snorkeling, boat trips, cave diving, and trips to Tulum. Daxone and I find a place among the other tourists, deck ourselves out on a beach chair, dangle our fingers in the golden sand.

The waves crashing gently against the shore lull me into a contented trance as the last few days of my life replay in my head and I thank the gods I made it here alive and with all my body parts intact.

I peer over the sunglasses' rim. "Cancún, Mexico. I can think of worse places to land."

"I'll take anywhere with you, but warm and tropical are a plus. Do you want some suntan lotion?"

"I should, but after the down under, I might need to inhale some sun, even if only for a few moments." I'm pondering whether my future youthful appearance or my need for sun is more imperative when I hear a familiar voice.

Chapter Sixty-Four

"Anyone for margaritas?"

I twist and stare at Titus. "You're on my vacation too?"

"Si la vida te da limones...¡pide sal y tequila!" His eyebrow quirks.

"Sorry, please translate."

"If life gives you lemons, ask for salt and tequila."

Becca walks up behind him in a bright-orange bikini. How'd she manage that? I do a double take. They appear happy, well fed, and well clothed in a casual, beachy kind of way. Titus's sunglasses rest on the top of his head. He's shirtless and sporting longboard shorts and leather sandals.

"Definitely need some tequila after seeing how relaxed and happy you two are." I twist in my beach chair. "Did you know we'd end up here?"

"I'm used to ending up in strange places and I've come to appreciate Death's sense of humor," Titus says.

"Death has a sense of humor?" I gasp. "I've never seen it."

"Guess I know them better than you do. I've been working for Death longer."

Putting my conflicted emotions about the Under-Lord aside, I raise the important question. "Does anyone want to order lunch? Death's credit must still be in working order." My backpack, slung on the chair upstairs in our room, hopefully holds all my essentials and possibly a new credit card or three. "You can have the honor of paying for us."

"I could use more food after the morning I've endured." A huge grin spreads across Becca's lips.

"Dirty devil," I screech. "You didn't."

Becca blushes, but joy radiates from both her and Titus.

"Time to celebrate." I hug myself. "We're one big happy family."

"One big happy family that can be instantly banished to purgatory if Death isn't pleased with the outcome," Daxone says.

I peer over the top of my sunglasses to give her the stink eye for ruining the mood. "We defeated zombies, alien spiders, shark-squids, hellhounds, and three bad-ass witches. Lilith will never rise from hell and humanity is safe. Humans will keep dying, souls can continue to be collected, and Death's job is no longer in jeopardy. What more could they want? We should be rewarded, celebrated, not banished back down under."

"I agree, but it's Death." Daxone turns to Titus. "You've worked for them longest. What are your thoughts?"

Titus shrugs. "Death remains a mystery. I still haven't figured them out after many millennia, but they'd never refuse us a good meal."

"What happened to the souls we rescued?" I ask.

"I got them to where they need to be," Titus says.

Nodding in approval, I point to the empty chairs next to us.

We order from the bar menu and celebrate our victory for the entire day. I swim, snorkel, drink, and enjoy the warm ocean breeze before I lounge and drink some more.

The need to shop arises thanks to my abundant lack of clothing options, and I buy a gauzy green dress, matching flip-flops, and dangling earrings that tickle my neck. When we head back to the room it's late. After showering and changing, the four of us meet up to dance.

Done with margaritas, I turn to wine and shots. We spin and bob until dizzy and fall into a discombobulated huddle of arms, legs, sweat, and laughter.

"We did it." I toast, clinking my shot glass against Titus's before throwing back the burning liquid. The room rotates. It's hard to focus on Daxone who sits next to me.

"I can't believe it's true." Titus punches my arm. "We rid the world of those pesky witches."

"Ouch." I rub my tender skin with my other hand.

"Amazeballs." Becca gushes slurred words my way. "That spell you cast must have been crazy powerful to deal with them."

"They were distracted." Three copies of Becca's face float in front of me thanks to the abundant alcohol. Her voice becomes my divining rod.

"You're being modest." She moves in for a hug, close and personal. The humidity and heat have not helped tame her or my curly hair. Hers has become an out-of-control dark mane.

"You're the fiercest warrior woman," I tell her.

She laughs. "Naw, but I'm a drunk one."

My thoughts are interrupted by another round of shots.

"To the power of love." Daxone wobbles on the stool next to me as she tries to hand over the next round of shot glasses.

"Let's drink to it." The liquid roars to life as it hits my throat.

Titus orders another round. I'm powerful, undefeatable, and deserving of a little celebration in my life. I'm also wobbly, blurry eyed, and inebriated. Being a witch doesn't affect my constitution for alcohol, and I've had one too many but forgive myself. There's a good chance I'm returning to down under at any second. Thinking about the gray and the chill and the cold stone house has me turning to peer behind me to see if Death is waiting, ready to banish me, but no, only some woman at the karaoke machine doing a bad rendition of Katy Perry. Thankfully, the bar is loud and crowded and her singing fades into background noise.

"We make a good team," I babble at no one in particular.

"We do." Titus puts his hand up for a high five.

The smack of our hands echoes through the air, but Titus doesn't even flinch.

"Ouch." I rub my hands together. "Thank you for saving me, by the way."

"I didn't do the saving. You did."

"But along the way you saved me from zombies and alien spiders. I owe you."

He smiles. "I'll keep that in mind."

"Put in a good word with Death for me. He trusts you and you're his right-hand man."

"Will do my best. You're not too bad to go into battle with."

"Gee, thanks." I stand. "I need some air."

The four of us desert the club for a walk on the beach. We stare at the stars, trying to identify constellations.

This is the life I want. The statement repeats in my head as I try to banish Death from appearing. A falling star sparks above me. It must be a sign of good things to come so I point it out, but everyone else is preoccupied by the tiny crabs scurrying along the shore.

Becca and Titus smooch, and soon they have a hard time keeping their hands off each other. We part ways. I'd love to do the same to Daxone, but I need a few minutes to sober up. We hold hands and walk along the mostly empty beach lit only by the moon and hotel tiki torches. A cacophony of sounds echoes from the inside of the resorts but they're easy to ignore, so focused on each other as we are.

"I'm a little hungry and tired. Want to head back to the room?" I ask.

"Hungry?"

"Food first, then I'll devour you before some sleep."

We make it back to the hotel and, once inside and settled, order room service. I figure a hot fudge brownie sundae will sober me up. When it arrives, I sit cross-legged in bed next to Daxone, and we take turns snacking on the ice cream.

The spoon smacks the bed when, in an instant, Death arrives, unfriendly face looming.

"What up, Boss Man." Maybe I should not have had that third or fourth shot at the end of the night, but Titus can be pretty insistent. Alcohol and sweets have always been my best and only therapy.

Daxone scurries behind me, body rigid. I want to protect her but there's no protection against Death.

"I'm having fun here. After all I went through with the witches, don't you think we could at least have a couple of extra days? Maybe a week in this paradise before returning to you-know-where for the remainder of eternity?" My voice rises a little with the last words. It's hard to control the swirl of sentiments. Those emotions want to come out.

My fingers shoot sparks. I stare, not sure what will stop the Fourth of July sparklers that exit my hands. After a long second, I blow on them, which does nothing. Turning to face Daxone, I mouth, "Help." She grabs my hands in hers. The gesture calms my soul and the light emanating from my fingers.

"You need to embrace and control the witch inside." Death's lips don't move but the voice is clear in my head. "You aren't doing either."

"I'll have plenty of time to embrace my magic once we're banished again." I can't help it, but a giggle escapes to avoid tears. "Is that anything like embrace your inner child or embrace your demons. Is there a twelve-step program?"

Death's robes heave in and out. "Pay attention. The world order depends on it. Lulu and her coven aren't the only people descended from the witches of Salem. You are as well. Your ancestors practiced witchcraft and now you possess their grimoire. Embrace your heritage, the past, their pain, and their wisdom."

"My mother wasn't powerful. She helped the people in our town."

Death ignores me and continues. "I allowed you out of Hades because you were the only one who could stop the three witches from resurrecting Lilith, but you must learn to channel your ancestors if you want to stay here."

I salute them. "Will do, boss." Then it sinks in with the squeeze of

Daxone's fingers against mine. Death said we could stay. "Wait, did you say we can remain here?"

"Not at the resort. You have proven to be a worthy warrior much like Titus. He will train you. Listen to him. He has walked the earth for more years than human memories stretch. Listen to your ancestors and learn their knowledge. Titus will not fail you." With those words, Death disappears.

There's a knock on the door and I'm suddenly sober.

I open it to find Titus and Becca. "Tomorrow bright and early," Titus says. "You need a lot of help, and this isn't going to be easy. If you want to stay on Death's good side, we have to train. You better be a quick learner."

Epilogue

Sometime in the Netherworld

Another report from the human world above lay open on Death's ebony, quartz-stone desk. With each word read, the stabbing pain in their skull heightened.

When done with it, Death pushed the information aside, opened a heavy drawer, and pulled out sheets of white paper. The stark blank pages of loose leaf appeared lurid against the black stone. An antique quill pen with a raven feather sat in the corner, and Death picked it up. It remained poised above the paper like a cobra ready to strike, but lacking prey.

Death turned to the computer on the other side of the monstrous long desk. Sure, computers and smartphones existed, but sometimes going old school was best.

Death jotted the letters C.A.R.E and wrote some notes. Maybe an acronym would make the *Reaper Employee Handbook* more effective.

C: Connect with the soon-to-be dead (SOD).

A: Abate anxieties. Death loved alliteration. *Accepting their fate is an essential part of the process. Reapers are integral in helping SOD recognize death has arrived.*

R: Reassure individuals about the transition. While reapers should never tell a SOD where they are heading or what that place might be like (a reaper hasn't been and therefore doesn't know), it is imperative to prepare the dying to the best extent possible.

E: Empathize with the dying. Every reaper stood in the same place as a SOD at one time.

With every movement, Death's bones sounded like tap shoes on the floor. All their efforts to enrich the employee handbook and explain the value of every soul energized them.

Next on Death's list of improvements to the handbook—an employee conduct code. Numerous reports from the human world above had brought to Death's attention more than a few reaper issues. These transgressions from reapers who inhabited the human world above included a soul sold for money and a reaper stealing a painting from a museum.

Both were unacceptable.

What was the present-day workforce coming to?

Death missed the days when ruling with an iron fist had been more than acceptable, and the employee handbook had amounted to a few clay tablets. Back then, reapers conducted themselves with dignity.

Death chuckled, accepting the lie. Reapers never changed, and history constantly repeated itself. The gods' endless existence had proven that. Not too long ago, there had been a rivalry between the Roman and Greek reapers—one of the worst, with a few deaths and even a beheading.

Death smiled. Reapers needed to be spirited employees, an essential requirement, though not one listed in the handbook.

The robed figure's bony shoulders clicked and clacked with a shrug. Lately, everything seemed different in this job. The increasing world population could be a consideration. Massive growth in a short period amounted to an overflow of souls, long work hours, and few rewards.

"You're providing a valuable service" only went so far. There was nothing else to do but follow protocol, amend the handbook, and hope the reapers followed the rules. If not, firing someone or punishing them with a stint in hell could be arranged.

Death pulled the most recent copy of the *Reaper Employee Handbook* from the large bookshelf covered with them—tablets, scrolls, printed manuals, bound books, an iPad, and other tech. Death hated technology and wished all of it could be banished to the darkest, hottest realm of existence, preferring pen and paper. While Death's ancient bones made any instrument smaller than a scythe hard to hold, the pains and aches, thanks to this endeavor, had to be tolerated for the greater good.

Turning to a fresh, white page, Death thought about some adjustments. He'd make the notes, and the admin could update the final version. That soul understood technology like no one else.

Revised Employee Conduct Code, Death wrote.

1. Professionalism: Employees must maintain a high level of professionalism in all interactions, both within the organization and with external stakeholders. This includes demonstrating respect, courtesy, and integrity. Employees must follow the newly enacted CARE clause at all times. They should follow all human and company laws and policies to the best of their abilities.

2. Confidentiality: Employees must respect the confidentiality of sensitive information pertaining to the organization, its clients, and fellow employees. Unauthorized disclosure of confidential information will be cause for reprimand, punishment, or dismissal.

3. Workplace Respect: All employees are expected to treat each other with respect and dignity, fostering a collaborative and inclusive work environment free from bullying, intimidation, or disrespectful behavior.

4. Attendance and Punctuality: Employees are expected to arrive on time for scheduled pick-ups, meetings, and other mandated activities and promptly notify their supervisor in case of absence or tardiness. Absences and tardiness are not an option.

5. Use of Company Resources: Company resources should be used responsibly and solely for business purposes. This includes equipment, demons, and magical items. Personal use should be minimal, and company policies should be followed.

6. Reporting Violations: Employees are responsible for reporting violations of this code of conduct or any unethical behavior they become aware of without fear of retaliation.

7. Compliance with the Reaper Employee Handbook: *Employees must comply with all applicable policies governing their conduct. Violations of this code may result in disciplinary action, including termination of employment and transfer to other realms, including the underworld, depending on the severity of the infraction and the employee's history.*

8. By adhering to these principles of conduct, employees contribute to a positive and productive work environment and uphold the reputation and values of the organization.

Death put the pen on the desk and chuckled. A work of art, no doubt, but they wondered if anyone would take the time to read it. The current manual stretched out for more than one thousand pages, and Death doubted anyone had read the entire thing. Even if they had, the rules changed so often on a whim and a prayer, so to speak, that the reapers probably weren't following the latest version. Plus, some of the rules Death had written purposely contradicted one another.

Death enjoyed keeping the reapers guessing. Existence got boring after the first few millennia, and the Employee Handbook was this god's little joke. The moment in orientation when the large volume thudded into a new reaper's lap and they peered up in fear never got old. Even a god had to have a laugh at the expense of their employees occasionally.

Death pursed skeletal teeth and wrote a list of names on a new sheet of paper. Reapers to watch. They circled one. Prudence Barlow. Gods and demons could only guess what was coming her way, but whatever it was, life for that reaper would never be the same again.

About the Author

Lisa Acerbo is the Director of General Education and Liberal Arts at Post University. Her short stories and poetry appear in *Scarlet, Sagebrush Review, Moonstone Arts, Poor Yorick Literary Journal, Ripples in Space, Universe in a Bottle* by Flying Ketchup Press, *Whatever Happened to Hansel and Gretel?* by Fathom Publishing (a finalist in the 2024 Best Books Awards in the category of Fiction: Anthology), and Birds of Vermont Museum. When not writing, you can find her walking in the woods with her rescue dogs.

Email
Laft100@gmail.com

Facebook
www.facebook.com/lisa.acerbo.7

X
www.x.com/Apocalipstick_

Instagram
www.instagram.com/laft100

Website
www.Lisaacerbo.com

We hope you enjoyed this book!

Thank you for supporting our authors. If you have a minute,

we would truly appreciate your review.

Website: NineStarPress.com

Facebook: NineStarPress

X: @ninestarpress

Instagram: NineStarPress

BlueSky: NineStarPress

Threads: @ninestarpress